SINFUL OBSESSION

GRACHEV BRATVA
BOOK 2

BROOK WILDER

SCHOLAE PALATINA, INC.

Copyright © 2024 by Brook Wilder

All rights reserved.

No part of this book may be reproduced in any form or by any electronic or mechanical means, including information storage and retrieval systems, without written permission from the author, except for the use of brief quotations in a book review.

Cover by Angela Haddon Book Cover Design: http://www.angelahaddon.com/

1

GALINA

I wonder how many different ways I can rearrange the potatoes on my plate without actually putting any in my mouth. So far, I've created a snowman, a three-legged dog, and a pretty decent interpretation of the Eiffel Tower. They're still warm, which seems impossible. Because I swear I've been sitting here forever.

My mother sits to my left—she hasn't eaten either, but she's on her second glass of wine. Yevgeniy watches us from across the table. His appetite is just fine. The food on his plate is half gone, and he stabs a chunk of steak, dragging it through the bloody juices before bringing it to his mouth.

My stomach gives a heave as his lips smack.

From the nearby room, Ruslan cries out excitedly. The noise of him clacking his toys together has been the only thing keeping the dinner from being entirely silent. He joined us for all of five minutes before he finished his meal and asked to be excused.

I've never seen a kid shovel down a meal as fast as Ruslan did. Yevgeniy watched the boy fondly, like he was proud of this gluttonous show, before giving Ruslan permission to leave the table.

If I could be excused by simply clearing my plate, maybe I'd force the food down.

But I don't want to leave my mom alone with this monster.

Yevgeniy glances over in the direction of his son. A faint smile crosses his lips before he looks directly at me.

"Is something wrong with your food?"

I set my fork down harder than I have to. "I don't have an appetite."

"Ah." He shrugs. "I can have something else whipped up for you if you like."

"What I'd like," I say calmly, "is to not be sitting at the same table as a murderer."

My mother releases a tiny, pressurized bit of air from her lips. It's the only sound she makes. I don't look at her—my attention is fixed on Yevgeniy—but I imagine her face is pure anxiety. Meanwhile, his is nothing but relaxed arrogance. He doesn't react or say anything. Hell, he doesn't even blink in response, as if my words are meaningless.

Lifting his glass, he takes a sip before replacing it on the table.

"Ruslan!" he calls.

There's some shuffling in the other room, and then the young boy runs into view. "Yes, Papa?"

"Go play in the basement," he says with a kind expression on his face. "I brought a new video game back for you. It's down there next to the PlayStation."

"You did?" Ruslan's face lights up with glee. "Thank you!" His laughter can be heard long after he's left the room. Once it fades entirely, Yevgeniy stares in my direction.

The kind expression still remains, but there's something

unmistakably sharp in his gaze. For a foolish moment, I'm afraid that if I stare too long, he might cut me with his eyes.

Stay strong. I swallow uncomfortably. *Don't show him any weakness.*

"You called me a murderer, *moya dorogaya doch*," he muses softly. "Why?"

I recoil at what he calls me—*my dear daughter*—and fight the urge to scream back that I don't belong to him. But I don't. I remain fixed in my spot, unable to answer at the moment.

Mom rocks in her chair, fidgeting from the growing tension. Her glass is empty. Gripping the bottle, she refills it, a few drops splattering from how violently her hand trembles.

Reaching over with a napkin, I clean the mess up for her. She gives me an appreciative, if weak, smile. It's enough to give me the strength to answer.

"What's to explain?" I ask as casually as I can. "Is that not what you are?"

"I suppose." His lips curl up slightly, and his tone remains disturbingly mild. "But this sounds less like a general accusation," he folds his fingers on the table, "and more like a specific instance you have in mind."

I spare another glance at my mother. She's looking down at her food like it's the most interesting thing she's ever seen. *This could be a trap,* I tell myself. *He might be baiting me, trying to get info. But this shouldn't be a secret ... He knows what he did, and I know he knows that Arsen has told me.*

Pulling my shoulders back, I sit up and speak with confidence. "You killed Arsen's wife, Kristina. His *pregnant* wife."

Mom ducks her head lower.

Yevgeniy's eyebrows crawl like worms, wrenching together like he's in pain. All the cold, calculating air around him has evaporated. In its place comes something more fragile, something ... vulnerable. He looks away, and for a second, he seems almost sympathetic.

I don't like it one bit.

"*Moya dorogaya doch*," he whispers. "There is so much that Arsen hasn't told you. So much that he's left out."

"He told me enough," I retort quickly.

"Enough for you to hate me," Yevgeniy whispers. "Enough to make him the hero of the story."

As much as I want to throw it back in his face, my own curiosity stops me from doing so. I lean closer. "What do you mean?"

"You'll learn more in due time."

"When?" I urge, my curiosity growing by the second.

"Once we're safe." His eyes crinkle from his sad smile. "From Arsen."

I'm taken aback by this. He's swiveled the conversation in a direction I never predicted. *He's playing games with me; that's all this is. Arsen is not a danger to me, only to him.* But a tiny part of my mind is frazzled by the implication of Yevgeniy's words. Arsen told me that Yevgeniy murdered Kristina. Mila confirmed the grisly details of what that monster did before killing her. Yet the look of pain that crossed Yevgeniy's face is real.

And that's enough to make me believe that Arsen left something out.

I still believe that Arsen is the good guy in this sordid story. But I'd be lying if I said there isn't a part of me that wants to know what happened on the other side. What could he mean when he said that Arsen told me enough to make him the hero of this story?

"Since you're not hungry," he says, wiping his hands on a

napkin, "you're free to go. Why don't you go entertain Ruslan? Get to know your little brother."

The words hit me like a slap to the face. It's like he delights in reminding me that I'm not Stepan's daughter but his. He's speaking in the same way that Arsen does: it sounds like a suggestion, but it's an order.

I fight the urge to wrap my arms protectively around my stomach.

I know better than to defy an order right now.

Slowly, I push my chair back. My mother starts to copy me, but that's when Yevgeniy holds up a hand to stop her.

"No. Katyusha," he says, "you stay. It's been *years* since I've seen you up close. And there are *years* of intimate conversations I missed having with you. We have so much to talk about. So much missing time to get to know each other once again." His grin tilts higher, at an angle, and he runs his tongue across his worm-like lips as he rapes her with his eyes. "Just like old times."

Mom shoots a terrified look my way, begging me for a way to save her from this. But both she and I know that it's an impossibility. Her lips press together into a bloodless line. Wordlessly, we communicate our shared fear. I fight the urge to grab her hand and drag her from the room. I start to reach for her hand, but she sits down heavily in her chair, settling the matter.

Yevgeniy rises from his seat and walks over until he stands behind her. His thick fingers gently caress her face before he grips her chin roughly and forces her mouth open.

"Oh," he tuts as he seizes a handful of her hair. "You have aged like fine wine, Katyusha. And I intend to drink you dry."

She closes her eyes, trembling, as a single tear rolls down her cheek.

She knows what's going to happen ... And she knows we can't fight it.

"Run along, now, Galina," Yevgeniy whispers as he yanks her forcibly to her feet. "Unless you want to stay and reenact the shame of that cuck who imagined himself your father."

I look at my mother, and through her tears, she forms a single word silently on her lips. *Go.*

Furious at how powerless we are, I turn away, rushing through the door to the basement where Ruslan is. I shut the door quickly behind me, wanting to shield myself from the hell that my mother is about to suffer. Anger courses through me, and I wish desperately that I had something—anything—that I could use to hurt Yevgeniy.

"Galina!" Ruslan shouts excitedly when he sees me. He's sitting on the floor in front of a TV as big as a picture window. In his small hands is a PS5 controller. "Are you here to play with me?"

Settling on my knees next to him, I return his eager smile with the best one I can manage, even as my heart shatters. My insides are still twisting, my brain still focused on what that monster is about to do to my mother. Ruslan has no clue what is going on above us.

And for his sake, I want to keep it that way.

"Sure," I say. "What kind of game is it?"

"It's a racing game! You can design your own cars, give them custom paint jobs, and even buy extra parts to make them faster when you race with other people. This is the one I made." He scrolls through the menus on the screen, displaying a very detailed racecar that has all the usual details that would appeal to a boy of ten.

"Wow, that looks really cool," I say, occasionally looking

up at the ceiling. *Am I imagining it, or did I just hear something scraping across the floor?* "Your dad lets you have whatever you want, huh?"

"Our dad, Galina." Ruslan grins even wider as he inadvertently cuts me with his words. "And yeah, he always gets me the best things. It's awesome." He passes me a controller. "Here, you can pick the track we race on."

"Thanks." *He's much sweeter than I expected him to be. I guess he didn't take on his dad's awful personality.* Grateful for a distraction, I sit down next to him, tapping my controller to view the different levels. "This is my first time, so I'm not as good as you. Please go easy on me."

"Dad is really busy these days." Ruslan's smile fades for a second, but I catch it nonetheless. "He tries to play when he can, but it's hard for him to make the time."

"Oh," I say gently. "It's a bummer you have to play by yourself."

"No, I play with others," he corrects me.

"You do?" Glancing up at the ceiling again, I frown as I picture the gun-toting guards hunching over the video game. "Who?"

"Papa has lots of girlfriends. They're really nice." He taps some buttons, focusing on the screen intently. "None of them stay around very long, so they never get good enough to beat me. I think it's because we move a bunch and they forget where we live. That's why they don't come around anymore. Pick a level, Galina, any level!"

Girlfriends ... lots of them... My heart jerks sideways. The only women I think someone like Yevgeniy knows are prostitutes. I remember Mila, her chained fox tattoo, and suddenly I taste acid on my tongue.

Yevgeniy's been bringing the women who are forced to work for him around Ruslan.

His son doesn't know the truth.

Looking at Ruslan with fresh eyes, I feel myself being crushed by the rush of pity. This poor boy has never had a real mother, probably never even a real friend. He mentioned moving a bunch. That makes sense. If they stayed in one spot, Arsen might find them. Does he go to school? Does he know anything beyond the lie that Yevgeniy has constructed around him?

Ruslan watches me eagerly, waiting for me to choose. Finally, I decide on a random level that looks like a tree-filled park.

"Oh!" Ruslan laughs. "Northwind Speedway! I'm really good at this one."

He's not boasting. Once the game starts, he loops me multiple times, winning every race. Even after he shows me all the buttons and some tricks, I still have no hope of beating him.

After my seventh loss in a row, Ruslan pats me on the back with a proud smile.

"It's okay, Galina," he says earnestly. "Maybe now that we aren't going to be moving anymore, you can actually practice and get good enough to beat me."

"What do you mean we aren't going to be moving anymore?" I ask warily.

"Papa says that now that Mom is here, we can be a family again," he replies. "Everything is going to get better because we're not going to be running from the bad man anymore."

Bad man ...

I don't have to ask. I know he means Arsen.

"I'm so happy to have both of you here," he rattles on. "I've always wanted to meet her. And you, of course! Isn't it great to have a family?"

Gripping the controller harder, I bite down on my tongue.

I had a family already. A wonderful one. Things were perfect until your father came along and destroyed them.

It's not rational to feel disdain for a child. But I can't help myself. The resentment I have toward Yevgeniy pollutes this moment with Ruslan. If Ruslan didn't exist, Yevgeniy would have no power over me or my mother.

He might even leave us alone.

But because of Ruslan, we're here ... forced to endure a facade of playing house.

Ruslan beams cheerfully at me. "I'm really glad you're here. I always wanted a big sister. Well, okay, I wanted a *little* sister because then I'd get to be a big brother. But you're still great!"

His naive honesty catches me off guard. Sapped of my misplaced anger, I let the controller fall from my hands. Ruslan picks it up, handing it back to me.

"Sorry," I say. "I didn't mean to drop it."

"It's okay. Papa will buy me a new one if this one breaks."

"He really cares about you, doesn't he?"

"Yeah!" Ruslan's grin is as big as the moon. "He's the best."

You have no clue what your father is really like, you stupid boy! It's surprising to me that Yevgeniy has shielded his son from the horrible life he leads. Is it possible for someone so cruel to still be a good father? Or is he just a master at keeping people in the dark?

"Let's play another round," I say with a smile. The more I'm left to my own thoughts, the more I might resent my little brother. At least when we play, I can distract myself with the lights on the screen and the rumble of the controller in my hand.

"Okay!" He rocks from side to side on the floor excitedly like a puppy.

As we start a new race, I push aside my grim thoughts. I want to focus on Ruslan and this moment. Maybe it's because of that, or just because I'm getting used to the game, but I actually manage to keep up with Ruslan on the course. Our cars race side by side. I brake, turning sharply, and fly across the finish line to beat him.

"No way!" he yells. Scowling viciously, Ruslan hurls the controller across the room, where it bounces loudly off the wall, then skids over the floor. The sheer abruptness of his actions, his explosion of rage, leaves me reeling. The little vein on his red face throbs.

In that instant I have no doubt that he's Yevgeniy's son.

He is capable of horrible things. I don't believe evil is genetic, and I'm sure Ruslan's behavior comes from the harsh world he's grown up in—absorbed even as Yevgeniy has shielded him from the worst excesses of the Bratva. But in this moment, fear stabs at my heart.

Will this child be destined to grow into a horrific copy of his monstrous father?

A surge of nausea attacks my belly. Clutching my middle, I double over on the floor, groaning. My mouth tingles to warn me, but it's too late to do anything about it, and I vomit on the floor.

Ruslan gasps. "Galina! Are you okay?" He comes closer, his anger replaced by panic and genuine worry.

No, this is bad. Swallowing down another wave of sickness, I search his face for some sign that he's figured out what's wrong with me. *He doesn't know; he's too young to know. But if he tells ... that could be enough of a clue for Yevgeniy to sniff out the truth that I'm pregnant. And if he does ...*

"I'm okay," I assure him with a weak smile. Sweat makes

my clothing cling to me. I want a bath—I want to get out of here.

"It's because of me, isn't it?" His chin trembles. "It's because I yelled at you. I scared you and it made you sick."

I blink. "Ruslan—"

"Please don't tell Dad," he begs me. "Please. I'm so sorry, Galina, I really am. I'll clean this up, I swear. Just don't tell Dad, okay?"

He thinks he's *the reason I threw up?* How can I be this lucky? Warily, I rest my hand on the little boy's shoulder.

"Of course not." I muster a wan smile at him. "This can be our little secret. Between brother and sister. Deal?"

His own fear is what will save me from being discovered. But as soon as the thought crosses my mind, I feel shame washing over me at the thought that I have to exploit a child's fear to keep myself safe.

Ruslan's smile lights up his eyes. "Deal!"

"Okay. I'll help you clean up this mess."

Nodding eagerly, he runs toward a closet and pulls out some paper towels. I watch him closely, trying to remind myself that seconds ago, he was a rage-filled creature, and now he's a sweet boy again. It's obvious that there are equal parts of my mother in him as there are of his monstrous father.

But the question is, as he gets older, which side will he grow up to embrace?

Later that night, I'm alone in the bedroom I'm supposed to share with my mother. But she's not there. I haven't seen her since Yevgeniy yanked her to her feet at the dinner table. I have no idea where they are, but I know that her absence is nothing good. *What is he doing to you, Mom?* I worry frantically.

I walk silently to the door and press my ear against it, listening for hints of footsteps.

But all I hear is nothing.

Cracking the door open, I gaze out, but I'm too nervous to go further. Guards might see me, and then they might decide to lock me in. When I left the basement, I spared a look at the dining room and saw that it was empty.

That was hours ago. *Are they in Yevgeniy's bedroom?*

Shuddering with raw disgust, I shut the door quietly and return to bed. Rolling onto my side, I hug my knees until I'm more curled than a snail's shell. My mind keeps throwing awful images at me, conjuring up things that Yevgeniy might be doing to my mother. *I could reach them if I tried. Guards or not, if I was quick, I could run past them.* And then what would I do?

I've never felt so helpless.

That's when the tears start coming, slowly at first, and then faster and faster until rivers run down my cheeks.

I burrow into my pillow, but my mind continues to torture me with vivid pictures of the vile things Yevgeniy is doing to my mom.

There's one person who could appear from the darkness, thrusting himself into the fray. Someone with enough strength and a drive for vengeance that would allow him to vanquish all my enemies and save both my mother and me from this living hell.

Arsen ... please ...

Come save us.

That night, I dream that he does.

But it remains just that—a dream and nothing more.

2

ARSEN

The bullet wound in my shoulder still burns days later. The cuts on my hands from shattered glass are barely healed. A normal man might have taken time to rest up and heal, but I don't have the luxury of wasting a single second. There are more pressing matters at hand.

Turning the wooden bat in my fist, I slap it into my opposite palm. Blood flicks from the bat, staining the front of my shirt. Mila stands behind me, watching with a bored expression on her face as I turn my attention back to the object of my fury.

"Stop, God, please fucking stop!" Sergei roars.

"Damn," I mutter. "Maybe wearing white was a bad idea. Then again, your black clothing isn't helping you much, now that I think about it."

Sergei's shirt collar and shoulders are soaked with blood from his broken mouth. Every wheezing breath he takes or desperate cry he makes sends more red splattering onto the material. "Arsen Kirilovich ... stop this. I'm begging you."

"Not until you tell me where Yevgeniy took my wife."

"I don't know, you bastard!"

"Wrong answer." Giving the bat a lazy swing, I take a few practice hits at the empty air. Sergei flinches during each one. "You know *something*. Otherwise you wouldn't have led us to the safe house. Galina *was* there. So were your buddies waiting to ambush us."

It was a miracle we got out of there alive. Mila was quick enough to narrow in on where the sniper was. She rolled next to me in the heat of the onslaught, snatching one of my guns from my belt. She managed to shoot him through the broken window while he was reloading. A single shot was all it took. Mila was deadly efficient, especially when neither of us knew just how many others there were.

And there *were* others. But by the time they approached the house, thinking we were injured and cornered, we were ready for them. Together, Mila and I left the would-be ambushers dead on the ground. We didn't bother to clean up the mess afterward—the cops could handle that for our troubles.

I had other pressing business.

Gritting my teeth, I rub at my bullet wound again. Between the warehouse and this last encounter, Yevgeniy's men are leaving more scars on me than I've earned in years.

"You were hoping we'd die in there, weren't you?" I ask.

"No." Sergei shakes his head rapidly. His eyes bulge, focused on my bat. "I would never hope that, Arsen Kirilovich."

Smiling with an echo of cynicism, I push the wet tip of the bat into his chest until I hear a discernible *pop*.

"You're a terrible liar, Sergei." My lips twist into a bestial smile. "I'm ashamed I didn't see the trap coming, in hindsight. So that's on me. But leading me to it ..." I take a deep breath. "That's on you."

I hoist the bat over my shoulder and slam it into

Sergei's rib cage, where I hear the satisfying sounds of multiple ribs breaking from the impact. He doubles over, spitting blood into his lap with a bubbling gag of sticky phlegm.

"Tell me where she is, Sergei. Now. Or I'm going to start breaking other things. Delicate things. Things that you don't want me breaking."

Heaving loudly, he looks up at me through the hair matted to his forehead by sweat and blood. "Fuck you, Arsen! You think you can beat me into talking? You have *nothing!*" he roars, and without thinking, I slam my fist into his chin.

Bursts of pain radiate out into my own arm. It was stupid to use my bare knuckles—they'll be bruised from the impact—but I wanted to shut him up without taking away his ability to talk. With as much force as possible, I swing the bat against his left knee. The kneecap shatters like dry kindling.

Sergei shrieks in pain, but I don't stop. The next hit is on his ankle. Then the other kneecap. Dipping the bat under his chin, I wait for him to finish moaning before I tilt his face toward me.

"Tell. Me. Where. She. Is."

"I don't know!" he coughs. A tooth tumbles from his lips, clattering on the floor of my basement. This section of my wine cellar has perfect soundproofing and temperature control. But even then, it does little to soothe the adrenaline-induced heat searing across my skin.

"This is a waste of time." Mila kicks the tooth aside with a look of disgust. "I told you we should've started with his toes, his eyelids ... the space beneath his nails." She waves a knife from side to side with a predatory sneer. "But I get first dibs on his balls."

"I'm doing the interrogation, not you," I grumble. I heft the bat once more.

Sergei's eyes widen as I prepare for round three. "I don't know where she is because he's moving her around!" he blurts.

I hesitate. "Continue."

"Yevgeniy has multiple safe houses. He's carting her from one to the next to make sure you can't find them!"

Frowning thoughtfully, I lean closer to him. "Which safe houses?"

"The old ones that were used as brothels." He licks his split, swollen lips. "You should remember them. They made us a mint before you shut them all down."

Being reminded of how I revolted against Yevgeniy brings me a satisfying thrill—one I desperately need. *Yes. I've beaten him in the past ... I can beat him again.*

Before I can ask for more details, Mila storms forward. She grabs Sergei by his scalp, forcing him to look at her from an awkward angle as she stands behind him.

"Do you miss them?" She traces her knife along his neck, leaving behind a thin red line in its wake. "Those houses of misery and horror?"

"Fuck you, whore," he sneers at her, finding a few last scraps of cockiness. "Maybe his precious Galina will be a better one than you. At least *she* looked like she could last a few rounds without falling apart like you did. And she looks like a better screamer than you."

Mila's eyes flare wider. I'm on the verge of crushing his exposed Adam's apple with the bat.

But instead, I consider what he accidentally revealed. *He doesn't know Galina is Yevgeniy's daughter.* If he did, he'd *never* suggest she'd end up in a brothel. *Now that's interesting.* Yevgeniy is keeping that detail close to his chest.

Turning on my heel, I toss the bloody bat aside, then head for the stairs. "I've heard everything I needed to hear. Do with him what you will, Mila. But make it painful."

Sergei lets out a whimpering, "Wait, what?"

"Oh, Sergei." Mila's delighted laughter floods the cellar. "How many rounds do you think *you'll* last in my hands? How loud of a screamer do you think you are? Because I'm betting you're a loud one."

I make it to the top of the stairs before Sergei's first blood-curdling scream reaches me. But once I shut the door behind me, the sounds fade away to nothing. Yes, the sound-proofing is *excellent*.

Rubbing my jaw anxiously, I mull over what Sergei said. Which old brothel could Galina be hidden in? There are so many of them, but it would have to be one that doesn't have any foot traffic these days. A place secluded enough not to draw attention from junkies looking for an abandoned space to shoot up or squatters hoping to make their home.

I should have drilled Sergei for more details before handing him off to Mila. Well, too late now. Entering the kitchen, I have to wipe the bottoms of my shoes, as well as a few bloody footprints, from the kitchen tiles. I'm messier than I realized. I wash my hands in the sink, removing the blood that's starting to scab over. It wouldn't be the first time I was spotted in my home covered in gore, but I prefer not to give off an overly violent image with my staff whenever I can.

Ulyana will skewer me for the mess in the cellar.

I take a quick shower after I go upstairs, and change into clean clothes. I'm in the middle of putting on new, blood-free shoes when Mila sways into my bedroom doorway. As if to spite my attempts at keeping the place from looking like a slaughterhouse, she trails blood behind her with every step.

"You look fresh as a babe," she says.

"Can you not track blood all over my carpets?"

"Don't get so pissy at me. I have good news." Crossing her arms, she leans on my doorframe. "Before I ripped his tongue out, Sergei gave up more info. It's amazing how quickly men start telling the truth when you have a knife at their balls."

"Spare me the details. What did you learn?"

"A list of potential safe houses Galina could be in."

My chest grows tight with joy. "Good."

"You're welcome," she chuckles. "In return, I'm blaming the footprints I tracked through here on you. Make sure Ulyana knows that."

"You think she'll believe that I was wearing heels?"

"That sounds like a you problem, not mine." Mila shrugs before she turns and walks away, heels clicking with each step and leaving distinct bloody dots in their wake.

I'm grateful that she had the presence to remember the mission. My brain has been fractured lately, making it a challenge to stay focused. All I can think about is Galina. It's impossible to chase the thought of her away from my mind. And each day I'm separated from her, it's harder and harder to keep myself as sharp as I normally am. The very memory of her dulls my senses.

Once I get her back, that will change.

"Get cleaned up," I call after Mila. "I want to work our way down this list immediately."

"You're in quite the hurry."

"We can't waste a minute."

"Last time we rushed, Arsen Kirilovich, we were cornered and you nearly died."

"I'm aware." Making fists at my sides, I work my jaw. "But we need to act fast. If Yevgeniy finds out that Galina is pregnant with my child, he *will* hurt the baby."

Mila's eyes soften. "I have a feeling he already knows."

A surge of despair careens through my blood. "What makes you think that?"

"He's a perceptive man. And Galina wears her heart on her sleeve. Even when she was here, she subconsciously tried to protect that unborn child from danger." Mila wraps her arm around her stomach to imitate Galina. "How long before she does that in front of him?"

Mila's words ring with harsh truth. "Then all the more reason we have precious little time to waste."

3

GALINA

Bruises come in more shades than I realized.

If the purple and green hues weren't patterned across my mother's throat and arms, I'd find them beautiful. Instead, I'm fighting down the urge to vomit.

"He did that to you?" I ask, seething.

My mother whirls around; she didn't know I was in the room. She was in the middle of changing clothes. Yevgeniy told us earlier that we'd be moving locations today. I wanted to pack everything, making sure to hide my father's rose carefully. I've been trying to keep it from being discovered. Now, I've discovered something Mom is hiding.

"*Malyshka*, please," she gasps. "I didn't want you to see this."

Shaking my head, I come closer for a better look. The marks resemble fingerprints. "He's sick. We have to get away from here, Mom."

There's a loud knock on the door. "Hurry up," one of the brigadiers yells. "We're leaving! Get your shit into the car."

Mom pulls the long-sleeved turtleneck into place, hiding all evidence of her "catching up" with Yevgeniy.

"Let's go," she says, shoving around me with her bag.

I don't have a chance to respond. I notice she's stripped the room of all our things, which weren't many. *She grabbed the brooch for me, just like last time.* Mom is in pain, but she's still looking out for me.

I chase after her. Ruslan and Yevgeniy are already in the car. It's a big van this time, enough room for all of us. Yevgeniy rides up front while Ruslan wiggles into the middle. He acts as a divider between Mom and me. His giant, toothy grin marks him as oblivious to the tension in the car.

"You said we wouldn't move anymore, Papa!"

"I'm sorry, *malchik*," Yevgeniy replies. "But the bad man found us again. But maybe this will be the last time. But as long as all of us are together, we'll be fine."

"Yeah!" he giggles. "Together."

We don't drive for long before we park in front of a squat gray house at the end of a cul-de-sac. The roof is sagging from water rot. When I step out, I stumble on the divots and cracks in the beaten-up driveway. This house looks more abandoned than the last one.

"It may not look like much," Yevgeniy says from the passenger side of the car, "but we'll be safe here."

I scoff internally at that. Safe isn't a word I'll ever associate with Yevgeniy.

Ruslan dashes from the van, grabbing my mother by the elbow. "Mama! Let's go inside! I want to see my new room!"

"It's not set up with your video games yet," Yevgeniy warns.

"That's okay! Mama and I can go play something else together!"

I tighten up and stare hotly at the small boy. His open possessiveness of my mother is making my hackles rise. *She was my mom long before you knew she existed.* I know it's silly to be angry at Ruslan, but after seeing how battered and bruised Mom was by Yevgeniy, I'm feeling protective. He's only a kid, and she won't chide him if he yanks on her bruises or sore muscles.

She'll take the abuse ... just like she does from his father.

She sees me looking and sends me a light smile. Her eyes assure me that she's fine. Allowing Ruslan to guide the way, she follows him into the house.

"Don't they look picture perfect?" Yevgeniy asks beside me. I didn't notice him creep up. His shadow drapes over mine on the ground. I hate even that part of us touching. I step to the side.

"Whatever you say," I mumble.

"You disagree?" When I don't respond, he puts his hands in his pockets, sighing. "A devoted daughter should be happy to see her family reunited."

"You're not my family," I growl.

"I'm the only family you have."

I whirl around to glare up at him. Yevgeniy watches me with infuriating calmness. "Just because you're forcing us together doesn't make you family. You'll never be my father."

"I shouldn't have waited so long to reunite with Katya." His eyes narrow slightly. "Stepan poisoned your mind against me."

"Stepan raised me!" I snarl. "And even if you raised me, I wouldn't be oblivious to what a monster you are. I'm not like Ruslan."

That makes him flinch. "I love my son. Just as I love you."

"You don't give a fuck about me."

"That's where you're wrong, *moya dorogaya doch*," he says softly, and there is no hiding the pain in his voice. "I will *always* love my children."

Turning, he strides into the house, leaving me standing in the cold, feeling more confused than ever.

THE BED IS STIFF, but it's clean. I'm pretty sure Yevgeniy must have hired someone to give the house a quick once-over before we arrived since the silken sheets don't match the grotesque exterior. He has enough money to uproot his life weekly. Paying a cleaner is chump change, I bet.

I'm lying across the bed when my mother enters the room. "*Mamochka!*" I blurt, sitting up sharply. "Are you okay?"

She waves a hand at me dismissively. Her arms circle her body as if she's cold, but the room is overly warm. "Of course."

"You've been playing with Ruslan for over two hours," I say pointedly.

"Yes, and what of it? He's just a child. He can't hurt me, *malyshka*."

"I guess not," I say cautiously, "not like his father."

She stiffens, then sits on the bed opposite mine. "I'm not as fragile as you think."

Standing, I move toward her, quickly wrapping her in a hug. She gasps slightly and I pull back. Her face is twisted in pain, and the sight of it makes my blood boil.

"You can't be alone with him anymore," I say seriously.

"Am I supposed to tell him no?" she asks hotly. "We're his prisoners, *malyshka*. Or have you forgotten?" She pulls away from me, facing the wall.

I sit beside her, putting my hand on her knee gently. "You're right. As long as we're here, we're all in danger. We have to find a way to contact Arsen."

"Arsen?" she hisses, gawking at me.

Now that the solution is in the open air, I lean into it eagerly. "Yes. He can get us out of here; he can protect us like he did before."

"Arsen is the reason we're in danger."

"What? No, he's the only one who can keep us safe!" I shake my head violently. "I'm an idiot for thinking that it was smart to run from him. I should have seen from the start that we were better off in his mansion."

"Oh, *malyshka*." Her eyes warm with empathy. She gently caresses my shoulder the way she would when I was a child. "Can you not see it? Our monsters may wear different faces, but they are the same."

Reeling away from her, I curl my upper lip. "You're wrong, *mamochka*. Arsen isn't like Yevgeniy."

My mother reaches for my face, but her fingers push back the hair around my neck until she traces the marks Arsen left on me from that time in the room detached from the house—when he made me beg for him to take me even as I screamed that I hated him.

She traces her fingers along the faded marks before she takes my hand and presses them to my belly. "He's *exactly* like Yevgeniy. And he has done to you what Yevgeniy did to me."

My heart flares with terror. "You can't tell him about the baby."

She wrinkles her nose, offended. "I won't do anything to endanger either of you. I'm—"

There's a sound at the door, and the two of us part just in time as Yevgeniy enters.

He's put on a long jacket, as if he plans to go outside or has just come from there. Jerking apart from my mother, I stand in front of her with my feet spread. He stops short. "You look like you're ready to fight me," he chuckles.

I make fists by my sides. "Leave her alone."

"You have the wrong idea, *dorogaya*."

Narrowing my eyes, I peek back at my mother, who's cowering on the bed. She resembles a beaten dog. "I know what you've been doing to her."

When I look back, he's staring me down. We're in a silent war. I realize I can't stop him from touching her, but that doesn't mean I won't try. His posture changes. "I'm not here for my Katyusha; she can rest. I'm taking my children to the park."

Children. Knowing he's referring to me sends nails scraping up my spine. The nausea isn't from my pregnancy. My mother is watching Yevgeniy closely, still curled up like she'll have to defend herself.

"You what?" I ask warily.

"Ruslan has a lot of energy to burn off. And I think we could all use some fresh air."

"But he was just playing with my mother for hours," I argue.

He waits a beat. "Would you prefer that I send him out alone instead?"

It's a trick question. I know I don't have a choice. *If he's with me, then at least he isn't raping Mom.* Lifting my head higher, I allow a sneer to dance across my lips. My voice is silky. "I'd never turn down a chance to get out of my cage."

His eyes flash, but he says nothing.

"Higher! Higher!" Ruslan's delighted laughter fills the crisp air. I can literally see it: puffs of white that dissipate with every thrust his body makes on the swing. His sneakers kick at the top of the arc, and when he descends to the bottom, Yevgeniy is there to push him back up.

It's a surreal sight. I'm struggling to reconcile the fatherly kindness I'm witnessing with the terrible things Yevgeniy has done. Even if I didn't want to believe Arsen—and I do believe him—I 100 percent believe my mother and the bruises Yevgeniy left on her body.

The man is a murdering rapist.

Ruslan squeals happily when his dad sends him flying higher on the swing.

A murdering rapist who's a wonderful father. If I took a photo of them right now, you could slap it on a Hallmark card. A perfect family picture ... without me in it.

Ruslan's maroon scarf floats as it defies gravity with each upward swing. He's bundled up perfectly against the chilly weather. His slate-blue coat is thick enough that it hides his shape, making him look bigger than he is, but not older.

I'm envious of how warm he must be. My jacket is meant for autumn, not the onslaught of winter. Burying my hands in my pockets, my eyes trek higher, to the gray-and-white mottled clouds on the horizon. We're the only ones in the park. The rest of the world senses the snow that wants to burst open on top of us.

It hasn't come yet, but it's waiting.

Yevgeniy says something to Ruslan before strolling toward me, where I'm sitting on the sidelines on the singular green bench. All my muscles bunch up when he settles beside me, his hands resting on his knees. The bench isn't big enough to give us enough space. Hell, being on the other side of the country wouldn't be enough, though I'd take that if it was an option.

"What has he told you?" Yevgeniy says.

He's speaking like we're resuming a conversation. In a way, we are, because I know who he's referring to. "You already know what he told me."

"You misunderstand me." His smile grows tense. "I want to know specifically what he told you."

You don't get to dictate everything I do. But I'm angry, and this is a chance to show it. "He told me you forced Kristina to beg for her baby's life before you shot her three times in the stomach."

His eyes turn toward Ruslan, his voice growing tender. "You must think I enjoyed doing that."

"Of course you did," I growl.

Somehow, his voice dips even softer. "That's where you're wrong. What happened with Kristina wasn't something I *wanted* to do. It was something I *had* to do."

Shivering, not just from the cold, I hug my body tight. "Nobody has to kill others; that's crazy."

"That's because you don't understand what Arsen took from me." Yevgeniy lets out a dry chuckle void of all humor. "He never told you that the only reason I killed Kristina and his unborn child was because I needed to teach him the true meaning of loss."

Ruslan's giggles fill the background. It's a strange soundtrack for the grim conversation.

The hard line of his neck flexes. It's as if he's holding his breath. Finally, he looks directly at me. His breath floats in the air like a wisp of a cloud.

"Because I needed him to understand what he took from me."

4

GALINA

Yevgeniy is staring at his hands. He links his fingers, twists them, creating every possible position his joints can manage.

"Once upon a time," he starts, "I had a son. Pyotr." His eyes close like someone threw salt in them, his lips making a sour frown. "I loved him more than anything or anyone in this world."

He had another son? The past tense is a megaphone. My blood seems to thicken in my veins.

Fondness enters his eyes, warming them. "Pyotr was always a wild child. That's natural, of course. He was a prince of the Bratva, and my future heir." His hands twist, the brittle mood returning tenfold. "Back then, Arsen was my brigadier. I trusted him with everything. With my life and my son's life."

My stomach drops out from beneath me. I know where this is going, and I need to stop it. I want to clasp my hands over his mouth or run away while covering my ears. But I can't move, and Yevgeniy presses on.

"He was supposed to keep my boy safe." Those hands

wring until all the blood flees his knuckles. He locks his eyes on me, the intensity, the pure sadness, stealing the air from my lungs. "And instead, he *killed* him. Butchered my son in cold blood and left the body to rot. He taught me *loss.* Honor demanded that I act. A child for a child. That was why I had to do it. That was why Kristina had to watch her child die inside of her."

I snap my head from side to side. "No. You're lying to me. That has to be it." *Arsen would never kill someone he was supposed to protect! Not a child!*

Yevgeniy sits up straighter. "I don't lie to my children."

Ruslan shrieks—we both look up. He's off the swing, running around the play structure, chasing imaginary friends and foes. He resembles my mother when he smiles. They share the same dimples. But seeing shadows of her on his face only makes me remember the bruises on her body.

"Why do you hurt her?" I whisper.

He keeps watching his son as he speaks, his voice clipped. "Because she denied me."

"What?"

"I gave her a chance to leave Stepan when you were born." My chest squeezes—so do my nails against my thighs. "She refused. She preferred to be a wife to a pauper than a lover to a king. She chose her fate, and for that, I will always resent her. And because she denied me, I'm driven by a *need* to possess her. To own her. To teach her that she can never run away from me."

I tremble on the bench. Rage, fear, horror ... It's all mixed inside of me in a thorny ball. Mom's words echo in my ear as I listen. *Our monsters may wear different faces. But they're the same.*

No, I tell myself. Arsen isn't like Yevgeniy at all. He can't be. He's better than him.

Is he? He murdered a child, *Galina!*

Yevgeniy faces me, studying me with a half-smile. "You think I'm a monster. I can see it on your face."

"Because you are," I hiss.

"Maybe." His shrug lacks commitment. "But can you honestly say that your precious Arsen is so different from me?"

He reaches up and pushes back my hair, revealing the marks Arsen's fingers left on me.

"See?" he whispers. "He's capable of hurting you the same way that you accuse me of hurting my dear Katyusha. And what's to say he hasn't done to you what I've done to her?"

I bite back a gasp. *Does he know about the pregnancy?* I wish I could read his face the way he reads mine. Afraid I'll reveal my secret, I remain silent. I don't budge an inch. A childlike fancy enters me: *if I stay still long enough, he'll forget I'm here and go back to playing with Ruslan.*

He tilts his head like an owl. "If you want to get your mother away from me, you'll need to get yourself away from Arsen. This war is only going to get worse." His eyebrows pucker. "It would be terrible to lose my daughter in the crossfire. I've lost one child to Arsen already. I do not wish to lose a second. And I have no desire to inflict that grief upon your mother."

The edges of my vision crackle with red and black. Panic mixes with disbelief. *He's talking like he cares about her. Like he cares about me.* I know it's just another lie. But for some reason, I'm stuck on what he said. *The war ... it's only going to get worse.* That part is true, but why tell me that now?

Yevgeniy slips his phone out of his jacket. His mouth is in a faint frown. He's reading something, and I guess he doesn't like it. But then he smiles again as if whatever he saw wasn't worth an afterthought.

"We'll see each other soon," he says to me without looking up. Standing, he shouts, "Ruslan! *Idi suda!* It's time to go!"

I start to rise, but before I do, he turns to me. There's something in his hand. "What—" I choke out, before he pushes the item into my palm.

"When the time comes, you'll know what to do," he says, backing away.

Opening my fingers, I stare at the tiny, hard square. It's a SIM card.

"Why would I ever want to contact you?" I seethe.

Yevgeniy ignores me, but the cryptic smile doesn't leave his face. Ruslan bounds toward us, his scarf looping through the air like a kite's tail. Yevgeniy meets him halfway, taking his hand. He whispers something to Ruslan, who casts a longing look toward me. The sadness is unmistakable on his young face, but he follows after Yevgeniy obediently. They move quickly toward the car we arrived at the park in. Everything is happening suddenly, and my brain is barely able to keep up.

They're leaving without me!

Jumping to my feet, I look on helplessly as Yevgeniy drives toward the nearby patch of trees. My heart is stampeding wildly. I'd be joyous, except that my mother is back at the house they're returning to without me.

"Hey!" I call into the dead air, confusion leaching into my tone. "What's happening?"

There's a crunch as tires roll over the road. For a second, I stiffen, thinking Yevgeniy has realized his error and is coming back for me. But this is a new car, and it's driving from the opposite direction.

The paint job makes it look like a chunk of midnight has broken from the sky. It stops right in front of my bench. The dark surface reflects everything around it, including my stunned expression. A familiar face appears in the crack when the door bursts open.

"Arsen?" I manage to whisper.

His intense eyes bring a familiar heat to my chest. The cut of his dark jacket fits him well, forcing me to remember how muscular and fit he is beneath. Just seeing him wakes my body up.

He's a blur of motion, and suddenly I find myself in his warm embrace. The friction of his jacket is pressed against my cheek, and his arms cling, holding me to his body. It's a tight embrace that steals the air from my lungs. Or maybe I'm simply too stunned to breathe.

Is this real? Or is it still only a dream?

I've thought about this moment every night since I fled his mansion. The frequency grew once Yevgeniy carted me away from our safe house. And now my dream has become reality. I'm in such a daze that when Arsen holds me at a distance, searching my face, I don't register that he's asking me something.

"What?" I utter.

"Are you okay?" he asks—no, demands. The fervor in his wild eyes screams. *Please tell me I'm not too late.*

"Yes," I assure him. Blinking, I place my fingers on his wrists, squeezing, feeling how solid he is. One hand has bandages wound around the knuckles. There are puffy circles under his eyes, possibly darker than my own. "How are you here?"

"Where is he?"

My heart skips. "He left just before you got here."

Arsen's eyes narrow, scanning the playground anxiously,

like he doesn't believe me. The intensity in his face makes my hair stand on end. *He's hunting.* My hand curls around the SIM card. *Should I tell him about this?*

Yevgeniy's words enter my head. *If you want to get your mother away from me, you'll need to get yourself away from Arsen as well. This war is only going to get worse.*

Arsen snaps his attention back to me. He hugs me again, tighter than before. My ribs creak from the pressure. But that's not my concern. The hug constricts me enough that it's hard to move. With a careful shift of my arms, I bring my hand near my pocket and drop the SIM card in.

I can't tell him ... not yet.

Not until I know what side I need to take in this war I didn't start.

5

ARSEN

She's safe.

So many things have become uncertain as of late, especially as my world flipped upside down over and over again. But from the second I jump from my car and wrap my arms around Galina, familiar certainty surrounds me once more.

She is safe.

A part of me knows that she won't be forever, not while Yevgeniy is allowed to run free. But in this moment, it's enough. Cupping the back of her head, I stroke her hair while my eyes search the playground. There's no one here but us. Unable to convince myself, I look again, scouring bushes, trees, and even the distant buildings fringing the area. My ears strain for the sound of Yevgeniy's wretched voice.

But still, nothing.

My hand slows its stroking of Galina's hair. "He wasn't lying."

"What do you mean?" she asks, turning her face upward at me.

I relax my grip enough for her to shimmy out from it,

even though it pains me to do so. "He sent me a text telling me to come here and get you," I explain. *I didn't think it was real.*

Somewhere nearby, Mila is stalking the grounds, hunting for any signs of an ambush to ensure that this happy reunion isn't about to become a tragedy in a split second. Two *boeviki* stand just outside my car, armed to the teeth and ready to intervene in a second.

My phone vibrates. It's Mila.

Mila: None of his men are here. The perimeter is clean.
Mila: Is she really there with you? He just left her?
Mila: What game is he playing??

"This makes no sense," I murmur, "why would Yevgeniy simply allow me to come retrieve you?"

How is it not a trap?

Galina grips my sleeves. Her eyebrows crinkle with worry. "Because he still has my mother."

I wince at the news. I'd thought as much—it was actually the best outcome, since otherwise, it meant her mother had met a worse fate. Gingerly, I cup her cheeks. "It's all right; we—"

"No!" she snaps, teeth flashing as she rips away from my touch. "It's not all right! He's going to hurt her! He's *been* hurting her!"

I'm taken aback by the ferocity she aims at me. This rage should be meant for Yevgeniy. Yet in this moment, I've become her target, and I can't figure out why.

Look at her, you fool. Look and see. She's standing with her feet spread apart, her jacket straining over her shoulders.

Instead of a frightened woman seeking reassurance, which I expected, she stands before me—shoulders squared—as if she's ready to fight.

I was foolish to assume Galina would simply rush into my arms, seeking me out as a source of safety. She's always been ferocious in her own right, since the very first time our paths crossed. On occasions, I've seen that ferocity rise to the surface. But here and now, in the flesh, she's reminding me that she isn't a damsel in distress.

Not by a long shot.

As I take in the sight of her, I can see the invisible barbs that have wrapped around her—signs of secret suffering during her time as a captive of Yevgeniy. The woman I love has been damaged and hurt, all because I was stupid enough to let her out of my sight.

Because I trusted that someone else could keep her safe.

I won't make that mistake again.

"What happened?" I growl. "What did he do to you?"

"Are you not listening at all?" She notices me scanning her and stiffens. "It's not me that we need to worry about. It's my mother and what he's doing to *her!* We have to go after him! We have to save her!"

"And we will," I insist flatly.

"Then why are we still here?" Her frown trembles at the corners. She darts her eyes from me to my Escalade. "Why aren't we chasing after Yevgeniy right now?"

My phone buzzes again. Mila demands my attention, but Galina needs it more. I don't have a satisfying answer for either of them; it's a no-win situation for me.

"Because I need to make sure you're okay first," I tell her. "And because we don't know where he's gone. Do you?"

"No," she admits hesitantly. "I tried to pay attention on

the drive here, but he intentionally took lots of weird turns and did a lot of backtracking."

That's not surprising. I dip my head in frustrated resignation.

"He's always been cautious." My temples thrum as I stare around us again, scanning for threats that still refuse to materialize. "Why did he bring you to a playground, of all places?"

Something flashes across Galina's face as she opens her mouth before shutting it quickly. Her expression changes in a split second, but I spot it just as it fades. *Guilt.* She looks away suddenly, as if she can't bear to look me straight in the eyes.

Suspicion pricks up and dances over my spine. A tiny voice whispers in the back of my mind that Galina is hiding something.

I swoop her hands into mine. "Galina, you have to trust me." She doesn't pull out of my grip, and I convince myself she doesn't want to. "I'll do everything in my power to get your mother back. But we can't find her by standing here. And I need to make sure you're okay. Let's go home. All right?"

She turns her eyes to the ground, the combativeness slowly melting away with each tumbling breath in the winter air. "If you say so."

I'd built up an image of the reunion in my head. In my imagination, it was a glorious moment where both of us crashed together like crashing ocean waves, the force powerful enough to polish stones into jewels.

Yet reality has a way of disappointing.

The only similarity to the ocean here is the chill I feel in my bones.

And a sense that I'm slowly drowning.

Opening the car door, I ease her inside before I slide over to join her. The *boeviki* in front give us quick glances. "Drive," I snap. The one at the wheel revs the engine, and the car peels onto the road.

Galina peers at the backs of their heads. She's looking all over the car, but never at *me*. Her legs clamp together, and her hands are wrapped in a knot on her lap. She looks equal parts vulnerable and wary—like a wolf that has to chew off its own leg to escape a trap.

I sweep her close, pouring my warmth over her as I greedily drink in her scent, her presence, and her sea of clashing emotions. *She's here. She's really here.*

I've been dying for this moment.

She nudges against my chest, softly at first, and then with increasing insistence. Reluctantly, I let her go, watching in dismay as she slips back until she's sitting as far away from me as possible. Pressed against the window, she turns and glares at me with wide, shining eyes. The moment feels familiar, and it takes me a heartbeat to realize that it's just like the first time I dragged her away from Tsar's.

The memory of that first night hangs as clear as a knife in my mind. She acted like I was a wolf, ready to tear her apart. I was equally suspicious of her motives and her reliability. Trust wasn't even a word that existed between us that night. She was a mystery to me, and I a threat to her.

Somewhere along the way, the walls between us came down and we allowed each other a glimpse of our true selves hidden underneath.

But right now, those walls have come back up.

And it pains me to think that this time, those walls might be permanent.

"When we get back home," I say, "tell me everything that's happened. All of it."

Galina turns from me to look out the tinted window. Her palm presses against it, dragging down until it leaves steamy streaks in its trail. When she speaks, her voice is cold and even.

"I'll tell you whatever will help me get my mom back."

The hair rises on the back of my neck at the way she phrases it.

What the hell did Yevgeniy do to her? What did he *tell* her? Most importantly ... what is she hiding from me?

6

GALINA

I don't have a home anymore.

That's the only thought running through my head as I stare up at the familiar sight of Arsen's mansion. The car rumbles along the driveway. The spiked gates look exactly as I remember. The yards with trimmed grass, the distant rose garden, the extravagant water fountains, and the perfect painted exterior ...

Nothing has changed since I was here.

But I have.

Both Yevgeniy and my mother are vying for my attention inside my head. Each of them whispers their own warning in the back of my mind.

He was supposed to keep my boy safe. And instead, he killed him.

Our monsters may wear different faces. But they're the same.

I want to silence the voices in my head, but I can't.

Once we park, Arsen clambers out to help me from the car. I ignore him to step out on my own. A wave of déjà vu washes over me. It feels just like the first time I arrived here.

I rejected his offer that time as well. The only thing missing is the blindfold he placed over my eyes.

His face betrays no emotions—but I know he's trying to hide his thoughts from me. His *boeviki* stand at attention, waiting for instruction. Arsen glares, releasing his frustration on them instead of me.

"Pay attention. You know your duty."

They dip their heads in acknowledgment before they return to standing as still as statues. I head for the front door, and Arsen matches my pace.

"There should be clean clothes in your room," he says when we pass the threshold.

The air inside is chilly, almost as if the heater isn't running full force. I'm grateful that I still have my jacket—thin as it is.

"Ulyana will have made sure your bed is ready for you," he continues. "If you like, I can have someone draw you a hot bath; just say the word."

But I'm barely listening. My eyes trace the familiar sight of the main room, trying to force me to feel the sensation of comfort I desperately long for.

But all I feel is hollowness.

The studio burned down. My mother and I were forced to flee my childhood home. Then we found ourselves stolen away from what was supposed to be a safe house in a game played by those who had their own aims. All of that just to be taken and then shuttled from one random house to another by the monster who laid claim to us.

Where do I belong? Am I always supposed to feel lost like this?

Has home become just another word to me now?

"*Ptichka.*"

That word ... That single damn word that has bound me

to Arsen since the moment our eyes locked across the negotiation table brings a torrent of emotions flooding through me. It tumbles softly from Arsen's lips, gentle as a caress and filled with promises that I know he cannot fulfill.

But it roots me somehow. It reminds me of where I stand.

Where I belong.

I turn my gaze forward, and Arsen stands in front of me. His hands are slack by his sides, and his fingers are twitching. The bandage on his hand catches my attention again. I don't know if he's hurt because of me—whether because he punched something in frustration or was hurt while he searched for me. But I know what his twitching fingers are a sign of: he wants to hold me. He was dying to hold me the entire car ride.

Part of me feels the same ache. But the other part ...

Our monsters may wear different faces. But they're the same.

"Sorry," I say after a deep breath. "What was that about a bath?"

"I can have someone draw you a hot bath," he repeats himself. "I've also called for a doctor. He'll be here any minute."

"A doctor," I echo.

Arsen looks at my belly and instinctively, I rub my hand over it. His fingers move again. Yes, he wants to feel proof that his child is alive and well. *No, not his child. Our child.* This baby has endured everything I have. A familiar fear clutches around my heart like an icy fist. A baby in the womb can't ask for help.

It could be hurt ... It ...

A rush of emotion slashes at me. I lean sideways, bracing myself against the nearest wall before the strength drains from my legs. Arsen starts to reach out, but I shake my head, refusing his offer. I know that if I were to allow him this single gesture, I'd fall back under his spell. I *have* to keep the walls between us up for as long as possible.

It's easier to block him out than allow him in when I don't know what he's planning for me.

It's the only way I know I can survive.

I'm not ready for any of this, I think in agony. *I wanted Arsen to save me, but now that he has, I'm back to doing everything I can to keep him away.*

All because of Yevgeniy and what he said about Kristina, about Pyotr, and about Arsen. I want to say that he's lying, but there was no hiding the hurt in his eyes when he brought up *his* version of the past.

Just who am I to believe? The monstrous man who fathered me? The one who claims he would never lie to his children?

Or the man who gave me the hope of being a mother again? The one who claims he would never lie to *me*.

"*Ptichka*, what's wrong?" he asks urgently.

"Nothing." Lying comes second nature to me these days.

"Don't lie to me, Galina." His eyes darken. "I know when things are not okay. I know when you're keeping things from me. And right now, I can tell that you're doing both."

I press my lips together, trying to think of how I can respond. He's not wrong, but I don't like being called out. If he suspects that I'm hiding something from him, then he'll keep prying at it until I spill the truth to him. But Arsen is a man who's willing to keep secret after secret close to his heart. Aren't I allowed to do the same? Don't I get to have secrets of my own?

A knock on the door distracts me, the door swinging open to allow an older man I recognize to come inside.

"Hello?" Dr. Helsan says. He's not dressed in the long

coat of his profession, just plain slacks and a green cardigan. He's carrying a heavy suitcase at his side, and there's an air of confusion on his face.

Whatever Arsen said to him, it must've sounded like an emergency.

The moment he sees me, his surprise transforms into a kind smile. "How are you feeling, Mrs. Isakov?"

My heart skips a beat at that name.

I haven't been called that in a while. The last doctor I spoke to knew me by a fake name, and all I wanted in that moment was for him to call me Mrs. Isakov. But now that I'm hearing it again, it feels ... different.

Everything feels different, having been polluted by Yevgeniy's words.

Reaching down, I brush my wedding ring. Throughout this entire ordeal, I never removed it. *He's here to check on my baby.* Slowly, I allow my shoulders to relax.

"I could be better," I tell Dr. Helsan. "Things have been hectic."

He smiles politely. "That's how life goes sometimes. Now, let's make sure your little bundle is growing into a big bundle."

Arsen shakes the man's hand before leading the way upstairs. I follow closely, moving carefully on the steps. Each step reminds me of that night when my heel wobbled on the edge.

But which specific night? The one with Simon? Or the one with Arsen?

Does it even matter?

In a guest bedroom, Dr. Helsan opens his suitcase. Within minutes, he converts the space into a mini-office. The long table is used to hold a variety of packaged items, and a surgery gown is draped across the bed.

"Go and get changed," Dr. Helsan instructs me.

Arsen hovers anxiously in the corner while I change. He keeps his eyes away, not peeking at my brief nudity. We're functioning like strangers instead of worried parents-to-be.

"Please lie down," the doctor says.

I do exactly that, settling on the blanket. I try to relax, but it's impossible. Lying down now, I'm made aware of just how *tense* I am. My spine is static, and my leg muscles cramp as I shift around. Dr. Helsan approaches with the small, familiar fetal Doppler.

I've done this already, I think, but not with Arsen. The thought hits me harder than I expect—*I've heard our baby's heartbeat. He hasn't.*

Arsen looks across at me. There's a wordless question he won't dare speak. Like ice in the glare of a radiant sun, I feel the walls I've put up crumbling away.

"Come here," I say gently and hold out my hand. Slowly, Arsen comes to life, and with long strides, he joins my side. Our fingers find each other, and a familiar heat flows from him to me, chasing away the chill that has enveloped me ever since he took me from that playground.

Together, we watch the screen next to the table.

Gently, Dr. Helsan gently runs the Doppler over my belly. The black-and-white scribbles on the screen shift like boiling water. Slowly, a shape forms, and a familiar pulsing echo fills the room. My baby's heartbeat floods me with warmth, and I feel Arsen squeezing my fingers when he recognizes the sound.

"There we are," Dr. Helsan says kindly. "Your baby is doing just fine. Just fine. Happy and healthy as far as I can tell."

"Really?" I ask, staring at the screen. After all I've endured, it's hard to accept some good news.

Air rushes from Arsen's lips loudly. He sounds like he's been holding that one breath for hours.

"Our baby," he says in awe.

My eyes find his. Even without speaking, mutual relief and joy pass through us. He smiles, and I feel my own eyes crinkling as the same gesture breaks on my face. My nose stings, and as much as I don't want to cry, I can't hold back the tears.

Dr. Helsan passes me some wipes to clean off the ultrasound gel. After cleaning myself up, I start to rise, but stop when a wave of exhaustion pins me to the bed. Arsen gently takes my elbow, and his voice is laced with worry.

"Are you all right?"

"Yes," I say earnestly. "I just realized how tired I am. Is that hot bath still an option?"

"Of course it is. I can have Olesya draw it for you."

"No need," I tell him. "I can do it myself."

"Are you sure?"

"Yes."

He looks at me like he wants to argue. But he doesn't. Instead, he helps me to my feet and leaves me to change while he speaks with Dr. Helsan in hushed tones. As I'm fumbling my shirt on, I feel a tiny hard shape in my pocket. *The SIM card.*

And just like that, the dizzying torrent of everything that happened today slams into me again.

Peering from the room, I check to see where Arsen is. He's halfway down the hall, still talking with the doctor. On quick feet, I find my way toward my bedroom without thought. The mansion may not feel like home yet, but I still know it inside and out.

But before I can reach its familiar door, a figure blocks my path.

"*Devushka*," Ulyana gasps.

She's dressed in her usual starched uniform, the long skirt dusting her ankles. The last time I saw her, she was helping me escape this place. My shoulders grow slack, and I'm overcome with a sensation of failure, like I've let her down by ending up here again.

"It's good to see you, Ulyana."

Her nimble fingers play with her skirt before she tucks her arms behind her back. She's struggling to keep her composure. Neither of us knows how to act anymore.

"You look well."

"I ..." I start, unsure of what else I can say, so I settle on the simplest answer. "I am."

I decide not to correct my statement. I'm *not* well, not really, but she doesn't need that burden on her shoulders.

"How have things been here?" I ask.

"Quiet." She quirks a crooked smile. "Too quiet. But I suspect that will change now."

My cheeks turn pink, but I smile back, appreciating the barb. It's her way of saying she missed me. "I was going to my room," I explain. "The doctor—"

"Yes. I saw him arrive." Her eyes move to my belly. "Everything is all right?"

I nod excitedly. My smile is genuine now. Being reminded of my healthy baby has brought me back to life in a way no other news could.

"I guess you'll get to see how it finishes, after all," I say softly.

"I suppose I will." Tilting her head, she stares over my shoulder. I peer backward, but no one is there. When I turn back, she's on me. Her hug is fast and stiff, as if she isn't sure how to perform it. It's over as soon as it starts.

Ulyana retreats, smoothing her skirt while clearing her throat.

"Come see me later. You need to eat. You look far too tiny for a woman about to have a baby. Understood?"

"Yes, ma'am." My eyes are twinkling. I feel the heat in them inside of me as it moves between us. Ulyana smiles once more before shuffling away. Talking to her makes me want to find Olesya next.

But first I have something important to do.

Something Ulyana reminded me of.

Safe in my bedroom, I do a brief scan to make sure I'm alone. The blankets have been switched out for new gold-and-green diamond patterns, and the curtains are black now, but otherwise, the place is as I left it. Heading into the bathroom, I turn the hot water on in the tub. Using the loud noise of the water as cover, I unscrew the knob on the wall cabinet's handle. There's just enough space behind the screw to tuck the SIM card into place. The knob doesn't seal fully when I twist it back, but it isn't noticeable to the eye.

Ulyana found the rose brooch when I hid it last time. I have to be cleverer this time.

Hopefully she won't run around plucking off every knob and panel in here. Feeling confident in my hiding place, I step back with a loud sigh. *Why am I hiding it? Do I actually plan to contact Yevgeniy?*

The things he said to me about Arsen continue to eat away at me like a million termites attacking a house. Each thought that I brush away is replaced by a new one. His voice and my mother's are warring in my head again. But it's that same damning statement from her that I keep coming back to.

Our monsters may wear different faces. But they're the same. He has done to you what Yevgeniy did to me.

Placing my palm on my stomach, I remember the sound of my baby's heartbeat. *Our baby's heartbeat. It's different ... We're different ... Arsen isn't Yevgeniy.*

Isn't he?

Frowning, I strip down and climb into the tub. The water is on the edge of scalding, but it's exactly what I want. I welcome the heat, hoping that it offers the distraction I need. But no matter how deeply I sink into the water, no matter how deeply its heat penetrates me, my worries refuse to vanish.

The only way to know is to find out the truth about Pyotr.

I need to know if Arsen murdered a child.

You can always ask him ... my own voice whispers. But I can't. I won't know that he's not going to spin me another web of lies. Even though Arsen said he wouldn't ever tell me lies, the fact that he kept Pyotr out of his story is enough to shake my belief in him.

I don't want to be scared of asking, but this dread I'm feeling tells me that I am. But just what am I afraid of? Of finding out which monster is telling me the truth? Yevgeniy or Arsen?

Closing my eyes, I remember the amazement on his face when he heard our baby's heartbeat. My brow furrows as another horrible thought bubbles up in the back of my mind.

What if he doesn't care about me? What if it's just the baby he wants? The baby will be Yevgeniy's grandchild, with a strong claim to the Grachev Bratva.

And once the terrible idea has taken root, it winds its way around my heart, poisoning my thoughts.

Will he discard me after the child is born? He'll have the heir he needs. He won't need me anymore.

Maybe he has done to me what Yevgeniy did to Mom.

Panic sets in like cement in my blood. The water can't soften it. I dunk my head, holding my breath, seeking some relief from my fear.

Am I destined to spend my life tiptoeing around Arsen, always unsure of what new secrets I'll learn? Will he become a monster like Yevgeniy with age? Will he always resent me for denying him—driven by a need to possess me, to own me, to teach me that I can never *run away from him?*

The tub feels ice cold by the time I drag myself from it. Drying my body off, I pause to study myself in the mirror. My belly is starting to round out now—not much, but noticeable to me. I smile at the sight, turning from side to side to get the full picture. What a shame that this dreamlike state is cloaked by the dreary reality that brought it to me.

I'm wrapped in a thick blue cotton robe, lying on my bed, when someone taps their knuckles on my door.

"Come in," I answer.

Arsen leans inside. The moment he sees my bare legs, he freezes, heat swimming in his hungry stare. "Can we talk?"

Crossing my ankles, I try to bury my own rush of excitement. I'm all too familiar with the animalistic hunger in his expression. And if I'm being honest, I feel it as well, even though I try to deny myself from him.

It's been weeks since we've been together, and my body is buzzing at the thought of being with him. Fighting back the urges inside me, I clear my throat.

"What's up?"

He shuts the door—the click resonates from the air into my skin. He doesn't come closer yet. Even at this distance, his presence affects me. "Dr. Helsan says that everything is fine with our baby."

"Yes," I agree, stroking my tummy. He watches me do it, like he's fascinated. I can feel his eyes taking me in, and I'm filled with fresh waves of adoration and desire.

Arsen settles his weight against the door. "But there's something he couldn't tell me."

"What's that?"

"How *you* are doing."

I straighten up in surprise. "I'm fine."

"Are you?" Crossing the room, Arsen stands beside the bed, looming as he studies me intently. "We haven't talked about what happened to you at the safe house or what Yevgeniy did when he took you with him. I know almost nothing about what you've endured. And you won't tell me."

He puts a hand on the headboard. The bandage wound around it draws my eye. "What about you? What have *you* been up to?"

Arsen frowns until there are grooves along his forehead. Flexing his fingers, he peels off the bandage to reveal bruises the same color as rotting grapes. They're centered on his knuckles. "I punched someone."

"Who?"

His eyes blacken like a storm is coming. It's enough to make me shy away. "A man who tried to get me killed. But that's not why I hit him." He shakes his hand out, making a loose fist. "He was one of Yevgeniy's brigadiers."

"That sounds like a good enough reason to me," I mumble.

Arsen's scowl shifts the spectrum until he's eyeing me with concern again. "Tell me what happened at the safe house Josh sent you to."

Pulling my knees to my chest, I sit up. *He's worried. Of course he is.* I should have expected this sooner. I can insist until I'm blue in the face that I'm fine. But if I were Arsen, I wouldn't believe me either. It would be simple to close myself off more. I can shrug off his questions, tell him to leave me alone, and drop the topic.

But I can't.

Peering at his face, I read his emotions as easily as words on a page. Arsen is genuinely concerned. This isn't a farce. *I've convinced myself all over again that I can't trust him. That might be true, but ... there's no denying that he loves me. That, amidst all this chaos, is real.*

"Yevgeniy showed up out of the blue," I whisper, hugging my legs harder. "He brought backup, men with guns who could see us through the windows. He told us that there was no other choice but to go with him."

"Of course he did," Arsen says, sitting on the bed. His hand drops to my ankle. The touch sends a jolt of electricity coursing through me. He pauses, clearly feeling it too. "You had no choice. He would have killed you for fighting back."

I shudder at the memory of that awful day. I crawled on the floor, wishing for a weapon, for some way to attack Yevgeniy. I hate how pathetic my rebellion turned out to be.

But above all else, I hate the fact that I'm out of his clutches, but Mom isn't.

"I can't stop thinking about the terrible things he's doing to my mother right now," I whisper. "How are we going to get her back, Arsen?"

"We'll find a way. I promise." His grip slips up my calf to squeeze my knee.

I swallow the knot in my throat. "You know what I was thinking when he had us on the floor of that kitchen?" Black terror swarms my vision and I close my eyes tight. "I was wishing you'd appear out of thin air. I prayed you'd save us."

He leans against me, circling me in a hug that could suffocate me if he did it wrong. Against my ear, he growls, "I wish I had. I should've never agreed to let you go." His breath rattles in his chest. "When I found these at the house, I worried that maybe you'd left them behind as a way to say I'd let you down, and you were done with me for good."

Something round and hard is pressed against my palm. I look down and spot the familiar prayer beads. He leans back to give me room to stare at them.

"No, Arsen. I left them behind accidentally."

His smile doesn't last long—not because his happiness vanishes, but because his lips crash against mine in a hungry kiss instead.

"I was afraid I'd lost you," he admits in a cracking voice, speaking between rapid kisses that get more insistent by the second. "Forever."

"You didn't." Cradling his jaw, I rub my forehead on his.

The sensation of our skin pressing together lights up my soul. *He was worried for me ... not just the baby, but* me. The next kiss begins, and my heartbeat grows faster as we deepen the kiss.

His fingers stroke my hair, and I think helplessly about the question I want to ask him. I'm desperate to know about Pyotr. But I'm too taken up in the moment, too paralyzed by our intermingling desire to bring it up.

I know that if I do, this moment will end.

And I need this too much to give it up.

For now ... our problems can wait.

7

ARSEN

If I could live the rest of my life with my hands never leaving Galina's body, I would. The space between us—tiny as it is—is pure agony. It leaves me feeling cold, as if I'm being covered in black frost. But I have to endure the distance for a few seconds longer, just enough time that I can slip the prayer beads onto her wrist again.

Galina lifts her arm and looks at the wooden beads with an inscrutable expression in her eyes. Seeing them on her wrist again slows my heartbeat somewhat. It looks right. It feels right. And I can't help feeling the same thought that rushed through my head during our wedding:

Somewhere along the way, Galina became mine.

Not just as something to possess, but as someone to treasure.

To shield.

To protect.

To love.

The thought goads me to action. I close the tiny gap between us, positioning myself over her on the bed. As soon as I do, I embrace her again, tightening my grip around her back and waist.

"God, I missed you," I whisper into her hair.

Her thick strands tickle my nose, and I inhale deeply at her familiar scent until I'm lightheaded. She whimpers in response. It's a small sound, yet to me it might as well as be a clap of thunder. It sends my blood singing, and I feel my cock stirring to life in response.

I'm overwhelmed by love, but my desire isn't far behind.

The frost around my heart begins to chip away. Galina's mere presence is waking up *all* of me. With a deft motion, I tug aside the loops of her robe to reveal her belly. I gasp when I see the tiny bump that's taking shape where there was once flatness.

Our baby. The words rise and echo like a liturgy in my head. *Our baby.*

My fingers gently brush over the tiny rise, marveling at the life budding inside of her. It's gorgeous. Miraculous, even. The two of us created life—innocent and pure—despite our own faults and secrets.

Sliding down, I plant a kiss on her stomach. She shifts on the blanket with a gasp.

"You are beautiful," I tell her.

"Even if my body is changing?" she asks, her voice soft like bells.

I level a serious stare at her. "Always."

Her mouth slips into a stunned circle, and then she does something unexpected. Her hand grips the back of my head and drags me upward until my lips crash against hers.

Her tongue pushes into my lips, and mine moves forward to meet hers. The kiss deepens, and my heart races at her urging. Her hands tug at my shirt, deftly unbuttoning it so that she might feel me, skin to skin. I push closer, swallowing the tiny moans bursting from her throat. My tongue swipes against hers as her fingers dig against my head, pulling me closer. She writhes beneath me, her warm body rising to meet mine as she slowly comes back to life by the second.

It's a challenge to take my time, but I'm determined to savor this—to burn this moment into my mind forever. My fingers entwine in her hair, tugging at those silken strands as I keep her locked to me. Reluctantly, I break the kiss, only to trail my lips across her face until I nibble at the lobe of her ear. Her breath quickens at the touch, and her body trembles against mine.

I dip my head lower until I'm grazing at her tender throat.

She gasps at the touch as I plant one kiss after another down her elegant neck. Her free hand tugs insistently at my belt.

"Arsen," she whispers.

"I missed you," I reply as I savor the feel of her skin, kiss away the beads of sweat dotting it, and intoxicate myself with the taste of *her*. "I've missed you so much."

"Arsen," she says again, gripping the back of my neck. "I missed you too."

Fire swells through my heart at the sound of her voice calling my name. There's nothing better than this. How could there be? I'd trade all my wealth in a heartbeat for a lifetime with Galina.

My lips part her robe all the way until her naked breasts gleam in the soft light. They seem rounder and fuller. Eagerly, I heft one, eliciting another appreciative moan from her lips. Her skin feels as soft as a rose petal under my touch.

Gingerly, I tug at her nipple, rolling it between my

fingers, and she gasps again. She's beautiful. Now, tomorrow, decades from this moment; it doesn't matter.

"More," she begs, arching upward to push her breast into my palm. My cock strains painfully against the confines of my pants, demanding that it be let loose to enjoy all the unparalleled delights Galina's body promises.

Growling, I reach down and loosen my pants, easing some of the pressure but refusing to let myself out.

Not yet.

I don't want this moment to end just yet.

With both hands, I palm her chest. I press into her, then pull back, kneading the soft flesh until she's moaning. My head dips and I close my lips gingerly around her right nipple, suckling. She cups the back of my head to hold me steady as whimpers and moans mix. When I ease the pressure to breathe, she yanks me closer.

She doesn't want me to stop.

Rolling her onto her side, I line our bodies up from behind. I don't let my hands leave her breasts. The sensation of her in my palms is like a drug, and I'm hopelessly addicted. She covers my fingers with her own, encouraging me to grip tighter, firmer.

What I'm doing isn't enough now ... not for either of us.

I'm reveling in her lust. Even as she pants helplessly, begging me for more without words, she's regal. The angle of her neck asks me to kiss it, so I do. The tip of her chin wants another kiss, and I go there. But she beats me to the punch. Winding around, her fingers catching in my hair as her face turns toward me. Our lips dance feverishly against each other.

I was sick without her. But this ... this is something else.

Slipping my pants down to my ankles, I kick them off the bed. Galina's bathrobe is half-hanging onto her arms by now. With a gentle tug, it comes free and pools with my clothes out of the way. The smell of the bath clings to her skin—lavender and lemons and the scent that is uniquely *her*. I inhale deeply, letting every tiny particle of her settle deep into my lungs, where I will never get it out.

Galina rubs her hips backward against me, grinding lightly on my hard shaft.

"Not yet," I tell her. "I'm not ready."

"I am," she argues. "Don't make me wait anymore."

A possessive growl rumbles forth from the back of my throat. Snaking a hand around her curvaceous hip, I trace the skin above her wet crease. She parts her thighs, urging me on, but I don't take the bait. I take my time to feel her body, to retrace the familiar routes where I left my marks on her. My fingers stroke her inner thighs, along the gap that makes a heart when her knees press together, and dance across the familiar contours that will slowly grow more curvaceous with each passing day. I toy with her navel, her hip bones, before I finally return to her slick entrance.

Her body trembles, screaming that it craves mine as much as I crave hers. I clench my teeth to control the wild urge to spread her legs and enter her.

From the tops of her thighs to the lines of her ribs, my fingers move over her like it's our first and our last time together. I know it won't be the last—I'll make sure of that. I have plans to kill every hand that has raised itself to block us from being together.

They'll die.

HE will die ...

But for now, I want to memorize the shape and feel of Galina so that if this were to be my last moment on Earth, I would die happy and fulfilled. She trembles each time my hands roam her body, her throat bobbing with arousal.

Kissing the side of her neck, then her shoulder blades, I release a gravelly growl.

"I can't wait anymore," I admit huskily.

The bed shifts. She turns around faster than I expected and pushes me back into the mattress. Her legs straddle me before I can react, and she rises above me like a goddess emerging from the sea. Her eyes are flashing with desire, and the only thing I see in her pupils is myself.

Her lips are slightly parted. Her breasts swaying above me are taut from desire.

"Then fuck me," she demands. "Fuck me and hold nothing back—"

I rise up on my elbows and kiss her before she can finish her sentence. When I pull back, she follows. Hiking her hips backward, she leans her full weight onto me. The plump roundness of her ass settles on my firm cock. I shut my eyes as I deepen our kiss before I whisper into her lips,

"We'll go at your pace."

"Is that right?" she asks lightly.

"Yes." My fingers explore her elbows, testing the hard edge before moving toward the soft skin of her wrists. Galina nibbles her bottom lip. I visualize her using her teeth on me and release a throaty hiss. "I'm yours to do with what you want, *ptichka*."

Her fingers lace into mine, and she pushes them over my head. I know that there's no going back now. I know she's in control. Once upon a time, I might've tried to fight her for it. But now, it's the only thing I want.

The only thing I need.

She rises and falls, teasing my cock with her slick pussy until our arousal becomes indistinguishable. My heart pounds as my ears ring from the pleasure of her torturous teasing. The tightness in my core is enough to snap me in half, leaving me helpless under her touch.

"I think," she breathes, as she rises up one final time until a bead of nectar falls from her quivering pussy over the angry red head of my rock-hard cock, "we've both waited plenty."

I can't disagree with that.

8

GALINA

SETTLING ON TOP OF HIM, MY THIGHS ON EITHER SIDE OF HIS hips, I tease his shaft behind my back. I'm fascinated by his face. His expression is one of wanton joy. I can feel his hands tighten their grip against mine, as if he's on the verge of fighting me for control.

Suddenly, I feel nervous. I'm too aware of my belly and how it's starting to protrude. The bump is subtle, but at this angle, I can see it clearly. The pregnancy is starting to change me, and although I have never been a shallow person, I'm feeling very much not in my own skin.

What is he thinking? He said I was beautiful, but ...

Arsen speaks, interrupting my thoughts. "Stop it."

I startle. "What?"

"Stop doubting yourself," he replies. "I can see it in your eyes. You're thinking about how you look. Stop it."

Blushing, I do the opposite and think more. I release his hands and circle my arms around to block his view of my naked body.

Arsen snarls, gripping my wrists to force my hands away.

"Arsen—"

"Never hide yourself from me." His eyes flash with a demanding presence that sets my blood pumping. I'm almost excited by how angry he sounds. "Understand? You're my wife, now and always. No matter how much you change, I will always find you beautiful. Irresistible. Because you're you. And that's what I'm attracted to."

I feel tiny buzzes of excitement shivering through my body like champagne bubbles. It's the same feeling I felt the night at the ballet, when he knelt between my knees and pleasured me in that empty theater meant only for us. Each swish of his tongue and each kiss he left against my thighs was a promise. The promise of pleasure. The promise of forever. The promise that he is a man who leaves no doubts on the table.

Lowering myself, I push my tender breasts into his hard chest and let my hair fall around us in a curtain to hide us from the world. I kiss him again and again until my lips go numb. His hands free now, he traces the familiar lines of my spine until they rest on my lower back. Holding me steady, he enters me with his massive girth.

I gasp and moan at the familiar sensation of him. *I really did miss this.* The moment he stretches my walls, I feel a new sensation filling my body. Not just pleasure. Not just desire.

But the feeling of being *home*.

It's a feeling I thought I'd never experience again. But in a single swift motion, Arsen has reminded me that I will always have a place by his side.

He rocks inside of me at a slow pace—a demonstration of his iron discipline. As much as we lust for each other, neither of us wants this to end.

For the first time in what feels like forever, I'm not thinking about my troubles. Danger and death are banished from my mind. Here and now is all that matters. Arsen's firm arms ... his gentle caresses, the way he finds the dimples on my hips and explores them as he slowly fucks me and draws out ripples of pleasure coursing through my core ...

This is my world.

This is where I belong.

He moans my name. And I moan his in response. Our voices entwine together like two strands of the same melody—simultaneously a promise and a wish for this to be all we ever want to think about again. The ability to form coherent thoughts flitters away from my mind with each second he buries himself inside me, and I don't care. Our movements are perfectly timed—he rolls his hips and I sit back onto his length. He pulls back, and I rise to tease him at my entrance.

It's as if the two of us can read each other's mind.

In that moment, you'd never dare to imagine that there could be secrets between us.

That there *are* secrets between us.

A bolt of pleasure—slowly rising since the moment he walked into my room—finally tears through my body. It starts in my core and radiates out, leaving delicious heat in its wake as it works its way over my skin. It blooms into being with each bead of sweat rolling down my face, my breasts, my legs, and my belly.

It leaves me breathless and gasping. My back arches instinctively. My toes curl as if they have a will of their own. I squeeze my eyes shut as stars explode across the darkness behind my eyelids. A deep, guttural cry punches from the depths of my throat. I couldn't hold it back even if I wanted to.

And I don't want to.

The wake of my orgasm leaves me trembling, and I collapse onto Arsen. But he's not done yet.

"I love you," I whisper, panting, into his ear.

He clutches me tighter, his speed increasing. "I love you too, *ptichka*." His teeth grit together. His strong arms grip, moving me along with him. His pace begins to quicken until it's a blur. I know he's not holding back now. My release has broken his control, and his facade is slipping with every thrust.

His brow furrows like he's exerting himself. It's the only warning I get before he holds me close and roars as he floods my insides. Reflexively, our bodies keep moving as if they are mindless automatons, sending shock waves of pleasure rippling long after we're both finished.

Eventually, my muscles begin to cramp. I wince, reaching for my calves. Arsen slides me off him and reaches down to massage my legs. The sensation of his powerful fingers kneading away the knots in my calves feels almost as good as sex. Slowly, he works up to my knees, then over my hamstrings until I'm positive my muscles have been churned to butter.

His eyes meet mine, reading my mood as he copies my smile.

"That was amazing," I say.

"You're amazing," he agrees. Kissing my forehead, he braces himself against me on the bed. We're both slumped in relaxation. My eyes flutter shut—I sway in and out of awareness. His presence is so comforting that I start to fade into sleep.

And when I wake, it's dark out. I don't know how much time has passed, and I don't care. The only thing that matters is that he's still here when I'm awake.

He's playing with the tips of my hair, letting them wind through his fingers, then drift away to land on my collarbone.

"There's something I need from you."

My smile is full of lazy contentment. "Anything."

He lets the rest of my hair fall. "I have to speak with Josh Sanders."

And just like that, he sends us plunging back to icy reality. Cold dread snakes through my body, chasing away the comfort he brought me earlier.

"Oh."

"It's important," he explains, watching me with expectation.

"I suppose it is."

"So." His eyes never leave me. "You'll do it?"

I shift on the bed to stare at the ceiling. "Why can't you ask him directly?"

"Because this is a meeting that has to remain secret. Because Josh can't trust the people around him."

That's probably true, I think. How else could Yevgeniy have found me and my mom so quickly when we were supposed to be in witness protection?

"But what if he doesn't want to meet with me?" I ask.

"That's why you're not going to ask him." Arsen's voice takes on an amused edge. "He won't dare keep his wife from seeing a friend that she thinks is dead."

I can't help the smile rising to my lips. One way or another, Arsen always finds a way. Even if it's something as unpalatable for him as working with Josh. The thought of Audrey also sends a twinge of guilt through me. She must be panicking after everything that's happened. She hasn't heard from me since the last time she saw me at the safe house. And if what Arsen said is true, then the next time she went, she would've found the scene of a slaughter.

If nothing else, I owe it to her to let her know that I'm okay.

That I'm alive.

"Okay." I nod. "I'll do it."

"Thank you." He curls me against his naked chest. But the feeling that I'm home is gone. Where this same exact spot once promised warmth and security and never-ending happiness, now all I feel is something else.

Something dark. Something cold. Something that frightens me.

9

ARSEN

The meeting is arranged quickly. Calling Audrey was the first hurdle, because as soon as she heard from Galina, neither of them could talk between the shouting and crying. It took longer than expected for her to convince Josh to escort her to my mansion.

Evidently, he's not as sold on seeing Galina in person as Audrey is. I suspect seeing her is a reminder that his way failed, and not because he was unable to protect her. It makes me respect him a lot less. But this isn't about him.

The meeting was supposed to start ten minutes ago. But for the last fifteen minutes, Audrey has clutched Galina in her arms, alternating between crying and chiding her.

"I thought you were dead!" she sobs for what seems like the millionth time.

Smiling indulgently, Galina pets her hair. She catches my eye, and I give her a look. *We're running short on time here.* She fixes me with one of her own that tells me to relax. But it's hard for me to do that.

Especially because Josh keeps tapping his pen on the

surface of the long wooden table in my sunroom like he owns the place.

I picked the place, thinking the pleasant sunshine would brighten the mood somewhat. But somehow, all it does is make everyone equally uncomfortable. The bright rays keep bouncing off the shiny table into my eyes, forcing me to squint. Damp patches of sweat are soaking through Josh's pale lavender suit.

It doesn't take a genius to know that things are already off to a rough start.

"Audrey," Josh mutters. "Can we focus, please?"

She wipes at her eyes with both hands, laughing self-consciously. "Right, right, sorry, everyone. I'm just overwhelmed." Giving Galina one last hug, she moves to stand by the window. Galina joins her, her eyes on us, but her hand is encased in Audrey's.

The sight of their closeness makes me jealous. Somehow, my own reunion with Galina—as passionate as it became—lacked the emotional intimacy that she shares with Audrey. And when she squeezes Audrey's hand, as if she's seeking a comfort that I can't provide, I feel my mood go from sour to black.

"Thank you for coming," I begin.

"Thank Audrey." Josh narrows his eyes. "If I had my way, I wouldn't have come at all, Isakov."

I force my smile to stay fixed in place. But given how flippant Josh is in my presence, it's a hell of a lot harder than I thought.

"Noted," I say through tight teeth.

"What are you up to, Isakov?" Josh asks, craning forward over the table, his eyes hooded. "Why invite me here?"

"Because we want the same thing."

"The destruction of the Grachev Bratva?" he sneers.

"You're a fool if you think that's possible." My neck becomes a roll of knots. "And an even bigger fool if you think it won't just set off more violence than you can ever know."

"Nothing is impossible!" He pounds his fist on the table. Audrey jumps, but Galina just glares. "The Grachev Bratva is a rot upon this city. Has been for years. This was supposed to be *my* chance to end it once and for all!"

"Is that all this is for you?" I ask pointedly. "Glory? Fame? A chance to be *remembered?*"

I know men like Josh Sanders. Sure, they may dress in fine clothes, parading their supposed power and influence in the daylight. But they are nothing but rats scurrying beneath those who hold the real power. The ones who operate in shadows. The ones who pull their strings, even when they don't realize it. People like Josh never want to put their own lives on the line. They're happy to scheme so others do the work while they claim the victory because they did the fucking *paperwork*.

"This isn't about any of that," he retorts. "This is about doing what is right!"

"You can't even hear yourself," I snap. "Do you imagine that the Bratva is so easy to collapse that taking *me* down will end it all? Do you think the corrupt cops who've gotten fat off Bratva money will simply *allow* their livelihoods to be threatened? Do you think the brigadiers who've been champing at the bit for their chance to taste power will just abandon that opportunity if you remove me? Do you imagine that all you have to do is kick in the door, and the whole rotten structure will come crashing down?"

"You don't believe in this city, do you?" He levels me with a haughty glare. "You've never believed in it."

"I've seen this city in ways you never could." I shake

my head in disgust. "I've seen it for what it is: a dirty, twisted thing that cares neither for its people nor itself. And here's the awful truth: you remove me, and you might get a year of 'peace' before things become infinitely worse."

"How do you know?"

I pause, knowing that every word I say to him can potentially incriminate me. *What does it matter?* I think savagely. I'm already a criminal. And there is room for both of us to help each other before we're back at each other's throats.

"Because I've seen it," I tell him. "Because I was the cause of the war that has been raging in these streets for the last ten years. Because I did exactly what you're trying to do now. Tell me, why do you think this is a *Grachev* Bratva and not an Isakov Bratva?"

"Why don't you enlighten me?" Josh crosses his arms. "Since you seem to hold all the answers."

"Because this Bratva once belonged to Yevgeniy Grachev," I confess to him. Behind Josh, Audrey glances at Galina. How much does she know? "Until I stole it from him."

"So what?" Josh licks his upper teeth. He'd spit, I think, if some part of his sense of civility didn't stop him. "Do you want me to thank you for sending so many people to their grave because of your little argument with this ... What's his name? Yevgeniy Grachev?"

He's so fucking smug that it takes everything in me not to grab him by his stupid tie and beat him bloody.

"For a man who gets off on telling people what to do, you should listen more."

"I *am* listening, Isakov." He shrugs. "But I know what you are, and nothing you say can change my mind about you. Criminals can't be counted upon to take down criminals.

And I have no reason to believe that if I put you away, I can't do the same for the rest of the Bratva."

You arrogant little shit.

"If you won't listen to my other warnings, then at least listen to this one." I lean across the table. "Yevgeniy has a mole in your firm."

"Impossible!" Josh's eyes flare wide. Audrey and Galina share his surprise.

"Is it?" I ask. "How else did Yevgeniy find Galina and her mother so quickly?"

Josh stands quickly, chest filling with air and wounded pride. I know the signs of a man who wants to fight. Wired with my own disdain because of how he put the woman I love at risk, I rise to meet him on the other side of the table. There's no barrier between us. I could easily wrap my fingers around his neck, and I'd watch in satisfaction as I squeezed the color onto his face.

He's a full half a foot shorter than me, and he seems to realize this as he gazes up at me. Surprise turns to hesitation; hesitation transforms into the shadow of fear in his eyes, and he reconsiders his decision. My hand twitches at my side. *I can grab him by his skinny gray tie and use it to strangle him. Or I could just slam it downward to bounce his face against my table.*

There are many options, and each one is more tempting than the last.

"Stop it! Both of you!" Galina slaps her hands on the table, glaring at us each in turn.

Josh recoils, his whole face wrinkling up like he's smelled something awful. He's eyeing Galina like she's the cause of his problems. My dislike for him grows stronger by the second.

But while Galina's words have created chagrin in me, my

annoyance with this man and his reaction *to her* keep me from calming down.

"You're a selfish son of a bitch," I say coldly. "Why did I ever think that I could reason with you?"

"Fuck you, Isakov," Josh snaps.

Now it's Audrey's turn to step into Josh's space. With a quick motion, she gives him a tap on the side of his head.

"Galina is right; you're both being unreasonable right now. At least hear him out about the mole."

Josh gawks, shrinking from her outrageous actions. It's such a ridiculous scene that I have to fight to keep myself from laughing.

"Our goal is the same," I say carefully to Josh. "To end Yevgeniy Grachev. Seek glory all you want, but your fight is with *him*, not me."

Josh considers me suspiciously before the lines smooth on his forehead. "Tell me about this mole."

"I have no name," I reply. "And the man who could tell his identity is six feet underground. But as long as this mole exists in your office, there is nothing the law can do."

"And what do you suggest?"

"Bring me every bit of information you've collected on my Bratva," I suggest. "Every last piece. Leave no copy behind in your office. If any new information arrives, I want it brought here and here alone. What Yevgeniy doesn't know, he can't act upon."

"You're asking me to break a lot of laws, Isakov."

"Better for you to break laws," I reply, "than to have Yevgeniy break *you* once you've outlived your usefulness. And trust me, you're getting dangerously close to that point."

Josh goes silent, and his face blanches. Finally, it seems the gravity of his situation is starting to set in.

"How do I know I can trust you?"

"You don't," I answer truthfully. "But Galina trusts me, and your wife trusts her."

Josh sighs, placing his hands on his hips as he considers my words. "I'm going to need some time to think about this."

You coward. "Fine," I say. "But be quick about it. You have a lot less time than you think."

My gaze tears away from Josh and his stupid lavender suit just in time to see Galina and Audrey step out of the sunroom. Josh is running his mouth as he launches into details about all the irrelevant things he'll need before he can agree with me, but my attention is no longer focused on him.

There's a reason Galina and Audrey stepped away from this room.

They're going to talk about something.

Something they don't want me or Josh to know.

Just what the hell could they need to talk about in private?

10

GALINA

THE MANSION HAS A SURPLUS OF ROOMS THAT ARE DECORATED but unused. Lately, the whole place feels like a ghost house. Things moving, being rearranged, but no people actually seen. I haven't spoken to any guards or much of the staff since being back. It's like they're avoiding me.

Or maybe I'm subconsciously avoiding them ... I haven't been the most approachable person. My mind is fixated on my mother, my baby, and nothing else. I'd avoid me too, I think.

Audrey glances around, then locks the door. We're alone, but her voice is a whisper.

"Okay." She pats the small, double-seated brown leather couch, sitting once I do. "What's so important that you pulled me away?"

Preparing myself to rattle off a hundred things, I'm surprised when I can't manage a single word. There's too much to discuss, and it's all tangling up on my tongue now that the chance to speak is finally here. Breathing out a few times, I try to calm myself.

"It's funny. I don't even know where to start now," I say, laughing weakly. "So much has happened."

"Why don't we start with you getting taken from the safe house," she urges. There's more than interest in her face.

From the way her brow is puckered, I know she's feeling guilty.

I put my hand on her knee and shake my head. "It's not your fault that I was taken. It's like Arsen said—Yevgeniy had a mole in Josh's office. One way or the other, he was going to take me and Mom."

She chews her lower lip. "Your mom, is she …"

"Still with him, yeah." My shoulders sink. "He's been hurting her. It's awful." Making fists, I bite back frustrated tears. "Waiting around to save her is killing me."

"Is *that* what you wanted to talk about?" she asks. "About how we can save your mom?"

I want to say yes. But that's a lie. I check her eyes, trying to read her. That's when I realize she's trying to read me. She knows I'm holding something back.

And I know exactly what that something is.

Pyotr Grachev.

Even though she's my best friend, I can't forget that Josh tried to use me to advance his own career.

"No, that's not it." I shake my head again. "It's something else. But I don't know if I can tell you. I don't know if I can tell anyone."

Audrey shoots a glance at the door. "Does Arsen bug his own home?"

I shrug. "He has cameras all over the place. His men are probably watching us right now."

"I see." Audrey nods. "Is this something that you don't want him to know about?"

"No," I sigh, flooded with fresh shame. "I'm pretty damn sure this is something he already knows about."

Taking my hand in hers, she makes me look at her as she smiles serenely. "Nothing you tell me will leave this room. But you don't have to say anything if you don't want to."

The tears I've been holding back start to well up in my eyes. Releasing her hand, I wipe them away. "No, I want to talk about it." *I need to talk about it.* "But it's just ..."

Audrey bends closer, her voice a low hush. "It's bad."

"Yeah."

"And Arsen knows?"

My whole body flinches at the sound of his name, as if merely mentioning it might summon him into the room. "He does."

Leaning away, she stands up and dusts her pants off. "You don't have to say anything if you're not ready, Galina."

I balk, eyeing her in disbelief. "What?"

"The only thing you need to say is if you're in danger." Running her hands through her hair, she locks her eyes with mine. "Because if you are, I'm going to help."

This act of kindness is why we're friends. Who else could pry so close to a juicy secret, then walk away before the lid is cracked to see inside? It's not the first time she's taken my cue and resisted pushing me. When Simon first started hurting me, I couldn't tell anyone.

I was too ashamed and convinced that it would get better.

Audrey saw my bruises and the signs of abuse. When she confronted me, I clammed up. Someone else would have pushed, shutting me down further. But she allowed me to come to her at my own pace. When I did, she was there for me with hugs, soothing words, and a couch to crash on until I got my life back together.

And right now, under her soft, reassuring gaze, I feel courage slowly perk up inside of me. Just enough for a single name to slip forth from my lips.

"Pyotr."

"Who?" She arches her eyebrows in confusion.

"Pyotr Grachev." I grab her hands and lower my voice in an urgent hiss. "I need you to help me find out if he's real. If he existed. And if so ... what happened to him."

She opens her mouth to ask for more details. But I put my fingers to my lips for emphasis. The message is received, and she nods quickly.

"Okay." She's talking quieter than before. "I'll do what I can."

"Thank you. I mean it."

Patting my arm, she eyeballs the door, sticking out her bottom lip. "We should go back and check on them. Before your husband kills mine."

I laugh, but it rings hollow. I'm too consumed with the possibility of finding out who has been telling me the truth—my monster of a father or my monster of a husband. Once I know, it will remove the burden of the secret I'm carrying.

I'll know for sure if Arsen killed a child in cold blood. And then I can be at peace about this.

But as I reach for the doorknob, another thought enters my mind.

No, I can't.

The truth won't remove my burden. Because there's always the possibility that Arsen *did* murder Pyotr. *That's* what I'm afraid of. Because *that* will be proof Arsen is exactly the monster I should fear. More importantly, it'll be proof that he's every bit the monster Yevgeniy told me he is. And if that's the case, everything I want from Arsen will crumble to dust.

"Galina?" Audrey asks warily. "What's wrong?"

"Nothing." Blinking quickly, I put on my cheeriest smile. "Just felt a bit lightheaded from the heat."

She looks at me with wariness in her eyes. I know she doesn't believe me, but she knows better than to keep pushing me for an answer I'll never give.

She knows when it's time to let things rest.

But more importantly, she knows when it's time to push.

She's always known.

I wish I could say the same about myself nowadays.

11

ARSEN
DAYS LATER

I'M TORTURING A LOT OF PEOPLE THESE DAYS.

It's not something I love, though violence has a special place in my heart, much as I'm loath to admit it. I was never so naive as to think that taking over the Bratva from Yevgeniy would be a bloodless venture. But to have to create precise suffering for my enemies is different than a battle for my life.

The upside is I'm quite good at it.

"Did you think that betraying me would end well for you, Mikhail?" I walk around my former brigadier, where Mila has tied him to a chair. The ropes cut across his tan, long-sleeved shirt, digging into his stocky muscles. The constriction is enough to leave his limbs numb without doing permanent damage.

I'd hoped we'd snag one of my defectors, but Mila surprised me by capturing one so quickly. She spotted him when he was ordering a hot dog from one of the many carts downtown and stalked him until he was out of view of anyone who'd care before she knocked him out and carted him back to my place on her motorcycle.

Now we're back in my wine cellar, the floors barely scrubbed clean of Sergei's blood, as we reenact the same scene. Mila watches from the shadows, her legs curled to her chest, where she sits on an oak barrel. She looks like a child waiting for her turn to play with a toy.

"I was making a smart choice." Mikhail glares up at me. "The only choice."

"By betraying me?" I grab him by the jowls, burying my thumb into his skin until I feel like I'm about to break something.

To his credit, Mikhail holds my gaze and refuses to show any sign of fear at what he knows is inevitable. I knew there was a reason I chose him to be one of my brigadiers.

Which is why his betrayal pains me more than I care to admit.

Releasing him in disgust, I spit on the floor. "You went to Yevgeniy, didn't you?"

"I did."

"Tell me where he is. The roach is hiding somewhere. Shine some light on him for me before I slit your throat."

"Why bother?" he chuckles dryly. "You're going to kill me anyway. Why not skip this unnecessary pageantry, Arsen Kirilovich?"

"You talk," Mila interjects, "and Arsen Kirilovich will make it quick. You don't, then *I* get to play with you." She tosses her knife up, catching it easily by the curved tip as a sharp smile dances across her red lips.

Mikhail's brow scrunches, the first hint that he's getting nervous. Putting my hands on either side of the chair, just outside his thick shoulders, I lean close until I'm all he can see.

"Which will it be? Me or her?"

"I don't know where he is. He's busy moving around

again. Probably has his face buried between the thighs of his new whores."

"He reopened the brothels?"

"He did."

Behind me, I hear Mila gasp.

"You didn't know, *devushka*?" Mikhail makes a face as he tries to look through me at Mila. When he can't, he turns his gaze back to me. "Did you forget that I was the one who brought you most of your intel, Arsen Kirilovich?"

I hate the smugness in his voice and the triumph in his eyes. Even now, as he tells me the truth, he mocks me to my face. Grabbing a fistful of his hair, I yank his head back, hoping to see fear dance in his eyes. Maddeningly, he continues to smirk through his grimace.

"You should know better than to taunt me like this," I warn him.

"Maybe." He shrugs. "But shouldn't I enjoy myself in my last moments?"

"How many brothels are there?" I inquire.

"Can't tell you." He clenches his jaw. "I'm bad with numbers."

This was a man I drank with, a man whom I trusted with my life. He had an engraved shot glass. He swore an oath to me. He was part of my inner circle. In another life, without the pressure of a brutal war hanging above, I would've counted him as a brother.

But now ...

I hold my hand out without looking back. "Mila."

A few soft steps, and she places the pommel of a knife in my grip. I bring the razor edge to Mikhail's chin. Finally, his eyes widen. Fear always takes hold of a man at the end of his life. A satisfying thrill rushes through me. Maybe I don't hate this as much as I try to convince myself I do.

"Fuck!" he roars as I glide the knife through his cheek, leaving a thin slash that weeps blood. "Fuck you, Arsen!"

Placing the edge to his other cheek, I wait for him to focus on me. Sweat droplets have beaded along his brow. His boldness has slipped away now that I'm reminding him of how it feels to be sliced apart, piece by piece. "How many brothels, Mikahil?"

"Fuck! I think there are ten, maybe twelve!"

"That wasn't so hard, was it?" Calmly, I nick him just under his left eye. He screams louder. "Where are they? Exact locations."

Over the next few minutes, Mikhail rambles out addresses. Mila records them, lingering just out of the corner of my eye. She's drawn to his suffering. And when he has expended his usefulness, I slit his throat quickly.

It's the only mercy I'm willing to give him.

But despite the treasure trove of information he gave, he refused to tell me where Yevgeniy was hiding. Perhaps he genuinely didn't know. But it doesn't matter. As I wipe my hands of Mikahil's blood, I know that Ulyana will chide me later for this mess.

I pass the knife back to Mila. She takes it, sheathing it slowly.

"This is going to have consequences," she says.

"We've killed plenty. What's one more?" I ask bitterly.

"He was one of your own."

"No, he wasn't," I say sternly. "Not in the end."

No one who betrays me can be called anything but a traitor.

I grimace, making fists at my sides. I'm fueled by the rush that comes with killing. It mutes the regret that gnaws at me for ending the life of someone I thought would stand by me until the end. *The war tests all of us.*

Mila looks at me thoughtfully as I walk to a wall of wine

bottles and grab a bottle. She offers me a corkscrew without prompting. I take it and open the bottle, drinking straight from it until my throat is a searing mess of fire. The heat spreads down my limbs. I felt no joy killing Mikhail. Not even relief.

It was just my duty.

Then why do I want to numb myself?

Refusing to dwell, I take another pull, then offer her the bottle. She doesn't take it.

"You need to tell the Bratva the truth about *her*."

My heart jumps. The thorny ball that saws through my insides isn't softened by the wine. I suck down more anyway, gasping for air after I've had my fill. "Why? What would that achieve?"

"Once everyone knows she's Yevgeniy's daughter, you will stave off future defections. And men like Mikhail, who already defected, might return. You know this as well as I do."

She's not wrong. But as I take another pull from the bottle and eye the lifeless body of a man I once considered a friend, I know the real reason why it will do me no favors to inform the men of Galina's true parentage. The alcohol gives me the push I need to speak the truth.

"The men who betrayed me can never be trusted again!" I growl, gesturing with the bottle. Wine drips out to join the blood. They mix, their reds impossible to tell apart.

"I'm not asking you to trust them." Mila approaches me with shadows in her eyes. "I just want you to put them in one place. Much easier to slit the throat of a full room than to stalk men one by one."

I lower the bottle in the middle of bringing it back to my lips. There's a chill moving through me, hair standing up as my instincts fire, warning me that there's danger nearby.

Mila won't attack me, but I know she's capable of it if she wants.

"Is this personal for you?" I ask softly.

Squaring up with me, she rips her shirt aside to reveal the chained fox tattoo. "Of course it is." The tattoo looks blacker than normal in the low lights. She hides it away again. "I haven't forgotten, and I know you haven't either."

The memory of our past rises like bile in the back of my throat. She was a tiny little thing once, sobbing in terror and pain as she prayed for a savior to rescue her from the endless nightmare of her own existence.

She won't be satisfied until *she* gets her revenge—a revenge that I've denied her. Looking down my nose at her, I nod. "I had to check."

"You should've never doubted," she reminds me.

There's a noise at the top of the stairs. Light filters down the steps. "Arsen?" Galina calls. "Are you down here?"

Mila snaps her eyes to mine, then we both stare at Mikhail's corpse. "Stall her," I whisper.

She obeys, darting up the stairs to intercept Galina before she can enter the cellar enough to see what we've done. I can't allow her to see this. Even though Galina knows I'm a killer, I don't want her to see that I've brought that home. The same home where we plan to raise our child.

She already thinks I'm a monster.

"Mila," I hear Galina stutter.

"Nice to see you, *Galina Yevgeniyevna,*" Mila drawls.

That patronymic makes me stiffen like wood. When Sergei screamed it out in the safe house before we were interrupted by bullets, I was able to ignore it. But now? Hearing it from Mila's lips makes me feel ill. Checking myself, I note a single spot of blood on my jacket. I yank it free, throwing it on Mikhail before adding a canvas sheet—one meant to protect the wine from dust—on top. The corpse in the chair is nothing but an odd lump now. Easy to ignore.

I rush to block Galina on the stairs. "Galina," I say.

She squints down at me from her higher position. Her face is sour—I don't know if it's because of Mila's comment or her suspicion of what we were doing in the cellar.

"What were you two up to?"

"Nothing." I shoot a look at Mila. She rolls her eyes with a slight grin. Taking Galina's hand, I walk past her, tugging her gently but firmly upstairs. "Mila, you can go; we're done here."

"*What* are you done with?" Galina asks sharply.

Ignoring her question, I lead us back up into the light. The wintry sun is unusually bright, making it feel like an entirely different world from the dark cellar coated in blood. How fitting. My home is split in half by the civil section that acts as a front for the world ... And underneath the light is the half that lurks with the demons of my awful actions.

I have to keep the two separated. For Galina's sake. I have to keep her from seeing the demons that lurk just within the walls.

Mila starts following us out. But I turn back, give her another look, and shut the door.

If cutting off the demons is impossible, I'll settle for locking them away.

12

GALINA

"What were you two up to down there?" I ask again, though it sounds less like a question and more like a demand.

They were clearly up to something in the cellar. Why else chase me out? Why else keep Mila from following? The last time I was among the wine casks, it was to have a secret meeting with Audrey. That place is designed for secrets.

And I'm not naive enough to ignore that when the Bratva is involved, secrets can hurt.

Secrets can kill.

Arsen is wearing a basic black button-up shirt. The kind he normally would pair with a jacket, especially in this weather. His hand is still on mine. And I don't pull away, not yet. Not until I know where things are heading.

"We found out that Yevgeniy has restarted his brothels," he finally says.

Horror jolts through my bones. "How did you learn that?"

He stares at the ceiling briefly before he turns to me. "Mila told me." He pauses a beat, like he expects more questions from me. Before I ask any, he adds, "It can't stand. We have to shut it down."

"But how will you do that?"

"Mila has some ... ideas." He works his jaw. There's something he wants to say, but isn't sure.

Gripping his hand tighter to reassure him, I whisper, "Tell me."

Watching me closely, he lets out a slow breath. "Your status as Yevgeniy's daughter both complicates and simplifies things."

I pull my hand from his. "I don't like where this is going."

Arsen stares hard at my fingers. He's wishing we were still touching. I do too, but the urge is smothered by my rising fears. The last time we discussed my relationship to Yevgeniy was in regards to marrying me for real.

That was a bad argument. I don't want a repeat.

"Several of my brigadiers abandoned me when they learned you were taken. They thought that I was vulnerable to Yevgeniy. So, they jumped ship to join him. But if they learn that *you*," he grabs my shoulders, and I tense up from the strength of his touch, "you, Galina, are his *daughter*, and not simply a pawn he is chasing, then they will return to my side."

The frost that was slowly consuming my heart thickens further.

"Will this be all that I am to you now? A way to control your men? A tool to keep you in power?"

His mouth drops open in shock. "No, of course not." He digs his fingers in as if he's trying to reach the part of me that I'm sealing away. It's a futile effort. He might as well be scooping at the snow with his bare hands to clear an avalanche.

"The men who defected will be punished. No one who aids Yevgeniy in his brothels or in harming you and your loved ones will be allowed to live."

The darkness on his tongue makes me shiver. Wrenching away, I recall our argument before I decided to flee his home. It's like fuel on the fire of my blazing anger. Arsen watches me, waiting for me to speak.

Good. Because I have plenty to say.

"I don't want revenge. I just want an end to this nightmare." Thrusting my hand flat against my chest, I narrow my eyes fiercely. "I want nothing except to go back to being *Galina Stepanovna!* I don't want to be treated like a Bratva princess or ever reminded that I share the same blood as that monster! Let me go back to living a life where nobody knows who I am! Just me, my mother, and peaceful obscurity."

I'm panting heavily from my declaration. Arsen watches me warily, his face a mix of concern and adoration. It's enough that when he takes a step closer, I don't retreat.

"You can be whoever you want to be. But as long as you live ..." His eyes drop to my belly. "And as long as you carry my child, Yevgeniy will never stop hunting you."

Then why did he release me? It's bothering me more than before. Arsen says Yevgeniy wants me in his clutches, but he set me free. Slowly, my mind turns to the SIM card he gave me. *When the time comes, you'll know what to do.* Did he foresee this moment?

A new thought suddenly takes shape in my head. I can slip it out from where I hid it, contact Yevgeniy, and get some sort of answers. But what would the questions even be?

And more importantly, would it help? Will any of this help?

Going to Yevgeniy won't end Arsen's plans. I doubt even *I*

can convince him to shut down the brothels. I'm in the same position as before.

I bite my tongue until I can taste blood. *This feud between them is endless. They'll always be enemies.* And just like that, my mother's warning returns to me once again. *Nothing is ever settled when the Bratvas are involved, stupid girl!*

On and on it'll go, this cycle of violence and vengeance. Once Arsen kills Yevgeniy, then it'll only be a matter of time before Ruslan starts seeking his own revenge.

Arsen stares at me in silence. At first, I think he's reconsidering his words. But the longer it goes on, the quicker I realize that he's waiting for *me* to start talking again.

But I have nothing else to say.

There's no magical phrase to get me out of this mess.

Abruptly he moves, his muscular arms capturing me, cradling me to his chest. His smell fills my nose. I remind myself I want to hate this. But God ... I don't—I can't.

He whispers hoarsely, his face in my hair. "No matter what happens, you will always be my *ptichka*."

That's the problem.

I can't escape the Bratva.

I'm trapped ...

Just like Mom.

Our monsters may wear different faces. But they're the same.

Arsen holds me tight; it takes some work for me to wiggle free. Once I do, he stands there with his arms at the ready, one step away from grabbing me again. It's incredible that he can resist.

"I need some time to myself. This is all just ... just so much to take in."

The pain in his eyes cuts me. I'm used to seeing his pain by now. Most of my soul is covered in scars from our emotional war.

Twisting, I realize we're not alone. Ulyana is standing in the doorway, watching us. Her hands are choking the front of her long, pleated skirt. Her concern rivals Arsen's, turning her blue irises pitch black, the rest around them a blinding, bulging white.

I've seen this expression before. She's terrified for us. The last time we fought, she had to help me slip away in a wooden box. And she has yet to tell me what punishments she suffered for helping me flee. I don't plan to escape like that again. If I leave, it will be out the front door with my head held high before I go in search of my poor mother.

As I storm out of the kitchen, Ulyana's eyes meet mine, then skid away.

She doesn't speak to me as I pass. She doesn't need to.

There's nothing she can do for me anymore.

13

GALINA

It's nice to have the freedom to explore the gardens. Ever since being back, I've noticed there are fewer guards lurking around. Arsen mentioned defectors. Perhaps that's why it's so barren now.

Wandering the rows of lush roses that hang, ever resilient, against the onslaught of winter brings me solace. But a cage is still a cage, even if you can see the sky.

What am I supposed to do?

Arsen has made his goal as clear as ever. It's changed very little from what it started as. Yes, he wants Yevgeniy dead. He also wants to dismantle his sordid business like he did years ago. Both are noble things, especially once I think about the poor women forced to work in the brothels. Are all of them marked with tattoos like Mila?

Strolling around the curve of a water fountain, I notice the stream has been shut off to make sure the pipes don't freeze. I wish it was still running at full force now. I'd have liked to sit on the edge of the smooth stone, listening to the bubbling water.

I've always loved the sound of running water. My mother

used to chide me for letting the bath go for hours, accusing me of wasting water. She was concerned with the bill, no doubt.

Can't blame her. We were too broke to indulge my silly fancies.

Sighing, I collapse onto the rim with my head in my hands. *Mom ... what's happening to you now?*

I'm not sure if she's in the same house or not. Yevgeniy could have moved her away with him and Ruslan. Just because I don't know the way doesn't mean he'd risk me figuring it out.

Are you missing me? Has Yevgeniy lied to you about what happened to me? The thought of her assuming he did something awful to me sends my pulse haywire. The bastard could easily lie and say I'm dead. Would that make her easier to control? Without me by her side, what could still give her hope?

Please stay strong, mamochka.

I'm coming back for you.

And when I finally do see her again, will her whole body be coated in bruises as a reminder of the horrors she had to endure in Yevgeniy's presence? That monster has a sick way of holding her accountable for her life choices. If it escalates, she could be left with more than bruises. The idea has my insides shifting. I twist, and I hope I don't vomit in the dry fountain.

"Galina."

Arsen has come up from behind a nearby hedge. The sun is low in the sky, mushing the clouds into a slurry of pastels. The color blends along his jawline and the tailored shoulders of his black wool jacket. It shines across his hair as the wind teases it. He's as beautiful as the roses ... No, more.

I jump to my feet. "What do you want?" I ask sharply.

He doesn't come closer. He stays by the hedge. "I want to apologize for what I did."

"You'll have to be more specific," I say grimly.

He flinches like I've slapped him, and I regret being so cold. "The way I explained myself, what I want from you—it came out all wrong. It's not a lie that your presence will help my position in the Bratva, but putting this on you without more ... courtesy ... was wrong. I made it sound like you have no choice in the matter."

"Probably because I don't have one." My laugh is dry and brittle. It goes on too long, echoing around the garden.

Arsen reaches for me, his pained frown and warm eyes promising comfort. I'm tempted to allow him to touch me. More than a small part of me longs for his warmth. But our conversation from before has reignited another fear that has never gone away.

He killed Pyotr. He murdered a child.

My foot slips back, pulling me away from him. Arsen lowers his arm, wilting like a flower deprived of water. That's what I am to him. He's dying without me.

Again, I fight the urge to throw myself against his chest. It would feel so good to work my hands into his hair, to place my ear on his ribs and listen to him breathe until I calm down. But I can't. Not until I know the truth and understand just where I stand in everything. All the niceties in the world can't fix that he's asked me to be a banner to rally more men to his side in this war.

He'll do anything to win. That's what it comes down to. He's motivated by conquest.

Is that why he killed Pyotr?

I should just ask him ... No. It's not possible. He'd want to know how I learned about Pyotr, which would lead to more questions. And if he starts asking questions, then I may reveal Ruslan's existence.

I can't do that if he's already murdered one child. What's to say he won't kill another?

Especially when that child came from my mother.

I can't have that on my conscience.

"Galina," he says, agonized, "you *do* have a choice."

"In what? I can't leave here." I gesture around wildly. "I can't call the cops to chase down Yevgeniy. I can't help search for my own mother. I can't even be who I want to be!" Mila calling me *Galina Yevgeniyevna* swims up in my memory bitterly, and I force my teeth together to stop my lips from trembling. "I'll be trapped in the Bratva until the day I die; it's just a matter of if that's sooner or later."

"No!" he insists, stepping toward me. "That's not true!"

The purple sky has darkened behind him like a bruised fruit. It casts new shadows on his twisted scowl. "As much as I wish I could keep you beside me forever ... if I knew you were safe, and ... if you were to ask ..." He pauses like this is something he doesn't want to admit. "I would let you leave my world. I love you, Galina. I would do anything for you. I've done it once, and you know I would do it again."

My eyes widen as my heart thuds violently. I can't sense a hint of a lie. After how hard it was for him to let me leave last time and how close I came to danger once we were split up, I was sure he'd cling harder than ever now that I'm back in his grasp.

He means it. He loves me enough that he would willingly let me go.

Looking away, I shake my head sadly. "You might be willing to set me free, but the men around you ... on both sides ... won't be so understanding."

"Which is why Yevgeniy must be destroyed." Arsen

approaches me, erasing the small gap between us. He reaches for my hands, not hesitating when he takes them. His skin is warm, comforting, and sets mine alive with a sense of thrill.

"Once he's gone, no one will threaten you. And if that's when you want to walk away from me?" His eyes dart to my belly, then back to my face. The determination battles with new pain. "Then I promise not to stop you."

He's saying he'd let me leave with our baby. Knowing how I could never, ever be separated from my child, I'm stunned. For him to suffer a fate like that is an act of sacrifice bigger than any I can imagine.

Holding onto his hands, I rub my thumb along his defined forearms. I trace his knuckles, where the bruises have mostly healed. The prayer beads rattle on my wrist.

"I don't have a choice." He starts to argue, but I cut him off. "Not until Yevgeniy is gone." I allow a slight smile to pass on my lips. "But once he is, give me some good reasons to stay around and I'll consider them for both of us."

He's shocked, but responds with a relieved smile of his own. "Of course."

"First, promise me one thing," I state flatly.

"Anything."

"Free the women forced to work for him." *They're more trapped than I am.*

"I will." His smile keeps growing. "In return, I need something from you."

"What's that?"

"I need you to get in touch with Josh Sanders again."

My eyes squint as confusion sets in. "Didn't you guys talk about everything you needed to last time?"

"I spent more time stopping myself from strangling him." He smiles darkly. "The thing is, for us to end Yevgeniy and dismantle the entire network, I need him to open a legal case without Yevgeniy noticing. Which is where you come in." He pulls me closer, his voice deepening. "Pass information to Josh through Audrey. This way, Yevgeniy won't know what hit him."

He yanks me against his body in an abrupt movement. He can't control himself anymore; he has to hold me. His shirt scrubs along my cheek. The scent of roses that saturates the air is warned off by his scent. Arsen has been working his way back into my life like an unstoppable storm. Caught up in it—in him—I can either weather the rain with a scowl or twirl in it with glee.

Winding my arms around his middle until my hands meet on the other side, I hug him fiercely. He locks up, as if unable to believe this is happening. Or perhaps he's trying to control himself from ravishing me right here in his garden.

"I'll do it. But you need to understand something."

"Of course."

Together, we're unstoppable. "If you break your promise—if my freedom and my mother's are reneged upon—I will never ... *ever* ... forgive you."

My grip begins to slacken—he catches my forearms, drawing me tighter than I could manage on my own. Arsen's assistance makes us greater than the sum of our parts, even in actions like a simple hug.

"I will never break my promise to you, Galina." Shifting his jaw through my hair, he lifts my chin. His kiss comes with less hesitation than the pause before a thunderclap.

Arsen tackles all my doubts with his teeth and tongue. The sky has left the last remnant of the sun behind. There are no stars yet, but soon there will be, and we'll still be here, kissing beneath them.

His mouth is warm ... soft ... welcome. Our kiss is all-encompassing, and nearly enough to quiet the clashing emotions inside my heart.

This is the right thing to do. Such an easy statement to make. But right for who?

The victims? My mother? My child?

Not least of all ...

Am I doing what's right for myself?

14

GALINA

Nothing tastes better right now than peanut butter and yogurt on top of a blueberry muffin.

I didn't have this epiphany until this morning, but I'm confident I'm right. Why else would I be slathering my third muffin in thick white yogurt, licking chunky peanut butter off my thumb while hovering over the sink in the kitchen?

Because you're a crazy pregnant woman.

Well, okay. That probably factors in.

Humming to myself, I wash down my mouthful of food with a glass of orange juice. It was freshly squeezed this morning, which boggles my mind because it's only nine and I've been awake for half an hour. Does the staff ever sleep? Or do they wake up fully functional at the crack of dawn? I could never. Especially not lately. I'm a walking ball of exhaustion mixed with ravenous hunger.

Running my palm over my belly, I sigh. Sure, my feet are swollen and killing me, and I'm eating weird things, but I'm living my best life.

If you ignore the mystery surrounding my husband-but-not-really-my-husband's possibly child-murdering inclinations.

Frowning as my mood takes a nose-dive, I stuff more muffin past my lips. I still haven't had the guts to ask Arsen about Pyotr. Audrey hasn't brought me any news either. I'm swimming in a sea of uncertainty as the baby I share with a possible murderer grows by the day.

"Good morning," a familiar voice says. Ulyana has joined me in the kitchen. She's dressed in her usual—she must have a closet full of the same-length skirts and blouses. Her blue eyes sparkle kindly at me. They match the gems ever present on her ears.

"I can make you a fresh pot of coffee. Decaf, of course."

"I'd like that." I rub my belly gently. "Thank you."

Ulyana moves through the space in that efficient way of hers. The bitter scent of coffee grounds wafts to my nose. I've become more sensitive to smells in the last week.

Sitting at the table, I wait for her to join me as the coffee percolates in the background. "Any plans for the day?" I ask.

"Take stock of the pantry, organize the spring collection of drapes, make sure that the girls scrub the first-floor bathrooms." Ulyana ticks off the tasks with her fingers. "Rotate the wine bottles in the cellar."

I'm overcome with a wave of unease. The wine cellar ... Just mentioning that place makes me recall the weird behavior between Arsen and Mila. The pair of them were being suspicious, but I dropped the topic because of other pressing issues at the time.

Why do I always feel like they're hiding ghastly things from me?

Because they probably are.

One is an assassin, and the other, the head of the Grachev Bratva. It would be weird if they weren't doing something ghastly that they don't want me to know about.

The coffeepot stops hissing. Ulyana rises and gathers

two small porcelain cups. She sets one in front of me, and brings over a silver tin of cream with a white cup of crystallized sugar cubes. The cubes remind me of the big chunks of sugar that gave the muffins their crunchy coating. And just like that, I'm hungry all over again.

She smiles fondly at me while stirring sugar into the dark liquid in her own cup.

"And you, *devushka*? Any plans with Arsen today?" she asks lightly.

"I don't know." Just the mere mention of his name sends me tumbling backward into the unease I've been fighting to quell.

Hunching over my coffee, I swirl it absently. The scent is burning my nose. I don't want it anymore. *I have to know about Pyotr.* I glance up from my cup. It's a risk, but at this point, I'll be eaten alive by anxiety if I don't find out *somehow.*

"Ulyana ... can I ask you about something?"

"You sound nervous, *devushka*."

I shift in my chair. "It's not an easy question to ask. It feels like prying."

Her head tilts and her earrings sway. "You can ask me anything, Galina."

I nod but don't speak. Not right away. I draw the moment out by adding sugar and cream to my coffee as I gather my thoughts. Ulyana grabs a cup and does the same as she waits. It's a big deal, what I'm about to ask. I'm dancing on an edge here, unsure if the nervousness I feel is because I'm about to fish for information I'm not supposed to know.

Or because I won't like what I find.

I can't just ask about Pyotr, not yet. I have to be cautious. "Kristina ... um ... did Yevgeniy have a reason for murdering her?"

Her hand stirring the coffee slows to a stop. "Because she was Arsen's wife."

"Right, but was there *another* reason?"

Sitting deeper in her chair, she takes a long sip of her coffee. The steam wafts around her face. "Why do you ask?"

Her sharp eyes catch every little twitch of my eyebrows and lips. My hands on the coffee cup slide to the table. She sees that too. Ulyana is too clever to be fooled like this. She can see right through me. *If I leave without explaining, I'll look more suspicious. What's the harm in revealing some of the truth?*

"I'll tell you," I reply. "If you promise to keep this a secret."

Her lips purse. "A secret from Arsen, you mean."

I nod. Who else can I keep secrets from?

Ulyana studies her nails for a while. I would count the seconds, but I'm distracted by making sure the cup doesn't shake in my hands when I pick it back up. I take a small sip, but the coffee tastes far more bitter than I thought.

"All right," she finally manages. "I'll do this for you."

Slumping from relief, I nearly spill my drink. "When I was with Yevgeniy, he told me that he killed Kristina as revenge. He wanted Arsen to know how it felt to lose a child ... because she was pregnant."

Ulyana stares at me without blinking. I let out a weak breath.

Now or never.

"Because Arsen killed Yevgeniy's son. Pyotr."

"Hm." Her eyes narrow ever so slightly. Not enough for me to figure out what she thinks, but enough to tell me that I'm not going to like what I'm about to hear.

"Is it true, then?"

"This is about more than the answer to that question, isn't it?"

"No," I say too quickly.

But Ulyana doesn't argue. Instead, she links her fingers over her lips and just *looks* at me. I can't tell if she's smiling or frowning. Neither would be good. *Of course it's about more than Pyotr. I need to know if Arsen is capable of killing a child!*

I need to know if he's capable of killing another one. I force my breathing to slow down. "You're right," I lie carefully. "There's more. Yevgeniy said that my position in this war isn't different than my mother's in regard to him. Do you think that's right? Am I blind to the fact I'm trapped with an abusive monster?"

"There is a *world* of difference," her hand falls to the table with a *thud,* and her eyes flash with anger, "between Arsen and that *monster*." She chews each word, spitting out the next. "Arsen has a moral code. Yevgeniy never did."

The steam of her coffee swirls around her like a righteous cloud of anger. Yet in spite of how worked up she's getting, it doesn't convince me. *This is it. There's no more point in delaying.*

"If he has a moral code," I say. "Then you should be able to tell me he didn't kill Pyotr."

She holds my stare evenly. Like a puddle in the rain, her doubt grows steadily. The pride she wore a moment ago is all gone. Settling back in her chair, she pulls her cup closer but doesn't drink from it.

"You know nothing, Galina Yevgeniyevna!"

"Then tell me," I argue.

Ulyana sizes me up. My conviction wins out, and she hangs her head in defeat. "Yes. Arsen killed Pyotr."

Her words hit me harder than I could ever expect. It's as if someone has shoved me face-first into a pond of ice and is now holding me there. My throat closes and I find it hard to breathe. *No. My God, it can't be true.* But Ulyana wouldn't lie about this. There's no reason.

Shivering, I grab my coffee cup, seeking warmth, but the hot drink isn't enough. Either it's gone lukewarm, or I'm too beyond what it can offer me.

He did it.
He killed a child.
And that means ...
He can do it again.

Recalling Ruslan's smile, so similar to my mother's, I fight down a ripple of nausea. I loathe Yevgeniy, but I have no wish for an innocent child—even if that child is his son—to suffer the actions of his father.

Why did I ask?

Because you wanted to know, stupid girl!

Now I do, and I can't forget it.

"Why?" I croak hoarsely. "Why would Arsen do that?"

Ulyana turns away from me to look out the window. There's nothing to see. The sky is flat gray without any defined clouds, but she studies it like it's a painting in a museum. "That's not for me to tell you."

"But you know!" I argue. "Why won't you tell me?"

"Because this is not for me to tell!" she says flatly. "If you want to know, then you must ask Arsen yourself. But know this: there will be consequences, Galina."

"There always are," I mutter.

"Not like this," she snaps, and I sit up in response.

In profile, her face is all angles. There's not a hint of softness here. When she twists, shifting her attention from the window to me, I hold my breath.

"The deeper you look into this," she warns me, "the more pain it will bring." The agony in her eyes has turned her sapphire irises pitch black. "Not just for you, *devushka*. But for everyone."

15

GALINA

THERE'S A STRANGER IN THE HOUSE.

I lean over the railing near the staircase to get a better look. Blonde hair down to her hips, a fur-lined ivory coat that doesn't hide how thin she is. She's shorter than me; I can tell because she's standing next to Mila and barely reaches her shoulder. *Small.* That's the word I'd use to describe her. Not only in stature, but also in how she presents herself.

I've seen beaten dogs who shake less.

"Come on, Madison," Mila says, her tone gentler than normal. "Arsen is upstairs."

She's here to see Arsen? Intrigued, I remain where I am on the stairs as the pair get closer. Mila sees me, her eyes going from wide to narrow. Madison, who has been pressing close to Mila like she's a source of comfort, stops short at the sight of me. The young woman can't be older than eighteen. Her face, unlike her thin body, has the roundness of youth.

"Did you need something?" Mila asks me with an edge.

Ignoring her, I smile kindly at Madison. "Hi there, I'm Galina."

Madison shuffles her ankles together and doesn't smile back. "Hi." Her voice is light as air. I glance down at her feet on the stairs. Her shoes are old and chewed up, one of them missing a part of the shoelace so the tongue flops loosely.

Mila coughs in a clearly fake way. "Excuse us, we've got business to get to."

"Yes. To meet with Arsen," I call out, following them as they move past me to the landing above. From behind, Mila's shoulders stiffen until they're as still as a wall. Madison peers back at me while Mila stays looking forward. "Why?"

"This doesn't concern you," she replies coldly.

Except everything concerns me. And she *knows* that. More curious than ever, I squeeze by them, standing in the hallway—not quite blocking them with my body, but not letting them escape easily either. I offer Madison another sweet smile. But she looks terrified.

"How do you know Arsen?"

"I don't," she whispers.

Puzzled, I check Mila's expression. For a second, I catch her looking at Madison with the immense, loving concern I saw earlier. But when she turns to me, her face grows cold again.

"Mila, do you know this girl?" I ask warily.

"No, but in a way," she snaps. Her neck tightens. "I do."

Both of them turn their gazes away from me toward the floor, as if they're somehow able to see the same thing. Something that I can't.

"Why are you taking her to see Arsen?" I ask.

Madison speaks up before Mila can. Her big brown eyes fix on me. "He's going to help me."

"*How?*"

"Madison ..." Mila whispers, but she doesn't interfere.

The blonde girl rubs her hands up and down the outsides of her frail arms. "I escaped a brothel owned by a terrible man."

The pieces click into place as I look between Mila and Madison. There's only one type of person Mila would be this protective of. "You're one of the girls that he …"

Madison pulls her bottom lip between her teeth. "Yes."

Mila's posture has shifted into someone ready to go to war. The tiny hairs on my neck prickle upward as she glares at me. I know I'm not why she's upset, but being on the opposite end of her fury is terrifying.

"I found Madison staggering in the dark. When she told me where she'd come from, I knew she had to speak with Arsen."

I nod. Mila's horrific past is only bearable because there is a distance between her and the tragedy. But Madison? Her trauma is fresh. Whatever hell she escaped still haunts her.

Arsen informed me that the business had been brought back to life. But there's a world of difference between knowing about the business and seeing the terrible scars that it leaves behind in person.

"Come on," I urge, motioning down the hall. "Let's go talk to him."

Madison manages something close to a smile.

As we walk, I drop beside Mila, letting her lead the way.

Mila shoots me a quick glance. "You don't have to be a part of this."

"Yes," I say solemnly, "I do."

Arsen is waiting for us in his office. The lack of surprise in his eyes tells me Mila let him know ahead of time that she was coming and who she was bringing. He surveys all three of us, lingering on me with a look I can't discern.

Finally, he focuses on Madison. "You know who I am?"

She swallows. "Yes."

"Why are you here?"

His gruffness leaves me confused. I try to catch his eye, but he ignores me. Mila, though, seems to be on the verge of speaking up. Her lips are pressed into a line so taut it could snap.

Madison trembles as she rubs her elbows through her coat. She can't be cold. It's not possible.

Arsen is the source of her shaking.

I glare harder at him. He still ignores me. Madison says in a reedy voice, "I need protection."

"From Yevgeniy?" he asks.

"He's going to look for me," she whispers, sounding miserable. "He told all of us that escaping was pointless. If we tried, he'd drag us back and beat us until we couldn't move. Then he'd kill us." She covers her mouth like she's going to throw up. "I saw him do it to another girl. I know he isn't lying."

"Yes," Arsen muses in a growl. "But I wonder if you are."

Mila steps forward, ready to challenge him. "There are no lies here. I believe her."

He holds her in an emotionless gaze. "That's not for you to decide, Mila."

She scowls as she flicks her eyes meaningfully at Madison. "There could be other girls like her."

"Which is why I need you out there," he says flatly. "In case there are more."

The gears in her head begin to turn. She's placated by this suggestion, but her voice comes out strained and clipped as she heads for the door. "Remember what I went through."

It's crystal clear what she's trying to say.

Treat the poor girl with kindness.

Someone has to.

I'm glad that Mila has taken such a big-sister position with Madison. I know Arsen respects Mila deeply. I'm sure he'll keep her trauma in mind while talking with Madison.

Or that's what I think until the door shuts and he squares up with the frail blonde girl.

Looming over her, his face a mass of shadows from how hooded his brows are, he talks in a tone above reproach.

"Who *are* you?"

She balks, shrinking where she stands. "I'm ... I'm Madison."

"No last name?" he demands.

"Pelante," she blurts. "But does it even matter? Nobody called me by that name. Sometimes they didn't even bother to call me Madison either."

My heart breaks for the girl all over again.

"Who else have you seen?" he demands. "In the brothels."

Madison shivers with such intensity that her joints could pop from their sockets. This is more like an inquisition than a safe zone. It's upsetting me to see him be so harsh with her. "Just men. Tattooed men. Rough men. Men that like to hurt." She pauses a beat, her eyebrows twisting as she takes a shuddering breath. "No, there *was* someone else. An older woman."

My attention peaks.

Arsen looks more irritated. "Who?"

"I don't know," she insists. "She came around to teach some of the girls how to dance."

Dance.

Mamochka.

The air goes out of me. I stare openly at Madison before

whipping my eyes around to look at Arsen. "Do you think that it's *her*?"

His frown melts at the corners. He's no longer angry; he's worried. He doesn't like how hopeful I'm getting. "There's too little detail. Plenty of older women teach dancing, and besides, the type they'd learn at a brothel isn't ballet."

"But it's possible!" I hiss, my excitement boiling over. *We can do it! We can find out where she is!*

"Madison!" Now it's my turn to demand. "Where is the brothel you worked at?"

Her skin drains of all color. If I held her to the window, I'm sure I'd be able to see through her skin. "I can't remember."

"Did it have a name?"

"I ... I don't know. I never heard one."

My hope is snuffed out like a candle in the wind. "Then you can't guide us there."

Mom ... no ...

Each time I get close, the taste of success is snatched away.

She exhales. "I'm sorry. I wish I could tell you. But there were guards everywhere so we couldn't get away. I got lucky only because the ones on watch got too drunk. They were passed out, and I ran through the back door. I sprinted down so many alleys and side streets I couldn't find my way back if I tried."

Arsen drums his fingers on his biceps. Walking to the office window, he peers out of it. "I don't like it."

"What do you mean?" I ask nervously.

"This is too convenient." He shoots daggers at Madison. "She could be a spy for Yevgeniy. Sent to get close to me."

"That's ..." I trail off, torn between his reasoning and the gut feeling I get from Madison. She's loitering by the couch, not sitting in it, though she should—her legs look ready to buckle. *A spy? Arsen, she looks like a frightened child! The details she gave are too clear for me to think she made it all up.*

"Mila believed her," I say bluntly.

"Because Mila *wants* to believe her," he replies bluntly. Folding his hands behind his back, he approaches Madison. She bends into herself the closer he gets. At this rate, she'll vanish.

"There's one way to know the truth."

"What's that?" she whimpers, her chin wobbling.

His shadow slides over her, turning the white of her outfit, the white of her skin, black as old blood. Madison's eyes are ready to fall from her skull. I know what is about to happen before it happens.

I remember the way Mila ripped open her own clothes to show me the chained fox forcibly inked on her shoulder.

"No!" I shout, holding up my hand to intervene. "Let me handle this."

He eyeballs me curiously. "Handle what?"

"I'll search her."

I look at Madison with a new swell of sympathy. The poor thing probably had plenty of terrifying men looking over her body. If Arsen were to do it ... it would break her after all that she's been through.

Arsen stands taller, his eyes becoming suspicious slits. "You don't know what to look for."

I face him without fear. "A fox on its haunches surrounded by chains."

His eyebrows shoot up. He must be surprised that Mila, such a closed-off, dangerous person, might share something so vulnerable with me. I feel him evaluating me with fresh eyes. There's interest and a new air of respect. "Then I'll leave this to you."

Thank God. The idea of Madison being examined like a horse at a trade show makes me sick. "Give us privacy, please," I say.

Madison darts her attention between us. She hasn't spoken in several minutes and that doesn't look about to change. But unless I'm imagining it, some color has returned to her face and she's breathing easier.

Arsen hesitates at the door. "The fox should have three legs."

"Three?" I repeat.

"Yes. The fourth, with the chain, is only added once a girl is trained and broken. She is neither." His long, dark stare at Madison communicates to me that he has also noticed how young she is.

The women who get the finished tattoo are changed forever.

I wonder helplessly what Mila was like before the last leg was added.

Arsen closes the door as he exits. Letting out a quick breath, I smile gently at Madison.

"Sorry about all that," I tell her. "He's been through a lot, so he's suspicious of ... well, everyone."

"It's okay," she whispers meekly.

She's so nervous ... How did someone like her find the courage to try and escape?

Silence stretches between us. I'm supposed to be checking her for ink, but the awkwardness of the situation is sinking in. Gnawing at my tongue, I debate how to begin the process. Madison is staring at me—has she blinked in the last minute? "Maybe we should take off your coat," I start.

She unzips the front, exposing the thin, ribbed purple sweater underneath. I flinch at the sight of the long sleeves.

Getting out of this without her stripping down isn't happening. To my amazement, Madison doesn't wait for my next instruction; she keeps going—the sweater is yanked over her head, sending her long hair into a cascade of waves. Static makes the thin strands cling to the sweater before it's set lightly by her feet. She's not wearing any undergarments.

"Here," she says, twisting to show me her back and shoulder. "This is what you're looking for, right?"

Madison's back is a canvas of bony ridges. I want to take her downstairs to the kitchen and plop her in front of a stack of Olesya's famous pancakes. But instead I stare at the canvas of pain and hurt spread across her body.

Painted on her right shoulder in stark black ink is the familiar shape of a fox on its haunches, its black body surrounded by thick, detailed chains.

Three legs, I confirm to myself. It's just like Arsen said. I'm not relieved. Finding out that she was definitely forced to endure life in a brothel is horrible. It would almost be better for her to be a liar. I try to imagine the things she's seen … the things that she's done. *If she were my daughter, I'd be so worried about her.* I touch my stomach, roiling with empathy for a parent I've never met, and for my future child as I picture it going through what Madison and Mila have.

Yevgeniy must be stopped.

Something on her left shoulder draws my eye. There's another tattoo. This one is a strange, thin rod. I can't make sense of what it's supposed to be. A bat? A baton? "Did they tattoo this on you as well?" I ask curiously.

She cranes her neck to see what I'm talking about. Pain flickers in her eyes for a moment as she shakes her head.

"I ran away from home." She hesitates, like she's overwhelmed by mentioning that word. I know the feeling. "My parents wanted me to see a tutor so I wouldn't fail sophomore year. And I didn't want to."

Sophomore year? My eyes flare wide. *Oh my God, she can't be older than fifteen!*

I'm infused by a brand-new wave of disgust toward Yevgeniy.

Fuck that man. He deserves to burn in hell.

"I snuck out," she rattles on. "And went to a tattoo parlor to get this. That's when I was kidnapped. I shouldn't have run away." Again, she pauses, her voice growing softer. "I was so stupid."

"But you're safe now," I say soothingly. Picking up her sweater dress, I hand it back to her with a sheepish grin. "And that's all that matters."

Madison puckers her lips together. Then, for the first time, she manages a smile. "Thank you."

"You're sure of what you saw?"

Arsen is pacing his bedroom. His shoulders are massive knots that throttle his neck. "Yeah, positive," I say. "It was definitely a three-legged fox. Are you satisfied?"

He pulls up short, staring at me like I said something insulting. All at once he drops his arms and sighs. "I'm sorry; I know I'm being paranoid."

Seeing how he recognizes his behavior and apologizes, the tension evaporates from my spine too. "I understand. Everything that's going on ... It's hard to know who we can trust."

You, for example.

I don't say it. I never could.

Arsen lets a tired smile cross his face. Ruffling his hair, he approaches me. "Thank you for checking her."

I let my eyes become downcast. "There's something else."

"What?" His voice is back to being anxious.

"She's only fifteen."

He says nothing. Lifting my head, I see the lack of surprise on his face. "How do you know?"

"She said something about not failing sophomore year. So I did some quick math."

Arsen grimaces. "Yevgeniy has always preferred teenagers. The younger they are, the easier they are to break."

I clutch my stomach so I don't heave. "Arsen, we have to protect her."

"We will. I'll tell Ulyana to set up a guest bedroom for her; she'll be as safe as anyone under my roof."

I smile in immense relief. Egged on by my flood of emotions, I move forward, wrapping him in a strong embrace. He stiffens in shock before hugging me back. At first, it's hesitant, but then it's firm and solid. He's eager for my touch.

"Thank you, Arsen." *Mila will be thankful too.* My attention shifts to his large bed. Since I returned to the mansion, I've been sleeping in my own bedroom. The questions in my brain, my own fears, have kept me from wanting to share his bed.

"Tonight," I say lightly, "can I sleep here?"

Arsen jerks back, holding me at arm's length. "You're serious."

I nod.

"Galina, I would love nothing more than to have you here beside me."

I smile shyly at his honesty. I don't tell him that I'm nervous ... that part of me still wonders about the core of his being. How dark are his sins? Can light ever shine on them? But I'm also feeling needy. I don't want to be alone, especially after listening to Madison. Her tragedy has made me want to seek out a source of protection.

There's no one more protective than Arsen Isakov.

I DON'T KNOW what wakes me up. I only know that the darkness I'm staring at isn't the familiar wall of my own eyelids. Everything shifts around me. Slowly, I recognize the ceiling, the walls, and the moonlight filtering through the gap in the drapes.

Arsen is breathing evenly beside me in the bed. It's a comforting sound. I rock sideways to hug him, eager for his presence to lull me back to sleep. The slope of his nose and strong chin glow in the starlight through the window.

And that's when I see it.

Someone else is standing over him.

In the diffused light, Madison's hair looks like cloud vapor. It drifts from side to side as she hovers over Arsen with something clutched in her fist. Something sharp.

Time is sluggish; it takes decades for me to draw enough air into my lungs.

Madison strikes downward. I scream simultaneously.

Arsen's eyes pop open. In a blur, he shoots his arm up, snatching Madison by her thin wrist just before she can touch him. Grunting, he twists his body, wrenching her violently. She lets out a cry of pain, and the item in her hand clatters to the floor.

My eyes have adjusted fully now and I can see the syringe.

Its metal tip glints where it lies on the rug.

"I'm sorry!" she sobs, her knees going slack. Arsen is the only thing keeping her on her feet. He rises from the bed, pulling her onto her tiptoes. "I'm sorry, I'm sorry, I'm sorry," she babbles, tears streaking her ruddy cheeks.

Arsen drags her from the room. Her desperate screams echo through the crack in the door, fading the further away he takes her.

She was lying. He was right; this was a trap.

He'll get the truth out of her by any means necessary.

And cruelly, a dark thought crosses my mind—a thought that frightens me.

I won't stop him this time.

16

ARSEN

Being right has its downside. Especially in this case.

"Please," Madison groans, cowering on the floor of my office. "Please, don't hurt me."

How odd to think we were in this room hours earlier while she barely uttered a sound. Now she can't seem to shut up.

"Quiet," I grumble, pacing by my desk. "The only thing I want to hear out of your mouth is an explanation."

She sniffles, hiding her face in a tangle of knees and arms. "Okay. I'll tell you everything."

Galina said she was fifteen, but right now, she looks even younger.

"How did you meet Yevgeniy?"

The door opens behind me; Galina leans in, sees my enraged face, and freezes. Amazingly she doesn't back out; she enters, shutting herself inside. Madison glances up to see who's joined us. Her puffy eyes widen. Galina looks at her with pity before turning away. "I just wanted to see what was going on," she explains.

I motion at Madison sharply. "Talk. Now."

"I told her the truth," she gasps. Rubbing her wet cheeks, she takes a shaky breath. "I was kidnapped at a tattoo parlor."

My heart jerks sideways before I aim my anger at Galina. "You *knew?*"

Galina tenses on the spot with her hands lifting in defense. "She has another tattoo on her that I was curious about. She said she ran away from home and got it as a way to rebel against her parents."

"And you believed her?" I snarl, bursting with ripples of hot frustration. *How can I keep Galina safe when she keeps details like this from me?*

Galina draws herself up like I've offended her. "I didn't think—"

"Exactly! You didn't *think*." I turn back to Madison, looming over her with new, deep-rooted rage. "Keep talking!"

She recoils as quickly as if I'd slapped her. "I was brought to a place called the Winter Palace. There were other girls there like me, all of us forced to undergo training."

The Winter Palace. That familiar name hits me like a truck. If she's trying to make me feel bad for her, it's a waste of effort. I won't allow any room in my heart to forgive someone who attacked me. *And someone who tricked not just me ... but ...* I glance at Galina.

I'm furious on her behalf.

Madison keeps talking. "After a few days, I met *him*." She peers up at me, then back at her feet. "Yevgeniy. He promised me my freedom if I did something for him. I don't know why he bothered with a reward though, since he also threatened to murder my parents if I didn't do it. I'd have done anything he wanted at that point."

Typical Yevgeniy.

"Let me guess. He wanted you to slip close to me with this story about escaping his clutches?" I ask coldly. "Then kill me with that syringe?"

"Yes," she admits.

I walk right, then left, my mind turning. "Show me the tattoo."

Madison licks her lips anxiously, but she has no fight left in her. She turns away from me and lifts her flannel pajama shirt—the one Ulyana let her borrow, which rankles me after her betrayal—and exposes her naked skin.

Crouching, I examine the oblong shape carved into her left shoulder.

"It looked like a baton to me," Galina whispers.

"It's not." Shaking my head, I rise to my full height. "It's a dagger hilt. The blade would have been added once she made her first kill."

It was meant to be me.

Galina goes as pale as Madison. "I had no idea," she says regretfully. "I'm sorry."

"If you hadn't stopped me from searching her myself, I would have seen this. I would have also found the syringe."

Her posture is infected by enough shame that she sinks closer to the floor. I loathe seeing her beaten down like this. *She's too naive! She should have listened to me!* Perhaps I'm being harsh, but that's the way the world—my world—is.

Galina needs to understand what's at risk.

But God, look at her ... cowering in front of me like this.

I know that I'm not in the right. But I can't say that right now.

I turn those negative feelings toward the source of this mess. Towering over Madison, where she shakes in a useless pile of limbs, I snarl, "I should kill you for this."

"Arsen!" Galina cries. "No!"

"Not because you tried to kill *me*," I seethe, my arm snaking down, gripping her by the collar of her shirt. The red and black plaid starts to rip when I haul her to her feet. "But because you betrayed *her* trust."

Galina freezes, realizing I'm talking about her.

"She believed in you," I go on, shaking the girl until her teeth rattle in her skull. "How dare you steal that away? How fucking *dare* you make her fight for you when you're no better than the scum on the bottom of my shoe?"

Madison grabs at my wrists, trying to get purchase. Her nails scrape, raising pink lines, but I ignore the hot pain. I keep shaking her.

"Arsen, stop it!" Galina cries, launching at me, tugging at my forearm. "This is insane! How can you be so consumed by revenge that you'd *kill a child?*"

Her accusation pierces me as deep as the syringe would have if Madison had attacked quicker. Wrinkling my nose, I glare down at Galina while Madison hangs limply in my grip.

"She was sent to kill me. Don't think she wouldn't have murdered you too if you'd gotten in her way."

"She's a child! A child who's been abused and frightened into submission! You can't blame her for how she is!"

"Of course I can!" I roar. "You're asking me to forgive someone who tried to end my life!"

"You don't have to forgive her, but you can try to understand!"

My chest rises and falls, each breath tasting like glowing embers. "You'd have me pat her on the head and send her on the way with a fucking bouquet of flowers." I drop Madison to the floor—she lands on her knees with a yelp.

Galina bends down to assist her. "Madison, are you okay?" she asks gently.

I watch with disgust growing like a tumor. "One day, your softheartedness will be the death of me."

She flinches—there's pure hurt in her wide eyes. As she cradles Madison like a baby, I'm assaulted by the odd image of the future. Galina ... hugging our own child protectively. Will she do that because I'm towering over them like I am now? Will she cradle our child from its monster of a father?

It cools some of my rage.

Jerking around sharply, I speak to the wall. "Thank Galina, Madison. She's the reason you're still alive."

Madison whimpers. "What will happen to me now?"

Yes, what will happen? To be only fifteen and go through so much so quickly ... I don't like admitting it, but Galina has a point. How can I blame this girl for what she was forced to do? The real culprit has been in my sights for years.

Yevgeniy ... the bastard ruins every life he comes in contact with. Thinking of Galina's determination to protect the girl, I let some of the tension slip from my body. My voice comes out smoother, less cut up by grit. "I'll find a way to reunite you with your parents."

Madison inhales loudly before covering her mouth. The air that's expelled sounds like a muffled cry of joy. Tears dribble endlessly down her splotchy cheeks. Undeniably, she didn't expect to live through the night. Once I stopped her attempt to assassinate me, she gave up all hope. Now it's bloomed again. She looks away from me, as if she fears one wrong move will change my mind.

Galina rubs the girl's back, rocking her, whispering in her ear. The pair of them talk in a hush. I don't linger. I'm possessed by a need to get away from the scene. *I came close to killing that girl. I really did.*

Only Galina stayed my hand. Maybe I should thank her for preserving what's left of my blackened soul.

In the hallway, I call Mila. "You need to come here now."

"What? Why?" she asks in an urgent voice.

My eyes track to my office door. "That girl turned out to be more of a problem than anticipated."

"What happened?"

"I'll explain later. Just get here. I want you to take her somewhere else until you can find where her parents are."

Mila is quiet for a moment. "Is it safe to bring her to them? Yevgeniy will want her back. He never lets his property go without a price."

Mila knows that all too well.

"Then I'll leave it to you to find a way to make sure they're all safe from him. By any means necessary."

"You always give me the hardest jobs."

"Can you get it done?"

"Oh yes," she chuckles darkly. "With pleasure."

GALINA STANDS IN MY BEDROOM, right in front of my window. The thin, silken bronze robe clings to her every curve. The light from outside forms a halo behind her long, loose hair. With her rounded belly and the soft glow of the light, she resembles a saint from one of the oil paintings in my hallway.

The sky outside is painted a brilliant scarlet. An hour has passed since Madison attacked me and Mila arrived to slip her off my property. I don't know where they've gone, and it's better if I don't know.

I don't want to think about that girl. She reminded me of how easy it is to let the beast out.

"Galina," I say.

She doesn't look at me. "I'm sorry."

"For what?" I ask, moving toward her.

Her chin tips to her chest. "I didn't realize how dangerous mercy could be."

Hair shrouds her cheeks from how she lowers her head, speaking to the floor, her voice growing more agitated with each choppy syllable.

"I was a fool to believe everything she said. If I'd let you or maybe Mila search her, or if I'd just told you everything she said and that I saw, none of this would have happened. You wouldn't have almost been killed, and I wouldn't be standing here wondering why I bother to give anyone the benefit of the doubt when I keep. Getting. Proven. *Wrong!*"

A sinkhole opens in my chest. The longer she talks, the more cavernous it becomes. I grab her by the arms, ignoring how she tries to shake me off.

"You didn't do anything wrong, *ptichka*. Madison was given the perfect set of words designed to appeal to good people like you." Stroking her cheek, I force her to look into my eyes. She looks ready to fight or flee. "The part of you that dares to allow others close to your heart isn't anything to be ashamed about."

Tears rise up, then spill over, turning her lashes damp like dew on tufts of grass. Galina collapses in my arms, allowing me to hold her and guide her back to bed. She weighs nothing, and it's easy to curl my body around her, settling on the blankets with her head tucked under my chin. She continues to cry, the tears staining her shirt and my hands as I wipe them away. But they keep coming.

"You'll be okay," I hush.

"It doesn't feel like it." Her voice is all cracks.

Hugging her protectively, I listen to her pulse as it flows between her skin into my own. I try to feel our baby's as well. I can't, not yet, but I know someday I will.

"I need to thank you. Tonight, your compassion kept me from killing a child."

All her slack muscles morph into rocks.

I continue while stroking her hair. "You alone had the courage to stand up not just against me, but for what was right." Breathing in, then out, I rub my cheek on her forehead. "Don't you *ever* apologize for that."

Other than her rapid breathing, she's gone quiet. In my arms she seems like a fragile thing I *have* to protect from all the cruelty this world has to offer. Yevgeniy has made her suffer again and again. He tests me through what he does to her.

I'll make him pay.

Galina stays in my arms without budging. She doesn't try to move away or shake me off, and I'm grateful because any attempt would be pointless. I'll never let her go. Not just tonight, as I wait for her to fall asleep, her chest rising and falling in an increasingly gentler rhythm that tells me she's slipped into unconsciousness.

Galina is mine.

She always will be.

17

GALINA

ARSEN IS DEAD.

I've never seen him so still. Even in his most brooding moments, he radiated life. But lying on the floor, his throat split apart in a clean gash, ashen skin coated in blood, he's as lifeless as a rock. The man who was constantly strong ... a symbol of power ... is no more.

And there's so much blood.

The trail of glistening red goes from Arsen to the tip of the knife in Madison's hand. She crouches over Arsen's body, legs bent like a gargoyle perched on a roof. She shifts almost imperceptibly to turn one eye on me.

Her lips twist into a smirk as if to say, *You're next.*

And it's true. Because what defense do I have against a trained killer? She took down Arsen with ease. I'll be a cakewalk.

"Madison, no," I whisper. My mouth is too dry; the words are too quiet. But again, I know it doesn't matter. Screaming won't stall her mission.

She rises, stalking toward me with the patience of a wolf cornering a rabbit. The knife flips into her other hand, leaving a trail of bloody dots on the ground. Behind her, Arsen stares at nothing. I'm about to join him.

"Please," I manage, just before she levers her arm back. Time dilates. I'm tortured by being forced to watch the infinitely slow way death comes for me. In a smooth thrust, the blade jams into my stomach.

I have a single, mind-splitting, agonizing thought about my poor baby.

I never even got to name it.

"No!" I manage to yell the word, sitting upright, clutching at my belly. I feel my skin, the lingering pain of the stab wound fading as I realize I'm not hurt. I'm wet from sweat, not blood. Around me is the familiar scene of Arsen's bedroom.

It was just a nightmare.

Frantic to confirm he's all right, I look over at Arsen. He isn't just alive; he's sitting up and gawking at me with his eyebrows pressed together so tight that they've become one.

"Galina! What's wrong?" he asks in a panic.

"I just had an awful nightmare." Trembling, but overcome by an urge to touch Arsen, I clasp his cheeks. "Why do you feel so cold?" I gasp. The imagery of his bleeding corpse swims up.

"I'm not. You're just overheated." He palms my forehead to remove some of my perspiration. "Let me get you some water."

"No, stay."

But he's already gone, hurrying to the mini fridge on the far side of his room. Returning with a small bottle, he cracks it open and hands it to me. The chill is good, but drinking it is heaven. "Tell me about the nightmare, Galina."

The tender way he speaks encourages me to be honest. I swallow down more water, then feel a wave of anguish as I relive the terrible dream, I force the words out. "It was god-awful. Madison ... she took a knife to your throat, dropping you to the ground. Then she came at me and—" Gulping, I rub my belly protectively. "It was so real."

"It wasn't," he assures me. His eyes warm over with fierce compassion. "It was only a dream."

The memory of Madison cowering on his office floor comes back to me, but the version of her in my nightmare doesn't leave.

"Would you have really killed Madison?" I whisper hesitantly. It's hard to look him in the eye.

I hate that he doesn't answer right away.

Frowning, he makes a soft noise in his throat. The hand that was on my cheek now runs through his own hair, like he's flustered. "I don't know."

My heart calcifies like limestone in a dark cave.

"What I do know," he says, looking at me with sincerity, "is that I would have felt haunted by her death. More so than any of my other kills." He presses his palm to his chest, as if to check that his own heart is still there. "Because each kill stays with you. Those memories will never leave."

My brain is looping back on itself, drawing at myriad concerning things. *Madison's death would have weighed on him more than Pyotr? Why is one child's death worth more than another's?* Arsen strokes my hair, trying to relax me, but I'm too wired. The adrenaline from the nightmare that had faded has been replaced by new anxiety over this question that continues to plague me. He killed Pyotr—I know he did —but *why?*

Ulyana said if I wanted to pry, I'd have to do it myself.

She also warned me this would unleash pain on all of us.

But I have to know.

Steeling my nerves, I shift enough to peer into his face. I need to see how he reacts. "Yevgeniy told me that you killed his son."

Arsen's jaw slips open. I spot every minor twinge of his lips and eyebrows. He's taken aback by my sudden question. But it's not shock I care to see from him; it's shame. I want him to *feel bad* for what he did.

I need him to.

It's so damn important to me and whatever future we're trying to build together.

"Yes," he sighs after a moment. "I did kill Pyotr."

Tension that had consumed me for days breaks off in sheets like ice on a mountain. I sway forward, our heads almost touching. We could be kids sharing stories after dark while hoping no adults catch us in the act. "Why?"

"Can we go back to discussing nightmares?" he chuckles wearily. "Those are easier. I've had plenty of my own."

I'm intrigued, and I do want to know what the dark dreams that haunt him are, but this is more pressing. "Please, Arsen. I have to know."

I have to know why you don't feel remorse for killing a child.

"More than ten years ago, I was Yevgeniy's brigadier." He sighs through his nose. "And Pyotr's bodyguard. It was a job that brought me honor and prestige, but not pride."

"Why?"

"Because that man was evil to the core. A rotten apple that didn't fall far from the tree."

My spine straightens sharply. "Wait, *man?*"

Arsen squints at my question. "Yes, Pyotr was twenty-two when I killed him."

The admission is like an anvil has been shoved off my chest. Not that killing anyone is okay, but the fact that Arsen isn't a child murderer is a relief. For some reason, I'd always imagined Pyotr as a different version of Ruslan. Impish, vulnerable, innocent to a fault.

It never crossed my mind that Pyotr was a grown man.

A rotten apple that didn't fall far from the tree.

"Sorry," I say, "Keep going."

Arsen rubs his fingers over his mouth. "Pyotr got his kicks by hurting those who couldn't fight back." He turns a wary stare on me, like he isn't sure if he should say the next part. "He took a particular liking to breaking the girls who were brought to the Winter Palace. He said it was like taking his vitamins each morning."

Gritting my teeth, I give my head a furious shake. "That's awful."

"One night," Arsen continues, "I stood outside, where he ordered, as he took a girl who was a wild child, even by Yevgeniy's standards. I could hear her screams through the door. And for the first time, I questioned just why the hell I allowed it to continue." His hands ball into fists. "I couldn't stand by anymore. The girl screamed for her mother, even though she *knew* her mother was dead."

Wait ... Somehow, all of this sounds oddly familiar.

Unbidden, familiar words whispered in the dark echo in my ear.

She left this earth long before I ever realized that I even had a mother.

"So, I kicked the door open and demanded that he stop." Arsen's eyes take on a faraway look. "He told me to leave. Told me that it was his *order*. That this terrible thing he was doing was his *right*. His *duty*. And that *my* duty was to stand guard outside until he was done. And that's when I saw her."

The chains are proof that I'm property.

"Pyotr had her tied down." Arsen is clutching the blanket so violently that it twists into a whirlpool of cloth.

The vein in his neck pulses quicker. "And he went back to raping her. The girl screamed, begging me to save her."

"I acted on impulse and ripped him off her." Arsen begins to strangle the blanket, saying, "He was furious. He got in my face, arguing that plenty of the other men ... other brigadiers just like me ... had been with her since she was a little girl."

I'm not a fragile little girl hoping for someone to come along and sweep me away into a happy home with smiles instead of sneers!

There isn't a vein in his body that isn't pumping with adrenaline. I ache to reach for him and comfort him, but I'm afraid if I try, he'll lash out. Not intentionally, but he's reliving a traumatic event, making it vividly real all over again.

Arsen ...

His mouth twitches into an open scowl. "I shot him without a second thought. Then I grabbed her, freeing her from that place. For good."

Whatever lingering disgust I'd felt toward him over killing Pyotr vanishes in the air between us. I reach for his wrist, and when I touch him, he doesn't lash out. Arsen looks at me with hollowed-out eyes. He's waiting to be judged. Asking me to tell him if what he did was right or wrong.

He does what he has to in order to save the helpless. This is what Ulyana meant when she said he had a moral code. It's admirable. It also makes him dangerous, because there's little to leash him from committing one crime to prevent another. "I understand," I say soothingly. "You did what you had to. For Mila."

"And for my act of mercy," his smile is sickly, "Yevgeniy murdered Kristina."

The reminder makes me pull my hand away; he catches my fingers, holding me so I'm touching his warm skin.

"Galina," he whispers, drawing me against his body, "I wish you'd asked me about this sooner. I get why you didn't; you were frightened of how I would react. I promise, there's nothing I will hide from you. You don't have to fear asking me about the past or the truth."

Sparks of joy open in me like blossoms in the rain. I drop the bottle of water; it rolls off the bed, forgotten.

Smoothing my palms over his face, I tug him down until our lips lock tight. His jaw is scruffy—he hasn't shaved in two days. It's a hint at the inner stress he's been suffering through. *I've thought about my own stress, but what about his?*

This man who is obsessed with saving me and my child and my mother ... what pressure that must be. How can he even stand up? I'd be flattened into the dust if so many lives relied on me to keep them safe.

Arsen doesn't stop kissing me—I keep hold of the back of his neck so he can't. Something passes between us, a silent acknowledgment of both the late hour and our exhaustion. We're drained of energy. He shifts, pressing into my curves from behind, hugging me with his chest to my spine. His chin nestles into the gap between my cheek and shoulder.

He mumbles something tender. I can't discern the words, but I can feel his intent.

His need to reassure me.

What am I going to do?

My body is weighed down by guilt. *He promised to tell me anything ... but I'm still hiding Ruslan from him.* I want to believe he won't harm the boy. It helps to know that Pyotr wasn't a child but a full-grown adult without a shred of redeeming value.

But then, I saw how he was with Madison. He couldn't tell me flat out that he wouldn't have ended her life.

And that's the thing. The monster capable of killing is always inside him. And it stirs to life every time a threat comes near.

But there's something else that crosses my mind.

Even if he doesn't harm Ruslan, he will definitely *kill Yevgeniy.* If Madison can be lured into committing crimes, then so can Ruslan. He loves his father, twisted and vile though Yevgeniy is.

What's to say that after Arsen ends Yevgeniy's life, Ruslan won't be tainted by the same desire for vengeance?

I wish I could convince Arsen to abandon going after Yevgeniy, but I can't.

Not when he has my mom captive.

All I can do as Arsen holds me close, whispering sweet, indiscernible words, is pray that there's a way to untangle this mess.

Because how can he rescue my mother ... and not find out about Ruslan?

18

ARSEN

"You're *going* there?" Galina asks me, her eyes wide, but her voice is torn between fear and hope. She hates that I'm putting myself in danger. I get it. But the reward at the end of this, if I do everything right, is something she's been begging for daily.

"I have to. The Winter Palace could be where your mother is being held captive."

Madison claimed there was an older woman there. Yevgeniy might have put Katya to work teaching dance. I can't discount the idea that this is a trap. *But what if it isn't?* I don't have a reason to believe a lick of what came out of that girl's mouth, but the Winter Palace was already on my list to investigate. Mikhail rattled off a few locations when Mila interrogated him.

This was one of them.

I haven't been back there since the day I killed Pyotr.

Galina, who's now staring at me with yearning, making her eyes sparkle, brought that bastard back to the forefront of my mind. I told her that every kill stays with me, and it's the truth. But I've never had to think about Pyotr because his was the only death that was completely justified.

Having her utter his name in my bed felt like having my skin peeled off with a dull knife.

The final image imprinted in my mind of him is still vivid. His body was slumped over the bed he'd been raping Mila in. The blankets were soaked black from blood. It wasn't a pretty sight then and it isn't one now, but I don't hate it.

It's comforting to remember that monster is dead. And that I did it.

"Please be careful," she tells me, clutching me around my middle. The hug is desperate. I want it to go on forever. For too long, our relationship has been fraying. Lately, I can see the border around the puzzle, picture how to re-lay the pieces. With steady hands, I can rebuild our happiness.

We'll be okay. Out loud, I say, "I'll be okay."

Mila catches my eye from where she stands by my front door. She's not normally so quiet. Her favorite habit is to send out snide barbs during inappropriate times like this. Lately she's been more withdrawn. More aloof. Madison's appearance and desperate actions have affected Mila deeply.

And from what I can see, far more deeply than even Mila herself expected.

I should talk to her about it. But I'm doubtful she'll want to listen.

She's never been great with heart-to-hearts.

I'm no different.

Her silent frown in my direction communicates that it's time to go. I hug Galina a moment longer before releasing her. "When I come back, it will be with Katya."

THE WINTER PALACE used to be a bus depot over half a decade ago. The rounded front hints at the interior that follows the same shape, the massive, curved walls designed to allow easy access to the buses that would line up along the streets in front and back. Those walls create a perfect acoustic experience. This was part of the reason Yevgeniy bought the building to turn it into a club in the first place.

I was with him that day. He strutted around the large rooms, his voice an intonation of pride as he waxed on about the money the place would bring into the Grachev Bratva. The music would lure in crowds. But that wasn't where the cash would come from.

"Noise up top drowns out what we're doing below," he explained with a smirk. Then he cupped his hands around his mouth, shouting to hear his voice reverberate, each echo softer than the last. "Let them get *loud!*"

All the sweating, dancing people, screaming to the beat ... yes.

No one would hear the poor girls. It was a perfect business, as Yevgeniy said.

"We should have burned that place down years ago," Mila growls beside me. We're crouched across the street on the roof of a flower shop. The fire escape built into the brick gave us easy access.

Eyeing her curiously, I keep my voice even. "Will you be able to control yourself in there?"

She juts out her chin and doesn't respond.

I watched the way she gleefully eviscerated Yevgeniy's men. It made me think she was getting satisfaction by fulfilling her need for vengeance. I thought she'd cool down afterward, but she never did. A Band-Aid was ripped off, but instead of being a healed scar, the wound still bleeds.

And after Madison, Mila's urge to hurt the ones in charge of the brothels has returned in full force.

No, it was never gone.

Following her gaze, I survey the Winter Palace with intense scrutiny. It's nearly midnight, but unlike the other businesses in the city, the club is just waking up. The signage is a vibrant neon blue and pink. It draws young people like moths to a flame. There's a line of people waiting to pass by the guards at the front door. Even at this distance, I can make out the unmistakable beat of music inside.

It's freezing out—I'm bundled up in a thick, long black jacket and gloves. There are women in the line wearing practically nothing. Skirts that graze their hips, heels that you could use as stepping stools, all to show off their bodies.

They have no idea that there are women in that building who wish they could cover their skin. I grit my teeth until my skull throbs.

Why am I worrying about Mila? I'm just as likely to lose control at this rate.

I scan the line closely, trying to pick out anyone who isn't here to just drink and dance. But on the surface, every man looks the same. They're all oblivious to the nature of the secret brothel just beneath their feet.

Or they might all have weapons.

Gripping my gun under my jacket, I let a puff of white air float from my nostrils. It vanishes on the breeze. "Are the *boeviki* in position?"

"Yes," Mila replies. "Kostya has them organized into groups. When you're ready, they'll move to the street level, then go around the back to break in."

I nod sharply. The goal is to slip into the club without being recognized. Once in there, we'll search for both Katya and Yevgeniy. They could be on the main floor. But more likely than not, they're underground.

I'm about to turn away when I spot something. "There. See them?"

"The cameras?" Mila slips out her small pistol. "I can shoot them, or—"

I fire off a shot before she finishes talking. The lens on the security camera that sticks off the far-right corner of the building shatters. The sound is muted by the club's music. Mila clicks her tongue in annoyance before taking out the second camera.

"Show off," she mumbles.

"It's not a contest," I say with a half-smirk.

"Better not be. If it was, I'd win."

"Not with knives, you wouldn't."

She spins her gun around her hand in a smooth motion. "Which is why I didn't bring any."

Shaking my head with a light chuckle, I stretch my legs to keep my knees warm. Crouching as long as we have has made me stiff. *I'm getting too old for this shit.* Sticking close together we descend to the street. There's good cover here, lots of dumpsters and cars parked by clubgoers that will probably end up towed by morning.

"Tell Kostya we're ready," I say to Mila once we're tucked behind some awful-smelling garbage. I check my gun even though I know it's loaded. But it never hurts to be sure. My blood is racing through my veins at such speeds I feel like I'm on fire.

Mila taps her phone, then peers over the dumpster. "We should go down that side street and circle through the alley. Otherwise, we risk being spotted."

Darting into the shadows, we rush silently across the pebbled pavement near the club. None of the people in line glance our way. We're not as interesting as their phones or the interior of the club they continuously crane their necks to see before the bouncers shove them back.

Still, there are enough pairs of eyes that I'm worried we'll get noticed in the open air.

How do we get from here to the side street? I wonder, judging the distance, the level of shadow coverage.

"Hey, man!" a young guy in a red leather jacket shouts at the bouncer as he puffs his chest out, seemingly annoyed by how he's being denied entry. "Do you know who I am?"

The guard grumbles something. I can't make it out. Then he pushes the jacket-wearing guy so hard he tumbles back into the crowd. There's a swell of voices.

Perfect. I point at Mila; she reads my silent signal. Taking advantage of the distraction, I rush down a back road with her close behind.

On a skinny street between two alley walls, we make a sharp turn. The section behind the Winter Palace is lit only by a pair of orange lights strapped to a huge set of rolling shutter doors. The music can be heard through the thick walls. Around us are construction-filled patches of dirt, projects that the city abandoned. We're not going to be seen by any civilians here.

Peering up at the bricks coated in graffiti, I count multiple barred windows. The giant shuttered doors are locked to the ground with padlocks. I'd hoped there'd be a back entrance guarded by someone in charge of deliveries, but there's nothing.

I'm gauging the best way to break in when I hear boots. "Tell them to move fucking quieter," I hiss at Mila. My men should know better.

"Arsen!"

Wrenching around from the urgency in her voice, I see what she does. From the left, where we came from, are several of my soldiers. Most of the group has met at our rendezvous. But the other figures rushing our way aren't faces I know.

But I recognize the uniforms.

Cops.

"Move!" I shout, reaching for my weapon.

Mila has hers out already; she sets off a bullet, and when the cop she aimed at spins to the street with a yelp, she dodges into the shadows. The darkness isn't reliable though —the gunfire lights up the world. There's nowhere to hide.

I frantically crouch in an indented section of brick along the building's edge. It's where people stand if it rains while waiting for their bus to arrive. It won't keep me safe for long, but I need to catch my breath and collect my thoughts. *Why are the police here? There are so many of them! It's almost like ...*

A bullet shatters against the brick by my face. Flecks of the wall slice my skin like shrapnel. "Mila!" I roar, pointing my gun around the corner, firing blindly. "It's an ambush!"

She doesn't reply. Over the barrage of bullets, I pick out the agonized scream of a man. The wretched sound cuts off early. Someone has died.

Peeking out, I quickly scan the situation. Twelve fucking cops, maybe more. It's hard to be sure with the flashing red and blue lights blinding me. Of my men, I count seven still on their feet. *Where the hell is Mila?*

Lifting my gun, I level the barrel. Down the sight, I take aim at the bobbing head of an officer who keeps firing his pistol while squatting behind a partially open car door. He jerks when my bullet penetrates his skull, sending his hat flipping to the ground. Another shot, and he joins the hat.

But it's not enough. My men are dying. Mila and I will join them at this rate.

Fuck! Galina, I have to make this up to you somehow.

"There he is!"

The cops have noticed me. Flashlight beams illuminate my chunk of brick wall, turning it from protection into a death trap. I can't dodge here. Against one opponent, it would be a challenge; with so many, I'm fucked.

A bullet sinks into my left leg; the hot poker sensation saps my strength, dropping me to my knees. Touching my hand to the wound, it comes away bright red. I hold my gun up and out. It slips from my bloody hands; I recover, gripping it tighter.

If I'm going down, it won't be quietly.

"I'm sorry," I whisper.

It's a message meant for the woman who'll never hear it.

There's more shouting. The long shadows of cops with guns float closer, like fingers in the dark. They're practically on top of me now. I shut my eyes, starting to smile and make peace. It's the only reason that I'm not blinded temporarily when the closest cop car suddenly explodes in a blaze of red flames.

The roar of the fire competes with the shrieks of the people closest to the explosion. Everyone is shouting, and I open my eyes to see most of the cops are scattered across the ground. More than a few aren't moving. Embers zip through the night air like snowflakes made of fire. One lands on my cheek, but I don't feel the burn through the other pain.

"Arsen!" Mila limps toward me with the flames at her back. There's blood on her chest, coming from a hole in her upper right shoulder. Her arm hangs loose. She's not alone. Kostya is holding her up, his face half-hidden by the shadows caused by the blaze that backlights them.

His severe expression holds firm when he sees the blood soaking my pants. "Can you run, Arsen Kirilovich?" he asks.

"Not fast, but yes." Grunting from the burst of pain that moving brings, I stumble forward. The car crackles, smoke pluming into the night sky. Men on both sides are stirring. In the distance, I catch the telltale shriek of fire engines. "Which way?"

Kostya leads us through the street, around the chaos. No one notices us. We pass multiple bodies in states of life and death. I recognize some of the faces. *If not for Kostya, Mila and I would be joining them.* I've been betrayed by many of the men I trusted.

Yet Kostya, someone who I always suspected hated my guts after how I humiliated him by breaking his fingers, wasn't one of them.

If he'd planned to, this was the perfect time for it. I'd be dead, and he'd be getting rewarded by Yevgeniy.

Instead, he's demonstrated his loyalty to me in the best possible way.

"You blew the car up, didn't you?" I pant.

"Yes," he replies. "I didn't see another option."

"If you hadn't, I'd be—"

"Don't waste your energy, my pakhan." Kostya stares straight ahead. I copy him, seeking solace in looking away from the blackened wreckage and corpses. Our mission was a failure.

But I'm going home to Galina.

19

ARSEN

Kostya's car is sticky from blood. Mila is slumped against the passenger door, her eyes open but staring blankly into the ethers. "How did the cops know?" she whispers.

I don't have an answer. My mind has been too tangled to puzzle it out yet.

We roll through the gates of my mansion. Every rocking motion of the car sends new waves of pain through my leg. I wiggle my toes to make sure my foot hasn't gone numb.

Kostya jumps out of the driver's seat. I see him through the window as he sprints to the front doors. I heard him on the phone as we sped here at top speed, so I'm not shocked when Ulyana, Dr. Helsan, and a few other staff and soldiers I left behind rush toward us.

I don't look at any of them.

I only have eyes for Galina.

She runs faster than the rest, her hair whipping behind her like a kite. Even at a distance, I spot the red rims of her swollen eyes. She's been crying. Her lips make the shape of a single word.

"Arsen!" she sobs, ripping the door open beside me. Carelessly, she leaps at me in the seat, hugging me as new tears dribble freely.

"I'm okay," I insist, though I fight back a grimace. Her weight on me is making the bullet in my leg pull, digging into the muscle. The sharp pain had become a distant ache, but moving forces the gash to shift along with me.

Ignoring the pain, I hug her back. I'll suffer ten times this if it means I get to bask in her existence. One bullet is nothing compared to being deprived of the woman I love.

"You're *not* okay!" she gasps, leaning away to stare at my blood-soaked leg. "What happened?"

"Got ambushed by the police. If it wasn't for Kostya ..."

"You could've died!" she yells.

"But I didn't." My smile is bittersweet. "I made it back to you. That's all that matters."

She stares, battling with her desire to hug me again or make space. The choice is taken from her when Ulyana grips her arm, guiding her away so the doctor can lean in.

Dr. Helsan looks down, scowling as he purges all semblance of proper bedside manner. "You look like shit."

Chuckling, I hiss between gritted teeth as he and Kostya assist me out of the car. Ulyana and Galina help Mila out behind me.

We've got quite the audience. Every member of my staff is crowded on the front steps or at the windows.

"Easy now," Dr. Helsan says. He and Kostya start to carry me, but I refuse to be seen in such a state of weakness in front of the people who rely on me. Though it causes explosions of gut-rattling pain, I make myself walk stiffly to my front door without their assistance.

Everyone clears a path for me. There's an air of unease shrouding my return. They only have to look at my bloody leg or Mila's wounds, or the fact Katya isn't with me, to know we failed.

The doctor is grumbling under his breath about me acting like a prideful fool. I appreciate that he keeps his voice low enough that only Kostya and I can hear him. When I reach a large, padded brown leather chair in the main room, I lower myself into it with a grimace. Colors dart behind my eyelids from the throbbing in my leg.

But Mila is in worse shape.

"It's cold," she gasps, breathing heavily. "Why is it so cold?"

Ulyana makes room for her on the love seat. "I'll get you a blanket."

"Take care of Mila first," I tell the doctor.

He gives me a long, uneasy stare. "You've got a bullet in your thigh, Mr. Isakov."

"And she's got one in her shoulder."

"I'm the doctor," he insists. "Let me decide how to triage this."

"Go over and help her. Now," I say crisply. "*Eto moi prikaz!* I'm fine."

My eyes dart to Galina, who is coming toward me, her face shiny and pale.

Now that I'm here with her, death can't touch me.

Dr. Helsan shoves a pile of gauze and bandages into my lap, then jerks away with another series of offended mutterings. This time he doesn't shield them from everyone else.

Galina glances at him as she passes before she runs the last steps, dropping to her knees beside me. "This needs to be cleaned right away. Give me the gauze."

Kostya bends close, offering her a small bottle. "Here. To stave off any infection."

Her brow furrows as she squints up at him. To my

memory, Galina has never liked Kostya. He has every reason to loathe her too, since she was the reason for his broken fingers. But for now, their enmity is forgotten. She gives him a quick smile and takes the antiseptic with a tiny nod. "Thank you."

My brigadier rubs the side of his neck awkwardly before shuffling away to help with Mila. Galina cranes closer to my wound, dabbing at it with some gauze she's soaked with the antiseptic.

"The bullet has to come out."

"Galina."

"I can't do it. I don't know how."

"Galina. Look at me."

She does, though I get the sense she wants to go back to tenderly fixing me up.

I search her face, trying to make sense of where her head is. "I'm sorry I couldn't bring your mother home."

Her brows make perfect little arches, her mouth going slack. "Arsen. I'm just relieved you're alive. I just ..." She frowns, hanging her head so her hair covers her face. "I can't lose you too."

"You won't," I reply grimly. *My men were murdered.* "But the fact that the police were there means we have bigger problems." I jump, startled, as she packs gauze into the bullet hole, patching it until the doctor can handle it. "Yevgeniy found the upper hand. It was a trap."

"Madison." Her face contorts with regret. She's reliving her part in allowing Madison to get close enough to nearly kill me. "He sent Madison knowing that she'd say the right things to get us to act."

"Yes," I agree. "He planned this from the start."

"He couldn't have known you'd spare her."

"He knew you would." I adjust in the chair, going rigid as

pain shoots through my body. Galina squeezes my knee with worry; I give her a reassuring smile.

"We have to tell Josh about this."

I nod in agreement. "Yes. For all we know, the cops are already on Yevgeniy's payroll."

"I'll get my phone." She half rises, eager to jump to the next step. Galina wants to put the fact that I nearly died on the cold, dark street tonight as far behind her as possible. But the mind doesn't work like that. Running from our mortality won't help us take big, full breaths the next time danger comes around. If anything, it will make her more skittish than ever.

Before she gets away, I stand up, wrapping my hands around the smooth skin of her forearm. "Wait."

She turns, ready to reprimand me for standing when I'm hurt. I keep pulling until she stumbles against me. When she lands in the chair, off balance, it jolts me with enough pain to leave me silent.

Luckily, I don't need my voice to kiss her.

Galina stiffens, but soon, she melts into my embrace. Her clothes will be stained by my blood, but neither of us cares. People are watching; we don't care about that either.

"When I was out there," I whisper against her lips, "standing in front of the police with their weapons drawn, I was terrified."

"Who wouldn't be scared of dying?" she asks.

I shake my head.

"It wasn't death I feared." Stroking each cheek in turn, I rub my mouth across hers with a shudder. "I was afraid that I'd never see you again."

Her arms circle my hair, my throat, my shoulders. She wants to touch every inch of me as if to confirm I'm not a ghost. I lift her arm, kissing the sensitive skin inside her wrist. She smiles until she notices the prayer beads she wears are stained red from my blood. "Oh no."

"It's fine." I study the beads before plucking them carefully off her wrist. "Let me wash them. I'll return them tonight."

"At this rate," Dr. Helsan grunts, appearing behind Galina, "you'll be in the hospital from sepsis before you're in your own bed. Let me get that damn bullet out."

Galina smiles with chagrin, moving away so he can get close with his bag of tools. Her eyes remain on me as she backs away, as if she's worried that I'll vanish if she loses her line of sight.

Fingering the prayer beads, I consider them for a long moment.

Yes. I know exactly how she feels.

20

GALINA

It's bright outside, and oddly sunny for winter. The glare through the car's windshield blinds me at certain angles. Arsen's sunglasses make it hard to catch the way his eyes skirt toward me before returning to the road.

"Where are we going?"

There's a wisp of a smirk on his lips. "You'll see."

"Why can't you just say?" I ask.

"Because the point of a surprise is to be surprised, *ptichka*."

I roll my eyes, but truthfully, I'm delighted. It's clear he's enjoying himself, so this "surprise" must be good. Plus, the last surprise like this involved me getting a bucket-list item of a ballet performance of a lifetime. *What could he be cooking up?*

Having something to take my mind off how stressful the last months have been is a welcome change. It's only been a few days since Arsen's foiled assault on the Winter Palace. From browsing the internet on my phone, I was able to find out that the news reported the incident as the cops intervening in some massive organized crime feud. Listening to clips of the chief of police smugly rambling to the camera about how proud he was of his team for suppressing such dangerous Mafia activity was infuriating.

No mention at all that the Winter Palace was running a secret brothel.

No mention at all of the fact that those dead cops were likely all on Yevgeniy's payroll.

I wanted to shake my phone and scream. *You're going after the wrong people!* I hope Audrey spoke with Josh, and if she did, that he was able to convince the police to pull back just enough.

I feel guilty for asking Audrey to get involved. It mirrors how she must feel toward me, to see a friend getting into the thick of the underground crime world.

But she can at least walk away.

I can't.

"See anything interesting?" Arsen suddenly pries.

Curious, I look out the window. I'd recognize these streets anywhere. I've walked them for my entire life. But they don't *look* familiar. It takes me a moment before I realize why.

"No way," I mutter.

Arsen is grinning like a madman. I spare a look at him before pressing my nose to the window as we pull up to the side of the building in mid-construction.

As soon as the car comes to a stop, I open the door to jump out, gasping in the cold air as I walk toward the sight of the impossible. The scent of sawdust and paint lingers in the crisp air. The windows that were last shattered into pieces are now perfect crystal rectangles.

He's rebuilding the studio!

"Do you like it?" Arsen asks behind me.

Without turning back, I gawk open-mouthed. I can't tear my eyes away. "When did all this start?"

He lets out a pleased laugh. "Almost immediately after it burned down." I get the idea he's trying to be modest. "Well? What do you think?"

Throwing my arms around his neck, I kick up my feet, hanging on with all my weight. He grins, supporting me by my middle, which, in spite of my rounded belly, is no trouble for him.

"This is incredible! I can't believe it! It isn't even painted, and it looks bigger and better than before!"

"Do you want a tour of the inside?"

"Yes!" Dizzied by excitement, I nod multiple times. Arsen beams as he helps me stand, then lets me lead him through the front doors. The lobby is bare of all the usual pamphlets and flyers that my mother would pin up like wallpaper. But I can see them in my head easily enough. My eyes turn toward the familiar spot where Mom would usually sit, and I feel a pang of sadness when I see nothing but empty space.

My feet carry me through the building like they know where they're going. Inside, Arsen has managed to preserve the familiar old layouts, but expanded the place at the same time. The cramped office packed with hoarder levels of boxes is gone. The room built in its place is big enough to fit two full desks.

"I have everything we could save from the fire in storage," Arsen says behind me. "I wish I could say there was a lot, but ..."

"No, this is perfect."

The fire destroyed a sordid part of the studio. The terrible things my parents were forced to endure in pursuit of their dreams.

It's better this way. Now, things can start afresh.

Well, as fresh as anything can be.

Turning on my heel, I flash him a smile. "We'll make enough new memories that this room will be just as packed as before."

His eyes soften. "Yes. I believe we will."

I must wander the new studio three times over. Each time I traverse the three different rooms, I'm inspired to do it over again. I'm trying to imprint this place into my body. To convince myself there must be some small flaw somewhere. But there isn't.

"It's perfect," I finally say. "It's everything the two of them dreamed it could be."

And just like that, sorrow that I'm not prepared for crashes through my veins.

Arsen stands in front of me. "Once I've finished with Yevgeniy and things are safe again, you'll be able to return here with your mother and teach your students. Old and new."

I begin to smile, but it's overtaken by a blanket of unease. The mere mention of Yevgeniy's name creates a foreboding sensation heavy enough to throttle my joy. I try and breathe in deeper, seeking more oxygen. But the pressing feeling on my chest doesn't go away.

No matter what happens ... No matter what changes ... It can't change who I am.

"Galina?" he asks gently.

I turn toward the wall of plaster with its pink insulation hanging out. Somehow, it looks organic—like the place is a living thing. Something that's regrowing and will continue to, even if Arsen hadn't paid people to shape it into what it currently is.

I bite back a wave of sadness.

"It's just ..." I start. "This studio was the dream of Stepan Rubinov. Keeping this place in his memory was supposed to keep *his* dream alive."

A tightness has built in my rib cage. I shift from side to side, but nothing dislodges the pressure. I say, "I wanted to keep his dream alive because I thought I was his daughter." I pause to swallow the lump in my throat. "Only, I'm not. I never was."

I close my eyes so that Arsen can't see the tears welling up in my eyes. Because if he sees them, he'll want to sweep me into his arms and promise me that Yevgeniy can't hurt me. But nothing he does can erase the fact that I'm that monster's daughter. That his blood flows in my veins.

"What right do I have to this place?" I finally ask, and my voice breaks.

Arsen edges closer to me, not shying away. Not even when I look at him with what must be enough regret to fill a funeral home. He keeps moving closer until he's touching my shoulders firmly, anchoring me like a ship tossed about on a stormy sea.

"You will always be Stepan's daughter."

"But—"

"I mean it." He cradles my face, the color of his eyes growing lighter in the brightness of the day. "Yevgeniy may have fathered you, but it was Stepan who raised you. He could have tossed you aside. He could have hated you. But instead, he loved you with everything he had. And you loved him. Stepan *is* your father. No one can take that away from you, *Galina Stepanovna*."

A shift of muscle and bone and grief moves through me. Biting back tears of thanks, I hug Arsen tight, seeking his presence for comfort. His words mean the world. But his actions—they've shown me time and time again that he truly loves and cares for me.

"Thank you," I whisper. "For everything. For helping me keep his memory alive."

"If all it took was spending money, nothing would die," he says softly. He kisses my forehead, stroking my hair.

I marvel at that before stepping away. My eyes track upward, just to take in one last look at the dance studio. My hope is the next time I see it, the mirrors will be in place, and students will be twirling across the floor.

"Huh," I say when I notice something.

Arsen pulls up short. "What is it?"

"The security cameras aren't here anymore." I point. "Are you going to reinstall them?"

He blinks a few times. Cocking his head, Arsen furrows his forehead like I gave him an impossible math problem without a solution. Suddenly, his expression changes and the lines all vanish at once.

"We have to go back home," he says. "I just thought of something."

21

ARSEN

THE FOOTAGE SCROLLS IN REVERSE. I STOP IT PERIODICALLY, staring so hard at the screen that my vision blurs. Galina peers over my shoulder while the man in front of me, tapping his computer keyboard, hunches ever closer to the screen.

Nothing ... Nothing ... Come on ...

"Arsen, what is all this?" she asks.

After leaving the in-progress dance studio, I didn't say much about what she sparked in me. I was busy formulating the plan while my excitement grew higher and higher. It's a miracle we didn't get stopped for speeding.

I rushed into the mansion, cornering the short, bearded man who often reminds me of a Schnauzer dog: Matvey, the tech guy who's in charge of all my networks. I texted him while driving back. Now, he's bent over his double monitors while I lean in close enough to smell his shampoo.

"Arsen," Galina prods again. "Talk to me."

"When you mentioned the security camera, I remembered the ones Mila and I shot outside the Winter Palace." I tap Matvey on the shoulder. "Slow down; that date looks right." He does as asked—I keep talking to Galina. "Matvey here has wormed his way into the data. We're looking for proof."

"Proof of what?" she asks tensely.

I turn to her. "Proof that it was a trap."

Matvey sips from a can of Coke as he scrolls through the long video clips. Each time we reach the end, he starts up a new timestamp. "Pakhan," he says, tapping away, "there are hours of footage to navigate."

"I know," I say simply.

He pauses, then continues to scroll. Watching closely, Galina and I examine the videos until my back begins to ache. My neck has a cramp.

Galina slaps my arm. "Stop! Look right there!"

I see what she did a split second afterward. On the screen, in only somewhat blurry pixelation, are a pair of people. One of them, a man, is dragging the other out of the front doors of the Winter Palace. I don't recognize Katya right away, but I'd know Yevgeniy anywhere. "Yes," I laugh sinisterly. "Here we fucking go."

Matvey freezes the frame as the woman looks at the camera. "That's Mom," Galina whispers.

"What's the timestamp?" I demand.

"Wednesday the twelfth," Matvey says.

My fist slams into my palm. "That's the day Madison arrived here."

Galina's expression morphs from excitement into slow distress. "Which means Mom wasn't at the Winter Palace at all when you went there with Mila."

Rubbing my jaw in deep thought, I walk around the room, stretching out my sore back. "Matvey, I need you to hack into the video feeds of every security camera in that area. I want to try and track Yevgeniy's footsteps to see where he took Katya."

The other man scratches at his beard and coughs. "Pakhan ... that's a tall order. Even with all of my team, it could take a day to complete."

My tone is hard as granite. "I want it done by tonight."

With a long, slow exhale, Matvey picks up his phone, swearing. "I'll call the boys."

THERE ARE five computers in the room. All of them are being manned. In every corner is another hacker crouched over a laptop. The constant tapping of keyboards would drive me mad if I wasn't already on the edge of my seat, waiting for news—any news.

Galina and I wander the space, staring at screens until our eyes water. Matvey was right; it's been hours, and we've barely put a dent in the amount of footage we have to review. Some of his team murmurs about ordering pizza, and I feel irritation dance across the back of my neck. I don't want to encourage any breaks, but if people burn out before the work is done, that's not helping anyone.

"I found something!" a young man shouts, motioning at us.

Galina and I rush over, squeezing close, our shoulders touching.

"Show me," I say eagerly.

"Well, there's Yevgeniy," he replies.

The sound of tapping stops. I peer at the screen. And sure enough, I recognize the unmistakable face of Yevgeniy Grachev. I feel my hands tighten into fists as the man continues to talk. The others are watching now too.

"From this network of cameras," he says as he brings up a map dotted with pins on his second screen, "I was able to triangulate his position. And then I found him along this road in this car ... *here*." He points as he moves through the video.

My heart is racing as I get snapshots of the car going through the city. It moves from different angles, depending on the camera. A front shot, a side, a rear view. Bit by bit, I'm getting closer to tracking this bastard down.

He's moving, if the cameras are right, to the southwest. They lose him for a bit, and my stomach sinks. But then the man taps a few more keys, and Yevgeniy's face is back on the screen. My pulse speeds up further when I recognize the park where I picked up Galina. Then there are back roads and houses in a cul-de-sac. There's no more footage once the bumper of the car goes half off screen.

That's the best angle the last camera can capture.

"That bastard hasn't moved ..." I breathe.

That arrogant fool.

"I know where to find him!" Galina blurts. "I know where that house is!"

I stand up and survey her with a burst of hope. "You're sure?"

"Yes!" Her eyes light up in wonder. "I thought for sure that he'd go elsewhere like he did before, but maybe he didn't want to upset—" she suddenly stops herself, darting a nervous look at me.

Unsure of what's gotten her so uneasy, I want to ask more, but now isn't the time. My body is thrumming with excitement that all of this is about to end right now. I'm ready to act.

"I'm going immediately."

"You're just going to show up at his house?" Her jaw drops.

"Much less noticeable than bringing a bunch of *boeviki* with me. Alone, I can sneak in, catch him off guard, and do what's necessary."

Plus, I need to save up my manpower after the last failed attack on the Winter Palace. But I don't want to admit that. I don't need to saddle her with more worries about things that she can't control.

Galina is chewing her bottom lip ragged. I take her hand into mine and speak to her in a gentle voice. "I'm going to save your mother and reunite your family. Just like I promised."

In spite of my encouraging words, she still looks anxious.

"You're dismissed," I say to Matvey. "I need a moment alone with my wife."

"Pakhan?"

I scowl viciously. He half falls out of the computer chair, waving for the others to copy him. They all flee the room, shutting the door, leaving us alone in the sweltering box full of glowing monitors and computer fans. The digital glow creates a halo around Galina's head when I tilt her back to stare into her eyes.

"You don't have any reason to be worried."

"Don't I?" she asks miserably. "Every time I let you out of my sight, you come back bleeding and hurt."

"I could say the same for you," I reply. Her narrowed eyes belay her annoyance. Pressing my cheek to her forehead, I breathe in and out. "Galina, I'll be fine. I promise."

She lowers her eyes away from me.

Cupping her chin, I make her look my way while speaking in a gentle voice. "Your future, our baby's future ..."

I lay my palm on her belly; she starts, but then leans into me. "That's all I see when I close my eyes. Soon, that's all I'll have to think about too."

"You mean it..." she whispers. It's not a question.

"With my entire being, I do." Through the years, I've learned many skills. Weapons ... schmoozing ... finances ... and lying. There's no better tool in the criminal underground than the ability to keep secrets with a straight face. Lying can be the difference between life and death. Because of this, I can convince anyone of what I want. I've lied convincingly to both friends and enemies. I've even lied successfully to a priest. More than once.

But when I tell Galina that her future is all I see ...

It's not a lie.

It never has been.

22

ARSEN

With my hand still on her stomach, I kiss her with the slightest of pressure—lighter than a leaf on a pond. Bit by bit, I sink in harder until our teeth touch. Her throat flexes, air leaving her nose in an intoxicating shudder. Kissing her never gets stale. I can taste her mouth for hours, perhaps days, the pair of us taking breaks only for water. I picture it now—the kind of lazing in bed a newly married couple does on their honeymoon.

We never had one.

Of course not ... It would have made no sense then. But now it pains me like an itch I can't quite sate. I *want* to spoil Galina. I want to see her stretched out on the sand with the blue water rolling behind her, her skin soaking up the sun. We'd fuck right then and there until both of us were red with sunburn, and then we'd retreat inside for round two.

"Arsen," she moans, opening her mouth wider, allowing me to sweep my tongue inside. My thumb on her jaw treads over the angle until I reach her ear. Curling a hand firmly into her hair, I tug her head back, eliciting a throaty gasp that drives me wild with need.

She's wearing a thick, form-fitting cable-knit dress the shade of a desert rose. It's lovely, but what's beneath is lovelier. With the fingers of my other hand, I hook her dress up until it shows her creamy hips. Her panties are dark from her juices.

"I need to taste you." Dropping to my knees, I inhale the sweet scent of her pussy. "You make me do insane things, *ptichka*."

"Do I?" she whimpers.

"Always." I tug her panties into her slit, enjoying how the fabric hugs her clit while showing off her lower lips. She moans loudly. "You put me so easily in a position no pakhan will ever willingly take. I'm on my knees for you."

Her hips rock from side to side as she anticipates what's next. "I don't want to make you do things you don't want."

"That's where you're wrong," I say darkly. Palming her ass, I yank her forward, my nose rubbing on her slit as she mewls. "I *want* to do this. I'm dying to do it. When you're close to me, all I want is to touch you, kiss you, feel you until I forget where I end and where you begin." I lightly spread my tongue over her panties. She jerks. I press her closer to my face until she can't move.

She's not going anywhere until I'm done eating her out.

I lap at her sweet slit until her juices and my saliva mix. Hooking the straps of her panties, I roll them down to her knees. Her pussy is the same pink as her dress. I'd planned to start out slow ... controlled. But something dark and primal possesses me now. Trapping her pussy against my lips, I lick along the length of her slit until my tongue swirls around her clit, and then I trace my path down, only to come back up again.

Galina's moans grow louder each time my tongue runs along the length of her pussy until moans become cries and cries become screams. But I'm deaf to it. Her pleasure soon becomes background noise as I lose myself in the rich taste and scent that is *her*.

I want to make her come, so I do.

I'm not a man who hesitates when he craves something. Call it a flaw.

Her thighs crush my ears, squeezing tightly as she loses control. Closing my lips around her, I feel her alluring taste flood my mouth. I refuse to let go as I drink down every drop of her nectar. She buckles, but I hold her up. Her clit is a hard nub that grazes my tongue. I suckle it a few times until her voice goes hoarse and those loud shrieks of pleasure die down into trembling whimpers. Her hands reach for my hair—now pulling me close, now pushing me away, now yanking me back as she struggles to decide what she wants.

Wiping my arm across my mouth, I gaze up at her with my blood singing in my ears. I'm tight all over, as if my skin is being stretched over the lust that's ballooning endlessly inside me. Moments like this bring me back to the present in a way nothing else but a fight for my life does. I prefer this to the latter, of course.

"Take it all off," I whisper thickly. "Now, *ptichka*."

Obediently she removes her dress, her hair coming undone in the process. The brown curls hang almost to her nipples. Her bra is thrown aside thoughtlessly. I stand, scooping her into my arms. We kiss again, and her tongue coaxes against mine as both of us share in the flavor of her pleasure.

When we break apart, I dive like a kingfisher, gathering her left nipple into my mouth. It's already firm, standing proud from her arousal. She whispers my name, among other lovely things as she guides her hands to the back of my head. In response, I suckle her nipple lightly, drawing yet another tender gasp from her pale throat.

I lift my head just enough to dampen my fingers. With my thumb and pointer, I roll them slickly over one breast while I lick the other. I can worship her breasts for hours. She makes it easy with how she moans lustfully. I take my time playing with her nipples—tugging, twisting, and grazing them lightly with my canines. When she starts to hiss like it's too much, I plant kisses as light as a butterfly landing on a flower on her trembling flesh as beads of sweat fall from my brow and burst into bloom on her flesh.

Slowly, I lower her onto the computer chair. It rolls back on its wheels. I grab the arms to bring it back to me. That's when I get an idea. "Spread your legs."

She bites her lip coyly, then tucks her knees up to her chest. Hooking my hands under her knees, I push them further until her ankles are over the top of the chair's arms. She's fully exposed to me—vulnerable and beautiful. Her wetness is soaking the cushions.

I'll have to buy Matvey a new chair.

A small price to pay.

The pressure of my cock in my pants is immense. Popping the top button gives some relief. I take my time inching my zipper down, glorying in the process. Galina watches raptly. This is a show she'd happily put on repeat.

My erection surges forward as I slip my boxers over my hips. Jerking the base of my cock lazily, I grin at her. "You can't get enough of this, can you?"

She shakes her head. "I might have a slight addiction."

"Good," I say huskily. I jerk my cock faster. "That makes two of us." I peel the bottom of my shirt upward, exposing my rows of abdominal muscles. She licks her lips, widening her thighs on the chair. The sight has my cock hardening more than I could ever get it to do by myself.

Dropping my shirt hem so it falls back over my navel, I lean down, balancing my hands on the arms of the chair. "Say you want me to fuck you."

"You know I want that."

"I also want you to *say it.*"

Her lashes flutter as she endures a rush of arousal. I felt the same thing. We're copying each other, turned on by the other being turned on. It's a dangerous cycle.

"I want you to fuck me, Arsen Isakov. I want you to stretch me open with your thick cock until I pass out from pleasure."

"What kind of monster would I be to tell you no?"

Holding the chair, I roll it—and her—toward me and bury myself in her inviting warmth with one swift motion.

"Oh!" she cries. Then she moans, the sound catching in her throat as I slide the chair away from me on its wheels. My cock is barely inside her perfect pussy. "Oh my God. Yes. Yes! Fuck me, Arsen!"

I sink into her with such force that I can feel my teeth rattle.

I've mapped this woman—my woman—out before. But we've changed, the two of us. In ways I don't understand ... and that I don't want to admit. She's shown me how strong she can be. Galina doesn't shy from taking what she wants or doing what's best. Priorities aren't her issue.

What are my priorities?

What do I want?

Revenge. Violence. Conquest.

Where do love and happily ever after fit into that?

Stop, don't think about it. I shake my head sharply, but the thoughts remain. I can't ignore them when Galina is right beneath me. She's in the air and in my blood. I want a world where she exists in it with me, because anything less would be desolate.

When she returned from being kidnapped by Yevgeniy, there was a barrier between us. Slowly, like ice near a flame, it's melted. But though it's changed, the wall still exists. Water can return to ice if the conditions are right.

I can't let that happen.

Driven by the idea of melting her down, I kiss her roughly, seeking to create more heat.

I'll keep the ice at bay however I can.

23

GALINA

I HOPE NONE OF THE WEBCAMS ON THE ARRAY OF COMPUTERS are recording.

If they are, they're getting quite the show.

The chair rolls over the floor, creating a pendulum that Arsen uses to fuck me mercilessly. My throat is raw from constant shouting. I'm not saying anything of substance, my mind devoted to focusing on the intense twinges of pleasure his cock delivers. His hips crank backward then forward, each thrust making my pussy tingle. The way he's moving forces my clit to grind on his skin.

I look up at the lavish sight above me. Arsen is perfection made human.

Like a perpetual motion machine, he fucks me in the chair.

"Oh God," I breathe, my toes cramping. "I'm close. Fuck, I'm going to come!"

"Then come." He shows his teeth as he grimaces, focusing through his own passion. His eyes are wicked embers burning into my soul, seeing how I'm about to climax on his cock. He knows me. He knows all of me.

There's no hiding from this man. "Come for me, Galina. Hold nothing back! It's only the second one."

His smugness tips me over the edge. Shrieking, I arch into the chair, pressing my ass upward to get all of him inside of me as I come. Against all odds, he pounds into me harder. The friction is mind-shattering; new pressure, so immense I think it will make me black out, speeds me toward another orgasm. Arsen abruptly retreats, pulling out of me before I reach the edge. I cry out from feeling so painfully empty.

"Easy," he chuckles, out of breath. "I said the second was fine. The third you don't get as freely, greedy girl."

Arsen bends over me, lifts his shirt, and tosses it aside. His tattoos seem to glow green in the lighting cast by the screens around us. I've seen them so many times, but they still fascinate me. The stars and the church and the spider. I'm inspired, wondering if someday I might get some body art of my own.

And if I do, it would be by choice. Nothing forced.

Surprising him with it would be thrilling. Does Arsen like tattoos on women? I bet if it was me, he'd love it.

My attention jumps lower to the stitches on his left thigh. The place the bullet pierced him.

Knowing he was in danger horrified me. But here, with the heady scent of sex swirling around us, the wound sparks something different. *He's powerful ... strong ... An army of cops couldn't take him down.* This man is like nothing I've ever known. And his desire for me—heart, body, and soul—makes me come apart at the seams. I don't want to be a damsel, but if I must be, having a hero like him at my beck and call has its benefits.

Propping one foot on the arm of the chair, he fists his cock inches from my face. His quad muscles are rows of delicious cords. The head of his dick is swollen and angry red. It wants to be buried inside my pussy. I want that too. I want it so damn bad.

But his serious stare says he expects something from me first.

Circling my fingers around the girth of his cock, I rub the slippery tip over my lips. He groans deliciously, my clit twitching. Shifting helplessly on the wet chair, I draw him past my lips and over my tongue, squeezing the base of his cock gently.

He moans my name on repeat. It's a beautiful song with a single lyric that I'll never get sick of. Using my hair for leverage, he encourages me to suck him down my throat. I go as far as I can before gagging. He pushes insistently, getting further the next time. My eyes burn with tears, but I'm anything but sad. My pussy is *soaked*, and the ache for release leaves me trembling. He denied my orgasm, and now my thighs are cramping as I grind the chair helplessly.

I reach up and cup his balls, feeling them flex under my fingers as I explore them. I run my nails over his calf muscles, over the steely bands of his hamstrings, amazed at the power coursing under his skin. My tongue traces the veins on his shaft, and I feel his balls swell and ripple in my hands. My other hand strangles his shaft, pumping without mercy as his musk overwhelms my nose. The salty taste of his precum fills my mouth, and I swallow him without second thought.

"Enough," he growls, yanking his cock from my lips. A string of saliva connects us. I suck in ragged breaths of air. Hoisting my knees up to my shoulders, he presses me into the chair. It starts to roll away from the impact—he puts his foot behind the wheels to stop the motion. Folding me in two, he rubs his cock over my pussy a few times, teasing my sensitive clit before sinking in until his balls slap against my ass.

The suddenness of being filled by his girth pushes me over the edge as if lightning has struck me through the wetness between my legs. My jaw pops open. There's no sound at first, and then the scream that leaves me is broken and ragged. Waves of pleasure course through my core until my heart thunders at my throat. My pussy milks his stiff cock, hugging him, begging for more.

He rips me off the chair, holding me by my hips, thrusting into me in the air. He holds me aloft while he pounds into me with sweat glistening on his chest.

"Kiss me," I pant.

Arsen does so dutifully.

The kiss deepens with increasing pressure, refusing to let up. He rocks to one side, losing his balance—something hits the floor; he's knocked an item off the desk. Inside me, his cock swells. He starts to break our kiss, but I grip his hair, letting him know he's not allowed. That this is for me.

That *he* is for me.

My tongue goes numb when he groans down my throat. Every tiny taste bud is awakened. Arsen tastes like almonds and vodka and sex and dreams. He nips my bottom lip, then my chin, creating enough suction just above my breasts to leave a mark—a reminder that I am his. The purple will match the bruises his palms are making on my ass. Maybe I'm becoming perverse, but the thought of his marks on me ... signaling I belong to him ... drives my heat higher.

"Your pussy just got tighter," he pants. "Why? Tell me."

"Your hands on my ass," I moan. "I like ... I like the way you grab me."

"And this?" His fingers shift until he traces one over my asshole. I tense, whimpering, my insides all tingling hot.

"Oh, *ptichka*, you love that too, don't you? Fuck me back. I'm so close." He thrusts more impatiently, his cock straining.

I do as my husband commands, gyrating my hips wildly just as his finger penetrates my ass. The sensation of being stuffed in both holes sends me soaring again. It's insanity. Pure, fucking insanity. No one should be capable of this.

With a husky groan, he pushes me against a wall, using it to brace himself. His hips pump faster, slamming, as he chases his orgasm while mine still trembles in lingering, tiny bursts. His shaft thickens, heating up and twitching. He kisses me right as the first thick, ropy burst of semen fills me up.

He comes hard, yet his knees don't buckle. He holds me steady as he finishes, guiding us both to the floor only when his cock stops pulsing. It takes some time. Or maybe it's me that's trembling, my inner walls trying to encourage him to wake up and go again.

I've become fucking insatiable around him. Has the pregnancy made me want him even more somehow? Is that even possible?

Or is this always what he's been capable of doing to me?

Rolling to one side, I wince—something hard is under my arm. Digging around, I hold up the wireless mouse. "Oh, this is what we knocked off the desk."

"Casualties happen," he laughs softly.

Grinning, I lob it lightly away from me. Arsen winds his arm around my middle, tugging me to his body. We're completely nude, grinding together, but the heat never fades between us. In fact, it starts growing again. If either of us pushes, we'll start all over. His cock is already hardening. It's good to know I'm not alone in being insatiable.

There is desire here ... There is lust and longing.

But there is also peace.

I sense it from how he breathes ... the pace of our hearts, the sparkles in our eyes.

When did this happen?

When did I fall back in love with this man?

The tinge of satisfaction from what we've done is leaving me slowly. I'm becoming aware of how hard the ground is under my hips. The heat of the computers thrumming around us is no longer steamy, but suffocating. In spite of reality returning to take hold, my heart remains in the clutch of love.

In *his* clutches.

Arsen smiles at me, his large arms folded behind his head like a pillow. He opens his mouth to say something. Laying my fingers over his lips, as if I'm pressing a stamp to an envelope, I keep him from speaking.

It's my turn.

"Don't talk. Not unless it's to answer this." He waits patiently, his eyes twin beacons that shine with curiosity. "Come back to me, Arsen."

I wait.

It's half a second, but it's enough to make my heart constrict.

Please promise, please promise, please.

If you can't do this much, then ...

"I will." Arsen holds my hand, keeping it against his mouth. He kisses my fingers twice. "I promise."

I want it to make me feel better. I hoped it would.

Arsen has promised me many things in our time together. He's kept his word more than enough to prove he's a man who takes what he says seriously.

But it doesn't matter. Not this time. Arsen is many things, but he isn't a god.

He doesn't have the power to control if he lives or dies.

24

GALINA

The sun is setting when he leaves. Our goodbye is brief, too brief, both of us lingering by the front door as he checks his guns under his jacket. He's counting bullets. Dutifully making sure the safety is on and that his weapons are where he wants them in easy reach. He flips them out multiple times, testing his speed before holstering again. Meticulous to his core.

Arsen is going to save my mother. Last time he tried, he came back injured.

This time he could come back in a casket.

"Wait," I say, grabbing his wrist on impulse. He's cracked the door, letting crisp air that warns of a winter storm creep inside the house. It feels like a bad omen. I grip him tighter. "Take Mila."

He shakes his head patiently, like he's already explained why he can't. "She's still recovering."

"At least take *some* backup—"

"I told you, the fewer people I bring, the better." His eyes grow big and gentle. "Galina, I know you're nervous. But this is the best way to do this."

The best way would be to clear the air before I lose my chance.

If you die before I tell you everything ... the guilt ... the shame ...

It will drag me straight to hell.

"Why do you look so afraid?" he asks me.

In a fierce, sudden motion, I hug him as hard as possible. Not just because I ache to feel him one more time, though I do, but because I can't let him see my face. He might read through me. As much as I want to tell him the truth about Ruslan, the fear isn't enough to shatter the chains around my heart.

"How can I not be scared? You're heading off alone into a situation where you could die!"

"I won't," he promises into my hair, kissing my temple. "I came back before. I will come back again. This time, with your mother at my side."

I want to believe him. It's the only reason I let him go, allowing him to slip away. Through the front window, I stare as his Escalade swerves off into the ink-washed grays of the horizon. It's darker than it should be at this time of twilight. There are no stars breaking through the dark, heavy clouds pregnant with snow. Stale air makes my skin go tight and my hair prickle and tremble. If it weren't for the yellow lamp lights perched around the house and throughout the large yard, I wouldn't be able to see a thing.

Chewing my thumbnail, I walk to one side of the foyer. The wall blocks me; I turn on my heel, going the other way. The large room has become too small. I'm suffocating as I move, feeling like an animal trapped in a cage.

Why did I let him leave? Because I need my mother safe. *But what if she's not there?* She has to be. *What if she isn't?*

No.

But if she is ... then so is Yevgeniy ...
And Ruslan ...

What will Arsen do when my secret is exposed without warning?

"You shouldn't fret so much," Ulyana says, startling me. "It's bad for the baby."

I jerk my eyes toward her. She's snuck up on me, standing by the bottom of the stairs. She's always been so good at surprising me. Maybe *she* should have become an assassin.

"Ulyana," I say, leaving it at that.

She considers me with her eyes half-lidded. "It doesn't get easier."

I do a double take. "What doesn't?"

"Waiting for him to come back alive."

Ripples of fetid fear work through my muscles. Clamping my hands over my stomach, I bend in two with a groan. I'm not in pain—not literal pain, at least. This sensation is a deep-rooted terror not unlike the floating sensation before a huge fall. The world below me is vanishing. The idea of Arsen not being in it makes me plummet.

"Galina! What's wrong?" Ulyana holds my shoulders, keeping me steady. I hadn't noticed I was collapsing until she kept me from hitting the floor.

Bracing my hand on a nearby table, I push myself up on unsteady ankles. "Ulyana ... I ... I need to tell you something, but I'm worried I can't."

Ulyana holds up her hand against my lips to stop me. Slowly, she gestures at my wrist and my eyes follow her hand until I'm looking at the prayer beads. Ulyana makes a gesture at me to look at them closely. And that's when I notice it.

There's a single bead that isn't polished wood, but lacquered plastic.

I look back at Ulyana, and she nods as she mouths the words, *He's listening.*

A bone-chilling cold seeps through my body as I stand there. I feel like I'm seeing myself from a distance. I'm a human being! You aren't supposed to track humans like this.

Has he always been listening? Or is this something new? And when did he do this?

And that's when I remember.

He took them from me after they were stained with his blood.

Hurriedly, I tear them off, and toss them across the room. But as soon as the beads leave my wrist, their missing familiar weight on my wrist nearly sends me rushing after them. It takes a remarkable amount of strength for me not to. I can't risk Arsen listening in on this.

I'll put them on later.

She stares hard into my eyes. "You've had a lot of moments like this with me lately."

She's right. I almost smile, but my anxiety is too heavy. "Can you keep a secret from Arsen?"

"I've kept a few already. What's one more?" she asks placidly.

I swallow loudly. "This one could destroy everything."

Her fingers squeeze mine before she backs away. The hardness in her eyes and mouth makes me certain she's about to turn, escaping up the stairs. She doesn't. Lingering in a long silence, Ulyana tips her chin upward until she's watching me in that perceptive way of hers.

"Yes. I can."

"Are you sure?" I pry. "It's been nearly impossible for me. He has a way of looking into my eyes like he can read my mind. I've been on the verge of spilling my guts more than once."

Ulyana's smile is as coy as a child hiding a frog behind her back. "Of all the people in his circle, I'm the only one Arsen can't intimidate."

I've seen the interactions she's referencing. Arsen doesn't seem cowed by Ulyana. He allows her more leeway, more sharpness and defiance, than anyone else he faces off with. "Why is that? Why are you the only one he can't terrify into submission?"

She dwells on my question. Lifting a hand, she brushes her sapphire earrings. "When he was young, he lost his parents. His mother first, then his father later. Nothing insidious, just a car accident and a heart attack. Not every death is a dramatic story." She chuckles humorlessly. "I was hired by his father as a nanny before he passed on. I'm not sure if Arsen ever truly saw me as a mother figure, but our dynamic was set from the start. I spoke, he listened. That hasn't changed as he's aged."

I nod slowly. "You stayed this whole time? Even when he was working for Yevgeniy?"

Her chest rises and falls gently. "Of course I stayed. He needed me more than ever then. His life was full of myriad, unpredictable dangers. I was the only constant in it. The power and money he gathered brought all kinds of people into his circle. He hired new girls to work for him here in this house." She gestures around. "One of them was a fresh face with grand schemes. Lyubova. She wanted to be in charge. When I wouldn't step aside, she tried to set me up. She hid jewelry that belonged to Kristina in my belongings."

I gasp in horror. "That's terrible."

"She fought to convince Arsen I'd stolen from him. But he knew better. As a way of apologizing for the situation since he hired her, he gifted the jewelry to me." Her fingers return to her earrings. "I've never owned a thing of worth. I don't spend on myself. Money is useless to me. That was the difference between Lyubova and me. She had aspirations to rise. Instead ... she was put underground."

My hands clasp over my mouth. "Arsen killed her?"

Ulyana grimaces at me in disbelief. "Of course not. After she failed to take over my position here, she went seeking glory with less ethical types. Yevgeniy let her in, but he knew she was a thief. Word travels. The poor girl was killed to send a message to other thieves in his circle."

Absorbing her story, I wonder again if I can trust her with my secret. She has an immense sense of loyalty to Arsen. He's taken her side on her word alone, and she on his. Would she really protect my secret from him?

But then again, she's never shown me any indication that she would ever betray me to Arsen.

And at this point, I'm out of choices. If I don't tell someone about this, my heart might simply explode. "Where can we go where no one else can overhear us?"

THE SNOW FALLS around us in gentle specks. Lifting my hand, I try to catch a few. Most of the flakes dodge my hand. The ones that land bring a brief, sharp chill before melting into nothingness.

"I think it'll stick this time," Ulyana notes.

Brushing the flakes from my hair, I drag my foot through the grass, making little tracks of green before the white covers them again. Maybe I can make a snowman later. I can't remember the last time I did that.

Ruslan could be making one right now. Mom might even be helping him do it.

Ulyana's breath is visible in the cold. "Galina ... what is this terrible secret you're keeping from Arsen?"

I flinch. This is it; time to come clean. I hope I'm doing the right thing. "Yevgeniy has another child. A boy of ten." I close my eyes and take a deep breath. "His name is Ruslan, and he's my brother."

"Another child?" she whispers, aghast.

I nod my head over and over. "My mother didn't even know he was alive. We found out when Yevgeniy took us. He's been carting Ruslan back and forth between different locations, so the poor kid has never known peace. He's always convinced that some dark monster is hunting him from the shadows."

"A monster?" she echoes, shoulders dropping. "You mean Arsen."

"Yes. He thinks Arsen will kill him—and maybe he might! Even if it's by accident while he hunts down Yevgeniy!" Words rattle endlessly off my tongue. Now that I've begun, I can't stop. "But even if he doesn't, even if Arsen kills Yevgeniy without hurting anyone else in the process ... Nothing will stop Ruslan from becoming someone desperate for vengeance. Someone like Arsen."

The snow around us muffles every sound, absorbing my voice like I'm in a white box. I breathe in, gasping, the chill hurting my lungs.

"And if that happens—if Ruslan comes after Arsen—then the cycle will never end." I swipe my palms protectively over my belly, clearing snowflakes away. "And in time, my child will pay for the sins of his or her father."

Ulyana stands in front of me with her lips pinched together. Her blue eyes and sapphire earrings are the only dots of colors in the changing swirls of snow. She shifts forward, grabbing me in her arms. I don't know why she's hugging me until the wind blows and I feel the tears freezing on my cheeks.

"Shh, shh," Ulyana shushes me. "It's all right, *devushka*. It's okay."

I'm being hollowed out the way a pumpkin is before being carved. Every rasp drags raw across my throat. My bones feel empty, as if the marrow has melted. A strong wind could lift me away into the clouds, and it's a marvel that I'm somehow capable of feeling any gravity to hold me down.

"You've carried this secret for too long," she soothes me. Her palm rubs up and down my back, patting occasionally. "Nobody should handle a burden as heavy as this alone. You're not responsible for what Yevgeniy does ... or Ruslan ... or even Arsen. They will make their own choices. Their sins, past or future, are their own."

"But their sins will leave lasting waves in their wake."

"Yes, and that is a consequence of the life that they lead." Ulyana cradles my face and smiles sadly. "But if Ruslan is truly your brother ... if he has as much of Katya in him as you do, then hope is not lost for him. Not yet. Not by a long shot. There are things that you can control in this world, *devushka*, and then there are things that will forever slip out of your fingers like flowing water. Worry not about the things that you cannot control."

My nose burns, and I don't know if it's from crying or from the cold. Scrubbing my eyes, I lean against her, sinking into the support she's kind enough to give. I expected her to chide me for hiding this. Ulyana has always been a mix of kind but firm. She has no room for games. For her to say those reassuring words with such confidence is an immense relief.

Shivering, I lean back a bit.

"Thank you," I choke out. "I've just been so afraid. Arsen wants Yevgeniy dead; I can't talk him out of that. But Ruslan ..." A bitter, broken laugh leaves my dry lips to hang in the eerie silence. "How do I tell Arsen about *him*?"

"That's something you'll figure out in time. It doesn't have to be now. And it's too late to tell him anyway."

Over her shoulder, I look back at the way we came. Fresh snow blankets everything, erasing evidence of footprints, the house, and the world outside of this moment. Faced with nothing but my inner thoughts and Ulyana's calm but firm warning, I'm overcome by supreme clarity.

I *will* have to tell Arsen everything.

That part is my responsibility. What happens after that rests on his shoulders. Not mine.

25

ARSEN

It's colder than a grave as the snow falls, muffling the world.

This weather is fitting. Dark deeds are best done in conditions like this.

I park my car about half a mile from Yevgeniy's house. It should be ignored on the street the way any other car would be, especially after nightfall. Plus, the drifts of snow will disguise it. Every car is going to look the same under the thick white blankets soon enough.

Taking a page from Mila's book, I've dressed in pure black, from my jacket to my boots. Moving like her is more of a challenge. Even if my leg injury wasn't sending a dull ache that forced me not to put my full weight on it, I could never slip as silently as she does through the shadows.

I don't need to be an assassin. I just need to bust inside without getting caught first.

Yevgeniy might have multiple guards around his property. I've considered what I'll do if I'm up against too many targets—which is a strong possibility. *If I act quickly and covertly, I might manage to kill three or four before the rest react.*

I doubt Yevgeniy has packed his house with more than six guards. But it's not an impossibility.

A dog barks in the distance.

My hackles stand on end as I crouch lower in the bushes. *Relax, it's too far away. It's focused on something other than you.* My nerves are on alert. Between creeping in the dark and the fact I'm about to face off with my enemy, my heart hammers at my rib cage like a piston in overdrive.

To calm myself, I reach to feel the gun hidden under my jacket. I've brought two, not planning to reload either. The backup pistol is the louder of the two. It's best to save it for after the guards have raised the alarm, when my cover is blown and the danger of being heard will matter less.

Ahead of me, the two-story house rises into view. Tree branches sway over the textured shingles already painted white by the thick layer of snow. I can't tell if the paint is yellow or gray. There's a single lamp illuminated above the porch, the windows shining light from the inside out. Snowflakes sparkle in the beams before vanishing in the night. Through a bottom-level one, I see a television is playing some movie.

I don't see any cars in the driveway, but it's clear there are people inside. My breaths tumble forth in the chilly evening and disappear into wisps on the wind. I watch them, counting backward from ten to force myself to relax.

No movement in the windows. Nothing out front. I peer up to the roof, my ears straining until I swear I can hear them echo. *No guards outside at all.*

Are you really this arrogant, Yevgeniy?

My calves are cramping from the effort of moving silently across the front yard. I'm trying not to slip on the slick patches of ice. *This can't be another trap. He couldn't possibly have known I was coming.* My fingers brush the trigger. *There are no guards posted because he's not afraid. This is his ego on full display, that's all.*

Comforted by this thought, I brace myself on the porch.

If he doesn't expect an attack, then that's his problem.

Thrusting forward with my good leg, I kick the front door open. It bangs off the inner wall, bouncing back toward me, but I'm already through. Turning to my right, where the TV is on, I aim my gun as I check for any attackers.

Nothing.

A quick turn, and I scan the other half of the main room. The lights are on, showing a small foyer laid out with white furniture and a shelf for stacking shoes. Above it is a coat rack built into the wall. There are two jackets and an umbrella draped on the pegs, the only sign that anyone lives here.

With my blood pounding in my veins, I rush toward the hallway. I'm halfway toward the base of the stairs when I spot movement in my periphery. I turn and point my weapon at the source of the motion.

And find a small boy with a mop of dark curls staring at me in fear.

He's dressed in plain jeans and a red shirt. It hangs to his knees on his thin frame. "Who are you?" he asks me. "What are you doing in my house?"

Freezing in surprise, I glance from side to side nervously. *Why is there a kid here?* Did I get the wrong house? Is that even possible? *No, Galina confirmed the address. This is the place!*

He blinks like an owl, saying, "I'm Ruslan. Are you a friend of Papa's?"

I lower my gun slowly. The boy stares at it like he's only just noticed it, his eyes widening further. My mind warns me of something. It's an odd feeling ... but he seems ...

familiar. The tilt of his eyes, or the angle of his mouth. I can't place it, but it feels like I've met him before.

"Of your papa's?" I ask harshly.

He recoils, picking up on my tone. "Yevgeniy Grachev. Do you know him? Are you also here to see Mom?"

Mom?

It's a struggle to keep my face emotionless as the realization hits me like a train. A hurricane of emotions consumes everything inside of me. I feel chunks of my heart break free, swirling in my stomach until all my innards are a mess in my chest.

It has to be a lie.
It has to be!

He rocks from side to side anxiously, his hands folding together in his long shirt. "Papa said someone was coming here to help find my sister. She's missing. Are you here to help me?"

I'm not ready to tell him anything until I know what the hell is going on. Working to keep my voice calm and failing badly, I crouch to his eye level. A terrible sensation settles in my blood. It presses on me heavily until my neck bends and my shoulders hunch. I lift my gun, balancing it on one knee. Ruslan can't tear his attention away from it. I should holster it, but his comfort pales next to my need to protect myself.

"*Where* is your papa now?" I insist.

"Why?"

"Just tell me!" I bellow.

Ruslan starts to shake. His bottom lip pokes out, pink and wet. He puts his hand on the banister of the stairs, his foot inching to the bottom step. I notice he's not wearing socks. The house is warm enough that he doesn't need them. Whoever left him here, they haven't been gone for long.

"You're not here to help me find her," he gasps. "You're not Papa's friend. You're the bad man he warned me about!" He clears four stairs before I react.

"Wait! Ruslan!" I shout, barreling after him. I shove my gun under my jacket, using both hands to grip the banister so I can climb the stairs faster. Ruslan is just ahead. I'm panting heavily, everything throbbing, pushing my body past its limits. If I wasn't injured, I could catch him for sure.

But maybe I still can. Maybe I can do it.

When he throws himself into a room at the top of the stairs, slamming the door, my heart sinks.

My weight pushes on the door. Jiggling the knob, finding it locked, I punch at the wood with my fists. "Ruslan! Open up!" *Shit, what do I do?* There's too much going on for me to think beyond my need to catch this kid. He has answers.

I'm here to find Katya! Where is she? Where did Yevgeniy go? And if this kid is his son, why leave him behind unguarded like this?

Through my hard pounding, I make out the sharp vocals of Ruslan's shouts. He's talking to someone. Is he not alone in there?

"Help!" Ruslan screams. "Someone broke in! I need help, please!"

He's on the phone! "Ruslan!" I roar, hitting until my fist goes numb. "Hang up the phone!"

I hear him rattling off his address. "He has a gun! Please hurry!"

Backing up, I prepare to try and kick the door down. Sirens wail in the distance, rising in pitch as they scream toward the house. Fuck! Fuck! Fuck!

Heaving air into my lungs in a panic, I spin and sprint down the stairs. My wounded leg is killing me, but I push past the agony. I dart through the front door, still hanging open from my break in, and slip into the darkness surrounding the house. My boots go out from under me on the slick porch. With a grunt, I come down hard on my hip.

In the distance, the dog is barking again, joining its noise to the cacophony heading my way.

Multiple police cars zoom down the street, their lights dancing over the hedges. I roll off the porch, cutting forward on my hands and knees through the snow. I duck lower, inching through the sharp leaves and twigs showering my hair with fragments of ice.

It feels like I've gone miles before I enter another backyard of a house further away. Sweat drenches me down my shoulder blades. But the cool night air gives no relief.

I scoot across the dirt on my belly. It's wet from snow that turns to slush under my body. The icy chill penetrates my jacket. My limbs feel heavy, as if they're waterlogged. Mud seems to glue me in place. Gruff voices with flashlights prowl not far from me.

I hold still, waiting, not daring to breathe.

Someone shouts, and they move back toward the house. I wait until the beams of light are gone, then I wait even longer. Seconds feel like hours, but slowly, I urge myself to move.

I don't relax until I make it to my parked car. Even then, the tightness in my limbs doesn't smooth out. I keep expecting a police blockade. I can visualize the red and blue lights in my rearview mirror. But nothing happens.

Yet I remain on high alert the entire drive back to the mansion.

Narrowly escaping the cops leaves my heart thundering, but it's only temporary.

The entire drive, all I can think about is what Ruslan

mentioned. My hands cling to the steering wheel. His voice. Those eyes.

I know why he seems familiar now.

Someone was coming to help find my sister!

His sister.

Galina.

26

GALINA

Headlights glow like a pair of wolf eyes as they pass through the gate. They skirt along the ground, predicting the path of the car seconds before its tires roll along, where it halts in front of the house. It's been over an hour since Arsen left to save my mother, and I haven't breathed easily since.

What happened? Did he rescue my mom? Did he kill Yevgeniy?

Did he kill Ruslan?

I need to know the answer to that final question as much as I need oxygen to keep my lungs working. I need to know just how far Arsen is willing to go.

I can't build a future with a child murderer. I just can't.

The driver's door opens in a wide swing. Arsen steps out, his movements stiff and slow. With his hand gripping the car roof, he cranes his neck until he's looking at my bedroom window. My light is on, so he can see my silhouette. His posture doesn't ease up. If anything, he looks more distressed. From this distance, there's no mistaking the hollowness in his eyes.

Mom isn't with him.

He failed in one task, but what about the rest? I'm relieved at the fact he's alive, but I can't calm down. Wrapping my robe tightly around my pale blue nightgown, I sweep my bare feet over the floor, halfway running down the hall. I slow at the top of the stairs, but only because my need to know isn't as strong as my deep-seated fear of falling.

The front door cracks open as I reach the last step. He enters and I cry out.

"What happened? Are you all right? Did you see my mother?"

His eyes lock on me. The grim shape of his mouth contorts until it spreads apart, allowing his gritty, hardened voice to stab into my ears. "Who is Ruslan?"

Shit.

I recoil. "What?"

"The boy." He stamps his foot down in my direction. I match it with another step back. The stairwell bumps into my hip. "The one I just met who insisted his father was Yevgeniy and that *you* are his sister."

I'm torn between relief and panic. *Ruslan's still alive. Arsen didn't kill him!*

"You spoke to him ..."

"What the hell is going on, Galina? Tell me right now."

I take a moment and actually *look* at him. The front of his jacket is filthy, the material made heavier by slush and mud. The lines across his forehead are drawn into deep furrows. It's as if he aged ten years in the brief time he was away.

Letting out a shaky breath, I nod. "Ruslan is my brother."

His lips curl back. "And Katya ..."

"Is his mother."

He cringes, running his hand over his mouth like he can wipe the anger off his face. It doesn't work. "How long have you known?"

It's time to come clean. Put it out there. Now that I've started, I can't hold the words back. "Since the day I was kidnapped."

"Weeks, then!" he roars, advancing my way. "How could you keep this from me? You had to know how dangerous this was!"

Approaching him warily, I lay my hands on his shoulders. He tolerates it, eyeing me so intensely that I expect him to rip away at any moment. "I wanted to tell you. I swear I did, but I was scared about what happened to Pyotr."

He wrenches away from me with a frown. "You thought I'd kill a child?"

My hands drift limply to my waist. "Can you blame me?" I ask meekly.

"Don't try to twist this around and make me the bad guy here. *You* hid Yevgeniy's son from me all this time!" He taps his hand against his chest rapidly, emphasizing every word. "Don't you understand what this means? Ruslan allows Yevgeniy to maintain control of the Grachev Bratva. If he succeeds in killing me, then the pathway of succession becomes clear."

I lift my chin defiantly. "And if you kill Yevgeniy, Ruslan puts your claim at risk."

Two can play this game.

"I'm glad we're on the same page."

"No." Whirling on him, I glare into his eyes. "We're not!"

He holds my stare steadily, even though it feels like the fire in me is lashing out. How can he resist being burned?

"I hate this bullshit about legitimacy and succession. By that logic, I have a claim to the Grachev Bratva too."

"A powerful position."

"That's all you care about? Power?"

"It's not about what I care about, Galina. It's about the fact that you *hid* Ruslan's existence from me! What the hell were you thinking?" he demands.

The flames curling in my guts spark higher and hotter with each beat of my heart.

"I was thinking about the innocence of a ten-year-old boy being stripped away because a bunch of grown men care more about how they'll rule the world."

His frown twinges like a bowstring, and I know I've finally reached him.

"The instant you kill Yevgeniy, Ruslan's heart will harden and his focus will become hunting you down to get his revenge. In exchange for achieving *your* vengeance, all you'll do is create *his* desire for revenge. This cycle will never end."

"You talk like you expect me to spare Yevgeniy after all he's done."

"I don't! That's the problem!" I point at him accusingly. "I want him dead as much as you. And that means Ruslan's hate for you will be inevitable. What does that mean for our future? If he kills you, won't our child end up with the same desire for vengeance? Where does it end?"

The air crackles between us. Arsen glances down. I notice I've placed my hands over my stomach. My protectiveness is second nature at this point.

"How did you expect to protect Ruslan from this?" he asks in a softer tone than before. "Hiding him from me could only work for so long. Knowing won't stop me from killing his father."

"I don't know. I don't know!" My feet cut over the floor, taking me toward the window.

The snow from earlier is a solid blanket untouched by any living thing. I watch it for a moment until I see my own reflection in the window's glass. The torment on it looks the same as Arsen's when he exited his car.

"I wasn't sure what to do," I whisper. "I thought I'd figure something out; maybe you'd never discover Ruslan, and then maybe there'd be a way for him to move on after you killed Yevgeniy … But clearly that was too stupid to hope for. I've seen them together, Arsen. He loves his father." I toss him a mournful frown. "And because of that, he will hunt you to the ends of the earth."

Arsen comes up behind me. I turn away, but I can still see his reflection. "You were trying to protect him without a plan."

"Because he's just a child, Arsen. A little boy."

Setting his hands gently on my shoulders, he sighs into my hair. "You're not wrong to fear the unending cycle of violence. I think about this all the time. I've always wondered, if Yevgeniy ever killed me, would my men try to avenge me? Would Mila?" His grip tightens. "Would you?"

Yes, I think instantly. *I would.*

"And his men," he goes on. "Surely some would risk their lives for his memory. Even before knowing about Ruslan, I knew these risks." Turning me with enough force that I can't resist, he makes me face him. His fingertips drag over my forehead, tucking a piece of hair behind my ear. "I *know* there has to be a way to break that cycle. And I will find it."

I don't need to see my reflection to know how miserable my smile is. "But will you find it in time? Whether he kills you, which I couldn't bear, or you kill him, this violence has no end in sight." Pushing out of his grip, I pace back toward the stairs. When I reach them, I drop down heavily on the second to last step.

"When did it all get so complicated? All I ever wanted was to be Galina Stepanovna. That girl had struggles, but they were honest, clean problems. But instead, I'm forced to be Galina Yevgeniyevna and live in this world stained with blood." I turn to look at him. "Forced to make choices I never wanted to make."

Arsen remains by the window. He doesn't blink; he simply considers me. Shrugging out of his soaked and filthy jacket, he lets it fall to the floor. His boots go next. When he's in just his dry undershirt and pants, he comes my way, standing over me with his hand on the banister above my head. "Whatever choices we need to make, I will make them with you."

"No, Arsen." Tilting my head, I shoot a bittersweet grin up at him. "You've made those choices *for* me. The moment you dragged me away from Tsar's Lounge, you forced me into this corrupted world without a choice."

All the stress of waiting to know what Arsen would do tonight collapses onto me at once. I fold in half, burdened by the load as it becomes sludge that drips through my muscles and bones.

"If I knew all of this was going to happen, I would have gladly allowed Mom to sign your contract and walked away."

"Galina ..."

Lurching to my feet, I climb the steps until I'm halfway up. He's below me, one of the rare times I can look down on the powerful man whose word can grant life or death.

"Like it or not, I'm bound to you now. I'm nothing more than your *ptichka*—a little bird locked up in a cage you built for me, too stupid to realize you've already broken my wings."

27

ARSEN

ULYANA HAS THE ABILITY TO TRAVERSE MY HOME WITH THE lightness of a mouse on tiptoe. I only hear her footsteps because I'm listening for them. My office door is open, her shadow slipping through the gap moments before she does.

"Arsen Kirilovich," she says to announce herself. Her posture is stiff, shoulders pulled back and jaw clenched.

She knows why I've called for her.

"Explain yourself."

"About what?"

She won't make this easy for me. Fine. Sitting forward in my leather chair, I place my elbows on my spread knees, my chin perched on my laced fingers. "You knew Galina's little secret. Didn't you?"

Gently, with just her heel, she shuts the door. "Her brother? I did."

There it is. The confirmation I expected but hoped to be wrong about. "It seems everyone is happily keeping secrets from me," I grumble, reclining back in my chair.

Her eyebrows lower to match her tone. "Can you blame them?"

My fingers, which had started to relax on the chair's arms, dig in fiercely enough to make the leather creak. "What?"

"You've created an environment where people feel like they *need* to hide things from you. They walk on eggshells, Arsen, terrified they'll upset you. Terrified of what you might do to them."

"It's good for them to fear me," I growl, pushing myself to my feet. "If they don't tremble in my presence, then they don't respect me. They don't see me as powerful. Only a ruthless pakhan can protect those who have entrusted him with their lives."

"Out there, yes." She turns her head like it will help her hear me better. "But not in here. In here, your people should trust you. They should be eager to come to you with their fears and worries and doubts." She pauses for emphasis. "Yet they don't."

A tingle ricochets up my spine as I read between the lines. "Galina doesn't fear me."

"Then why did she keep Ruslan from you?" she asks coolly.

"Because she doesn't understand!" Throwing my arms up, I begin to pace in front of Ulyana. My office, a place normally spacious and comforting, has become a cage. *Like the one Galina accuses me of trapping her in.* I feel hot all over and wipe at my neck, expecting to find sweat, but my skin is dry. "She's confused, and so set on saving every life around her that she doesn't realize she's putting more of them in danger."

"If she wasn't afraid, she would have spoken to you right after you picked her up in the park."

The muscles in my back cramp up. I say nothing, just stare at her as she continues to speak. "She held her secret close, and only when she thought you might die or murder the boy, did she share it with *me*. Do you know why she did that?"

One answer jumps to my mind. "Guilt."

"Maybe a measure of it, yes," she admits, "but ultimately, she wanted me to soothe her fears about *you*. She wanted me to assure her that you would not harm the boy. That you would not stoop that low."

"And what did you say?" I pry eagerly.

"I'd told her before that you had a code. You didn't hurt the boy tonight, did you?"

"No." I finally stop pacing, standing before her with my arms hanging at my sides. I curl my fingers, unsure what to do with myself. *But I could have. I could have killed him.*

"Then that's all that matters," she says sharply, cutting through my inner turmoil. "You *didn't* harm him."

The tendon in my neck pulls tight. "But I might have to. He threatens everything, Ulyana. I promised Galina I would end this war and the endless violence along with it. How am I going to do that if Yevgeniy's son is allowed to live!?"

"I cannot help you with that answer," she whispers. "I can only tell you to go speak with Galina, and talk to her calmly. Work with her to create a real plan instead of empty promises that you know you cannot uphold."

Pushing out my jaw, I trace the lines of it as I fidget. Realizing what I'm doing, I force my hands behind my back, squeezing my fingers together. "Do you really think a solution exists?"

A gentleness passes through her eyes. I've seen it before, this tenderness she offers me with such rarity. The years haven't softened her, but the tragedies we've shared have created moments like this where her emotions rise to the surface.

"I do," she says. "And I believe you'll find it with Galina."

I'm no longer the wild boy who needs a firm hand. I've grown into a man tortured by his many sins, a man who forgets he has a heart.

I'm grateful Ulyana is here to remind me.

Sometime later, I leave my office to seek out Galina. The conversation with Ulyana still plays through my head on a loop. The last thing I want is to inspire fear in my household. Respect, yes, but fear was never my goal.

But the secrets ... Whatever the reason for them, they must stop.

Scraping my nails over my neck, I walk quietly through my hallway. The staff has gone off to bed; I'm the only source of noise. Each of my steps echoes in my ears. As loud as it seems to me in the night, my inner voice is louder.

Why does it bother me so much that Galina lied to me? It goes beyond a basic sense of insult. Nobody wants to be lied to, least of all me, but what she did has remained lodged in my belly like a burr the size of a plum.

I pull up short before I turn the corner near her bedroom.

Of course. It's because of who I am ... because of what *I am.*

A lie between ordinary people can be waved away. A thing of simplicity solved with an apology or a cheap gift. But here in this underworld I've spent my entire life in, lies are dangerous.

To deceive someone here among the corrupt and cruel is to declare war.

If one of my men lied to me, I'd assume their plan was a betrayal.

By hiding Ruslan, Galina triggered my survival instinct. I know how quickly a silver tongue becomes a sharp blade. Being stabbed in the back is old news to a man like me. But never once have I looked at Galina and seen her through that lens. She's hurt me, yes, but it was always to protect herself or our baby.

But now ...

This single lie of hers—even if she lied by omission—wasn't meant to protect anyone but my enemies.

I arrive at her door, yet I don't open it. I don't try to knock. Lingering on the threshold, I war with the awakened part of my brain that's telling me the woman I love on the other side of this door might actually be capable of betraying me.

And with it comes a much more terrifying question.

One that I don't want to answer:

What will I do if she does?

28

GALINA

When I was a kid, brushing my hair always brought me comfort. Doing it before bed was a ritual that started before I knew what the word even meant. I'd sit on my mattress, my knees tucked beneath, music piping gently in the background, and throw my hair over my shoulder. Mom used to do it for me. She was patient—which was rare—as she ran the boar-bristled brush over my thick locks until they glowed like honey in the sun.

I wish she was here to do it for me now.

Mom, I hope you're okay.

Stroking the brush down to the tips of my hair, I try to let it relax me, but it's not working. It was a long shot, all things considered. Too much terrible stuff has happened in such a short time. If I could just brush it away, it would be a miracle. People like me never get those.

A soft tap comes at my door, and a moment later, I hear Arsen's voice on the other side.

"Galina?"

Sitting up, I drop my feet to the floor. *What could he want at this hour?* I have an idea, but I don't know if I'm ready for a deep conversation right now. There have been so many of those lately, and every one of them has left me drained.

"Come in."

The door opens, and I catch the way his eyes settle on me, widening a fraction as he takes in my bare legs under my nightgown and my thick hair coiling over my naked shoulder. He hides his reaction behind a quick blink.

"I was looking for you," he says.

"Well, I'm easy to find. Not like I have a lot of places to go these days." I gesture around my bedroom with a bitter smile.

Arsen's nose crinkles up like I've thrown dirty water in his face. But if you ask me, that verbal jab was well deserved.

"I wanted to apologize."

I sit up at that. *Well, that was unexpected.* I was ready for another tongue-thrashing about how I lied to him and put the Bratva in danger. But certainly not this.

His contrition is refreshing, but I'm not ready to let my guard down.

Not yet.

"You had every right to keep Ruslan a secret from me." He moves further into the room as he talks. "I shouldn't blame you for it. And it was wrong of me to snap at you. I'm sorry, Galina."

Folding my hands over the hairbrush, I rub my thumb over the smooth handle absently. "It *was* wrong how you snapped at me. But ..." I take a deep breath. "I admit that keeping Ruslan's existence a secret was wrong too. And I owe *you* an apology for that." I smile hopefully. "Are we even?"

Letting his shoulders loosen, he visibly relaxes. "Yes, very even." Two more steps of his powerful legs and he's standing over me. His eyes are half-lidded as he observes me in his thoughtful way. "I can't imagine how hard it was for you to keep that secret to yourself."

A resigned laugh that sounds more like a scoff tumbles from my lips. Clutching my stomach, I toss my hairbrush aside, where it lands soundlessly on the mattress by the headboard. "Well, if I gave myself an ulcer, I'm going to blame you."

Arsen doesn't answer my lame attempt at a joke. Instead, he stares hard at the bed, seeming to be debating with himself. He eventually sits, his legs spread, hands clasped in between. "I love you, Galina. You know that, right?"

"Of course I do." Warm ripples swim through me like small fish on their way to a bigger pond. "But Arsen ... I didn't hide Ruslan because I didn't think you loved me. It had nothing to do with that. I just wanted to protect a scared child." Tugging at my bottom lip with my teeth, I scoot closer to him. Our hips are almost touching, but not quite. "How was he?"

"Scared. He thought I was going to hurt him."

"Did you?"

He snaps his head around, eyeing me with uncertainty. "No." His eyebrows unfurl and his frown becomes a soft shape. "But I did kick down the front door. That would scare anybody. Galina ... he kept mentioning you and Katya, like he'd known you his whole life."

"Blame Yevgeniy," I grumble. "That asshole has deprived Ruslan of any form of stability since the day he was born." Recalling how Ruslan brightened up when talking about my mother and me returning, my voice grows tender. "He seemed to think that us showing up meant his life would change for the better, that we'd all become one big happy family. Yevgeniy probably told him that's how it would be."

That monster was using us for his own purposes before we even knew.

"You said before that Katya didn't know he was alive."

"That's right."

"How can that be?"

I fidget, pressing my hands between my knees to halt the movements. "It's ... hard to say out loud."

"Please try," he urges me. "It's important."

I glance upward, finding that he's looking at me. I want there to be some softness, some understanding, in his silvery blue eyes, but they're flat and cold.

He's not thinking about the deeper implications of what I just told him. My heart shudders as I realize that in this moment, I'm not talking to the man who loves me, but to the head of the Grachev Bratva.

Shutting my eyes, I fight back a harrowing wave of sadness. I've wanted to avoid this conversation since the day I learned the truth. It hits too close to my own past. But there's no avoiding it now. Arsen's eyes drill into mine, and though he doesn't say anything, I know I'm expected to answer.

The fresh wound breaks open as I begin to talk, my tone hoarse and gritty.

"Yevgeniy raped her," my voice cracks as the words are dragged out from the depths of my soul, "the same way he did when she got pregnant with me. But unlike how he left me with my parents—"

I catch myself with every intent to correct it to *my mother and Stepan* but decide not to. *That monster has taken everything from me already. He can't take the man who raised me. He can't take my dad.*

Arsen's hand reaches out to cover mine, pouring his warmth into me as he gives my hand a soft squeeze. The gentleness of his gesture gives me enough strength to continue.

"When Ruslan was born," I tell him, "Yevgeniy stole him away. Mom convinced herself he was dead because it was easier that way than to picture her child somewhere out in the world, existing without her."

Arsen sits in silence for a long minute, never letting go of my hand. "How did she react when she met him?"

"Shocked," I say. "But she knew right away that he was her son." Opening my eyes, I look at him, imploring him to understand. "She *loves* him. It doesn't matter to her that Yevgeniy is his father any more than it matters that he's also mine. Ruslan is *her* baby."

"And he loves her?"

"God, yes." I chuckle lightly. "He's obsessed, like he's making up for lost time."

Arsen's mouth moves as he mulls over everything I've told him. "Obsessed ... That's an odd way to describe it."

"No, it isn't. He's a boy who has only heard stories of his mom, and one day she's finally in front of him. It's natural." I hesitate, reliving the moment Ruslan lashed out when I beat him at a video game. There *was* something different about him—a hint of the darkness that lives in his heart, similar to Yevgeniy's.

"Galina?"

I shake myself quickly. "It's nothing. Trust me, he's just an innocent kid. He's not like his father."

"He's more like Katya, then?"

"They have the same exact smile." That brings a twinge of melancholy. "It's a little surreal."

"I saw some similarity to you too." Bracing his free hand on the bed, Arsen leans back until he's gazing at the ceiling.

"You only spent a few days with him, but you're convinced he doesn't take after his father?"

"Why do you need to know?" I ask warily.

He drops an eye on me. His tone is bleak. "Because it's important."

I don't like how that sounds. Not at all. Placing my palm heavily on his knee, I squeeze just enough that his muscles tighten and his attention drops to what I'm doing.

"Why, Arsen? What does it matter if Ruslan is more like my mom or Yevgeniy?"

"It's my job to understand our enemies so I can keep us safe. Keep *you* safe, Galina."

"Enemies…" I pull my hands away from him with a scowl. "Arsen, how many times do I have to tell you that he's just a child?"

I scoot further across the mattress to create distance. His eyes narrow as he notices, and his voice is clipped.

"Every boy grows up into a man one day. Maybe he's a killer in the making. Maybe Yevgeniy will come to the surface sooner rather than later. When you were around him, did he act entitled? Did he give off any indication that he expects to get his way, and if—"

"Stop it!" Leaping off the bed, I clutch my nightgown tightly around my body. "I'm not someone you can interrogate at your leisure!"

He hunches in my direction with a scowl. "I'm not interrogating you."

"That's exactly what you're doing."

His eyes widen, the black dots of his pupils shrinking until they're pinpoints. Winding his fingers in the blanket, he remains seated, but I know he wants to stand and follow me. He feels the space between us the same way I do. It's cold, empty, troubling. But this discussion is worse.

"Galina ... I'm just trying to protect you."

"Please, go." I point at the door, not moving my eyes from his. I won't be challenged. I'm not going to fold to his demands anymore. "I need some space to think."

The lines by his nose deepen, and his jaw draws downward. "You don't understand that you're walking straight down a shooting range. There are guns all around, and people are fingering the triggers. Don't be so willfully oblivious."

"You keep saying you're trying to protect me." My nails burrow into the flesh of my upper arms when they cross over my chest. "From whom? Myself?"

"If I must," he says plainly.

I can't hug myself any harder than I already am. Desperate for comfort, I face the window. There's nothing outside, but I look anyway. "I see how it is."

"Galina," he growls.

"Are you going to sit there and force me to answer your questions until you're satisfied? I thought I was your wife, not your prisoner."

The bed shifts loudly, the headboard colliding with the wall from how fast he jumps to his feet behind me. "You *are* my wife!"

Curling in on myself, I fight the urge to become a tiny ball. I make sure my chin and head are held as high as possible. "You'd never guess it from how you're treating me. Yevgeniy kept me confined too, or did you forget that?"

Arsen says nothing. In the window, I catch a glimpse of his reflection. The massive man is shrinking ... his head lowering, his hands dangling; he's doing exactly what I'm trying not to. The shock of my words is sinking in.

"I'm sorry. I'll leave you alone." He vanishes from my view when he moves toward the door. It's a challenge not to turn and watch. I hate what he's saying, and I also hate not seeing him. Even when I'm upset, his existence is a comfort.

The doorknob clicks as he grips it. "But I meant what I said. I want to keep you safe at all costs."

When I don't respond, he closes the door behind him.

On impulse, I hurry over and lock the door. It's like I'm protecting myself from doing something stupid. *If he comes back, you'll forgive him. You can't do that, not until you think this through.* He said a lot of things, and all of them have to be dissected.

He loves me. I know that.

He wants to protect me ... I believe that too.

He thinks I'm a danger to myself. He thinks Ruslan is an enemy.

I'm not ready to believe those.

Dropping heavily onto my bed, I flop backward, throwing an arm across my face. If I was tired before, I feel boneless now. My elbow clicks on something hard—the hairbrush. Picking it up, I study the bristles. My finger traces over the soft tips, recalling again the childhood memory of my mother brushing my hair. *Is she alone or with Ruslan?*

Or is she with Yevgeniy?

Shuddering, I lay the hairbrush across my belly. The side of my wrist rubs my skin where the nightgown has shifted aside. There's nothing to listen to but my own heartbeat. Nothing to distract me when a firm, solid kick jabs against the inside of my belly—softly at first, like a flutter of gas. But then it comes again.

And again. More insistent than before.

Oh my God!

Gasping, I sit upright, the hairbrush toppling carelessly to the floor. My head throbs from how fiercely I'm concentrating with both hands clasping my belly.

The baby kicked for the first time.

Wet droplets appear on my nightshirt. Sniffling, I clear the tears away. *My baby ... my sweet baby, you're so strong. I can't believe it. This is the most amazing thing ever.* For years, I wished for this. Having a child meant everything to me. When I came so close in the past, only to be robbed of the joy by sheer chance, I convinced myself that being a mother wasn't meant to be.

Simon created a tower of guilt I didn't expect to ever leave behind. He made me think losing our baby was my fault. That I didn't deserve another.

Yet here I am ... getting what I wished for.

I thought people like me didn't get miracles. But clearly, I was wrong.

All because of Arsen.

That frustrating man has brought me untold levels of chaos. The turmoil, the stress, all of it has been overwhelming. In spite of that though, he's also brought me the one thing I always wanted.

That has to count for something.

Right?

29

ARSEN

STEPPING OUT OF MY SHOES, I THROW THEM CARELESSLY TO the far end of my bedroom. My overshirt goes next. I'm in nothing but my pants and a sleeveless undershirt when someone knocks on my door.

Drawing my hand over my face, I stare at my reflection in the closet door mirror. I'm haggard, to put it politely. *If it's Ulyana knocking, she's going to take one look at the messy state of my room and conclude I'm becoming a slob.* Finding the energy to be tidy isn't easy. This listlessness goes beyond mere exhaustion.

I'm bone-tired after my talk with Galina. Every conversation we have feels like a battle. I'm not winning any of them, though I don't think I'd feel better if I did.

The knock comes again—more insistent. Sighing, I grab the brass knob and yank. "What do you—" I stop talking. Galina stands in front of me in a thin lavender silk robe she's thrown hastily around her shoulders. "Galina, what's wrong?" After telling me she needed time, I expected she'd avoid me until tomorrow.

"It's the baby."

My heart stops. *Something is wrong.* I experience a split second of terror before she finishes speaking.

"It kicked," she says, motioning for my hand. "Here. Feel."

Allowing her to hold my wrist, I gingerly press my palm to her rounded belly. All the blood in my body is rushing to my brain. I can taste the metallic excitement on my tongue. Time slows down to a crawl. I've never been so impatient for anything in my life.

I'm about to ask if she's sure the baby kicked when it happens.

The movement is tiny, as subtle as a butterfly landing on a flower petal. But to me, it feels like someone just knocked over a mountain.

"I felt it," I gasp.

Galina's eyes light up, mirroring my own thrill. There's color high on her cheekbones, her lips slightly parted like she's out of breath. This woman is the embodiment of *glowing*. She reminds me of another time years ago when I felt joy just like this.

Another lifetime ago, Kristina pressed my hand to her stomach. She welled up with tears when I twitched in surprise from feeling our baby kick. That was when I learned the meaning of serenity.

An overwhelming warmth wells up from my center. It presses at the back of my eyeballs. "I've only felt happiness like this once before," I whisper, gently trailing my fingers over her belly. "When I felt my baby kick inside Kristina."

Her smile falters. "Oh, Arsen."

There's enough love in her eyes that I could fill an ocean with it. It soaks into me, and while it brings me a different sort of joy, it also makes me kick myself internally. *She loves me so much, yet I keep hurting her each time I mention Kristina's name*. Dropping my hand, I hang my head in regret. "I never meant to make you feel like a prisoner. You're my wife, and if anyone is a prisoner here, it's me. I'd do anything for you. I mean that."

She watches me quietly before reaching back, closing my door, and shutting us inside. Whatever she wants to say, she wants privacy. "You keep calling me your wife, but I can't forget that our marriage was just a tool."

"At the start, yes," I agree. "But it's become real—more real than anything I've ever given myself over to."

Lighter than the kick of our baby, she rests her hand on my cheek. I lean into her touch—not on purpose, on instinct. The craving I have for her is incredible. It's more compelling than hunger or thirst. It's the kind of feeling that could drive a man insane.

We're watching each other, waiting for one of us to make the next move. My desire to kiss her has my mouth tingling. I have to clench my jaw, my hands, every muscle to resist grabbing her face and capturing her lips.

I won't make the first move.

Not here.

Not after she told me she needed space.

Galina runs her nails slowly down my jaw. "Do you love me?"

"With every fiber of my being," I reply. I don't have to think about it.

Her eyes search mine hastily. "Are we really on the same side?"

That word ... *sides*. It carries a weight with it that settles on the back of my neck. In my life, there have always been two sides—those with me, and those against. Galina belongs with the former. So why, then, are my hackles standing on end?

Our fighting has been boiling down to our principles not aligning. That kind of thing ... can it even be fixed? Can we reconcile our differences when they're so stark? I want to throw back my head and scream *yes,* but my gut won't let me.

My world is dangerous, and I've learned to thrive in it. Part of that is because I've been able to see the plots against me before they can become reality. I haven't always succeeded, unfortunately. And tragedies have given me a sharper sense of preservation.

That's why ... as I mull over her question... my paranoia is going haywire.

Galina won't betray me. I think it, but the fear doesn't vanish. If I try to say it out loud, there'll be no conviction. As much as I want to believe she'll always choose what's best for me, I can't.

And I hate that.

I hate that I can't bring myself to trust her even as my heart screams at me to do exactly that.

My hands start to rise, but I force them back to my hips. *I want to touch her ... God ... this is torture!* "We want the same things."

"Do we?" she muses sadly.

"Your future ... mine ... our baby's. It's all I think about. I swear, Galina. I swear it."

Tell me you think about it too. Please. Please.

Her lips glide apart. I expect more words. She's been arguing with me fiercely for so long; surely she's not done yet. Galina digs her fingers into my hair, leveraging herself forward, dragging me toward her until we crash together in a kiss.

The resistance inside me splits apart. Grabbing her by her shoulders I thrust us together, seeking more of her mouth ... more of everything. The thin robe does nothing to stop the firm tips of her breasts from rubbing against my chest. My undershirt is just as useless. The clothing feels the same as skin.

Her long hair tangles in my fingers, soft from how she brushed it earlier. Winding it in my fist, I force her head back to deepen our kiss. She opens her mouth for me, and I slide my tongue along her teeth, tasting the mint lingering from her toothpaste.

Galina parts her lips and moans a soft sound. I think it's my name. Backing away to give her enough room to know for sure, I stare eagerly into her eyes. "What was that?" I ask.

Her cheeks are flushed, her eyes blurry, like she's having trouble focusing. "Kiss me again," she says.

In this moment I would do anything she asked. Anything.

Pushing her robe down her arms, I kiss her left shoulder, enjoying how smooth her skin is. She presses the back of my head, trying to force me to go lower, but I'm not ready yet. As eager as I am to see and taste every inch of her body, I want to draw this out. I need to make this last as long as possible.

All around us in the air, mixing with the passion, is the heavy shadow of fear. I can't explain exactly what I'm scared of, and I don't dare take the time to figure it out. Discovering the shape and the name of the monster hanging over my head would mean admitting it was real. Right now, all I want to do is to be in the moment with my wife.

She is my wife, I think seriously. We are partners. We're working together, and all I want to imagine is the future for us. *For us*, I press my hands to her belly. A primal sensation wakes up inside of me. Galina is more than my wife; she's my *everything*.

She's carrying my baby. I have to make sure that she's safe, that she's cared for. Normally, to me, that means guns at the ready, a wall of spikes, an army at my beck and call.

Right now, caring for her means making her body feel amazing.

"I love you," I whisper, before pulling her robe completely off her. She groans and hugs me closer. When my mouth gets near to her throat, I kiss her there, moving downward until I lick her collarbone.

Her fingers scoop at my shirt, trying to get it over my head. She's struggling because I won't move back far enough to create the space. I refuse to allow even an inch of air appear between us.

"Arsen, take this off," she demands.

Ignoring her, I reach behind her shoulder blades to unclasp her nightgown. The straps dangle, the rounded tops of her breasts teasing me. The material dangles on her hardened nipples until I tug it, letting it hug her rib cage.

I kiss her right breast, then the left, and then the right again. She gasps at each touch. "Please," she begs. "Don't make me wait anymore."

She sounds desperate and I relate. I lean back just enough to pull my shirt over my head, throwing it across the room. Galina glances at my muscular body, but then she arches her head back, unable to see straight because I've cupped her perfect breasts in my hands. This is her weakness.

It's also mine.

"You're so fucking beautiful." Grabbing her nipples between my thumb and forefinger, I twist them from side to side. She shivers visibly as I play with her. Lowering my head, suckling at her right nipple while toying with the other, I feel her flex up into me. I know exactly what she likes, and not just because she's so vocal, but because I pay attention.

I want to drive her crazy; it's my favorite thing.

Lifting her up, I carry her to my bed and set her on it. She takes the opportunity to wrap her legs around my hips as I stand between her knees. "I love you," she swears to me. With how she's gazing up from down below, it sounds like a prayer. She aches for me to believe what she says. I do ... I do believe she loves me ... but that almost makes it worse.

You have to trust that she'll stay on your side. Stay—as if she hasn't already swayed. *There's no proof of that!* I argue with myself, except there's plenty.

She hid Ruslan from me. She defended Madison, a stranger, because she's a good liar.

No, you fool. Because she's a good person. She's not a monster like you.

I kiss Galina to quell the chorus of warnings in my skull. She's surprised by how I ravish her—hands on her neck, her chest, her spine, and hips. I can't get enough of her. I'm trying to chase away my inner fears with the passion surging in my blood. It's almost enough.

"Say you love me," she whimpers.

"I love you." *I do I do I do.*

"And you always will?"

I kiss her mouth, sending the word *Yes* down her throat. She swallows it and doesn't ask again.

The bed shifts when I press her flat onto it. She doesn't loosen her thighs from my waist. I don't need her to. Peeling her black satin panties over her plump ass until they're stuck between us, I give them a rough yank, tearing the fabric. Her eyes flash with a spike of arousal.

Her nightgown is pooled on her waist, the upper band rolled over her sternum and below her exposed breasts. It's sexier than if she was naked. Settling my weight on her, I lick her left nipple in a slow, patient circle until she's panting. Without looking, I navigate my jeans, popping the button, lowering the zipper. My cock is engorged to the point of pain. I shove my boxers to the side, setting it free, sighing in relief. My shaft is thick and hot in my own fist.

Galina rakes her nails down my shoulders, then downward, searching for my cock. I hiss through my teeth as she circles it in her grip. She squeezes lightly, testing me, watching my face. I don't tell her to stop ... I give her no instructions as she starts jerking me off.

Pleasure radiates through me in jagged stripes. I resist the urge to close my eyes and toss my head back, because then I'd have to stop looking at her. It's an incredible challenge to stay locked on her flushed face when I'm going blind with desire. Muscles in my core bunch, then tremble as waves of heat take me prisoner. My cock is stiff as fire-hardened steel. I break our stare for a split second, too tempted to look down and see her hand pumping my cock. The visual makes me dizzy.

"Fuck," I pant.

"I'm ready," she moans, guiding my cock head toward her. She's right—her inner thighs are glistening with her juices. I barely thrust forward, and the slickness lets me push inside her warm walls. Her back makes a perfect arc, heels jamming into my spine as she tries to fill herself with more of me. "Oh my God!"

Holding my breath, I endure the slow way she eases me inside of her. I could thrust forward, stuffing myself in to the root, but I refuse. This way lets me experience every millimeter of her soft, tight, flexing pussy. I'm doing all I can to keep this moment from ending.

Every stroke of my cock draws a cry of pleasure from her.

The pressure of her milking me creates a knot of tension that continues to build. It's endless, the force pulsing in me, threatening to tear me apart. I don't know if I'm going to cum or explode into a thousand pieces.

"I'm close," she whimpers, driving her hips into me with more insistence. I *know* she's going to cum; it's inevitable. If she didn't want to, it would still happen. She's that far gone. I see it in her heavy-lidded eyes ... her slack mouth.

Seeing how delirious she is turns me on more. A scorching wave washes over me, making me grit my jaw. My skin is sensitive enough that I feel every single droplet of sweat gliding over my back. One drips from my chin, landing on her chest. I bend down to lick it off, then swing sideways, suckling her nipple.

Her pussy clenches suddenly, and I know she's going to cum even before she screams.

30

GALINA

Everyone in the house must have heard me scream. I don't know how they wouldn't—the sound is echoing off the walls, the ceiling, and bouncing back into my own ears. I could grab a pillow and muffle my cries, but I don't. Deep down I want everyone to know what we're doing. At least then there'll be proof beyond us. The world will know that, for a little while, we were happy together.

Stop that ... Don't think like this is all you'll get from him. It isn't.

It might be.

The Bratva war isn't over. Arsen has nearly died more than once. I know there's tension between us. His need to achieve revenge and my pitiful hope that we can have a future without more bloodshed are in conflict.

"You're perfect," he whispers, shutting me off from my internal demons. I can't ignore his eyes darkened by lust. He holds me close, bending me to him until our ribs are interlocked. A tornado couldn't rip us apart.

Little ripples vibrate through my insides. My climax has

left me dazed, but it hasn't sated me. "Get on the bed," I tell him.

His eyes twinkle with curiosity. Wiping his sweat-soaked hair from his forehead, he shifts until his knee is on the mattress. Without pulling out, he hefts me upward, then flips over, so that in the end I'm straddling him. I gasp as my own weight sinks me deeper onto his cock. "Like that?" he chuckles.

"Yeah, just like that." Spreading my hands on his chest, I explore his solid shelf of muscle. I vaguely remember how shy this position once made me. Now, gazing down over my swollen nipples past my rounded belly into Arsen's transfixed eyes ... I'm flush with pride.

I can tell he adores me. He's said it many times, but it's how he looks at me that tells me the truth of it.

Lifting myself upward on my knees exposes half of his shaft to the air. He groans deep in his throat, then gasps when I drive myself back down. Colors flash in my vision. I repeat the motion, loving the colors. It's like chasing fireflies.

Arsen takes hold of my hips, controlling my speed. I move like a piston, each impact harder, faster, until our breathing melts into one shared rasp. "I'm coming!" he roars, pushing himself off the bed with such force the springs creak. The headboard bangs the wall like someone is trying to break in.

His cock flexes wildly. I sit my ass down hard, wanting him to be as rooted as possible when he comes. Grinding my clit helplessly on his pelvis, I resist the urge to shut my eyes or stare at the ceiling as another of my own orgasms surges forth. I want to watch *him* when he comes. Seeing his face wrapped in the rapture of our moment is better than a glorious dream.

His lips peel back over his perfect teeth. He grunts, voice

husky and thick. Burying his fingers into the plump skin of my thighs, he flexes his ass. Spurt after spurt of hot cum fills me up. I bite my bottom lip, then switch out my knuckle, digging in. I need a small burst of pain to help me focus or else I risk falling away into nothing. I'm carving his expression into my mind like a sculptor's knife cutting into marble.

Arsen reaches for me, pulling me until I flatten on top of him. He strokes his hand over my sweat-soaked spine, feeling the long groove until it ends above the dimples of my rear. We hold each other until our breathing returns to normal. And when that happens, we hesitate, clinging on an extra minute or five.

Finally, he eases me off him with a low hiss. His cock pops free, wet from what we've done. I'm slick as well. We're both a mess and could use a shower, but instead, we curl up together on top of his blanket. Washing up would erase what we've done here. Neither of us wants that, though we don't say it out loud.

A warm weight settles on my stomach. Arsen has put his hand there. He traces back and forth over my skin, his head on the pillows, his eyes shut. He looks like he's concentrating. *He's feeling for our baby.* Putting my hand over his, I sigh softly. Arsen opens his eyes to watch me, his lips in neither a frown nor a smile. Every time I think I understand him, I'm reminded that he's an enigma.

"What is it?" I whisper.

His hand flattens slightly. "Can I sleep like this? Will it bother you?"

The way my heart trembles verges on agony. "Please stay like that." There—he finally smiles. That's how he remains for the next hour. I know because I'm awake the moment he drifts into sleep. My mind is too restless to allow me any relief.

When the baby kicks again, he's snoring. It should be funny. Why isn't it?

You don't know what's going to happen, I remind myself sadly. Linking my fingers with Arsen's, I study his face, looking for a sign he'll stir. He's oblivious to my touch. *Arsen ... you said we're partners ... but did you mean it?* I wish I knew for sure. If I did, the lead balls in my chest would melt away.

I haven't breathed easy in months.

He wishes to end this war; that's all I should be focusing on. The violence will end. It has to.

Not knowing how it's possible to create peace for us without more killing, I shut my eyes and snuggle against the father of my child. *He's not a liar ... We're on the same side. We are.*

I fall asleep without believing it.

31

GALINA

I'VE DEVELOPED A SLIGHT OBSESSION WITH BABY FORUMS. My mother is out of reach, Ulyana has never had kids, Olesya is too naive, and Audrey ... I *should* be able to talk to Audrey, but ever since her husband was roped in to help with the cops, our relationship has been awkward. Each chat has a heavy air around it, like discussing the baby is inappropriate.

I've wondered more than once if she's not actually excited about the pregnancy. Her opinion of Arsen isn't a glowing one, after all.

Sitting downstairs in a patch of sun on the long green couch by the massive windows, I scroll through my phone idly. There are all kinds of messages on the forum. People post about how far along they are—they love comparing their babies to the size of vegetables and fruit—and talk about if they're having a boy or a girl; they even complain about their in-laws. That's a very popular topic to vent about.

I'd take that problem over the ones I have, I muse cynically.

I'm reading the live chat, and half the posters are going on about planning baby showers—something I feel a pang of regret about, because I doubt I'll get one. Suddenly someone drops a link to a video. I sit up, squinting while reading the barrage of all-caps messages.

What is everyone freaking out about? Curious, I click over. The link pops up, revealing a video screen with a big red *live* button. There's a blonde woman speaking into a microphone as she stands in front of a large building downtown.

"Breaking news. We're coming to you live from downtown in front of one of the most popular nightclubs in the area, the Winter Palace."

I'm assaulted by a jolt of adrenaline. *The Winter Palace? What's going on?* The woman keeps speaking. I push my nose to my phone, listening with rising unease.

"This was the place to see and be seen, but just last night, police performed a raid on it. What they found will shock you. A dozen or so bodies, all women, were found in the bottom level of the high-end club."

Clapping my hand over my mouth, I muffle a loud groan. *No! Bodies!? What the hell happened!*

The reporter fades away as the camera zooms in on the building. There are police cars parked all around, blocking much of the view. "The location, which police revealed doubled as a brothel, was shut down immediately. According to our insider, the brutally murdered women had various messages carved right onto their bodies. This is what the police commissioner has to say."

Oh my God. Did she say carved ... onto their ... I tighten my hand over my mouth in case I vomit.

A portly man with a white mustache and the tell-tale black uniform of a police officer appears on my screen. His voice is a reverberating, gritty baritone. "Late last night, we raided the Winter Palace on a tip. The scene was horrific. In all my years, I've never seen anything like it. We're still investigating, but our current evidence points the blame in one direction—the Grachev Bratva."

"Arsen!" I shout, not lifting my eyes from the screen. "Arsen, come here quick!"

Footsteps pound through the home. It takes him all of ten seconds before he cuts around the corner, searching for me with wide, worried eyes. "What is it? What's wrong?"

"Just look!" I yell, thrusting my phone in his direction. He hurries over, crouching over the back of the couch to watch my screen. His eyes widen, darting from side to side before narrowing to tight slits.

His hands clutch the couch as he lets out a hot breath. "Yevgeniy is behind this."

"What?" I ask, lowering my phone. "Why would he ruin his own club?"

"To pin it on me. That bastard would raze his business to the ground if it meant he could take me down in the process." Straightening up, he walks back and forth with his hand running over his hair. He stares into the air, his brain on overdrive. "He's going to send the cops straight to me."

A mild ringing rises in my ears. I hear the reporter's words again. *Dead women. Bodies carved with messages. A secret brothel. The Grachev Bratva.*

"He's going to get away without a single scratch," I whisper. My eyes dart to Arsen.

My phone buzzes, startling me so much that I almost drop it. Navigating away from the news video, I answer the call when I recognize the caller is Audrey. "Hello?"

"Galina! Did you see—"

"Yeah, the Winter Palace? It's awful. Those poor girls."

"I know, but spare a little pity for yourselves because the

cops are on your tail. Josh says he's having a hard time keeping them from driving straight over to Arsen's place right now."

My jaw drops wide. I look at Arsen, and he catches my fear, coming closer to where I am. I reach out and he grabs my hand, squeezing it. It brings some comfort. "Are you serious?" I ask Audrey.

"He's doing his best," she says, "but the police are being extra aggressive. I mean, can you blame them?"

Recalling the quick visuals of the scene on the news, I shudder. "Arsen, Audrey says the cops are itching to arrest you. Josh is barely holding them back."

"I appreciate his efforts, but it's pointless. Nothing he says or does will stop them after this. We need to leave." He pats my wrist, and when he starts to pull away, I cling on. He gets the hint and remains where he is.

"And go where?" I ask anxiously.

"There are several Bratva safe houses located far enough from here that we can hide out at, stay under the radar."

I gesture around the empty room to indicate the entire household. "What about everyone else?"

He manages a small, indulgent smile. "They'll be fine. This isn't the first police raid this place has handled."

"But—"

"Galina, trust me. Ulyana knows how to handle it." His eyes darken like he's been shrouded in shadows. "The cops are going to regret wasting their time."

"Did you hear that, Audrey?" I ask. "We're going to go to a safe house."

She's silent for a while, and for a moment, I'm afraid that the call has disconnected. But after a moment, she says, "Okay. Be safe, Galina."

"We will." I end the call and push myself off the couch.

Arsen comes around, holding me like I might collapse any second. I smile to show I'm all right. "Well ... I guess we should pack."

THE SNOW HAS TURNED the landscape into a blank canvas. The only color in front of us is the dark swatch of road that swerves like an undulating snake. We've been driving for an hour, and in that time, we've taken turns choosing the music. Arsen's crunchy brass jazz is a severe contrast to the lilting flow of my instrumental orchestras. The songs are as different as us. In spite of that, I easily appreciate the refreshing life the jazz brings, and Arsen smiles fondly as I hum to "The Sea and Sinbad's Ship."

Arsen grips the steering wheel with one hand, reclining casually in the driver's seat. You'd never guess we were fleeing from the police. He's acting like this is a drive through the country. But when he doesn't notice me looking, I catch the way he churns his jaw ... the furrow that makes his brow heavy.

His free hand, placed on the middle console, flexes now and then. It's not from the rhythm of the music. Gently, I place my hand over his. Arsen starts, giving me a curious side-eye. I just smile and keep humming.

"Oh!" I gasp, sitting forward as the car takes a curve, escaping the white hills and trees that filled my view this whole time. In front of us is a huge lake. The water mirrors the periwinkle sky with its puffy clouds. Winter hasn't been able to freeze the lake into ice; a few geese scoot along the water as they search for food.

On the edge of the water is a small wooden dock. There are no boats, but one of the stumps is wrapped in an old, frayed rope as thick as my wrist. But what really holds my attention is the cabin. It's a single level, but that doesn't diminish the size. The polished, gold-tan wood helps it stand out from the field of white all around. Someone must have plowed the snow away because the road that leads to the driveway is cut in clean chunks that nature could never do overnight.

"This is where we're staying?" I marvel.

"I take it you like it."

"I love it," I say honestly. "I always wanted to stay in a cabin by a lake."

"It's nothing fancy."

"It's perfect," I state firmly.

Arsen hits the brakes a little harder than needed, as if I've surprised him. He smiles at me, cutting the engine then opening his door. "I'm relieved. I was worried that making you pack up and rush here would be a miserable experience."

"The reason we have to is bad, yeah, but I'm not upset about the change of venue."

He chuckles to himself before helping me from the car. The ground is clear of snow, but the wooden stairs into the cabin are slick. I appreciate being able to lean on him to make sure I don't fall. I've become hyperaware of how easy it would be to hurt myself—and my baby—with a wrong step.

The interior of the cabin is even better than the outside. The ceilings have a steeple shape, the beams crisscrossing elegantly. There's a chandelier crafted from deer antlers. Arsen flicks a switch by the front door, lighting it up. The main room is expansive, set up open-floor style so the kitchen is on one end, the stone fireplace and maroon couch, big enough to fit eight people, on the other. The wall in front of the couch is one massive window that overlooks the lake.

"Are we the only ones here?" I ask.

"For now. I'll have some of my men come by so we can plan our next steps." He catches my slight frown and hurries to add, "But I have cameras set up outside. No one will break in without me seeing them coming, so don't worry about a lack of guards."

He's misread my frown. I'm not worried about protection. I was hoping we could escape all the reminders of our situation, but apparently, even now, we can't.

"Are you hungry?" he asks me.

"Starving," I admit. I haven't eaten since breakfast and we hurried to pack, so lunch was skipped. It's been a few hours since I ate and I'm only just realizing it.

Rolling up his sleeves, he walks toward the large, stainless-steel fridge. "I'll make us something."

"Wait," I laugh, "back up. First, how is there food here? This place is far away, and no one lives here. Second ... since when do you cook?"

"I've always cooked," he says, looking offended. "For the rest, I just messaged my team before we left the house. I needed someone to plow the snow so we could reach the cabin, a cleaner to get things perfect, and groceries and supplies so we could stay for a while."

I nod in amazement. *He's always prepared. It's second nature to him.* I tingle with a mix of appreciation and love. Cradling my tummy, I watch Arsen in the kitchen, enjoying this home-maker side of him.

He catches me watching. "Sit," he motions at the couch. "Relax. I'll even get a fire going."

"You're doing too much."

"Hardly." He comes around, gently pushing my shoulders until I relent and settle on the squishy couch. He bends over the large stone fireplace; his muscles flex deliciously as he hefts a few thick logs into the cavernous opening beyond the grate. He presses a small button, and the flames burst to life. "There. That should get things warm."

I'm already warm, I think with a coy smile. I don't say it because I'm hungrier than anything else—I don't want to distract him from cooking. Yet.

He stacks four russet potatoes on top of a wooden chopping block built into the counter. It's big enough that once he's done peeling and chopping the potatoes, he still has room to dice some shallots. Their purple chunks, all perfectly uniform, are scraped to one side. He moves with skill, the definition in his forearms obvious in the overhead lights.

Reclining on the couch, I settle into the cushions, enjoying the gentle sound of his knife work as it clicks on the wood. The fire crackles nearby, casting yellow across the polished floor, the heat making me sleepy.

This is the first time we've been alone like this. Half-shutting my eyes, I smile fondly at Arsen where he's begun arranging a heavy copper saucepan on top of the stove. *The first time we act like a normal couple without his staff scurrying around. There's no one here but us.* I stroke my belly with a little sigh. *I wonder if this is what it will be like when we're finally a family?*

Picturing our baby but older, toddler-sized, pressing his or her nose against the big window and giggling at the geese ... It has my heart overflowing. It's easy to forget we're in hiding. Outside these walls, there are multiple people who want Arsen dead. Some of them wouldn't mind if I was dead too.

I start to drift off as the heat of the cabin and plushness of the couch overwhelm me.

"Galina?" Arsen calls gently. I pop my eyes open, yawning and stretching. He's standing by the kitchen table, where two plates have been loaded with food. The scent of it reaches me—paprika, shallots, and olive oil. There's steam wafting off the food.

"Did I fall asleep?" I ask, smiling sheepishly.

"Only for a moment. I didn't want to wake you, but you said you were hungry."

"I am," I laugh. Smoothing my hair and outfit, I push off the couch with a grunt. "What did you make?"

Placing his hand on the middle of my back, he guides me to one of the chairs, pulling it out so I can sit. "Potato and mushroom Stroganoff."

Inhaling the steam drifting off the food, I let out a gentle moan. "It smells amazing." Plucking up a fork, I stab one of the circular potatoes. It's clear he's made this dish before. The potato is thin enough that I can hold it to the light and see through its transparent surface. When I pop it into my mouth, chewing experimentally, a rush of flavor coats my tongue. It's mild but delicious; saltiness enhances the gentleness of the potatoes without overwhelming them. "Oh my God," I manage, before scooping up a bigger mouthful, wanting to get some of everything. "This is incredible!" I mumble as I chew.

Laughing, Arsen leans forward in his chair, like he's trying to get a better look at me enjoying his food. "I'm glad you like it."

"Seriously, I wish you'd cooked for me sooner. I didn't know you were so talented."

"What sort of man doesn't know how to feed the people he loves? There's more to being a protector than shooting a gun."

Mulling that over, I twist my fork into the short, flat

strips of pasta until it's too much to swallow in a single bite. Chewing half of it, I arch my back with an exaggerated moan. "It's crazy good. I can't get over it."

"That makes me happy," he says, his voice growing soft. Lowering his eyes, he pokes at the food on his own plate. I'm reminded of a time that seems so long ago ... a dinner where he ate greedily, and I refused to touch my meal. He sets his fork down. "I've been worried about you since the moment you left for witness protection. And even after you returned."

Oh, that's what's on his mind. "I was surprised you let me leave, honestly."

"Don't misunderstand," he says, waving a hand for emphasis. "I struggled with it. Ulyana stopped me from getting in the way."

I'd brought my glass to my lips, but instead of drinking, I freeze up in surprise. "She did?"

His shrug is aloof, like he wants to pretend Ulyana's involvement was less impactful than it truly was. "She has a way of knowing what's best."

"Yes," I agree, putting my glass down with a mild smile. "She does."

Arsen shifts in his chair. His eyes roam to his food, his hands, the large window. He works his jaw, trying to summon the words he needs. "Terrible things happened because I wasn't there to shelter you."

"Arsen—"

"Even so ... I don't regret letting you leave." He faces me, his eyes searching mine in that eagle-like way of his. "You're your own person, Galina. You should be allowed to make your own choices. But, my God, I was a wreck. I kept picturing the worst scenarios and ... and I had a vivid nightmare."

That's right, he almost told me. It came up after Madison nearly stabbed him with a syringe. I wanted to pry but resisted. "What was your nightmare about?"

Lacing his hands together, he hunches lower in his chair. "For a long time, I've had nightmares about Kristina. They're always the same thing—me coming across her body and being unable to save her as she bleeds out. But this time, it wasn't her corpse I picked up." His attention snaps to me. "It was yours."

"How did I die?"

"I killed you."

Ice spreads through my bones. The deliciousness of the meal evaporates. "What?"

"You died because of me. I was responsible. Galina, the very thought that I could lose you is unbearable."

Reaching over the table, I grab his hand in mine. "You won't."

"Predicting the future is impossible," he argues sourly.

I clench his hand tighter. "Yes, but I know *you* won't be the reason I die."

The lights on the chandelier flicker, then go out. I yelp in surprise. "What happened?"

"Shit," Arsen mutters, scraping his chair backward. The firelight makes one half of the cabin red and orange; the window paints the rest in washes of blue and somber purple. I didn't notice it earlier, but there's a scraping, wheezing noise, tiny taps as something small and hard brushes along the window. He moves to a metal plate on the wall—I could barely see it if not for the fire's glow. He fiddles with it. "The snow has started coming down again hard. Must have taken the power out."

"Will we be okay?" I ask nervously.

The tension in his face smooths away. Smiling kindly, he

comes my way, taking my hands in his. "We'll be fine. I'll check the main breakers when the storm calms down. Let's finish our meal by the fire."

Together we carry our plates in front of the roaring flames. We eat mostly in silence, allowing the storm to provide the conversation. Snowflakes skirt across the glass. I watch in amazement as the trees outside, their shapes blurry, all chunky black limbs, sway in the wind. The lake is invisible. The geese are long gone, I hope.

When we're finished eating, Arsen pulls out a heavy green-and-gold checkered blanket from a closet. Wrapping up in it, we sit arm to arm in front of the fireplace. Though we're pressed together, the mood is edgy. There should be peace here ... but there isn't.

There won't be until we finish talking. Arsen has a lot on his mind. The weight of being in charge, and the drive to keep me safe, has crushed him into the dirt.

He thinks constantly about the Bratva. He even thinks he'll get me killed because of it. I know he won't. He'd never. But ... there are choices, and then there are accidents. I need to know where I stand on the line he's drawn.

Slipping my hand into his under the blanket, I look him in the eye. "If you were forced to choose between the Bratva and me ... which one would you pick?"

His eyes widen. Gripping not just one of my hands but both, he tugs me toward him under the blanket until our knees grind together. His voice comes out hoarse.

"I would burn the world down to keep you safe. But ... the only way I can do that is by staying in control of the Bratva." He frowns sharply, then barks a pale excuse for a laugh. "I feel like I'm losing my grasp on that. I worked as hard as possible to lead those men. Now, one by one, they're running off with Yevgeniy. At this rate, I won't have a Bratva left to lead."

A jagged pain rips through my heart. I knew he was burdened by all of this, but I didn't know how it was tormenting him. Not truly.

Lowering his chin until I see the top of his head, he speaks to the floor. "Who am I if I'm not the pakhan?"

Gripping his chin, I force his head up until he's looking at me. The pain in his eyes turns them blacker than the storm outside. More than ever, I want to erase that pain.

"You're my husband. You'll *always* be my husband."

Our kiss is light and gentle. Not hesitant, but patiently sweet. He pulls the blanket tighter around us, using the material to sandwich us together. His lips graze over mine; he kisses me once more, then stares into my eyes. The darkness within his eyes is gone.

"I want to be more than that."

"You don't—" He silences me with another kiss, pushing himself on top of me until I'm beneath him on the wooden floor. The blanket acts like a barrier around us, binding us tightly. Firelight sways behind his head above me.

He stops kissing me, catching his breath. I have a chance to press my question again, but I bite my tongue. Now isn't the time. I want to heal him, and the only way I can think of is to unite like this. If we're nothing but soft limbs and hot skin, our only concern bringing each other pleasure, then our other problems don't matter.

We want to forget. It might be our last chance to do so.

"Galina," he whispers, clutching my face in both hands. His kiss has some teeth this time. The hint of feral danger thrills me, making me thrust my hips up into him on impulse. The wind bangs on the window, but we ignore it. The storm can't touch us.

The only issue with the blanket is it makes it a struggle to undress. Arsen pulls at my shirt to get it over my arms, then gives up, sliding his hands beneath. Decadent heat swirls through my body, making me press my knees together as I whimper.

I can't see what we're doing beneath the blanket. It's a cocoon that envelops us, hiding our actions from even ourselves. Somehow this heightens everything Arsen does; his fingers are firmer, my skin awake and hypersensitive. His thumb pad brushes my right nipple, and I swear I feel the friction of the minuscule grooves embedded in his skin that identify him as *him.*

Wet snow pelts the glass. For an awful moment, it sounds like bullets—I tense up, trying to look. Arsen cradles me closer, bringing me back to him, to the moment, with a fervent kiss. He kneads my muscles until I'm soft again.

I can't tell if the heat is from the nearby fire or the boiling lust building inside me. "Arsen," I try to say his name. His mouth eats the noise away. He consumes all my groans and whimpers and heavy breathing, feeding them back to me. I'm suffocating under the blanket, but I don't care. He pulls it over our heads, engulfing us fully.

If this really is a cocoon, I wonder what I'll metamorphose into when he's finished with me.

Grabbing my waist, he yanks me against his pelvis. His cock is stiff through his pants; I fumble for it, working as quickly as I can without sight. He helps me by tugging my leggings out of the way. We're not naked, our actions similar to a pair of hasty teens trying to have sex without being caught.

His cock is heavy and hot between us. There's so little room that he's digging into my navel—it hurts, but in a way I luxuriate in. He's blessed with size, but when I can't see him at all my brain turns him even bigger. I start to breathe faster, nearly nervous with anticipation. I know he'll fit—he has every time before—but there's doubt in the darkness.

"Shh," he soothes into my ear. Goose bumps prickle along my arms and thighs. "Relax. It's fine. I promise."

I don't know if he's talking about sex or something more important. My heart swells regardless. Circling my arms around his wide back, I spread my legs as much as possible under the blanket. It's enough for him to sink the tip of his cock inside. I tighten, gasping at the surge of pure pleasure. Another inch, then another, until I lose count. He's stuffing me to the brink. Arsen kisses my temple, then my neck, stretching me out with another push of his hips.

It's an endless stroke. I lose all sense of time, my brain fuzzy with delicious pleasure. He's grinding on me firmly, his stomach brushing my swollen clit. By the time he finally sinks in to his full length, I'm shaking with the need to come.

"Oh!" I sob, hugging tight to his muscular shoulders. He starts to withdraw, the friction driving me wild. I can't budge with how we're positioned. Unable to make him move faster or harder, I'm forced to endure the patient way he fucks me. It's beautiful in tempo ... but infuriating because I'm buzzing with a need for release. "Harder, please," I whisper.

He doesn't obey. He keeps his pace.

A burst of wicked heat attacks my center, moving downward until my pussy tightens. I'm fluttering inside ... muscles rippling as the dam holding my orgasm breaks. He doesn't need to go fast or hard. And he knows it. He knows if he slides into me a handful of times, it will be enough to send me over the edge.

"Yes. Yes ..." I gasp. My toes curl, heels tapping the hard floor. Frozen in place as I am, I experience every tiny flex of my own pussy, every twitch of his cock. My pulse was racing before, but it stampedes now. There's another rhythm that matches mine—his heart.

Whatever was holding him back before is gone. His jaw clenches against mine, breath hot steam on my ear. Arsen fucks me with renewed energy, like he's just realized what he's doing. Or he's decided he's done resisting the urge.

The storm raging outside has come here, inside him.

He doesn't speak, but he makes plenty of noise. Snarls rumble in my head; growls packed with exertion roll down my spine. I'm coming again before I feel it rising up. Screaming under the blanket, sweat pouring from every pore, I let him take me the way he wants.

In the blackness, he kisses me. His lips lock on, tongue chasing mine, making shapes that don't belong anywhere else but the secret alphabet of our desire and love. His cock stiffens deep inside me. It pulses, stretching me out further as his orgasm begins to peak. New, fresh heat fills me up when he finishes.

Gasping for air, he throws the blanket off us. His hair is a mess; mine must be a sight. Staring at me, he searches my face for something. *Maybe he's wondering if I've changed. Have I become a butterfly?* Of course I haven't, but he smiles anyway.

A tired smile ... but a real one.

Lifting my hand, I drag my palm from one side of his face to the other. My thumb traces the corner of his eyebrow. "Earlier, you said you wanted to be more than my husband. You already are. You're going to be the father of our baby," I whisper. "That's more than enough."

His lips shift around, warning of the words that yearn to burst free. I can hear them now. I can feel them rising from his chest, across his tongue, into my ears. *It's not.* That's what he's going to say. I'm so sure of it that when he closes his eyes, ducking his head, and does nothing but exhale, I still imagine them.

He wanted to say them. He didn't.

I wish that made me feel better.

32

ARSEN

"Tell me everything," I say.

I'm standing in one of the large bedrooms in the cabin. There are four, but this is the biggest. It's the only space that can comfortably fit me, Mila, and six of my brigadiers. Kostya has placed himself dead center in the room, his shoulders pulled back, head high and static. The rest sit behind him in an arrangement of chairs I've had brought in from other rooms.

Mila is the only other one on her feet; she's picked the back right corner, huddling into the gap like she wants to be ignored. She keeps her arms tucked around her chest, her lips scrunched up.

Kostya clears his throat. "Three days after you left, the police raided the mansion. They searched it up and down, turned it inside out, but of course, they found nothing."

"I assume they interrogated the staff?" I ask.

"Nobody said a word, of course."

Not surprising; my people are loyal down to their bone marrow. "Good. What else?"

Kostya glances over at Nikolai. The lanky man jumps to

his feet to speak next. "The police left after they failed to get any evidence against you."

"They'll be back," Mila cuts in, pushing off the wall until she's standing in the middle of the room. "The Winter Palace massacre was too newsworthy for them to give up."

Kostya eyes her thoughtfully. She eyes him back, and he tenses up, like he's become aware he's within reach of a rabid dog. "Mila is right. Eventually they'll track you down here," he says.

"We could move you to a new safe house," Nikolai suggests.

Maxim snorts derisively. It yanks at the scar worming over his face. "That would delay things at best, or put Arsen at risk if they're watching the roads and they catch him traveling."

"That's why we'd be cautious," Nikolai huffs.

The group descends into rising levels of debate. People who were sitting now stand with their chests puffed out, gesturing for emphasis. This is the result of us all looking over our shoulders, waiting for the hammer to fall.

I hold up my hands to stop the arguments. Instantly, everyone quiets; they constrain themselves at my command. It's good to remind them that I'm in charge here. "Mila is right," I say. "We're on borrowed time until we can clear our names."

She graces each of them with a smug grin. Facing me, she opens her arms, making herself both vulnerable and appeasing. "The solution is staring us in the face: we have to kill Yevgeniy. Nothing has changed. I don't know why we're discussing other options."

"It's not that simple," I say flatly. "There are other things that need to be done."

They return to bickering among themselves. I allow it,

but only because I need a minute to gather my thoughts. Scratching at my temple, I walk across the room until I'm near the California king-size bed. *They're fighting about logistics ... but there's much more to this situation.*

I haven't told any of them about Ruslan yet. I'm not sure how to present it. Or if I should. The boy is a curveball none of them can predict. All the planning is a waste of time until they know what we're facing.

There's no avoiding it anymore. Lifting my eyes, I scan my brigadiers. Kostya catches my eye first; he stiffens, ending his heated talk with Nikolai. Maxim sees me next and turns away from Lev, the younger man's face a deep shade of red. Whatever Maxim was saying has riled him up. He works to calm himself when he sees I'm waiting for the room to quiet down.

Mila hasn't stopped staring at me. Her eyes are harder than diamond, fixed on me with as much intensity as an owl about to strike. *I have their attention,* I think grimly.

Here we go.

"There's one major complication," I say. "Yevgeniy has a son. Another one."

"How did you learn about this?" Mila gasps, taking a step toward me.

I shake my head quickly. "It doesn't matter. His name is Ruslan, and he's ten years old."

"Ten years old ..." Kostya whispers, his eyebrows scooting up his bald head. His concern is mirrored on the faces of my other men. They've all realized what he has. "That means there's a chance he'll be initiated soon."

"Exactly," I agree solemnly.

Mila moves again, nearly on top of me. Her voice is a breathy warning. "Arsen, we can't let that happen. *You* can't let that happen."

"I'm open to suggestions."

"Kill him," Maxim says simply. "Before he becomes a problem."

"*Nyet!*" I reply instantly. The word is stronger than I meant it to be. It makes Maxim grimace. "He's just a child," I explain carefully. "There are better options. Let's think this through from every angle."

Kostya and Nikolai share a look. "Why?" Nikolai asks. "He's a boy now, but he won't stay that way forever."

"I said we aren't killing him," I snarl.

Curling his upper lip, Maxim rolls his shoulders like he's loosening them up. He looks ready to spit at my feet. "You've gone soft."

"He's right," Lev says in a harsh grumble. "I thought the man I served would do whatever it took to lead the Bratva."

I didn't realize I'd moved, but suddenly I'm face to face with Maxim. Glaring down my nose, I don't try to curb the fury in my tone. "I *will* do anything."

His scar crinkles from his scowl. "Then stop being ruled by your emotions and embrace the ruthlessness that being a pakhan requires. I didn't choose you over Yevgeniy by a coin flip. You're one of the most powerful men I've ever known. Or you were."

The veins in my skull are throbbing. If I bite down any harder, my teeth will crack. His words are worse than if he'd taken out a knife and buried it in my ribs. What hurts more than that though is how my brigadiers are all watching me with the same shade of disdain.

They agree with him.

Searching for some proof that I'm not alone in my decision to spare Ruslan, I turn toward Mila. She's holding her breath. Not even the dip in her throat flexes.

Mila meets my eyes, then turns away.

Clenching my fists at my sides, I back away from Maxim. He lifts his chin higher, clearly thinking he's scored a point. I can't allow that. Weakness here among my men is shedding blood among sharks.

They'll devour me.

I have to stop this before it gets out of control. Marching to the front of the room, I survey the group with careful precision. They manage to look at me, but the energy is all wrong. They're questioning themselves ... questioning *me*. Lifting my arm, I point at Kostya; he flinches. Nikolai is next. One by one, I go down the line.

"Who among you would be willing to slit the throat of a child? Hm? Who here wouldn't hesitate to spill his blood while looking into his innocent eyes? You call me soft, but what you're demanding I do is the exact thing we'd condemn Yevgeniy for."

Maxim holds my cold stare. Abruptly he ducks his eyes to the floor. I jump on that the way a jackal would rip out the neck of a gazelle. "No one should be able to murder an innocent boy without blinking," I state firmly. "But fine, tell me there's no other option. Force my hand. If all of you tell me that I have to kill Ruslan, that you'd do the same, then I'll consider it."

"You won't!" It's not any of them that cry out. The voice comes from behind me, simultaneous with the door bursting open. Galina's eyes are dilated with fury. "You will *not* touch that boy!"

"Galina!" I snap, whirling on her. "Were you listening?"

"Of course I was! I could hear the arguing through the walls." She waves her arm to indicate that doesn't matter. "You promised me that you wouldn't and yet the moment I turn around, you ask that of your men?"

"You can't be here," Kostya says, moving to block her

from reaching me. Galina flares her nostrils—I swear she's about to slap him out of her path.

"It's okay," I say, putting my hand on his shoulder to move him out of the way. "Galina, you don't understand the situation."

"The situation?" she mocks me. Her hair flies from side to side like a lion's mane, her eyes flashing with a similar feral hue. "You can save him the same way you promised to save my mother! It doesn't have to be this way!"

Something black and slim shifts beside me—Mila, moving like a shadow. Her hands clasp Galina's elbow, tugging her toward the door. "You need to leave."

"No!" she shouts, wrenching her body sideways, using all the force she can summon to halt Mila in her tracks. "Someone has to stand up for Ruslan!"

"Galina," I urge gently.

"He is a *child!*"

My brigadiers are muttering to themselves behind me. I pick up slips of their conversation, words like *weak* and *pathetic*. They already suspect I've gone soft from how I argued against murdering Yevgeniy's son. Now they're watching me be challenged by my wife.

I've never felt my position being tested so clearly. Galina, with her furious eyes, pink-lipped scowl, and rounded belly. My men judge me with their eyes on the back of my skull.

I can't let them worry that my backbone is gone. They have to see that I'll put the Grachev Bratva first. Galina has to understand. She has to. Mila catches my eye; she lets go of Galina, backing away, letting me fill the gap where she was. "He's not just a child. He's on the cusp of being initiated into the Bratva as the sole heir of Yevgeniy."

"Initiated?" she repeats cautiously. Suspicion creates wrinkles along her forehead. "What does that mean?"

Mila's laugh is dry as sand. "He'll be made to rape, kill, or both."

Bringing her hands to her lips, Galina moans in shocked despair. She turns away from Mila, searching my eyes for a hint of compassion. "If we get him away from his father before that—"

"*If*," I say the words like I'm cursing. "We can't risk our lives on a bunch of ifs."

Her face falls. Her hands go next, hanging in fists at her hips. "So you're willing to risk it all to kill a ten-year-old."

"I'm risking it all to save your mother and end this war!" I yell it out. I need her to hear. Everyone has to hear. *I* need to hear it. "Everything I do is for you and for the good of the Bratva!" Galina cranes her neck to look up at me as I loom over her. She's expressionless. It's like I'm talking to the frozen lake outside. "Ruslan is a Bratva prince. If he lives, he'll be what Yevgeniy's men rally around. He might not want it, but he will be forced into it just by his very existence. Killing him isn't something I relish, but it's going to happen sooner or later. Will it make you feel better when he's a full-grown man like Yevgeniy's last son?"

There are pleased murmurs from my men. It sends a thrill up my spine to know they're rallying around me. My speech reached them.

That's what I wanted. That's the goal. I need to be the pakhan they deserve.

My blood pumps quicker. I stare at Galina, waiting expectantly for her to show me a hint that finally, she understands as they do. I'm doing the right thing.

"You sound like him," she seethes.

"Who?"

"Yevgeniy."

All of my joy melts away. "Galina—"

Her hair flips around her shoulders like a cape as she spins. She's taken to wearing it down recently, I think because she knows I like it. And I do like it. But seeing it sway as she vanishes out the door is torture. The pit in my guts grows so large I think I'll turn inside out.

She hates what I'm doing. Nothing I said can convince her this is how it has to be. I was sure if I used the right words, she'd come around. It was a foolish mistake to forget that, whatever she's been through, Galina doesn't belong in my world. She never will.

"My pakhan," Kostya says gingerly.

Unclenching my fingers, the knuckles cracking, I look over the room. All eyes are on me. The air of doubt has drifted away. All that remains is their quiet obedience ... their eagerness for my next command.

My voice is steady. "We're proceeding with the plan."

33

GALINA

Killing him isn't something I relish, but it's going to happen sooner or later.

That sentence chases me through the cabin. It follows me down the hall, past the ice-fogged windows, around the carefully crafted wooden benches built into the walls. It's on my heels like a dog on the hunt all the way to the bedroom I've been sharing with Arsen.

I stare around at the space for half a second before retreating.

No, I can't be in there.

I can't be anywhere that feels like him.

The cabin is large enough that ducking into a guest bedroom isn't hard. I have my pick from the bunch. They're all similar in design. All I care about is the white bed in the middle of the room.

Killing him isn't something I relish, but it's going to happen sooner or later.

How can he say that? My head is being pulled apart by pressure. I'm trying not to cry from frustration and disappointment. From the pocket of my sweater dress, I tug out my phone. I'm halfway to dialing when I remember the obvious. Plucking the prayer beads off my wrist, I stuff them under the pillow. Arsen shouldn't be able to spy on me now.

"Audrey," I say into the phone. My voice is tight and high, even though I'm trying to whisper. I suck in air, shaking, working to calm myself down. "I need to talk."

"Hey, yeah, of course!" she replies quickly. "I'm here. Tell me what's going on. Are you crying?"

Wiping my eyes, I force the tears to stop. "It's about Arsen."

There's a quick beat of dead air. "Wait, wait, first thing, are you safe?" she asks in a low tone, the speaker crackling. I can picture her pushing the phone tighter against her ear.

"Yeah."

"Okay, just making sure," she sighs in relief. "Go ahead."

"I'm not even sure how to start. It's a lot."

"Just take your time. Did Arsen ... do something to you?"

She can't see me do it, but I shake my head vehemently. "No. Not exactly. It's more about what he *might* do."

"All right ..." she trails off, leaving the word hanging in the air.

Sucking in a large breath, I ease it out through my pressed lips. *Just tell her. It's not like it's a secret anymore.* "Do you remember what I told you about Pyotr? How he was Yevgeniy's son and Arsen had to kill him?"

"How could I forget?" she asks grimly.

"Well, Pyotr wasn't Yevgeniy's only son. He has another one, a ten-year-old named Ruslan."

"Wait, this other kid is *alive?*"

"Yes, though at the rate things are going ..." I stop myself before I head down a road that will start me crying again. "Audrey," I say seriously, "Arsen says what he's doing will save my mom and end the war, but part of his plan involves killing Ruslan."

Her sharp inhalation hurts my ears. "Is he serious?"

"Yes," I groan in agreement. Tucking my legs under myself on the bed, I hunch tighter around my phone. My eyes dart to the door, worried someone might walk in on me. "Ruslan doesn't deserve any of this; he hasn't done anything wrong."

"But why does Arsen want him dead? Yevgeniy I can understand, but this?"

Picturing the group in the other room plotting away, I frown. "He said something about Ruslan being initiated into the Bratva. I don't know how that works. But it's clear what the implication will be. Once initiated, he'll take over after Yevgeniy dies. I don't understand the logic here, but I also don't care to." Bracing myself for my next reveal, I swallow the lump in my throat. "And one more thing ... Ruslan is my little brother."

"Galina!" Audrey cries out, loud enough that I cup my hand over the speaker nervously. "What the fuck!"

In a hushed tone, I say, "I have to save him no matter what, but I don't have any idea how to do it."

"Can you do anything from where you are?" she asks.

Remembering how I was rebuffed in the room by Kostya, then Mila, I grit my teeth. "No."

"Then the first thing we have to do is find a way to get you out of there. Arsen is too dangerous."

My neck twinges painfully. "This isn't about Arsen."

"Isn't it?" she shouts. "He's the one planning to *kill* a ten-year-old!"

"Like I said, it's complicated!" I hiss under my breath.

Her sigh is long and exaggerated. It makes me blush to have her casually hint at how ridiculous I'm being by begging her for help while still defending Arsen. "It's really not, but fine; let's just focus on how to get you away from wherever you are."

"I'm at a safe house. I don't know the location."

"Is there anyone you can talk to who does?"

Chewing the corner of my lip, I look at the ceiling. Finding no answers, I gaze around the room while racking my brain. I see the inside of the bathroom from where I am. There's a cabinet with handles that reminds me of the one in my bathroom back at the mansion.

Wait. I perk up excitedly. "Not anyone that *I* can talk to, but you can."

"What?"

"Ulyana must know this place. Audrey, I need you to do something for me."

"Of course. Just tell me."

"There's something in my bathroom at the mansion. Something that Ulyana knows about. I need her to bring it to me." I freeze, thinking my plan through carefully. "There are security cameras around the cabin. She'll have to come up with a ruse for why she's visiting ... Tell her to bring me something, like some really comfy compression socks. My feet are killing me with all this water retention, so it's not even a lie."

"Wait, what is it?" she asks.

I don't have to tell her this. Biting the inside of my cheek, I weigh the upside to keeping this part of my plan a secret. "The less you know, the safer you'll be. I promise."

God, I sound like him!

"Galina! You can't be serious. Are you actually keeping secrets from me now?"

"I'm sorry, Audrey," I say. "But it's the only way."

Turning my head slightly, I stare at the wooden walls.

Through them, some distance away, Arsen is in a room, debating the pros and cons of murder. My fingers tighten on the phone and my breath comes quicker. "It's the only way to stop Arsen from crossing the line that he'll never come back from."

Hours pass before Ulyana arrives. Arsen has already departed with Mila and his brigadiers, off on some mission for intel so they can track down Yevgeniy. There's no one posted to stop her from walking straight to the door and knocking.

In a way, this location is more vulnerable than the mansion. There are no hordes of armed guards, no miles of razor-tipped fence. All we have are a few cameras and a single guard that Arsen left behind. A guard who's already fallen asleep while watching TV streaming on the spotty wi-fi on his phone.

"Ulyana!" I gush, grabbing her in a grateful hug once she's inside.

"How are you?" she asks.

"I'm fine, but what about you? I heard the mansion was raided by the cops."

Her eyes crinkle from her pleased smile. "They thought it was a raid, but it was more an excuse to have someone else turn over all the furniture to save me the work. The place has never been so clean, not a spot of dust anywhere."

Laughing with my whole chest, I step back from her, my hands still on her shoulders. "I'm glad you're all right. Did you bring—"

"The socks? Of course." She passes me the bundle, looking at me meaningfully. I take the socks, feeling through the middle. My thumb rubs the hard edge of the tiny SIM card. Anything caught on the security cameras won't spoil my plan.

"Thank you," I say genuinely.

"I hope they help your swollen feet. Arsen should be taking better care of you."

I manage a mild smile. "He's doing what he can. It's safe to talk if we whisper. He isn't here, the guard is passed out, and those cameras can't catch our audio." I saw that for myself when I spotted Arsen reviewing the footage with Mila earlier. They complained that they needed to upgrade the tech at this location.

Ulyana ducks her head and crinkles her eyebrows. "In that case, *devushka* ... I know what that thing is. Are you *certain* you've thought this through?"

My pulse skyrockets at this. I study her face, trying to work out how she could possibly have figured out what I'm up to. Did Audrey tell her? *No, wait. Calm down. She knows it's a SIM card, but she can't know it's to contact Yevgeniy.* "Thought through what?" I ask innocently.

"Please don't insult my intelligence." She grips my hands and squeezes them. It's a pleading gesture, but it also hurts, like she's trying to shock me awake. "I've spent my life in proximity to the Bratva. I know what you're about to do."

Our eyes meet—she frowns, and I know she's seen through my game. Dropping my hands, I let out an exhausted sigh. "If Kristina was alive, she wouldn't want Arsen to taint his hands with the blood of a child."

"Yes," she admits. "But have you thought about the consequences?" Ulyana suddenly looks very drained. The energy has been siphoned from her, and I feel awful for not noticing until now. Between covering for me, dealing with the police raid, fighting with Arsen, and keeping more of my secrets, she's gone thin as stretched chewing gum. If I'm not careful, she'll tear.

"You're about to make a deal with the devil," she says softly.

Scrunching up my nose, I hug the socks tight to my chest. "I know, but what choice do I have left?"

She cradles my face and starts speaking again. "Actions have consequences, *devushka*. Unintended ones. Think about the lives you'll be risking. Your mother—"

"Is a survivor," I cut her off. *I am too.* "Please, I have to do this."

Her shoulders round lower. "I understand. I just wish I could talk you out of it."

"I know how frustrating it is to not be able to reason with people." I smile sadly, thinking of Arsen. I speak clearly and calmly as I smile at Ulyana. But she doesn't smile back. "Thank you for helping me. You should leave before Arsen returns and sees you here. He'll have questions that are harder to dodge in person."

"Then I suppose we're back to sharing secrets."

I cringe as new thorns prick my heart. "I'm sorry."

"Don't be. Just pray these secrets don't cause more harm than good." The frozen air invades the house when she opens the door. It swirls around me, but I'm already cold. A shiver runs through me; it's erratic, and my teeth chatter.

Like she's trying to warm me up, or perhaps because she's afraid this is the last time we'll speak, Ulyana grabs me in a solid hug. She rubs my back the way my mother used to.

"Good luck," she whispers. "Galina Stepanovna."

34

ARSEN

Winter has wrapped the world in its fist. Though no more storms have arrived, the weather has been stark. The kind of cold that steals the air from your lungs if you stand outside and take too deep of a breath. From the window of the back bedroom, I stare over the lake. Its ivory surface melds with the land. I only know it's there because parts of the wooden dock are visible. The thick rope extends out before vanishing into the nothingness.

"I was patrolling one of the areas you gave me, pakhan," Kostya says from my side. He arrived ten minutes ago with Mila. I wasted no time rushing them into this private place for some news. "We have a location on Yevgeniy."

I twist around to stare at him with interest. "Well?" I demand.

"He was moving Katya and the boy, Ruslan, into a black vehicle. A Mercedes. They proceeded to drive west while I pursued. The place they stopped at is a house in another suburb, one that's still under development, very secluded. Lightly defended too, at least currently. If we move *now*, we might be able to rescue Katya and kill Yevgeniy in one blow."

I rub my hand over my jaw anxiously. "This is an incredible opportunity."

"Exactly," Mila agrees. She flashes me a wild grin. "We can't delay."

Nodding to myself, I pull out a map from a stack of papers on the desk by the window. "Show me the path they took and where they are now."

Bending over the colorful spread, Kostya begins sketching lines with a pen. The black lines are clean, drawn without any hesitation. "If we circle in from this side of the street, there won't be a way for him to slip out. We'll have him cornered."

Studying the map, I tap a few spots. "It should be easy to post snipers who can pick off any of his soldiers that try to provide backup." *This is perfect. We've got a real shot at ending this now!*

"Arsen ..." Mila warns in a dark hush, "your *wife* is listening to our conversation." She looks pointedly at the door. I follow her gaze, my neck hairs prickling. Kostya straightens up as well.

Both of them eye me expectantly. Taking a calming breath, I push the door open, nearly running into Galina. She retreats with wide eyes. "What are you doing?" I demand.

The guilt in her face at being caught red-handed twists on itself. Narrowing her eyes, she jabs me in the chest with her finger. "Are you still going through with this?"

"I don't have any choice."

Her eyebrows arch as high as possible. "Of course you do! You always have a choice!"

I'm hyperaware of Mila and Kostya watching us. It's

almost worse than the last gathering with all my brigadiers, because now they know I've told Galina what I plan to do. She's had everything laid out for her, been chastised for spying, and still, she rebels against me. *I can't look weak.* With ice on my tongue, I speak in slow, pondering words meant to drive my point home. "I promise his death will be quick."

Every last drop of blood drains from her face. She's whiter than the snow outside. "You're going to regret this."

I was already on edge, but her warning triggers a new burst of paranoia. Goose bumps rise along my arms. *She's capable of interfering. She's done it before.* "Mila, confine Galina to her room."

Galina's eyes pop wide open. "Arsen!"

Turning away, I look directly at Mila. She stares back at me with dark curiosity. "I want her under lock and key until I return."

"You can't do this!" Galina argues.

Mila looks put out as she approaches Galina. "I'm not babysitting her. There's no way I'm missing out on the action," she says.

"Then assign another man to guard her," I agree coldly.

"Mila, don't help him. Please," Galina begs. The pain in her voice cuts me to the core. It's good that I'm not looking at her but the map. Because if I look at her, I'll want to agree with her.

"Come on," Mila sighs as she takes Galina's arm.

Focus on what needs to be done. Remain strong.

"Arsen, stop this right now!" Galina yells.

"Someday," Mila says flatly, "you'll understand that ugly things need to be done. Think of the bigger picture."

"You don't care that he plans to kill a child?" Galina argues.

"Ruslan is more than a child." Mila's patience is running out. Her voice sounds strained. "Don't make me drag you by your hair, Galina Yevgeniyevna. I'd hate to do it, but I will."

Kostya lets out a little grunt of surprise—unlike me, he's watching the scene. I can't resist anymore. I peer over my shoulder at the women. Mila has Galina by her arms, pinning them behind her back, forcing her into the hallway.

Galina grimaces, thrusting forward and fighting back. Her eyes find mine—the panic transforms into bitter hate. "Did you know he almost killed Madison?" she suddenly shouts.

Mila freezes like the air has gone out of her in a great push. She flicks her vengeful eyes at me.

It's a long moment in time. I'm not sure if Mila will turn on me. She's always been loyal, but I knew from the start that Madison was special to her. She related too much to the suffering of that girl.

Stay the course, I think fiercely, trying to send my thoughts into Mila's brain.

Her brow sinks, her eyes narrowing further. Instead of asking me to confirm or deny, she closes her eyes, then rounds on Galina. "Last chance. I really don't want to do this the hard way."

All the strength fades from Galina. It seeps first from her angry eyes, then to her limp arms, her hanging head. Hair dangles in her face. I can't see her expression. I should be grateful, but instead, it makes my heart shrivel.

"Galina," I call. "When I come back, it will be with Katya."

I won't fail again.

Mila is the only one who looks at me. Galina shuffles all the way into the hall without a single word. Not even a sigh.

"Pakhan?" Kostya prods me.

In desperate need to do something with all the energy inside of me, I grip the desk, crushing it until my knuckles throb. "We'll wait for Mila to rejoin us."

"Of course," he says.

It's not long before the assassin returns. She enters, shutting the door and effectively shutting off all reference to what just occurred. She glances at me from the corner of her eye, and I try to get a feeling for where her head is at after learning about Madison. She doesn't give me a chance; she nods at the map.

"No time to waste, you were saying?"

Easing my cramped hands off the desk, I trace the lines of ink Kostya drew. I go over a quick rundown of each unit, who will be posted where, and when we'll strike on the house.

Finally, I stand to my full height and consider them both with grave seriousness. "When we encounter Yevgeniy, there's a potential for things to get messy. Katya isn't to be harmed." I work my jaw as a flicker of wicked excitement takes hold. "Kill whomever you want, but Yevgeniy is for me."

"And the boy?" Kostya asks.

The excitement dampens like autumn leaves rotting in the sun. "Make it quick and painless for him."

It's mercy, I tell myself.

But I don't believe it. I never have.

The snow outside shifts in a gust of wind that pushes drifts of it off the dock. A new kind of white flashes; four geese have landed on the ice. When they spread their wings, they remind me of angels.

Why think of heaven? I chide myself. *It's a place I'll never go.* Men who condemn children to death have no right to keep their souls. I don't need God to condemn me; I've already done it.

And if not me, Galina surely has.

Kristina would have done the same.

The idea splits my throat apart, making me choke on a gritty cough. Mila and Kostya eye me, but I wave them off. I'm beyond help in every sense of the word.

No one will forgive me for what I have to do.

But ... even knowing that ...

I pray Galina will.

35

GALINA

"This is ridiculous," I scoff. "Mila, you can't go along with this!"

Ignoring me, the black-haired woman speaks in a hurried, authoritative voice to the young man in the hall. "Arsen wants her locked in here. That means she doesn't leave until he says so. Understood?"

"Mila!" I argue.

The guy glances at me nervously.

"I said, do you understand, Yeremey?" Mila asks hotly.

"Yeah, I got it," he insists, lifting his hands to calm her. "I'll stay right here. She won't go anywhere."

Squaring off with the pair of them, I hold up the prayer beads accusingly. "Did you know he's been listening to my conversations?"

With a bitter smile, Mila just shrugs. "Of course I did. Who do you think put those there in the first place?"

The fight sags out of my shoulders. *Mila knew? This whole time?* Just how little *does* Arsen trust me?

"And don't think about doing anything stupid, Galina Yevgeniyevna," Mila continues. "It's more than just a microphone in those beads. There's a GPS tracker as well. In case you're taken again, Arsen will have ways to find you."

"Of course he does." I turn my face away.

"I know what you're thinking," Mila says. "I don't agree with it, but like it or not, you're a danger to yourself as much as you are a danger to us. But you need to remember something: Yevgeniy is a devil through and through. And although Arsen is one too, he is different. He has you as the angel on his shoulder."

Can devils even have angels? Is that even possible?

"I'm not exactly doing much to stop him, am I?"

"You're doing enough that he's having doubts. And I—no, we—need him to be the opposite of that."

Then, she pushes me backward, shutting the door fast enough that the blow-back sends my hair fluffing away from my forehead. I grab for the handle; there's a metallic *click.* One wiggle and I know she's locked it. "Mila!" I cry, pounding my fists on the wood. "Mila! Come back here! Mila, please!"

There's no answer. She's gone.

Spinning around, I place my thumbnail between my teeth. *I have to do something, and I have to do it fast!* I've been praying I won't have to go forward with the plan I orchestrated through Audrey and Ulyana, but the situation has gotten dire.

Marching over to the single window, I test the sill. It doesn't budge. *Shit, has this always been locked?* I've never tried to open it before because of how cold it's been. Whether Arsen had it sealed intentionally or it's just jammed from old age, it doesn't matter.

I'm officially trapped.

Recalling the icy way Arsen spoke to me, I hug myself and tremble. *He promised me Ruslan's death would be quick.* It's the kind of promise that taints all the others he's made for me.

Because mercy or not, he's going to kill a child.

From the drawer of clothes I packed, I withdraw the fluffy thermal socks Ulyana brought and pull out the SIM card from the inner cuff. Slipping out my phone, I carefully push it inside. The screen flashes. Yevgeniy's name is the only one in the contacts list.

My thumbs are a blur as I type rapidly.

ME: It's me. Arsen is coming for you! You need to get Ruslan away from there!

YEVGENIY: I think you should come join us for a family reunion.

ME: Don't you get it? You have to run before Arsen kills your son!

YEVGENIY: You must miss your mother.

ME: Please. Leave.

YEVGENIY: If you want your sweet mother to live, you'll have to come to me.

ME: Are you crazy? What about Arsen?

YEVGENIY: Have faith in me. I have a plan to ensure you, myself, your family ... OUR family ... can be together.

I'll see you soon.

I sit on the bed in stunned silence. Something grazes my thigh—the prayer beads. On autopilot, I twist them in a circle. *Arsen ... I swear, I'm doing this for you. I hope you'll forgive me.*

Pushing my phone into the pocket of my oversized pink sweater, I chew at my nails again. Yevgeniy wants me to meet him. How can I make that happen when I'm stuck in this room? Outside the window, I spot motion. Moving closer, my cheek to the chilly glass, I watch Arsen's black Escalade and another silver vehicle drive through the plowed snow until they're out of view on the main road.

This is it. They're going to do it. I eye my door with a deep frown. *That means it's just me and Yeremey in the house.* If I'm going to do anything, it has to be now.

When I start to nervously gnaw my nail again, I flinch; the edge has become sharp from my chewing. I stare at it as my brain begins to twinge. *That's it!* Sliding my leggings down, I stare at my pale thighs. *Don't hesitate! Just act! Ruslan is counting on you!*

What I'm going to do is awful. Not just because it will hurt, but because it will trigger one of my deepest fears. Dragging my nails over my skin, I press in harder and harder, flinching as the milky skin splits apart. Red droplets bead upward. It's not a big cut, but it's enough for my purpose.

Smearing the blood all over my inner thighs, hands, and pants, I waddle toward the door. I glimpse myself in the full-length mirror; the gruesome sight is convincing. Enough so that my stomach flips around. I've had nightmares about miscarrying.

Gathering myself, I raise my voice as loud as I can. "Help! Please, help!"

There's shuffling outside my door. "What's going on in there?" Yeremey asks warily.

"I'm bleeding! Oh God, I think it could be a miscarriage!"

The door explodes inward. Yeremey takes in the scene with his eyes threatening to pop from his skull. He looks younger than before—terrified of me. "What should I do?" he asks.

I wave my red-stained hands. "Take me to the hospital!"

His face falls. "But Arsen Kirilovich said—"

"We have to go before it's too late! The baby could *die!*"

He turns in place, frozen by indecision as he realizes the impossible choice I've forced upon him. "Hold on, let me—should I carry you or—"

He's falling apart under pressure. It makes me feel bad for the charade. I wobble closer, reaching for his arm. "Help me walk to your car. I think I can make it if we go slow."

He handles me like I'm made of eggshells. Bit by bit, we move through the house, him fretting nervously, me adding an occasional moan of pain. I want to sprint, but it would ruin the act I'm putting on. "Don't worry, I'll get you to the hospital quickly. I'll call Arsen on the way so he knows where we are."

"No!" I blurt. He blinks; I grip my stomach, covering my anxiety with a fake, exaggerated groan of agony. "Please, no. I don't want him to get distracted on his mission; it's already so dangerous."

"Yes, you're right, of course."

The air outside tastes like static. Snowflakes are falling, spiraling down like little dancers in white. Once he eases me into the back seat of the dark blue Tesla, I tuck my legs close to my body. To the plain eye, I'm soothing myself through my suffering. "What hospital are we going to? How far away is it?"

"Saint Juniper's. It's just five miles. I'll drive as fast as I can. But it's going to be at least a half hour."

"Thank you." In the shadow of my jacket, I tuck my phone in my lap and begin to text Audrey. I know her number by heart.

ME: Meet me at Saint Juniper's. I should arrive in half an hour with this snow.

AUDREY: Okay, I'm coming now. Should I bring anything?

ME: A disguise of some kind. I'll duck into one of the bathrooms. Just wait in there for me.

"You doing okay back there?" Yeremey asks. He peers at me in the middle mirror.

Curling over on the seat, I suck on my teeth. "How much longer?"

Snapping his attention between the road ahead and his phone's GPS, Yeremey makes his tone as cheerful as possible. "Real soon, I swear."

He's a nice guy. Lying to him really does suck.

And I hope Arsen won't punish him too harshly when he realizes my ruse.

How long will it take Arsen and his group to arrive at Yevgeniy's house? I'm terrified that I'll be too late. To go this far and have it all be for nothing ... It makes my stomach hurt. I was already hugging myself, but I do it for real now. Yeremey watches me occasionally in the mirror. He looks worried.

The snow makes it too dangerous to hammer on the gas. In spite of this, we pull into the large parking lot of a massive multilevel hospital in the next ten minutes.

"Okay, we're here. Let me pull up to the emergency drop-off." He slows to a halt. The tires grind on the salt that's been laid down in front of the red-painted curb. Before he can cut the engine, I jump from the back seat. "Galina Yevgeniyevna, wait!"

"I can't, I'm going in!" I yell without looking back. *Please, please let me be faster than him!*

My plan won't work unless I can escape into the bathroom without him noticing. Once the doctors and nurses get involved, slipping away will be that much harder. Darting through the sliding glass doors, I feel the eyes of the front desk on me. "Sorry!" I groan, patting my belly with a sheepish grin. "Baby's pressing on my bladder, can't wait!"

The woman flashes an understanding grin. She can't see any blood with my jacket hiding the evidence; to her, I'm just a soon-to-be-mom about to pee on herself. From the corner of my eye, I glimpse movement; Yeremey has reached the glass doors. My shoe nearly slips out from under me from how sharply I turn down the hallway. The restroom sign is a beacon of hope. Panting heavily, I push the door open, stumbling into one of the three stalls.

Okay. Okay. I did it, I'm here! Now I have to hope my guard doesn't get bold and come investigate. The front desk didn't see us together. With any luck they'll send him away. If he waits for me in the lobby, that's a different issue, but one I have a solution for.

Squatting on the lid of the toilet, I hunch over my phone. *Come on, Audrey!* I'm about to text her for an update when the door to the bathroom swings open. Shoes shuffle on the tile, turning in place, as if unsure where to go. I stand warily.

"Galina?" Audrey asks in a soft hush.

Popping the stall door open, I jump into her arms. "Oh my God, you made it!"

"Did you think I'd bail on you?" she laughs, hugging me back. "Come on now. Are you all right?"

"Sort of. Did you see a guy out there acting cagey?"

She peeks back at the door she came through, puckering her lips. "Yeah, the front desk was telling him if he didn't calm down and leave, they'd call security on him. Let me guess, he's with you?"

"One of Arsen's men," I explain. "He won't be a problem if you brought—"

She holds up a backpack. "You can always rely on me."

My immense relief makes me feel like I'm glowing.

"You're amazing," I say, taking the bag. Digging through it, I begin lifting out the various hats and shirts.

Audrey cranes her neck as she watches me. "I didn't know what you wanted exactly, so I brought a few options."

Flipping a fluffy white winter hat with a fuzzy pompom into the air, I shove it over my hair. "This is perfect. Yeremey won't recognize me at all."

"Galina, what exactly is your plan?"

I measure one of the sweaters against my chest. I'll have to layer a few on to stay warm. "I have to save Ruslan."

She gnaws at her bottom lip, hands wringing. "Is this really the best way? Can't you just call the cops, tell them where everything is going down?"

"If I do that, they're likely to shoot Arsen in the chaos. Or just because they want to. Oh, this is nice." I've stuffed myself into a second sweater; this one is a pretty shade of pine green.

"Galina," she nearly groans my name.

"I have to do this alone," I say bluntly.

She stares at me like she wants to argue more, but instead she backs down. "How are you going to get to where he is?"

Taking her hands in mine, I slip on my most winning smile. "You said I can rely on you, right?"

"Oh God."

"I need your car."

Audrey throws her head back to stare at the ceiling. She shuts her eyes, staying like that, as if she's gathering her courage. Letting go of my hands, she grabs my shoulders, staring at me hard as she talks in a serious whisper.

"When you bring it back to me—and you *will* bring it back—it better be in one piece."

"Thank you, Audrey. I don't deserve a friend like you."

"Funny," she laughs dryly. "I was just thinking the same thing."

Yeremey has folded himself over the front desk. There are two police officers speaking to him in soft, patient voices. The woman sitting at the computer in front of him looks extremely uncomfortable. "Listen to me," Yeremey begs. "I'm looking for a pregnant woman."

"Yes, sir," she says lightly. "We have many of those here."

Yanking my hat further over my face, so that it's nearly on my eyelashes, I speed-walk toward the exit doors. Yeremey is too distracted to see me. Even if he did, I look like an entirely different person. The double sweaters are plenty warm—too warm, thanks to my nervous sweating. It's a relief to burst out into the chilly snowflakes.

Okay, she said she parked in the left lot. Scanning the cars all sitting in nice rows, I half-jog over the pavement. The snow has made it slick; my shoe kicks out from under me, one knee buckling. Gasping, I grab onto the hood of a red hatchback to keep my balance.

Be careful, I chide myself. *Don't go this far only to bust your ankle and lose everything!*

Looking up, wiping snow from my eyes, I spot Audrey's familiar green Subaru. I've been in Audrey's vehicle enough times to know it by sight.

Yanking out the keys she gave me, I stick them in the driver's side door. The car opens for me, letting me close myself inside. It's not cold—she must have had the heat blasting in here before she parked.

I put the car keys in the ignition, where they jingle loudly. There are two empty containers of Jamba Juice in

Audrey's center cup holders. I pause, considering them with a funny sense of sadness. Audrey has always struggled to keep her car clean. I'd chastise her when we went on joy rides together, and she'd laugh it off, insisting she'd clean her car the next time we went out.

Of course, she never did.

The empty drinks are a stark reminder of the predictable life I left behind. A life I might never get back.

I'll never get anything if I don't do this.

Pulling out my phone, I message Yevgeniy.

ME: Where do you want me to go?

36

GALINA

The snow is coming down in sheets. With the wipers going at top speed, I'm allowed a few seconds of vision before I'm blind again. My jaw is clenched for the entire agonizingly long drive. White-knuckling the steering wheel, I take a right turn into a dark section of road. If my GPS is right, Yevgeniy's location is closer to the hospital than Arsen's cabin. There's a chance I'll beat him there if he's spent enough time organizing his men before moving to strike.

Please don't let me be too late.

My wipers are working less now—the snow is slowing down. Turning into a development with lots of unfinished houses, I start to ride my brake. *I'm close ... Where is it ...* The pavement is slippery from the storm. I take each turn with the utmost caution. I'm moving at barely a mile per hour, my headlights glistening wetly on the ground, when I see the house.

It's as quiet as the rest of them. Not a single light is on. There's one working streetlamp, and it casts a pale-yellow glow on the snow-coated sidewalks, flickering like it's ready to die. To my right sit a number of large pieces of construction equipment, their surfaces heavy with chunks of ice.

Parking Audrey's car, I remain where I am, trying to decide what to do next. There's no sign of Arsen, but that doesn't mean anything, because I don't see Yevgeniy either. *Is this the right place?*

The tap on my window makes me scream.

Yevgeniy smiles at me through the glass, waving his black-gloved hand.

"Welcome home," he says, muffled by the window.

I reach for the keys, wondering, not for the first time, if this was the right move. *I'm here. There's no point in running now.* Before I cut the engine, I crack the window. "Where's my mom?"

He gestures at the house behind him. "Inside. Come and join us."

My hand clenches the keys. Tension thrums in my whole forearm. *What choice do you have?* Bracing myself, I turn the car off.

He gives me enough room so I can step out and shut the door. We're in near total darkness, the streetlamp glinting on Yevgeniy's right side, making his jaw sharper, his eyes darker. "It's been a while, my dear daughter."

Filling my chest with dignified air, I stick out my chin. "Stepan is my father, not you."

"Hardly," he snorts. "And why would you even *want* that?"

"Because I'm proud of him. Proud of who he raised me to be. I'll always be *his* daughter," I say fiercely.

Reeling back, Yevgeniy eyes me like I said the funniest joke ever. He barely controls a full-throated laugh. "Stepan did *nothing* but watch me fuck his wife. He was weak."

Heat spreads up my neck until my whole face burns red.

"He wasn't. He was using you as much as you thought you were using him."

"Is that right?" he says crossly.

"My father was smart enough to resist the urge to enter a fight he'd lose."

He can't contain the laughter anymore. The sound echoes through the development, bouncing off the snow until the awful noise becomes endless. "Oh, stupid girl, he was anything but smart. Otherwise, he'd have noticed he was being poisoned."

My heart gives a quick double thump. "What are you talking about?"

"Stepan not realizing what was happening is one thing, but it's amazing no one else did." He shrugs dismissively. We could be discussing the damn weather. "But that's the beauty of a good poisoning."

"I don't understand what you're saying," I whisper, my voice rising at the end.

"Did you really think his cancer was natural?" He laughs, shaking his head in a slow swing. "That man's illness was deliberate. All it took was a tiny piece of Cesium-137 taken from a medical imaging device and soldered to the bottom of his favorite mug. So small that you would never even know it was there. And it was only a matter of time. Months, years, it didn't matter. He was *always* going to die."

His favorite mug? I remember the white and gray mug he would always drink out of. And when I told him about my pregnancy with Simon ... I remember holding the mug in my hands, cradling it over my belly as I told Dad excitedly about what my future held.

A new chill snakes its way into my heart and something heavy shifts inside of me—it's like the baby is moving, but this feeling is slimy and prickly and ghastly.

No ...

NO!

YOU BASTARD! YOU MURDERER!

My mouth tingles, and I feel like I'm on the verge of vomiting. "You're evil," I hush.

All this time, I thought my miscarriage was a tragic accident.

But it wasn't.

Somehow Yevgeniy managed to find a way to twist my father's love for me into something vile. Something horrible.

He really is *the devil.*

Spreading his arms with a fond smile, Yevgeniy waits for me to throw myself into his embrace. "I'm just a father who wants what all fathers want: their family to be reunited. Now come here."

I step backward until I make contact with Audrey's car. "How could you think murdering someone I love—someone my mother loves—would make us want to spend a minute near you?"

His arms dip an inch. "The man you thought was your father was pathetic. By removing him, I've *freed* you." He approaches me. I try to retreat further, but I can't. His eyes are slits, his smile full of sugar and razors. "You can embrace your roots ... your heritage ... the power of our bloodline. You are Galina Yevgeniyevna and not Galina Stepanovna, and you should be grateful for that."

"I'll never be who you want me to be," I spit at his feet. "I fucking hate you."

Slowly, he lowers his arms to his sides. The smile remains, but the sweetness is gone. There's nothing left but the razors. "Perhaps you'd change your tune if I had Arsen's welp cut from your belly? Or would you prefer to see me kill it in front of you?"

An unbearable urge to run away takes hold of my legs. I'm moving before I think it through, shoving around Yevgeniy, bolting toward the construction equipment. I don't have a destination, just a drive to *escape*.

I won't let him kill another one of my children.

Sucking in ragged breaths that appear in the air like shifting ghosts, I hold my belly in both arms, running into the snowbank. I make it a few feet before something stops me. It's not Yevgeniy grabbing me in the night. And it's not me slipping on the unstable ground, though that does happen. I'm on my knees in the snow, ready to rush forward again, when my mother shouts my name.

"Galina!"

Contorting so fast that my neck tweaks, I spot her standing beside Yevgeniy. She's dressed for the weather, her small frame bundled up in an unfamiliar midnight blue jacket that tickles her ankles. It looks brand new. Yevgeniy must have bought it for her.

With wide eyes, she stares at me across the road. Her fingers rise to her lips, nearly touching her nose, which has turned pink from the chilly wind. "Galina?" she asks again.

"Mamochka!" Running toward her, I grab her tight, not wanting to let her go as tears start falling from my eyes. "Oh my God, you're okay!"

She hugs me in return, the warmth of it sapping my energy. I forget why I was running. I can't think of anything but how she's here with me. We're together again.

Yevgeniy rips me away from her by my hair. I scream, struggling to get free, to reach my mother as he yanks harder. "You can enjoy your reunion later," he snarls.

"Let go of me! Let me go! Mom!"

"Stop resisting!" he snaps, tugging my hair until my

scalp burns. "This isn't a game! You arranged this meeting, now be a good host and wait for Arsen to arrive."

I quit pulling; the pain is too much. He takes me over to the house, leading me like I'm a dog on a leash. Through the window I glimpse a flash of light, a small shadow. There's someone inside, hovering beside a lamp. *Ruslan.*

Yevgeniy finally lets go of me.

My mother joins us in front of the house. She moves to stand near me, but a single glare from Yevgeniy sends her scuttling to his other side.

"What are you going to do?" I demand.

Vapor exits his tightly pressed lips. He looks at Audrey's car, then further, into the distance. "I'm going to show you the consequence of your own soft heart."

It feels like the world is shaking, but it's only me. The tremors travel from my feet to my guts, ultimately settling in the center of my chest. *My soft heart.* I've heard that before. It was a warning uttered by the man I thought I was coming here to help. Arsen stood over Madison mere minutes after she tried to kill him. She got close. Too close.

All because of me.

It's happening again.

37

ARSEN

"*Mi gotovi*," Mila says. *We're ready.*

Casting my gaze over her head, I look around in the low lights. The snow has stopped falling, but the heavy clouds remain. The homes on the street are as quiet as graves. Just around the bend is the division that's currently under construction. It makes sense for Yevgeniy to have set up here. There's no one else living in the other homes. Most aren't even finished being built.

Once we move ahead, there'll be no one to hear what happens. We'll be acting under near-total cover of darkness. There are streetlamps here, positioned one after the other like kids lined up for school, but around the corner there's only one. The plan to use snipers was scrapped when we realized there wouldn't be a good line of sight. It's a small setback.

"Arsen?" Mila prods.

Pulling my black gloves tighter against my wrists, I peer back down the road. None of my men are visible, but I know where every single one of them is positioned. "Go with the second team. I need you with them." *If things go wrong ...*

"I'm not good with a team, you know that," she grumbles. "Let me go in alone. I'll kill any soldier he's put on guard before they know I'm there."

"Not this time. I won't have a repeat of the Winter Palace." My brigadiers have formed a perimeter around the area. I'm certain we'll have the upper hand. But if not, we won't make it easy for Yevgeniy.

Mila scowls openly at me. She's dressed herself differently for once; pure white from her ski mask down to her boots. Not a single strand of her black hair escapes. She's right that no one will see her coming. "This won't be like last time."

"I know," I agree coolly, staring pointedly at her, "because you're joining the second team."

"*Blyat*." Crossing her arms, she holds out for a few seconds. When she accepts that I'm not changing my mind, she stalks past me toward the opposite end of the street, away from the division. "You're lucky I trust you."

"Yes," I whisper, soft enough that she won't hear. "I am."

Doing a quick check of my arsenal under my jacket, I begin walking down the street. Unlike Mila, I'm not dressed to hide. I want Yevgeniy to see me. I want him to shake with rage as he watches me approach.

There'll be no question who killed him when this is done.

The snow crunches under my boots. The road hasn't been plowed here. I slow down, noticing tire tracks. A car has come through recently. *His men? Or Yevgeniy himself?* It's not one of mine, that's certain.

Frowning, I grip my pistol in its holster under my jacket. It brings me some comfort as I creep along the road. My toes are going numb, but I don't slow down. Rocks could start falling from the sky and I wouldn't walk away. *I'm too close to ending this.* Galina's face flashes in my mind—the way she looked at me as I forced her from the room with Mila holding her tight.

You're going to regret this.

That's what she said. And she might be right. *I'll do what I have to,* I think, slipping my gun into the air. I check the safety before inching around a large, raised hill of snow. With it gone, I can see straight into the developing neighborhood. The massive diggers and bulldozers look like old relics, patches of yellow paint gleaming in the streetlamp where the snow has slid away. The houses are in various stages of construction; most are just framework, their hollow insides exposed to the elements.

The tire tracks I noticed swerve in a long, snake-like trail, ending at a green Subaru. I hardly notice it. My attention is fixed on the group just beyond the car. They're standing in front of one of the unlit houses, the only people around. Waiting for me.

Yevgeniy wraps his arm tighter around Galina's throat. She's gripping his forearm, eyes big and shining and staring right at me.

Galina! I think, not daring to utter it. *How did she end up here?* Beside her is Katya. And just behind her is the small boy I met a few nights ago.

Ruslan looks terrified.

I lift my gun high in the air. "Using your own daughter as a shield? I shouldn't be surprised. Where are your men? They're the ones meant to protect you."

Yevgeniy's chuckle echoes into the night sky. "They're around. Same as yours, no doubt."

"Arsen!" Galina shouts.

The rage I'd been trying to keep a hold on surges forth. He has no fucking right to touch her. My finger twitches on the gun's trigger. I'm salivating to put a bullet in his brain, but I can't risk hitting Galina. "Let her go, Yevgeniy."

"Why would I do that?" he scoffs.

Galina tries to shuffle forward, but Yevgeniy pulls her back. "Arsen, please, just run!" she begs me.

My throat tightens up when I speak. "It's going to be okay, Galina. I promise."

"How sweet," Yevgeniy says. Pressing his head against Galina's, he releases a light sigh. "I'd never be capable of such kindness toward someone who betrayed me."

The tip of my gun lowers an inch. "What are you talking about?"

A flash of shame works through Galina's face. Her eyebrows tilt downward, copying the shape of her pink lips.

What did she do?

Tugging at Galina's hair absently, Yevgeniy smiles viciously at me. "How did Galina know where I was? How did she end up here before you did?"

"Arsen ..." she whimpers plaintively.

"She says your name like she actually loves you!" he laughs. "She's a very good liar, isn't she?"

Shoving at his arm, Galina tries to break away, but Yevgeniy clings to her even tighter. "I'm not a liar!" she cries.

"Galina didn't betray me," I tell Yevgeniy. "You can't trick me into believing that."

"I don't have to trick you. Here, see for yourself." He tosses something toward me. My grip tenses on my gun; I almost aim at him, ready to fire on instinct alone. I hold back because I might hit Galina or Katya. The phone slides to a stop in the snow at my feet, leaving a small wake.

"What's this?" I demand.

"Go on, have a look," he coaxes me.

Crouching without taking my eyes off him, I pick up the phone. My attention flicks between it and Yevgeniy. The screen blinks to life at a press of my thumb. There are messages, lots of them. *They're all between Galina ... and Yevgeniy?* My stomach begins to turn itself inside out the longer I read. "No," I whisper.

"It's like I said." His smirk could cut glass. "She's a *very* good liar."

The phone falls to the ground. Everything feels numb, but not from the cold. Clenching my fist, I try to warm my sluggish muscles. Betrayal has slowed me down, making me confused and weak. *How could she do this?*

"Galina ... why?" I ask in disbelief.

"Arsen! It's not what it looks like!" she screams, her voice shattering.

She came here by herself ... She planned this ... all of it ... right under my nose. And for what? To stop me from killing Ruslan? She chose his life over mine?

I lift my eyes, glaring savagely at Yevgeniy. *She won't stop me from ending this, not when I've come this far.*

Galina thrashes in Yevgeniy's grip, pulling toward me. Her eyes drip with tears. Both her cheeks and nose have gone a blazing red, as dark as her lips, which are curled back as she sobs. Lifting my gun, I stare down the muzzle, trying to hold it steady. It wavers between Galina and Yevgeniy.

I have to kill him.

This is my chance.

I can't shoot ... not when I might hit her.

Galina ...

The tip of the gun angles downward until it's pointing at the snow. No amount of hurt I feel could make me risk her life. As long as Yevgeniy is using her as a shield, I can't fire. I have to think—I need a plan, and fast. There has to be a way to—

A roar splits the air. It echoes through the wind, bouncing off the snow and ice and through my teeth. It's so loud it hurts.

No, it's not the noise that hurts. It's more than that. This is …

The pain billows up and out. The intensity spreads from my ears to my flesh. Helplessly, I watch as my gun drops to the ground. The feeling has vanished from my hand like the nerve endings have been sliced straight off. I try to kneel and pick it up, but no part of me is listening anymore. Messages from my brain to my body are getting stopped.

"Galina …" I gasp, dropping limply to my knees in the snow.

She is shrieking my name. But she sounds so far away.

All at once the agony strikes me—I inhale sharply, placing a palm to my side where the pain is radiating from. It's warm and wet. My fingers come away, soaked in red.

And that's when I realize …

I've been shot.

38

GALINA

I'VE SEEN THIS BEFORE. THIS EXACT SCENE. ARSEN LYING IN A pool of his own blood, dying right in front of my eyes. The last time it was just a nightmare.

This is real.

"Arsen! Arsen, no! Arsen! Get up!" I cry.

Yevgeniy keeps his hold on me as I struggle to escape. He ignores how I fight, turning around to grin wolfishly at Ruslan. "*Molodets*, son! You got him!"

It clicks with me then—I understand what's happened. No longer struggling, I instead turn, staring in disbelief at Ruslan. His face is pale as old milk. He's gripping a pistol that looks massive in his tiny hands.

"Ruslan?" I whisper.

He sniffles, starting to shake, the tremors coming faster and more violent by the second. "I ... I ..." he stammers.

Beaming with sadistic delight, Yevgeniy turns again so he can see Arsen. "You should have fired when you had the chance, Arsen. I guess you don't have the courage of a ten-year-old. Or maybe you're just weak. Did Galina's kindness soften your backbone? Hm?" He cups his ear. "No response?"

Arsen lies in the snow. He doesn't budge. Clutching my mouth in horror, I throttle down the bloodcurdling scream that wants to break free. I'm scared that if I start, I'll never stop. *Oh God, Arsen ...*

"I didn't mean to," Ruslan whispers. His voice is fragile, on the edge of panic. "I thought ..." He drops the gun, gawking at it like it's turned into something else. It might as well be a king cobra for how he looks ready to flee. "It was real. It wasn't supposed to be real."

"Ruslan?" my mother asks, as aghast as he is.

He rolls his eyes toward her. He hasn't blinked in far too long. "I'm sorry. I'm sorry."

"It's okay, it's okay," Mom whispers to him. She cradles the boy, trying to stabilize him as his shaking grows worse.

"Stop crying," Yevgeniy snarls. "You should be proud of what you've done." The sirens that split the air make him freeze; he stands tall, staring at the sky, then back toward the road. "We need to move. Everyone get in the car. Now."

I keep waiting for Arsen to get up. For Mila and his men to burst from the bushes, rushing to his aid. Arsen's blood stains the snow all around him. But nothing happens.

This is my fault.

I did this.

"I said let's go!" Yevgeniy snags me by my elbow, forcing me up into the driveway. There's a black Mercedes parked with only a light layer of snow on top. He shoves me into the back, then shouts for my mother and Ruslan. Mom shuttles the boy into the back seat, holding him in her lap. He's still crying.

Yevgeniy hurriedly swipes snow off the windshield before jumping into the driver's seat. We're not even buckled in when he starts the car. I'm thrown back from the force. He's speeding, rushing to escape the area before the cops or Arsen's men close in on us.

Ruslan's sobs fill the vehicle.

"Shut up!" Yevgeniy roars. "Stop crying! You have no reason to cry!"

"I'm sorry, I'm sorry, I'm sorry," Ruslan sobs. Snot pours from his nose, his whole face cherry-red. We're free of the suburb, and the car spins on the black ice. It's a miracle we don't fishtail into a tree. Once we reach drier, clearer roads, Yevgeniy speeds up. The tires scream, but Ruslan's crying is loudest of all.

The brakes squeal sharply as Yevgeniy turns us around a corner into an alley. The car jostles to an abrupt halt, sending my mom and Ruslan falling to the floor.

"Mom!" I gasp.

Yevgeniy leans into the back seat and slaps Ruslan clear across the face before wrenching him from my mother's arms.

Ruslan stops crying, the utter shock of the assault robbing him of his voice.

"No son of mine will be a crying *suka*! What we did back there, what *you* did, was vengeance! Hold your head up high with pride!"

"Leave him alone!" I snap, pulling Ruslan back to me. "He's not heartless like you!"

A terrible darkness swirls in Yevgeniy's pupils. He considers me with disdain, saying nothing for a full minute. The only sounds are the faraway sirens and Ruslan's heavy breathing.

"If you think you can protect him from his own destiny ... or from *me* ... you have no idea how wrong you are."

Ruslan clutches me like I'm the only safe thing in the

world. Tears run down to my chin. I resist the urge to rub them away.

"You're a pathetic man who makes a boy do his dirty work."

Yevgeniy narrows his eyes curiously. "Are you crying because Arsen is dead?"

"He isn't dead!" I yell defiantly, my voice going hoarse. Mom watches me with abject fear written on her tired face. She's not afraid for herself ... She's afraid for me.

Yevgeniy's sneer grows like a weed. It's a twisted shape from ear to ear that only stops when it can grow no bigger, and I'm surprised I don't see fangs or a forked tongue when he speaks.

"He *is* dead. But don't worry, you'll see him again."

My pulse quickens. Ruslan stirs in my arms, his wet cheek turning into my body. He's seeking comfort, and I wish I had some to give. "What?" I ask worriedly.

I was wrong. His sneer *can* get bigger. "Haven't you figured it out by now?"

That's when I understand.

He's going to kill me.

39

ARSEN

It's cold.

A thousand hands crush my skull, pressing in, trying to crack my bones and pierce my brain. They're holding down my shoulders... my arms, my calves. I feel like I weigh a thousand pounds, I can't move no matter how hard I try, and hands shove me downward like they're preventing me from springing straight into the sky.

Through it all comes the pain.

It slashes at my skin in precise strokes, leaving me stripped and exposed. Every nerve is on fire. If this is dying, I wish it will come to an end soon. I'm craving the kind release of death so much that I've stopped thinking about how I got here.

Through a fog, I hear my name.

Someone is shouting it. Over and over and over.

Sharp cracks, like wet wood in a fire, explode near my ear. Slowly the weight lifts off of me. Numbness fades enough for me to open my eyes. I'm not on fire—the burning comes from the cold of the snow I'm lying in. My cheek is buried in it. When I breathe, slush floods my mouth and nose, forcing me to cough in pain.

The haunting cry of my name lingers in my ears. *Galina?* It must be her. It has to be.

Thinking of her terrified face forces me back to this painful existence. Clarity returns, and with it, come brighter bursts of pain. I look around. In front of me is a dark shape. It's blurry until I squint harder, making myself focus.

A face.

A corpse.

Kostya?

Inhaling in shock, I stare at the wide-eyed, blank expression frozen on my brigadier's face. His waxen face is dull in the dim light of the street lamp. Red lights flicker off of it. They mimic the blood surrounding him in the snow.

How did this happen? And then I remember. Ruslan, his mouth wide with disbelief and fear... the clap of thunder as he pulled the trigger... And then I fell, unable to do anything but watch helplessly as Yevgeniy fled with Galina and the rest.

What happened while I was unconscious? How did Kostya get here, and how did he die?

"Pick him up, we have to move!" a gruff voice demands. Multiple figures hoist me off the ground. I cry out from the unprecedented flares of agony. Each sway of my body tear at the bullet wound, and sends fresh stinging pain searing through my body.

"Get him on the stretcher, and *let's go!*" another voice shouts.

"Who? What?" I groan, trying to understand the chaos. I'm lifted onto something firm, laid flat, and strapped down. I can barely move before but now I'm restrained. The metallic tang of panic fills my mouth.

"Put me down, stop," I gasp.

"Relax." A gloved hand pats my arm. "We're here to help."

Twisting my neck I squint into the flashing red lights. They belong to an ambulance. *Paramedics. They must have heard Ruslan's gunshot and come to check it out.* Against all odds, I'm condemned to live.

They lift the gurney; I see Kostya splayed in the snow like a rag doll. Bitter shame swells in me, muting my pain. "Wait! Don't leave him here!"

"He's dead," one of the men holding me says. It's delivered as a simple fact.

I can't accept that Kostya, who risked his own life for mine, could be forgotten in an abandoned suburb like this. It's wrong—he deserves better.

The gurney jolts roughly, blinding me with pain. My view of the red lights and dark sky shifts, becoming the inside of the ambulance. It's crowded, multiple faces swaying close to mine. Some avoid meeting my eye. One of them, a gaunt man with a full mouth and ear-gauges, is strangely familiar.

He catches me staring—looks at me, then away, quick as a blink.

Do I know him?

"Hurry up," someone shouts, banging on the divider between the rear of the ambulance and the driver's section. "We can't waste time. He'll die before he's supposed to."

Something's not right.

Focusing on the man from earlier, I dig through my memory, trying to remember where I've seen him. One of the others is fumbling with an oxygen mask. He pokes a button, sets it off, scrambles to shut it down as the others laugh mockingly.

Sharp fingernails creep up my spine. The ear-gauge man

glances at me again—and suddenly I remember. I've met him before, long ago, when I was still Yevgeniy's brigadier.

Shit.

My pulse speeds up; I tense on the stretcher, curling my hands into fists. *These aren't paramedics! They're Yevgeniy's men!* Rocking side to side I struggle to break free of my bonds. Everyone notices what I'm doing, two of them launching forward to hold me down.

"Get away from me!" I wheeze. Moving is making the bullet wound stretch; warm blood gushes through my shirt.

"Hold him still!" Hands seek purchase on my shoulders. Another pair grips my knees. I'm weighted down as heavily as when I was fading into unconsciousness in the snow. I can't break away, but I'm sure as hell going to try.

Gritting my teeth, I flex my biceps, shifting my weight from the right to my left. The men loosen their hold on me; I rock again, the other way. The gurney crests upward as it sways. Yevgeniy's men gawk with rising dismay. Their worry gives me strength. *If I can just tip over, the restraints might snap!*

A sharp prick in my inner arm startles me.

"That should calm him down," someone laughs.

I spot the needle just as it withdraws from my skin. A man sneers down at me and flicks the needle away.

"Enjoy it, Arsen Kirilovich, it's the last peaceful rest you'll experience before what the *real* Pakhan has planned for you."

"Fuck you," I rasp. I try to reposition myself. Nothing happens. The others look relieved, moving away to lean on the walls of the ambulance. *Come on! Move!* I scream internally, working to force my hand to make a fist. My fingers tingle as they go numb.

I do my damnedest to flex my legs, my neck tensing from

my effort. *Move, come on, move!* The only motion comes from the vehicle as it drives over the road.

No... this can't be happening. Once Yevgeniy gets his hands on me, I'm done for. All of my efforts over the years to bring him down have been wasted—ended by a scared child. *I was planning to kill him.*

Maybe this is karma.

The ambulance jerks sideways so suddenly that medical supplies topple off the wall, raining around us. "What the fuck!" a man cries. The world inverts—I'm floating. I've never felt so light, and though everyone around me is shrieking, I'm relaxed—detached from reality—like all of this is a dream I'll wake up from any moment.

Everything slams to a halt. All the men in the ambulance somersault around in boneless heaps, their cries cutting off abruptly. Metal crunching on metal fill my ears; it's all I hear. Glass shatters, shards of it bouncing against my face and limbs. Some of it dusts into my hair.

The sensation of flying continues on even though we've stopped moving. Around me comes the soft groans of those lying in piles of twisted legs and arms.

The sedative continues to course through my veins, taking the last of my strength. I can hardly turn my head to blink blearily as the back doors of the ambulance burst apart. Through my fuzzy vision I make out the shape of someone entering the vehicle. They're white as snow—something bright flashes in their grip.

Pop pop pop! My ears ring from the closeness of the gun going off.

Blood flicks onto my chest from the skull of the man nearest me. He collapses, his mouth agape.

"I've got him!" A woman's voice yells. I think it's familiar, but my ears are buzzing, making every sound an echo of itself. A white ski mask and a pair of dark eyes fill my world. Mila rips the mask away, reaching for me. "Jesus, you look like shit."

"Mila?" I whisper.

"Help me with him," she says to someone just behind her. Men—my men—fill the ambulance. They kick aside the corpses until there's enough clearance to lift my gurney onto its wheels, then they cut my straps away.

My heart beats quicker as relief floods me in a dizzying rush. "What are you doing here?" I groan.

"Saving your ass," Mila says. "Move him to the car, and fast."

I try not to grimace when three men hoist me under my arms and around my ankles. I'm carried like a sack of corn out of the ambulance. As we move over the snow, I see a silver car parked nearby, its headlights blinding me. Another car—a black Tesla—is crammed against the ambulance. Its whole front is crumpled in. One of my men is reversing it out of the snow and back onto the road as two others push the front of it to help.

As I'm placed in the rear of the silver car, I let out a ragged groan. "Apologies, my Pakhan," the man holding my feet says, trying to ease me in more gently.

Mila rips the other door open, sitting beside me. She works to ease me up, but I'm struggling to move my own head. My eyelids won't obey either, they keep drooping.

"The fuck did they do to you?" she growls.

I spread my lips—no sound comes out. She grabs my shoulder, shaking me. Now *she's* moving her lips and no sound is exiting. My whole head is throbbing. The pain is finally slipping away. It's taking my energy with it.

I'm going to live. I'll be able to stop Yevgeniy. He won't win, he can't *win.*

I won't let him.
I'll... I'll stop him and I'll... save her.
I have *to save her.*

"Hey!" Mila's voice sounds like it's a hundred feet above me. "Stay with me! Wake up!"

I can't see anything. My eyelids are too heavy to lift. With the last of my strength being sapped away, I manage one word before sinking into nothingness.

"Galina."

Galina twirls across the stage, her long hair barely keeping up with her. The fullness of her skirt is white as the moon. There's no music that I hear, but she spins to the rhythm, in tune in a way only someone who grew up dancing could be. Bright lights illuminate her movements, blocking out everything else. I can't see beyond the pitch-black shadows around the edges of the stage.

"Galina," I utter, taking a step towards her. My legs feel wrong. I'm jittery all over. She spins further away, not once looking at me. "Galina!" My legs give out, knees slamming onto the hard surface of the stage.

I look at my hands where they brace on the wood. They're bare. My wedding ring is gone.

With ice in my stomach and my heart in my throat, I lift my head. Galina continues to twirl, her skirt practically glowing. But when she stops short, heels together, and pivot to face me, the blood is easy to see. Red streaks across her stomach. It's not rounded with our baby anymore. It should be round. It should be fucking *round.*

"Galina!" I gasp, sitting up sharply.

Mila chuckles to my left. "He rises from the dead."

Hunching forward, I look at the blanket stretched over my lap. I recognize the blue cotton that pills too easily—I'd wanted to have it replaced but kept forgetting to tell someone, other issues always taken precedence over something as small as linens.

I'm in the cabin by the lake.

"When did we?" I whisper in amazement.

Mila releases an annoyed sound. "Not that long ago."

Lifting my arms in front of me, I study them curiously. Small bandages stick haphazardly all over my flesh. My wedding ring sits firmly on my finger.

"The glass didn't cut you that bad," she says, misunderstanding why I look relieved.

There are more bandages wrapped around my chest. I brush them, wincing when I graze the tender spot that the bullet entered. Someone has packed thick gauze beneath the wraps there. I'm naked except for a pair of loose tan joggers. "Whoever patched me up did a decent job."

"You're welcome."

"Did anyone follow us?" I ask.

She shakes her head, stretching herself like a cat in the chair by the window. "Corpses don't move very fast."

I grimace at the word *corpse*. "Kostya..."

"I know," she seethes. Mila stands from the chair, wandering closer to my bed. She's no longer in the white gear I last saw her in. She's dressed down to basic blue jeans and a loose teal shirt that's frayed around the sleeves. It's too big on her; it makes her look smaller. Younger. Too much like the screaming girl I saved all those years ago.

"It's not your fault, Arsen."

"What happened out there?" I can't keep the anger out of my tone as I demand answers.

She turns away, unable to look me in the eye as she talks.

"After you were shot, we tried to move in and help. But cops started swarming around us. They did just enough for Yevgeniy to escape. I told everyone else to bail until we had a plan." Her shoulders rise upward, the crease of her jaw deepening. "Kostya refused. That bastard actually ignored orders, can you believe it? He ran into the fray to try and drag you out." Her words become more clipped. "He went down fighting."

Closing my eyes, I take several big breaths. Kostya had to know he wouldn't get out of there alive. Even so, he'd jumped in with both feet.

"He'll be remembered." Shifting on the bed, I start to slide my legs over the edge. Pain radiates from my chest; I lock up, clutching at my bandages. Hot air exits my teeth in a quick burst.

"Don't try to get out of bed," she scolds me. "You're not out of the woods just yet."

I chuckle grimly. "Ruslan has good aim."

Her brow scrunches upward, then down just as fast. "The boy?"

"Not important." I wave my hand dismissively. "Tell me more about the cops helping Yevgeniy."

Mila watches me warily, expecting that I'll make another attempt to get out of the bed. When I remain still she sits back in the chair beside me. "Seems they've struck a deal with him. They might as well be his personal army now."

Well, that certainly explains some *things.* Remembering the fake paramedics makes my skin crawl. I rub my arm where the needle pierced me. "And what's in it for him?"

"Immunity." She spits the word out like it's poison.

The cops would put him on a throne before they put him in cuffs. "I need to speak with Josh. If we don't act quickly, the entire police force will be on Yevgeniy's payroll."

"You think he'll talk to you? After this?" Mila laughs derisively. "He only tolerated you because of Galina."

I mash the blankets until my forearms cramp. "Do you know where she is?"

"No fucking idea. But we're looking." The aloofness in her dark eyes melts into pity. "She's alive, Arsen."

"I know that," I growl, furious at the suggestion of anything else. "Which is why I need to talk to Josh. Now."

"Just how do you plan to convince him to help you?"

Rubbing my bandages, I laugh ruefully. That small movement causes my ribs to ache, but I keep laughing in spite of the pain.

"I'll make him an offer he can't refuse"

"And how do you plan to do that?"

"With your help, of course."

40

ARSEN

"You sure you should even be out in public?" Josh asks me flatly. He's not concerned about my safety—I think he's actually trying to make me feel threatened.

Sunlight streams through the half-gaped blinds over his office windows. They create a striped pattern across his torso, reminding me of a prisoner's uniform. He's not the one who has to worry about jail.

I smile coyly. "Let's get down to why I'm here."

"Where's Galina?" Audrey blurts. "Is she okay?" It's the first thing she's said since I entered the room. Dressed in a maroon, long-sleeved turtleneck and pale pink ankle-skirt, she's the opposite of Josh's cobalt-blue ensemble. The one thing they share is the same narrowed-eye disdain for me.

Oh, now you care about her? Mila informed me that the car at the scene belonged to Audrey. It's hard not to tear into her for helping Galina meet up with Yevgeniy. I resist because being at odds with Audrey won't endear Josh to my side.

"I'm working on finding that out," I say. "It would be easier with your help."

"How?" Josh asks dubiously.

Folding my arms behind my back I walk around the long table. As I draw near to him, Josh clinches up from his lips to his knees. "The police is hunting me down, but they're chasing the wrong person. It's not me they're after, but Yevgeniy. I need the commissioner to understand that."

"Let me guess." He lets out a hollow laugh. "You expect me to convince him?"

"Yep." I shrug like I'm bored. "Otherwise, Yevgeniy will control the entire police force in a short time. If you think he's dangerous now, wait until he doesn't need criminals to do his dirty work for him."

Audrey flicks her eyes at her husband. He pointedly ignores her, focusing harder on me. "The police aren't as corrupt as you're implying."

"Says you?" I sneer. "And just how would you know?"

He stands taller with a sour grin. I've seen rotting Jack-o-lanterns that look more pleasant. "Coming here was a mistake."

I take another step towards him, causing him to retreat; his shoulder rattles the blinds.

"Don't take this lightly. Your life is already in danger."

"What did you say?" His eyes flash before his face turns red. "Are you threatening me?"

"I don't need to threaten you. But I've told you that Yevgeniy's spies infiltrated your firm, or do I need to remind you that Yevgeniy found where you'd hid Galina the first time?" He turns a darker shade of red at that. "They've already told the other cops not to trust you." I pause, noting how he's pressing his lips together in a white line. I have his full attention. "As far as they're concerned, you're in bed with me. Which, in a way, you are."

He slaps the surface of the table, making the carafe of water none of us have touched rattle. "Fuck you, Isakov!"

"Josh..." Audrey whispers nervously. She's not as doubtful of my claims as her husband.

He storms forward, his shoulder bumping mine as he passes. His hand chokes the handle on the office door, opening it wide. "It's time for you to leave, Arsen, before *I* call the cops on you. And believe me, I'm *real* fucking close to doing it."

"Oh, I'm aware." I gesture around the room vaguely. "But there's a reason I came here in person." I look up at the security camera tucked in the corner of the ceiling. "Nice setup you got here. How do you think Yevgeniy will feel once he sees that I'm here?" My voice drops to a true baritone. "Hell, I bet he's already getting ready to do something."

Josh slams the door shut; Audrey yelps. "You piece of shit, you tricked me!" He comes at me so fast I brace myself, expecting a punch. Josh stops short, his lips wrenching back over his teeth and gums.

Keeping my words steady, and my hands behind my back, I say, "You can go back to hating me once this is over. But right now, I need you to keep the police away until I can rescue Galina and her mother. And then I'll deal with Yevgeniy."

There are more lines around Josh's nose and eyes than on a sheet of notebook paper. I glance at his fists, watching his knuckles gleam and swell and flex. He's barely controlling himself. One wrong move and he'll swing on me. He'd lose in a fight, I'm nearly twice his size, but the fallout is what concerns me more. I need him to work *with* me not against me.

"We've already tried that," he says. "And you nearly died. I'm not falling for this again."

"He's right," Audrey calls out.

Josh whips around to gawk at his wife. "Audrey, you can't be serious!"

Folding her arms over her chest, rubbing her shoulders, she goes quiet. She's gathering her words carefully, not wanting to take my side, or go against her husband, but she wants to save Galina just as much as I do.

"We can't stand by and do nothing, Josh."

"This is blackmail!" he snaps.

Her downcast eyes rise up to meet mine, hanging there, judging me. I wonder what she's weighing. Crossing the room, she stands in front of her husband. "We said we'd help *before* we were put in this position. I'm not going to turn my back on Galina." The hate in her glare scalds me. "Even if we have to work with the devil himself."

Josh looks ready to explode; his face is shiny with sweat, verging on purple. Audrey places her hands on his. A ripple moves through his body. The pair don't speak—and still, I know they're communicating. Slowly, Josh relaxes. He shuts his eyes and Audrey squeezes his hands. She's soothing him better than anyone else is capable of.

Watching them creates a painful longing in my chest. I miss Galina more than ever.

Sighing in exasperation, Josh frowns at me. "Fine. I'll consider it."

"I'm glad to hear we're on the same page."

"I said I'd *consider* it. I want proof first."

"The proof will come. Probably sooner than we expect." Digging in my pocket, I hand him a burner phone. "Yevgeniy will be acting fast since he failed to kill me. Use this to call me."

He fixates on the phone, studying it like he's worried it

will hurt him somehow. Eventually he picks it up. "You're a real cocky asshole, Isakov."

Josh can insult me all he wants—the fact he took the phone is all I care about.

"I should go," I say, glancing at my own phone.

Audrey pokes her heel at the floor. "We'll walk you out." Josh shoots a *are you kidding me* brand of look at her, and she shrugs. "We were going to leave for dinner anyways."

"Thank you," I say earnestly. We step into the elevator, Audrey and Josh taking the furthest corner possible from me. It's an awkward, silent ride down to the bottom floor. And they're the first to jump out of the elevator when the doors open.

The main lobby is nearly empty; the woman behind the front desk doesn't bother to glance up from her computer at us. Josh takes the lead, pushing the glass doors wide. It would be a polite gesture if I didn't know he wanted me out of his sight as fast as possible.

"And here we are," he says.

Scanning the sun that's eager to set, I squint down the street. There are a number of cars parked in front of the building. Not an empty meter in sight. "Call me the second you know anything, or if you're in trouble."

Josh throws his head back, laughing while we wander down the sidewalk. "Your concern is appreciated, but there's no need for that."

He pops his keys out, jingling them, pressing the button. A dark blue Mercedes *beep* ahead of us.

And then swells like a balloon in a fireball.

The roof cracks apart as the windows shatter from the explosion. Orange flames blossom into the air like a flower in bloom. Every other car alarm goes off, the cascade of noise mixed with the crackling fire rising along with the smoke from the Mercedes. Then the shockwave hits the three of us, knocking us to the ground.

"Holy shit!" Josh gasps as he scrambles up.

Audrey screams.

"Get back!" I yell while shielding them with my arms. Corralling them towards the building, away from the smoldering car, I glance back at the chaos. Black fumes billow upwards, blocking out the sun. Sirens shriek in the distance. Someone has already called 911.

"What happened?" Audrey stammers, clinging to me. "What... what was..."

"What the fuck!" Josh shouts. He jumps out of my grip, standing on the sidewalk with his hands buried in his hair. "What the actual *fuck!*"

I drop my hand heavily onto Josh's shoulder; he stares up at me, his pupils tiny dots. He's slowly sinking back into his own body. "Are you okay?" I ask him.

He blinks rapidly. "Yeah." He blinks again. "I almost died."

I don't say anything.

Audrey gawks at the flames with her mouth dropped open wide as a trumpet bell. "How could that happen? Cars don't just blow up!"

Josh's eyes narrow—he's connected the dots. "Yevgeniy. You said he'd act fast, but I didn't think..."

I tilt my head, listening to the sirens draw closer. "I can't stay here with the cops coming. I'd offer you a ride with me, but that's not wise, I think."

"No," he agrees quietly. Something passes his face, then he tightens his jaw, staring at me with new determination. "I should have believed you from the start."

My thumb moves in a blur over my phone as I message

for a private taxi. "The police will want to talk to you. I suggest you take the opportunity."

"And do what?" he asks.

"Find cops who are honest. If you're lucky, some of the ones showing up might be exactly that." Tucking my phone away, I hurry towards the nearby alley. "Be safe, both of you."

"You too," Audrey calls after me.

This time, she means it.

The squeal of cop cars and the honk of a firetruck peaks nearby. I resist the urge to jog. Exerting myself pulls at the bullet wound still freshly healing under my bandages. Sliding around a rusty dumpster, I exit the alley onto a side street. Unlike the front of Josh's building this section is void of vehicles—other than my own, that is.

I reach for the driver's side door, preparing to unlock it.

"How'd it go?"

Mila is leaning on the stained concrete wall opposite my car. Her ankles are crossed, her black boots glinting in the fading sun. When she stretches her arms over her head with a yawn, her motorcycle jacket rises off of her waist, letting me see the handle of a knife. It's a decoy to distract from the many others she's hidden on her body.

I tap the hood of my car with a scowl. "You used too much fuel. It wasn't supposed to draw the attention of every firetruck in the damn city."

"Did it work?" she sighs.

Peering over her head, I note the smoke still floating in the distance. "Yes. Josh is willing to help us."

"He's going to be pissed when he realizes you lied to him."

"Fuck what he thinks," I say, unlocking my car. "I need him to buy us some time."

"Not worried about the long term?" she asks suspiciously.

Mila strides toward me until she's on the other side of my car, eyeing me over the top of it. "Guess it's easier to not be alive for the blowback than to say you're sorry, huh?"

I don't respond.

"Arsen, I'm just fucking with you." She bends her knees like she's about to leap over my car and tackle me. "But what I want to know right now is if you're going to do something suicidal." She's waiting anxiously for me to expand upon my plans. The smoke continues to sway in the air behind her, curling, ever lengthening.

It reminds me of Galina's hair as she danced in my dream.

I slip inside my car. Before I shut the door, I reply curtly. "No."

Were it so easy.

41

GALINA

Ruslan hasn't stopped shaking. He's been like this during the whole car ride. I have to half-drag and half-carry him into the large townhouse, all the way down a dark hall that Yevgeniy shoved us through. As my mother and I huddle in the small backroom we've been stashed in, Ruslan continues to shake.

"I didn't want to do it. I didn't, I swear I didn't," he mutters. It's all he's been able to say.

Brushing his hair from his forehead, I push him to my chest. "You're okay. I'm here."

He whimpers, mumbling into my shirt, as if he didn't hear me. I'm worried he's gone into shock. The reality of shooting Arsen, nearly killing him—because I refuse to believe Arsen is dead no matter what Yevgeniy says—has broken his little mind.

I look up, seething with hatred at the sight of Yevgeniy. He's pacing the room, occasionally checking his phone. He seems to be ignoring us. It's a small favor, but I'll take it.

"*Chyort*," he hisses, crushing his phone in his fist. He

arches his arm like he plans to throw it. At the last second he stops himself.

Bad news? I wonder... and hope.

Ruslan lets out a wretched sob. His voice is raw from crying so much. "I'm sorry... I'm sorry... I didn't mean to... please."

"Enough!" Yevgeniy whirls on us. My mother retreats into the corner, trying to hide behind a curtain of her own hair. I don't blame her for being afraid. It's not her job to stand up to this man.

But someone has to.

"Stop it!" I snap. "You did this to him."

"Did what? Turn him into a man?" Stomping over to me, he lurches down, grabbing Ruslan by his shirt. "Get up, boy!"

I try to cling on but he rips him away from me. "Give him back!" I demand.

But it's useless.

Yevgeniy hauls Ruslan—wide eyes rimmed with red—onto his feet. He reaches for me desperately, trying to cling to me even as Yevgeniy gives him another hard yank. My heart leaps to my throat. Jumping forward, I swipe at his small hand. But our fingers can only graze as Yevgeniy drags him through the door and slams it in my face.

It's my turn to shake.

"What is he going to do to him now?" I ask out loud.

"I don't know," Mom whispers. "*Gospodi,* I don't know."

I move to the door, putting my ear to it in an attempt to hear some hint of what might be happening behind it. My plan is to try and hear some hint of what's happening down the hall.

At first, there's only silence.

And then the screaming comes. I don't have to strain to hear it.

Jerking backwards, I put my hand to my mouth. "Ruslan?"

Mom stares at me, her silence confirming my fear. My little brother is shrieking. The awful sound careens through the air, searing itself into my brain.

"What's happening? Mom?"

"I don't know..." she's shaking harder than before, and tears are running in streams down her face. "I don't know."

I tug at the door but the knob won't budge. I pound it with all my might as I scream. "Stop it! Stop hurting him!"

The screaming stops.

My heart sinks into my guts like an anchor on a ship. *Oh no...*

This can't be good.

In desperation I twist the knob over and over. But it's useless. The knob refuses to turn, and the door refuses to open.

"C'mon," I whisper, fighting back tears. "C'mon!"

Suddenly the knob shifts as the door is unlocked. Someone is opening it from the other side. Leaping backwards, I brace myself, ready to attack Yevgeniy.

But when the door opens, only Ruslan is there.

He shuffles towards us, dragging his feet while his arms are wrapped around his upper body. His head is bent low, and his eyes are blank as they stare ahead.

Relief and worry war in my heart, and the strength drains from my legs as I rush towards him. "Ruslan?"

He doesn't lift his head.

I drop to my knees, cupping his cheeks. "You're okay. Everything is okay."

I reach for his shoulder and he screams, yanking backwards. "No!" he sniffles.

"What is it?" I ask anxiously.

He continues to dodge my gaze as he stares at his feet.

"Ruslan, you can talk to me." I gently take his hands. On my knees we're face to face. "Ruslan."

His eyes rise to lock on mine. With a great shudder, his face crumbles and he starts crying—deep choking sobs that seem to be dragged from the depth of his soul. Slowly, he turns away from me, tugs at his shirt, and lifts it up.

There! Pristine and raw, is a new tattoo on his skin.

A black crown on his shoulder.

My mouth goes dry and suddenly I can hear Ulyana as if she's standing here with me: *Tattoos. Every man of the Bratva has some. Some signify their past deeds, terrible or great things they've done, and their ranks.*

It doesn't take a genius to know what the crown means.

I'd suspected Yevgeniy planned to kill me, but now I know for sure.

And yet, I'm unable to feel pity for myself, not when this little boy is pale from the horrific trauma his own father has imposed on him.

"Ruslan?" Mom's voice rises up, trembling, behind us.

"It hurts," he whimpers.

"Oh, my sweet boy," Mom opens her arms and Ruslan falls into them like he belongs there. It's strange to think that, not long ago, I was jealous of him trying to steal her away. But he was never doing that. He's just a boy who never knew what real love was.

Until now, when it might be too late.

Ruslan sobs as my mother pets the back of his head. "You're okay, *malchik*," she shushes. "I have you now."

"Why did Daddy do this?" he cries. "What did I do wrong?"

"Nothing." God, my heart can't fracture anymore. "You didn't do anything wrong."

"Then why? Why me?"

My mother and I share a look over his head. Her eyebrows crawl higher, her stare more pointed.

Yevgeniy ruins everything he touches! He hurt you, too, Mom. I try to tell her with only my eyes. *Remember that? There's no good in that man.* Running my hand lightly over Ruslan's back, I take a breath. When I stray too close to his tattooed shoulder he recoils away from my touch.

"Your father..." I start. "Do you understand what he does? What he *really* does?"

"He never tells me." Ruslan wrinkles his brow. "He's just says that he's going to protect me."

I swallow down the hard lump forming in my throat. "He's a liar. *He* is the bad man that he's always warning you about." I take a breath. "He's a killer. He hurts people"

"He says he only hurts people who want to hurt me," Ruslan argues weakly.

I shake my head. "He hurts anyone he feels like." Without meaning to I look at my mother. She flinches.

Ruslan notices, staring between us. "Did he hurt you, Mom?"

"I—." Mom starts. But she's having a hard time saying it.

"Yes," I cut in, giving my mom a glare that says *he needs to know, stop sheltering him.* "He has."

"Did he hurt you too?" Ruslan asks quietly, burying his hands in his shirt, and twisting the material over and over.

"Not yet," I tell him. "But he will. I'm sure of it."

I unconsciously cover my belly with my hands. *He's going*

to kill me. But I don't say it out loud. Because if I say it out loud, it'll be real.

Ruslan opens his fingers, staring at his palms, squeezing them at the air. He's holding something I can't see. "Because of that other man?"

The vision of Arsen splayed out, blood staining everything like syrup on a snow cone, makes me ill.

"Yes, because of that other man."

Ruslan tugs at his shirt near his shoulder. "I don't want to be like him."

Hugging Ruslan to her chest, my mother rubs her cheek in his hair. She fixes her solemn gaze on me. "You won't. I promise you that you won't"

"How?" I whisper to my mother, low enough that Ruslan can't hear. "That tattoo means he's chosen Ruslan as his heir. There's no going back now."

"Is that man really dead?" Ruslan asks urgently. "Did I kill him? I didn't mean to, I promise I didn't!" His breathing picks up again, and I'm afraid he'll start crying again.

"I don't know," I whisper, my voice coming apart as I admit it. "I want to believe he's alive."

"I... I don't want to be here anymore." With eyes shining from fresh tears, he looks up at me, chin shaking. "Get me out of here, Galina. Please. I'm afraid."

Me, too. My baby punches inside of my belly. I don't know if that was a fist or a foot; I picture a minuscule array of toes, a pair of footprints on the birth certificate, and bite back a hot swell of tears.

You can't cry right now. You have to be strong for all four of us.

I don't have the luxury of letting myself be consumed by my own misery.

With an indulgent smile I cup Ruslan's cheek. My

thumb makes streaks over the tears that have dried on his skin. "We're all going to get out of this. I swear. But I need you to stay strong and brave and fearless. Can you do that?"

He bites down until his chin stops wobbling. "Yes," he says, with all the confidence of a child who doesn't know how unfair the world can really be.

I tug at my prayer beds nervously. I've tried whispering into them multiple times, hoping Arsen can hear me. If he's listening, I want him to know that I'm alive. I wish I can tell him something more useful than that.

I don't know where I am... but if the beads are doing their job, that won't matter.

He'll track me down.

He'll find me.

He'll bring us all home.

42

ARSEN

The lake is frozen solid, blending into the land. Everything covered by a uniform blanket of snow. The only markings on the surface are the triangular tracks made by geese and other animals in search of food. My own bootprints cross on top of them as I make my way slowly over the ice.

I'm cold enough that I can't feel the tips of my ears or nose. But I don't mind. The mild pain is worth it. This weather is clearing my head. My bare hands clench in my jacket pockets, feeling for my phone, trying to summon a call from Josh or Mila or, God willing, Galina.

Galina... please be okay. You have to be okay.

If she's still wearing the prayer beads, I should be able to track her location. But I can't do that from my cabin. *The cops need to get away from my mansion. I can't do anything until they're off my back.*

A sharp *honk* echoes through the air. Craning my neck, I watch as a flock of geese, their black heads contrasting against the white clouds, soar overhead. I marvel at how effortlessly they sync together. Wordlessly, they fly as a unit through the sky like they were born to be there. One by one, they land on the far side of the lake, wanting to be as far from me as possible.

Pulling my hands from my pockets, I breath on them to warm them up. The clouds overhead split enough to create a few beams of sunlight. One of them dances on the silver ring wrapped around my finger.

I stare at it hard, like it's the first time I've seen it. Holding my hand high with my fingers spread, I frown at the memory of that day. *If I hadn't forced her to marry me... Yevgeniy might have left her alone.*

My phone buzzes to life. Ripping it out, I press it to my ear. "Hello?" I ask eagerly.

"It's me," Josh says.

I don't bother to keep my voice calm. "What is it?"

"It's done, just like you wanted. The police are backing off for now."

My pulse rockets higher. "You're sure?"

"The current task force the commissioner put together to hunt you down is temporarily suspended."

"That's good."

"Don't get too excited. It's only temporary. They're looking for any and all reasons to get it back up and running in full capacity."

"You couldn't convince them I'm not the problem?"

"It's hard to make a case for you when *I'm* still not sure what to believe. I've staked a lot of my own reputation for you, Isakov."

"Fuck your reputation. Your life is on the line," I remind him. "Yevgeniy wants you dead just as much as he wants that for me."

"So you say."

"You'll thank me when this is over."

"I doubt that very much. But it's not like I've got much of a choice at this point. What are you going to do?"

I start walking across the ice, my strides as quick as I can risk without slipping. "I'm ending this tonight. But since we're erring on the side of caution, keep the cops off my back for forty-eight hours."

Without another word, I hang up and start running.

The geese see me and begin to cry out in alarm in the crisp cold air. I watch as they launch themselves back into the sky, wings flapping against the canvas of golden clouds above.

Scaring off the peaceful animals wasn't intentional.

I wish I could have watched them a while longer.

"Arsen?" Mila asks when I burst through the front door. She was reclining on the large couch... the place Galina took a nap our first night here.

"We're leaving," I say, moving towards the kitchen table. I unzip the black bag I'd set there earlier, checking the contents.

"*Kuda?*"

Lifting out a rifle, I make sure it's loaded. "Back home." *Assuming nobody gets in the way. But if they try...* I chamber the gun, put it back in the bag, and sling it over my shoulder.

Mila jumps off the couch, rounding on me with her eyes wide in shock. "That son of a bitch actually did it?"

"I'm as shocked as you are, Mila."

"What do you need me to do?"

"We need as many men as possible. Organize everyone, and tell them to meet me at the mansion, then call Kos—" I stop short. For a moment, I'd forgotten he was dead.

Mila watches me closely. I lift my head higher, trying to keep my voice as flat and emotionless as possible. "Call

Maxim and have him collect men across the city. We're ending this *today*. Do or die."

"Do or die," she agrees, more enthusiastically than she needs to. "I'm on it."

I nod and make my way towards my car. There's no time to get buried under regrets. Not now. Another time will come to mourn for all the lives that we've lost.

And by morning, I'm sure there will be many more graves to dig.

Ulyana dips her head. "Welcome home."

She's not alone in the foyer. Word of my arrival has spread fast. I spotted the faces of my staff through the windows of my mansion, watching eagerly as my car rolled up. Many of them have chosen to arrange themselves in the main room, but the staircase is lined as well.

Ignoring their gazes, I focus my attention on Ulyana. "Is Matvey here?"

"He is."

"Good," I say, passing her by and nearly sprinting up the stairs. The two maids by the banister press against the wall to give me space.

"Arsen?" Ulyana calls out. She watches me with her body in a stiff line. Her outfit is as crisp and perfect as ever. She's acting like this is just another day, but the angle of her lips and brow says otherwise.

"Bring her back. This place is too quiet without her."

I allow myself a tired smile. "I will."

Dashing up the stairs, I dodge more of my staff. All of them offer kind smiles or happy bows. My home is *packed* with people who are invested in my existence. And yet, as full as every floor is, it feels... wrong. It's in the smell of it, the quiet, pregnant pause that grows as I walk across the lengthy rug.

I pass a door—*her door*—and pull up short. Staring at my own warped reflection on the brass knob, I hold my breath. Logically, I fucking know she isn't inside. Yet I thrust the door open anyway.

The bed is pristine and perfect and miserably empty. Everything is clean, and the stringent smell of disinfectant hangs in the air, reminding me of a hospital. Her scent has been eradicated.

There's no evidence she was ever here.

This may be my house. But as long as Galina isn't here, it's not my *home*.

My hand trembles as I shut the door. I can't bear to be in that room a second longer. Not without her. Marching further through the house, I arrive at the computer room. The door is half-open, three computers lit up, the glow of their monitors make me squint uncomfortably.

Two men in wheeled office chairs spin to face me. Matvey rips his headset down to his neck. "Arsen Kirilovich."

I motion at the computers. "Pull up Galina's tracker."

"Already have it." He taps the keyboard, then the screen, indicating a flashing dot on a darkened program. It's a top-down view of the city, the buildings and roads outlined in pale gray. "She's there."

Hunching over the back of his chair, I frown in disbelief. "She's only fifteen miles away?"

"The tracker is." He hesitates before he corrects me. "I can't say if she's with it or not."

I fight down the urge to snap at him. I can hear Ulyana's words again. *In here, your people should trust you. They should be eager to come to you with their fears and worries and doubts. Yet they don't.*

"She's there," I finally say after I compose myself. "I'm sure of it." Yevgeniy *could* have removed the bracelet himself. Galina, too, if she thought she had no other choice. I have to hold out on hope. It's all I've got at this stage.

Well...

That, and an army.

"Send this location to my phone," I continue as I exit the room. I can't linger any longer. There's no time to lose. My head is abuzz, like a bloodhound that has caught a scent. *Galina... I'm coming for you.*

I step through my front door; the sunlight on the snow blinds me briefly.

"Pakhan!"

Shielding my eyes, I barely make out the stern face of Maxim. He's waiting for me in front of my car in the driveway. Behind him is a full double row of men, all of them standing at attention. On their hips, or strapped over their chests, are guns of every shape and size. From young faces to the stern and scarred, muscular frames to lean, they all share one thing—their attention is devoted to me.

"We're ready," Maxim says with pride.

I nod sharply. "Let's go pay Yevgeniy a visit he won't fucking forget."

When I arrived, I was alone in my black Escalade. Ten cars leave my mansion. We form a single line, bumper to bumper, along the quiet strip of asphalt that leads from my secluded mansion towards the city. From above we'd form an elegant shape. *Like the geese,* I think suddenly. The image sticks in my brain.

I'm at the front of the pack, and when we reach the first split, I speak into my phone hooked up to my car's Bluetooth system. "Split up and maintain dispersion. We don't need to look *too* obvious. I want every bit of surprise we can get"

"*Ponil*," Maxim responds, and relays the order to the others.

When I pull down a backstreet, an engine revs loudly near my tail light.

A motorcycle pulls beside me, the helmet a mix of white and blue. It matches the moto jacket zipped to their chin. The rider turns to me and signals me to roll my window down. When I do, she yanks the helmet off, and shakes out her hair. It's Mila.

"When did you get the new gear?" I ask her.

"How I spend my money is none of your business. I'm going to go ahead, scope the situation out."

"Be careful," I warn her. "*Eto moi prikaz.*"

Instead of answering she covers her face again. The motorcycle roars like a grizzly bear, and she zips off around the corner, leaving my sight. At the speed she's going, she risks getting pulled over. I stare at the streak of rubber she left. *She's eager to get to the scene.* This fight isn't just about Galina.

Mila wants Yevgeniy to rot in a hole as much as I do.

She's the one who's been accusing ME of being suicidal.

Is that why she splurged on brand new motorcycle gear? To enjoy it in case this was her last ride?

Crushing the steering wheel, I press harder on the gas. I refuse to allow her to die for me. I'm done burying my friends.

It's not long before I dip through a section of the city that borders a number of old factories. The ocean frames my right side, the waves loud as they crash, refusing to be frozen by the icy weather. It's a relief it's not snowing—and I pick up speed around another bend in the road, passing by a number of barren stripes of dirty land.

The road splits again and I glance at my tracker, turning further away from the water. Yevgeniy has positioned himself on the outskirts of everything. Before I see the actual building, he's barricaded himself in, I spot Mila.

She stands on the edge of the road, her helmet hooked on the handlebar of her motorcycle, waving frantically at me.

Parking behind her I jump out of my car. "We're still half a mile from where we need to go."

Her lips shape into a severe frown. "He's got a whole damn perimeter of cops around this place."

All the muscles in my upper back clench. Gazing over the horizon, I try to glimpse what she's talking about, but there are too many half-finished buildings blocking the view.

"Looks like Josh wasn't as effective as he made it sound," I grumble.

"You think he's gone back on the deal?" she asks.

"No. If they're here, it's because they were already Yevgeniy's men to start with." Popping my trunk, I unzip my large bag, shouldering my rifle. "Time to see if they're really that willing to die for him."

Mila taps her fingertips on her mouth. "That's risky."

"There's no other option."

Gravel crunches behind me; one by one the cars packed with my soldiers arrive. They park quickly, and exit even faster.

"At least we have the element of surprise," Mila chuckles.

"That we do," I say, motioning at the multitude of armed men all lining up in the road, ready to heed any instruction I give them. "I forced Yevgeniy out of his position as Pakhan once. I'm going to make it permanent this time."

My men's faces light up with pride when they hear me. Maxim cocks his gun, his chin high as he waits for more instruction. Some of the others let out soft murmurs of excited agreement. Each of them is a coiled spring, ready to leap forth.

"Boys." Holding my rifle overhead, I point it down the road. "Are we afraid of a few little piggies?"

As a unit they shout *NO!* Shaking their heads or spitting on the ground, they pledge themselves to the cause. My heart floods with appreciation for my soldiers.

Using my gun like a flag, I wave it over the road. "*Davai!*"

They don't hesitate—they rush forward, lips pressed in scowls, some in wicked grins, their eyes alive with the fire of men ready to shed blood. This is what we've been building up to for years. I can't call them back now no matter how hard I try.

I start to follow them. Mila grabs my shoulder. "Not you."

"What do you mean?" I ask curtly.

"Let me direct the fight."

My eyes widen, taking in the solid way her shoulders are set. She fingers the knife on her hip. "Mila—" I start to argue.

"Let me finish!" She digs her hand into my shoulder tighter. " Your job is rescuing Galina. Leave me and the boys to do what we do best."

I'm already shaking my head furiously. "I need to be here for this."

"If something happens to her because you got there too late, you'll never forgive yourself. Even if we manage to take Yevgeniy down, if it comes at the cost of Galina, the Bratva will fall apart. *You* will fall apart. That's no victory."

Biting my molars together, I gaze at the last of my

soldiers as they head over the asphalt. The first gunshot cracks the air. Then a second, a third, until each staccato gunfire turns into a steady shriek.

"Let us be the distraction you need," she pleads with me. "So you can do what you must."

The song of battle grows. Mingled with the crack of gunfire are the shouts of dying men. How many will fall in my name? How many are going to die because I brought them here?

Their deaths can't be for nothing.

I nod.

"Get it done," I tell her as another rattle of gunfire splits the air.

A savage smile twists on Mila's face. With a serrated knife in one hand, and a pistol in the other, she sprints over the hard packed dirt to join the fight.

Checking my earpiece, then my rifle, I follow after her towards the fray. Red and blue lights flash in a quick tempo as I crest over the hill. It's just like Mila said—there's a whole damn perimeter of cops blocking the road. They spill onto the gravel, the cracked mud, insuring there's no gap between them and the townhouse in the background.

I swear as a bullet flies past my ear, snapping in the air. Ducking onto my belly, I check around, searching for the shooter. No one is aiming at me. The shot was a random one—the police are fighting for their lives, and in doing so, are blind to the actions of a single figure like me.

I get on my knees like a man in the midst of prayer. And in a way, I am. I'm praying for the safety of everyone I know, I'm praying that I'm not too late, and above all, I'm praying that by the time the sun rises in the morning, this will all be over.

And with that, I sling the rifle onto my back, and stare down at the situation.

As long as I don't shoot back, I'll be a ghost.

Knowing it's the only way to save Galina, I begin to crawl.

43

GALINA

"What's that noise?" Mom asks me nervously.

Cocking my head, I listen with my pulse quickening. "Gunfire."

"Someone's shooting at us?" Ruslan shudders, scrambling towards my mother where she's sitting on the bed. She spreads her arms to welcome him into her lap, the action warm and natural.

I move towards the one window in the room. Parting the thin, yellowed curtains, I peek through the glass. I can't tell what's happening, there's a large tree branch with stubborn frost crusted to it blocking the way.

"What do you see?" Mom asks urgently.

"Nothing. I don't know what's going on." But I have a feeling. One so delicious, so exciting, I try to ignore it because the pain of being wrong would tear me apart.

The door bangs open, hitting the wall, bouncing back into Yevgeniy's grip. His lips are curved in a wretched snarl. "You! What did you do?" he shouts at me.

I let go of the curtain, my heart tap-dancing into my

mouth. I don't like the manic expression he's wearing as he shuts himself inside the room.

"What are you talking about?" I ask.

"The police I arranged to guard this place are under attack!"

The gunfire outside seems to grow louder. It isn't, not really, it's just that I'm listening to it with more interest. *It's Arsen! It has to!* The part of me that was afraid to hope grows big enough that it lifts my lips in a helpless smile.

"Scared?"

"Fuck no," he growls. Storming towards me at a rapid pace, he blocks me against the wall with both hands. His breath is humid on my cheeks. "I care more about how he found us!"

I cringe away as much as I can. "I didn't tell him anything."

"Liar!" He snatches my wrist, hauling me onto the tips of my toes. "I'll kill you!"

A crackling sensation spreads up my neck as every hair on my body stands at attention. Yevgeniy is close enough that I can see the red veins webbing in the whites of his eyes. His chest rises and falls; he's worked up.

Afraid.

"Why are you *smiling?*" he demands, shaking me.

"Because Arsen is alive. He's going to save us." I laugh so hard I begin to hiccup. *He's here, he really came! We're going to be okay!* My hand drifts down to my belly. *All of us.* "And he's going to *kill you.*"

Yevgeniy goes still as the surface of a fetid pond in the heat of summer. His fingers burrow into my wrist until the burst of pain breaks through my joy, forcing me to cry out.

"You think you're saved? You really think I'd let him get what he wants after all of this?"

His shoulder bunches up. My eyes bulge in terror, my body racing to react to protect me in time. I'm too slow—he slams me into the wall, my skull bouncing off the solid plaster. Pain explodes behind my eyes from the force of the impact. I can taste blood in my mouth.

"Galina!" Mom shrieks.

I scrape at his arms, and when he doesn't release me, I go for his face, but he simply holds me further away. "There's nothing you can do to stop him," I wheeze.

He slams me into the wall again. It's like my brain is being knocked back and forth. My eyes start blurring, unable to focus on anything but the pain along my spine. I can't see or move, and all I manage to do is bury my nails deeper into his wrist.

"You fucking cunt!" he yells. I can barely hear him from the throbbing headache. I don't hear the gunfire anymore. I don't know what's up or down or if I'm blacking out.

Is this what dying feels like?

"Leave her alone!" Ruslan jumps onto his father's leg, yanking at him with all his might.

"Ruslan!" Mom's voice cracks.

All the pressure vanishes from my arms; Yevgeniy has let me go. Unable to stand, I collapse against the wall at his feet. He turns away, looming over Ruslan with hatred blackening his stare.

"You ungrateful welp!"

My vision is still swaying when Yevgeniy backhands Ruslan. My mom screams, her fear and my own bringing me to my senses. Everything is in hyper focus. Veins bulge on Yevgeniy's hands, saliva drips from Ruslan's gawking mouth.

"Get away from him!" I shout.

Ignoring me, he crowds over Ruslan, holding him flat to

the floor with one wide palm on his tiny chest. He hits him again, the sound wet and awful.

"I was too soft on you." His knuckles land on the boy's jaw, splitting his lip. "You want to die to protect that cunt? Fine! I can always start again and make a replacement. And next time, I won't make the same mistake I did with you!"

"Get away from him!" Mom yells, leaping onto Yevgeniy's back.

Hunching like a bull ready to buck, he half-rises, spinning as my mother hangs on desperately. "You too, Katyusha?" In a single easy swing he loops his hands around her and slams her to the floor. The whole room shakes—it resonates in my teeth. He turns back to punching Ruslan.

Rage courses through my blood. Reaching inside my shirt, I feel for the small object I've kept close to my heart—the rose brooch from my father.

Clutching it like a dagger, I run at Yevgeniy, stabbing the sharp end of the rose brooch into his shoulder. "Leave him alone! You fucking asshole!"

He shouts, surprised by the assault. I wrench my arm back, stabbing him a second time, and then a third. The wounds are small but his grimace and the blood they draw are satisfying. My mother crawls back to us, joining me in trying to force Yevgeniy away from their son.

Together, we're able to maneuver him towards the window.

He's not talking anymore, just making a low grinding noise in his throat. I'm using all my effort to hold him back now, panting until my throat is dry, occasionally losing my grip from my sweaty palms. Mom has her whole body tangled on his waist, her hair hanging in her face. We're doing it—we're protecting Ruslan.

The solid impact of Yevgeniy's fist into my stomach

knocks me back. I stagger, landing on my backside, the rose brooch remaining in his skin. There's such vicious hatred in his eyes that it's like he's still punching me.

Quickly, I cradle my belly, wrapping myself around it like I'm tying myself in a knot.

No... my baby!

"Galina!" Mom yells.

"Galina," Yevgeniy mocks her, twisting with his free arm to pull the pin from his arm. He throws it at me; it skids into my leg. Fisting my mother's hair, he tears pieces of it free, the strands floating away as my mother cries out in pain.

I watch helplessly as he slams her to the floor again. She tucks her knees to her chest, curling into a ball, trying to protect herself from his next assault.

But he doesn't punch her. He doesn't kick. Straddling my mother, Yevgeniy wraps his hands around her skinny throat and starts squeezing. She bats at his powerful forearms as her face starts turning blue.

"No..." I heave as a sharp pain rushes through me. "Stop it... Mom..."

Yevgeniy's breathing becomes labored, his grin widening until it makes his jaw click. This isn't simple revenge—he's *enjoying* this.

I inch across the floor, not caring that I'm getting rug burn. *Please let me move, please! I need to help her!* My body won't obey, each small movement is sending another jagged agony in my stomach.

Mom's hands start slowing down. The feral grin on Yevgeniy's face widens.

No! No! No!

I'll never reach her in time.

The door is kicked inward, the hinges breaking off on the bottom, causing it to swing at an angle. Yevgeniy whips around to see who's interrupted us. His eyes protrude, his hands loosening on Mom's throat. She coughs weakly, sucking in oxygen while her skin changes back to normal.

"I expected you would show up eventually," Yevgeniy says flatly.

At first I don't believe what I'm seeing. There's a man in the doorway. He's gripping a rifle as long as his torso. When he turns his silvery blue eyes at me, relief floods through my bones, my muscles, giving me enough strength to rise onto my hands and knees. "Arsen," I breathe.

He spares a glance at me before aiming the gun at Yevgeniy.

"Ah-ah-ah," Yevgeniy taunts, wrenching my mother tighter to his chest as he rises to his full height, dragging her along, not caring how she struggles. "You wouldn't want to hit her."

Arsen's fingers curl firmly around the butt of the rifle. Every finger except the one on the trigger. He's in a standoff with Yevgeniy, one he plans to win. He could end Yevgeniy's life in a simply flex of his hand. Years of his seething hatred and lust for revenge finally sated in a split second.

But I can see in the depths of his eyes... in the way his brow furrows ever slightly... that he's not going to shoot.

He promised to save my mother and me, he's not going to break his word. The gentle rasp of nervous breathing reaches my ears. Looking over, I spot Ruslan. His whole face is a swollen mess, his bottom lip cracked and bleeding onto the front of his shirt. His small body quivers from both pain and fear.

He locks his eyes on mine. *Be strong,* I mouth.

His shaking recedes; he swallows, like he's gathering himself up. Glancing at Arsen, then towards Yevgeniy, he stumbles forward. I'm the only one watching when he launches himself onto Yevgeniy's back. He doesn't make a sound, but his father does. "What are you doing?" he demands, craning his neck to see.

Ruslan clings on tight, even when Yevgeniy backs up into the wall, crushing his own son. Yevgeniy shifts his arms, holding my mother with one around her throat while snatching at Ruslan. He catches the boy's shirt, ripping the cloth. The black crown shines when it's exposed to the light.

Using both his thumbs, Ruslan digs into his father's face. His knuckles and nails grind in, deep as possible, the liquid *squish* turning my stomach.

"Fuck!" Yevgeniy roars, releasing my mother.

She falls forward, hitting the floor and lying limply on her side. Yevgeniy tugs desperately at Ruslan's arms, trying to dislodge him to no avail. "You little shit! I'll make you pay for this!"

"Ruslan!" Arsen shouts. "Let go!"

Ruslan obediently does as Arsen commands, rolling on the ground in my direction. I scoop him into my arms, holding his cheek to my chest protectively. He doesn't see the rifle go off, but I do.

Blood sprays from Yevgeniy's chest, running down in rivulets that pool at his crumpling knees.

His lips move soundlessly. Wiping his hands over his ribs, he raises them up, staring in shock at the red on his palms. Arsen angles the rifle down. He could keep studding Yevgeniy with bullets, and honestly, it's a wonder he doesn't. This awful man murdered his pregnant wife... he's caused Arsen untold levels of pain for years. In his shoes, I'd empty the entire clip.

Instead, he just stares at Yevgeniy, who angles his chin up as if he's going to say something.

But the only sound that emerges from his throat is a wet

cough, sending crimson spittle everywhere. And then, just like that, he tumbles forward.

Dead.

Ruslan whimpers in my arms. "Are you okay?" I ask him.

"Yes," he says into my shirt, before shifting around.

I grab the back of his head. "Don't look."

"Let him," Arsen says. "He should see what's become of the monster that was his father."

I start to argue, but Ruslan wriggles firmly out of my arms. The boy who was trembling and broken a moment ago is gone. This child has a serious, grim face, his mouth a hard line. He looks pointedly at his dead father, quietly judging him where he lies. His hand rubs on his tattoo. I hold my breath, waiting for him to cry, but he only closes his eyes and nods.

Arsen shoulders his rifle, then helps my mother to her feet. She gives him a grateful smile.

"I'll be fine," she assures him. Her hand gingerly brushes the bruises already forming on her neck. "Check on Galina. She's hurt."

A new wave of fire lights up in Arsen's eyes. If Yevgeniy wasn't already dead, he'd be tearing him apart. Crossing the room in just two long strides, he crouches before me, scooping my cheeks into his warm palms. God, I've missed these hands. "Galina, what—"

My lips press onto his before he finishes the question. He tenses up, his hands locking on me tighter. There's no hesitance when he kisses me back, his fingers seeking my hair, my jaw, my shoulders. I do the same, because I want to make sure this is real. I need to feel his solid existence, because if I don't, my heart might deflate. *This is real. He is real!*

"I wished for this," I croak as I end the kiss. "I hoped so

badly that you'd show up and save us, and you did it. You actually did it."

"Of course I did." He traces his thumb over my cheek, just under my left eye where the tears are pooling. "I was never going to let him take you away from me."

"I can't believe it," I whisper, "It's over."

The joy leaves his face. "No," Arsen says. He guides me to my feet, makes sure I'm steady, then moves to the window, peering out at the world. "There's more left to do." He considers all of us one by one. "We need to get out of here. Can you run?"

He's asking everyone, but really, he's asking me.

I step forward—a searing pain tsunamis through my belly. It forces me to suck in air, catching my breath and bracing for more of the awful sensation. Nothing happens.

"Galina?" Arsen asks warily.

"I can," I say confidently, "I have to."

He smiles in relief, but my mother catches my eye.

She knows I'm lying.

Something could be wrong with my baby... the idea haunts me, the cold claws of death playing with my mind. As we leave the room, I run my hand anxiously in circles over my belly, over the spot the pain occurred. Each step tugs at my innards. Never mind running, walking is a challenge. But I have to push the agony aside.

Arsen risked his life to save me.

If he needs me to run...

I'll run.

44

ARSEN

Night has become day from the fires of the chattering rifles. Each time a muzzle flashes I can see the face of the man firing it. Whether an enemy or one of my own *boeviki*, they all have the same feral expression.

Everyone is fighting for their life.

Including me.

"This way," I urge Galina, holding her by her wrist. We wasted enough time hovering inside the front door of Yevgeniy's hideaway. I had to get my bearings, but I know we can't linger. As helpful as this chaos is, someone is bound to come and check on Yevgeniy.

Not every one of his men is a corrupt cop, some are as loyal to him as my own brigadiers.

Galina tugs backwards. "Wait!"

"No time," I argue, stopping on the front step. She's gawking at the fighting behind me. Her eyes shine with flashes of guns going off, the sound loud in my skull. Katya and Ruslan crouch behind her. They're just as afraid. "If we stay here, we'll be found, and then—"

The wood of the door-frame explodes next to my ear.

Splinters stab into my temple and cheek. Grunting, I lurch away, ducking inside the house with my body shielding Galina.

"Look out!" I warn, eyeballing the fighting over my shoulder. I wait for another shot. When it doesn't come, I feel safe enough to breathe. "That wasn't someone aiming at us," I explain, "it was an accident."

Katya presses her lips together. She's pale to the point I'm wary she'll faint. "Who cares if it wasn't on purpose? A bullet is a bullet!"

"Mom is right," Galina agrees. "Is it even possible to run out there without getting hit?"

"I don't want to die," Ruslan says. He's not crying, his young face looks older, like what happened upstairs has aged him. There's a twinge of guilt running through me. I had no intention of ruining his innocence, but Ruslan was always destined for this hard life. One way or another, he's going to have to confront the reality of being born into the Bratva.

Gauging the fire-fight, I grit my teeth with a frustrated growl. *We need to run, but dodging bullets is impossible!* Holstering my gun—I refuse to let go of Galina with my other hand—I touch my earpiece.

"Mila, I've got them. All of them."

There's a static crackle. My pulse goes haywire the longer the silence stretches. Is she going to respond, or did something happen to her?

"Mila, come in."

"I hear you," Mila finally says.

Exhaling loudly, I peer through the open doorway again. "We're coming out the front, I need you to clear us a path!"

"On it!"

Hoisting my rifle once again, I tighten my hold on

Galina. "Everything will be okay." I don't know if I'm trying to convince her or myself.

She squeezes me back, her hand warm and welcome. "I trust you," she says earnestly.

Calming myself with a few breaths, I square up with the door. "Everyone, stay close to me. Don't slow down, don't hesitate. Got it?"

When I hear their murmurs of agreement, I bound forward. My first steps are patient and careful. The instant we're exposed to the crisp night air, the shelter of the building's walls gone, I start to run.

Blood thrums in my eardrums like the crashing waves of the sea—nostalgic and familiar, a reminder of a simpler time in my life when all I had to worry about was if I'd hook my thumb while threading lures with my father on the docks.

Bullets crack overhead. The snow in front of us has been tamped down into mud and slush. The red blood of fallen bodies swirl in the mix of gray. Everywhere is the copper-penny scent of death.

"I see you!" Mila yells in my ear. "On your left!"

Jerking sideways, I pull Galina out of the way, aiming my rifle at the cop about to jump on us. My muzzle flashes, casting light over his wretched scowl. Half his face vanishes in a spray of blood and bone. Katya screams, but Galina and Ruslan don't make a sound. They're becoming numb to the violence. Or maybe they're still in shock.

Galina wipes at the blood splatter on her shirt. I give her a tug.

"Look at me." When she does, I say, "Don't think about it. Just grab my hand and look at my feet. That's all you have to do."

Jutting out her chin, she nods and drops her stare to my boots.

Another cop rushes at us—one of my men takes him out before he gets close. Two more have spotted me. The *crack-crack of* a pair of perfectly aimed bullets is the only warning before they both fall in a heap.

"Keep moving!" Mila's voice in my ear guides me. "Another hundred feet! I'm straight ahead of you!"

Hanging on to Galina with my rifle aimed forward, I lead us across the yard. The slick ground is only half the problem; I trip on the corpses that have piled up. I make a note of every one of my soldiers. I'll acknowledge their sacrifice properly when the time comes.

My chest is searing from exertion, but I keep pushing onward. Adrenaline is what keeps me moving at this point. That... and the knowledge I'm almost there. I've killed Yevgeniy, rescued Galina and her mother, and ensured our future all in one stroke.

It doesn't matter if I'm exhausted—I'll run for another hundred miles if I have to.

A scream as ragged as the edge of an old saw-blade floods my ears. Galina's grip on my hand goes slack—she's not running anymore as she pulls me down to the ground.

Terror grips my heart before I look to see what's happened.

Galina is on her knees in the snow, one arm folded over her ribs. The blood is dark and bright and it's all I see. "Galina!" I cry.

Her mother, aghast at the sight of her daughter's injury, falls beside her. She tries to help Galina to her feet. Ruslan looks on in dazed confusion. The bullets haven't stopped darting around us. A cop stands nearby, his gun letting off steam in the cold air. His smug sneer is the only proof I need to know *he's* the one who's done this.

Diving to the ground, I yank Ruslan low to the ground, and then level my rifle. The cop shifts his aim to me, but he's too slow. My shot hits him square in the chest, and he crumples like a sack of potatoes from where he stands.

I drop my rifle, scooping Galina into my arms. "Galina, Galina!"

There's blood on her lips, her eyes are wide but unfocused. The only thing she's actively doing is clutching her stomach protectively.

Just like in my nightmares.

"Mila!" I roar. "Galina's been shot!"

"On my way!" she replies, so loudly the static crunches.

My rifle remains by my feet. I need both arms to lift Galina. Hoisting her close to my chest, I search the distance for a sign of Mila. I'm more vulnerable than ever.

"Follow me!" I snap, not looking to make sure that Katya and Ruslan obey.

Sprinting around dead friends and foes, I bend forward, straining to make my legs pump faster. I've never run so fast in my life. The sound of their heavy breathing and stomping feet confirms that Katya and Ruslan aren't far behind.

Mila, please, where are you? I glance down at Galina. Her face his white, like all her color has spilled onto the front of her clothing. *Don't die, don't you dare fucking die!*

Tires screech, high-beams blasting me in the face. The tell-tale red and blue lights on the top of the police car send me into a panic. Even if I *had* a free hand to draw a weapon, I left mine far behind.

"Arsen!" Mila yells out the driver's side window.

"You stole a cop car?" I ask her in surprise.

She looks beyond me. Lifting her pistol, she fires off

three quick shots. The cops who were trying to close in on us groan, gag, and fall. I didn't see them coming.

"Just get in," she shouts. "Before the rest of them figure it out!"

"You're a fucking angel." Katya and Ruslan climb inside the car. I join them, clutching Galina in my lap in the backseat. Her chest rises and falls erratically, her breathing more tremor than air.

"Galina, do you hear me? Galina?" Carefully I remove her hand from where it clutches her ribs. The wound gushes—I flatten my palm on top with a hiss. "Go, Mila! Get us to a hospital now!'

She takes off, sending sludge everywhere as the car's tires spin. For an awful moment I think we're stuck in the mud. The vehicle jostles, twists, then we're tearing over the ground onto the cracked street. The gunfire continues in the distance, I can hear it long after we're around the curve in the road.

"There's a lot of blood," Katya whispers, looking worriedly at me. Ruslan cranes his neck from the front passenger seat. His eyebrows contort tightly, his jaw shaking as he bites back tears. I think he's trying his best to be brave. Is it for himself, or for Galina?

Linking my fingers in Galina's with my other hand, I kiss her forehead. She's clammy, cold as ice. The only part of her that's warm is the endlessly seeping wound. Her lashes flutter like the wings of a moth struggling in a spider's web.

"Arsen?" she whispers weakly.

"Yes, *ptichka?*" I fight back the hot pressure of devastated tears. "You made it. We're going to the hospital now."

Her smile takes a full five seconds to form. I hate how pale her lips are. "You'll take care of them, right?"

I tense up. "Take care of who?"

She swallows. "Mom and Ruslan. Someone has to make sure they're alright, they don't have anyone else."

"Don't," I scold her gently. "Don't you dare say your goodbyes right now."

Galina turns slightly, her eyes finally clearing enough to focus on mine. She lifts her hand, wincing as she does it. When she tries to reach my face, she starts to shake—I grip her hand, pressing it to my cheek, and she sighs in appreciation. "Thank you for everything."

"Don't," I whisper.

"You should show her the cabin," she says, her voice getting quieter, each word a struggle. "Mom would love to see that lake."

"Galina, stop talking like this is the end!"

"I love you, Arsen. Through everything that happened... I never stopped. Not once. I need you to know that."

"Galina—"

"Tell me you believe me."

I breathe in shakily. There's something thick in my throat making my voice raspy. "I believe you."

She smiles sweetly before shutting her eyes.

"You're going to live, Galina. I love you and you're going to make it! You and our baby both. Okay? Do you hear me?"

She doesn't respond.

"Galina?" Katya asks nervously.

I roar at Mila until my neck twinges from the force of my distress. "Can't you go any faster?"

"I'm going as fast as I can!" she assures me. "Almost there!"

The sirens are blaring. Nobody blocks us as we speed into the parking lot of the hospital, the entire vehicle jolting violently as Mila slamming on the brakes.

I move in a nightmarish haze. The world around me

transforms into a blur, like someone has smeared Vaseline over my eyes. I carry Galina into the hospital, yelling over and over for a doctor, not stopping when my voice shatters into razors that slice my vocal cords apart.

A sea of scrubs rush at me. Two of them take Galina, setting her gently onto a stretcher. It's just like the one I was strapped to when Yevgeniy's men kidnapped me. The sight of it sends a cold ball of dread sinking through my gut. I can't get a full breath, can't decide if I want to rip her away from these strangers or beg them to wheel her away.

I'm robbed of the choice when they begin to move her towards a set of double doors. I'm following, until a hand grips my shoulder, forcing me backwards. I nearly backhand them, recognizing Mila at the last second. Her face is grave, commanding me to *stay.*

"Let them help her," she explains. "There's nothing you can do anymore."

Katya and Ruslan gaze at the awful scene. A nurse approaches us, asking for information, trying to understand what's happened. When I don't answer, Katya lifts her head higher, summoning the strength to speak to the woman.

Mila pulls at me again, encouraging me towards the sitting area. I don't budge, I'm too busy watching Galina, spread out and vulnerable, being swept out of my sight. She's nearly gone through the doors into the hallway when the machine attached to her that a doctor is wheeling alongside begins to screech.

The urgency in the air is suffocating. My hair stands on end, heat spreading up my back, into my skull, until I expect my head to split. *She's flat lining.* I told her she would be okay...

"No." I try to scream it, it comes out as a fragile croak. I collapse to the hard tiles on my hands and knees, crawling forward as the last of my energy leaks away.

"No... dear god... please, no..."

Hanging my head, I fill my chest with so much air that my lungs swell painfully. Everything hurts. I don't care—let the agony come. I'd die a thousand times if it meant Galina would live instead.

With the torturous squeal of the machine in my ears, I lift my eyes, hoping I'm wrong. *Let me see her... let her sit up and smile and laugh. Let the love of my life be alright. Her—our—baby please...*

PLEASE!

But instead, all I hear is the single piercing note of the flatline.

It's happening again.

I'm going to lose everything again.

I defeated Yevgeniy but he still won.

With my hands in fists, I pound the tile, throwing my head back. The barrier that made my voice crumble is gone. That time, when I scream, the sound fills the hospital until it drowns out every other sound.

I scream helplessly until my throat goes numb, and then I scream some more.

I don't think I'll ever stop.

45

GALINA

MY TOES ARE PERFECTLY POINTED AS I STRUT ACROSS THE stage. A simple ankle-turn and I'm pivoting, another and another and I'm a flurry of motion, my white tutu fluffing like a dandelion on the breeze. I was born to dance. I know this in my soul.

Curtains flutter around me, brushing me as if they want to hold me close. The only person I want a hug from is the man sitting in the audience.

Dad beams proudly, never taking his eyes off of me.

I'm so glad I decided to do this performance! I'd been terrified when Mom suggested it, the moves were advanced for a ten-year-old like me, but she would always click her tongue and insist that *she* did ballet like this when she was my age.

But Dad?

He caught me fretting in the studio, staring at myself awkwardly in the tall mirrors. He'd come to me, knelt, and told me not to be afraid of the stage. *Even if you make a mistake, it won't matter to me. If you get nervous, just look for me in the audience, malyshka.*

Lunging forward, I hold my breath, chest high. Every

time I've tried the Fouetté, I've failed. Days of practicing it have filled me with confidence. *Dad is watching, you can do it!* I start the spin, hands held high, one leg whipping forward. For a moment I'm weightless, perfectly pointed from toe to fingertips.

My ankle flexes wrong, sending me stumbling off balance. Crying out, I hit the stage on my knee, skidding a foot on the polished wood.

"No!" I whisper furiously, hanging my head low. My hair is bound back in a scalp-tingling bun. I grab the elastic, yanking at it until my dark tresses tumble everywhere. "No, no, no!"

Footsteps thud heavily on the stage. "Galina, are you alright?" Dad asks, kneeling beside me.

Tears boil in my eyes; I wipe them away roughly, but more replace them.

"Why do I keep messing up? Why can't I do it?"

"Everyone makes mistakes, *malyshka*" he chuckles kindly.

"But *I* shouldn't make that mistake! It's not fair!" I challenge him with a petulant glare, my cheeks as fiery as my shout.

He watches me for a moment, the depths of his dark eyes warming with love. "Oh, *malyshka*." Taking my messy hair in his hands, he carefully winds it back up, tying it into a bun as he speaks. "It's not about fairness. Sometimes life just doesn't go the way we want it to."

"That's happening a lot, lately," I complain.

"It happens to the best of us. Even you."

Pouting, I cross my arms and look pointedly at everywhere but him. I don't *want* to accept that it can happen to me. All my mistakes... all the lies I've told... all the ways I've hurt people.

Something loops through my brain. The scent of roses... a black tattoo... a ballet stage, like this one, but bigger. It's a memory that's trying to hook into my brain. But before it can, I shake it off and raise my head to find Dad smiling at me.

"What should I do?" I ask in a quiet hush.

His hands leave my hair. The bun is tight, but random strands have escaped it. It isn't perfect. "Just get back up. That's all anyone can do. Don't think about your mistakes, just think about trying again. That's what matters the most."

I try to stand, but my legs are numb, like they've fallen asleep. My father coughs into his fist. I squint at him, noting the hollows shadows around his eyes, the yellow tinge to his skin. *He's sick. But he'll get better. He has to! He always gets better.*

I brush my hands over my tutu, but it's gone now, and all I see are rose petals. They look like the ones in Arsen's garden. My heart staggers in my chest. Lurching, I hug my body with a whimper. "Daddy, why does everything *hurt?*"

"You're alright, *malyshka*," he soothes me, cradling me closer. "You're okay, I'm here."

The curtains flutter around me again. But this time, I can tell that something's not right. The stage doesn't look as real as I thought. And Dad... his face continues to change. His eyes sink deeper into hollow pits. His face becomes sallow and stretched.

I'm no longer a ten-year-old girl.

And the pain. Oh God, the pain. It hurts so much.

"None of this is real," I whisper as realization hits me. "You died."

And then a worse realization hits me.

"You're not my real father," I whisper. "You never were. I

am Galina Yevgeniyevna... And I can't change that." Hot tears roll from my eyes even as I try to stop them from falling.

His gentle hands brush my temples. Familiar wide fingers that belong to strong hands tuck my hair behind my ear. He's worked himself to the bone from the moment he arrived in this country until the day he passed away. Gently, he plants a kiss on my forehead.

"It doesn't matter, *malyshka*. You know who you are in your heart," he says. "And nobody can take that from you. As far as I'm concerned, you will *always* be Galina Stepanovna."

I blink back a heavy shower of tears.

"Arsen says that, too," I sniffle. "I wish you could've met him."

"Tell me about him," he says.

"Where do I start? He's selfish but protective. Smart yet bone-headed. Kind in his own way yet terribly jealousy. He does what he thinks is best and it's not always right. But he'd die for me, he'd burn down the world for me, even if I begged him not to." I place my hand on my stomach. There's a strange twinge of pain—the world around me wobbles like steam has entered my eyes. "And I'm going to have his baby."

My father considers me in curious silence. "Does he love you?"

I don't have to think, I simply nod.

"As long as he loves you," he says. "That's the only thing that matters, *malyshka*."

Falling forward into his arms, I embrace my father with my full strength. The roses have vanished; all I smell is his familiar stringent soap, the shaving cream he used that I'd sometimes steal to make a fluffy beard on my face.

His grip loosens against me.

"There's not much time left," he whispers sorrowfully. "You'll have to go back soon."

"I don't want to go." I beg, my hands burying into the front of his shirt. I loop them around his shoulders, gripping my own wrist, locking in. "I don't want to lose you again."

"You must, *malyshka*." Gently, but firmly, he pries my arms off of him. There are tears in his eyes, but he's smiling. "I'll see you again, and when I do, I want to hear more about Arsen and all the wonderful things you've done together."

His face begins to glow. So bright that I have to squint. The pain I felt before returns, but it's dulled now. Swallowing, I try to call out for my dad. I manage a weak groan. The curtains swirl around us, and soon they fade into the light as well.

Along with Dad.

"Galina, you're awake!"

Turning slowly, I see Arsen watching me intently. His handsome face is a welcome sight, though his features are etched with worry.

"Where am I?"

"The hospital. How do you feel? Are you in pain, do you need anything? Let me get the doctor."

He starts to move, but I manage to grab his wrist. I see mine for the first time—the medical bracelet clipped into place.

"No, wait, stay. Just sit and stay. Please."

Hesitating a bit, he eventually sits back beside me. "I thought I'd lost you. You were hurt... bleeding... and it was *me* who put you in that situation. I'm so sorry, Galina. You should never have experienced any of that."

I shake my head. "You saved me."

Placing his other hand on top of mine, he hangs his chin, not responding.

"Oh, you're up!" a cheerful voice calls. A man in green scrubs with a cloth mask on has entered the room. He holds a clipboard, flipping the papers and reading them quickly.

"You should have told me immediately, Mr. Isakov." I try to shift his way and he shakes his head. "Don't move around, please, you're lucky to be alive."

That's right. The shoot out. Gazing down hurriedly at my belly, I cross my fingers on top. "My baby, is..."

"The baby is okay. *You're* okay," Arsen assures me. He's lifted his head, and for the first time since I've woken up, he's managed to smile.

"What about Mom and Ruslan?"

"Everyone is okay, Galina. Because of you."

I exhale through my nose, closing my eyes to calm myself down. My mind has cleared up, giving me the ability to remember everything that happened. The fear is smothered by relief with this news.

Looking at the doctor, I ask, "Can I have a moment alone with my husband?"

For a second, he seems to want to argue. After eyeing Arsen, then the chart again, he acquiesces. "Yes, yes, of course. Press the button if you need anything."

Once we're by ourselves, I make a desperate grab for Arsen. "Come here." He hugs me back, leaning over the hospital bed, making it hard for me to breathe. I don't care. I don't care at all. Against all the odds we made it out of this mess *alive*.

"I love you, I love you, I love you," he murmurs into my neck. My skin is damp, but I'm not the one crying.

With one hand on my belly, the other on his cheek, I sink into his warmth. "I love you, too."

46

ARSEN

"It's taken months, but I think we're finally about to root out all of the corrupt cops on Yevgeniy's payroll," Josh says as he paces in front of his window. It's a new office, one that's on a higher floor and bigger than the last.

Whatever his complaints about me, our connection has helped lift him up in his career.

I nod as he finishes talking.

"Thank you for working so hard at this."

"Please, it's my pleasure," he chuckles, spreading his arms. "With the new police commissioner's help, this city will be scraped clean. This is a day that's been decades in the making."

Galina casts me a sly look from where she's sitting across the room. She sits everywhere now, her stomach jutting out as the baby threatens to come each new day. Her eyebrows wiggle; she's trying to tell me that Josh is a piece of work. I agree.

"What happens now?" I ask him.

"All the paperwork is being organized, the records of the

Grachev Bratva should be corrected in time. But you need to keep a close lid on things."

I arch a single eyebrow. "Oh?"

"Make sure nobody in your little group steps out of line," he threatens.

If Josh was demanding before, now he verges on insufferable.

"Sounds like my Bratva have become enforcers for this city you love so much," I taunt. "Almost like a second police force."

He recoils like I've slapped him. "Just because the city owes you a debt of gratitude doesn't mean you should get cocky."

"They're not the only ones who owe me their gratitude," I say lightly, shrugging.

Josh narrows his eyes. "One of these days, the Grachev Bratva *will* be dismantled."

"One of these days." Moving towards Galina, I help her to her feet. "But it's not today. I'll keep the peace. See you around, Josh."

He has no biting remark. Taking the elevator, I hug onto Galina from behind. My hands instinctively go to her belly where I can feel our baby kicking. It's the best sensation in the world.

"He can be a real prick," Galina giggles.

"Yes. But he's just scared."

"Of what?"

"Of losing what they've won." I escort her through the doors as they open. "Of what they treasure the most."

For Josh, that's prestige and respect. And for me? Well...

Summer has finally come into its own. Outside, the trees that cluster the sidewalk are saturated with green, waxy leaves. I hold Galina's hand as we walk towards my car, our steps slow as she struggles along.

"Arsen."

There's a tremor on her tongue. I pull up short, squinting at her with concern. "What is it?"

She looks down; the front of her leggings are darkened by fluid. She stares up at me with her eyes widening further by the millisecond. "Baby's coming."

I'VE LIVED through many things. I was sure, in my arrogance, that there was no emotion I hadn't felt.

Until I'm holding my son.

Blue eyes, deep and mysterious and ever changing, watch me from the face of the smallest human possible. He's minuscule in my arms. I worry that if I breathe wrong, I'll break him. I'm also certain I'll never, ever let any harm come to him. It's a love I've never felt anywhere else.

It rattles me, as if I'm holding my own heart outside of my body.

"He's perfect," I hush.

Galina watches me from the bed with tired eyes. "He really is."

Sitting beside her, I trace my finger over the boy's small arm. It's like pink satin. I try to wedge my finger into his palm, marveling at how little his own fingers are in comparison.

"How did we manage this?" I don't mean to ask it out loud, it just happens.

"Manage what?"

"This." I don't have a better way to phrase it. Galina quietly considers me, ruminating on the question. I consider trying again, but know it's pointless. "We never had time to talk about naming him," I say to change the subject.

"Well," she replies softly. "I just kept avoiding the topic." She sits up on the pillows, reaching out to hold our baby.

"Why would you do that?" I ask. I give him over, feeling the absence of his weight the second he's gone. The primal urge to touch him is powerful.

Cradling our child, Galina rocks him gently, her eyes warm with adoration. "Each day I woke up expecting something bad to happen. I kept thinking that the other shoe was bound to drop eventually. But here we are. Here he is."

My mouth dries out from hearing her sad explanation. "You shouldn't have had to worry like that."

"I'm not worried anymore." Kissing our baby's brow, she sighs gently. "And I have a suggestion for a name."

"Oh?"

"What do you think of Steven? For my father."

"Steven." I smile as I hear myself say it. "I like that. Steven Isakov."

Galina clenches up, the sorrow returning to her eyes. I want to banish that emotion from her forever. "I was worried you wouldn't be for it."

Swinging my head side to side I wrap my arm around her shoulder. We're cuddling on the bed, gazing at our baby. My other hand seeks out hers, linking so our wedding rings click. "Too much of our relationship has been about us being afraid. We didn't enjoy any of the fun parts of marriage or making a family. Hell, we didn't even have a honeymoon."

"True, that usually happens before the baby."

"We're anything but usual." I smile. "Where would you like to go?"

"What?" She laughs, like what I said was a joke.

"Our honeymoon."

"Oh, you're being serious."

Kissing her cheek, I then kiss Steven's. "I want to take you somewhere special."

Our bodies bend together. We form a triangle, a symbol of strength... a harmony unlike any other. Galina's tone is light as star dust, but her hand clutches my own like steel. "As long as we're together, wherever we go, it will be."

47

GALINA

I've never seen so many shades of blue and green. The ocean is like a stained-glass painting, stretching for endless miles until the border merges with the cerulean sky, making it impossible to tell them apart. It's the most amazing thing I've ever seen.

But I can't enjoy it, not with my heart wedged in my throat.

"Are we almost there?" I yell over the buzz of the seaplane's engine.

The white and red plane looked sturdy when I first laid my eyes on it. Now, though, with the air yanking at the wings, jolting the plane from side to side, I feel like it's about to split in two. I wish it was as big as the one we took to the main airport. The flight to the Maldives was long, but thanks to Arsen splurging for first class, quite comfortable.

This is *anything* but that.

"Excuse me?" I yell louder, trying to get the pilot's attention. "I asked how much longer until we're at the Reethi Rah resort?"

"It's okay, Galina." Arsen gives my hand a squeeze, pulling me closer to him in our seats.

"Maybe we should have taken the boat," I lament.

He laughs in my ear, his breath stirring my hair and my warm core. "The boat would have taken *much* longer?"

Comforted by his touch, I risk a quick glance out the window. In the distance I spot a flash of opal. The island's pristine white sand might almost be mistaken for mid-winter snow.

"Is that it?" I ask.

Arsen nods, wrapping an arm around my shoulders. "Close your eyes, it will be better not to watch us come in for the landing."

Taking his advice I squeeze my eyes shut, pressing into his body to envelope myself in his inherent aura of safety. It helps, but when the plane dips low, sending my stomach somersaulting, I squeal.

"We're almost there," he assures me. His leg grinds against the outside of mine, his chin on my hair. "You're safe, I promise."

I promise.

Tension melts from the back of my neck. If there's anything I trust, it's that Arsen will never break a promise. Through half-cracked lids I peer at the water rising towards us. We hit the ocean, bouncing up, then down, the motion constant and never ending. I'm not afraid, but I know I'm tinged green.

"For the record," I say as the engine grows quiet, the propellers no longer spinning, "I also hate roller coasters."

Arsen laughs with his whole chest. Helping me to my feet, he leads me out of the plane. A floating dock sways on the waves made by the plane's landing. The captain has descended, yelling at a few young men who hurry across to unload our luggage from the bottom section. He offers me a wide grin, waving at the island.

"Welcome to Reethi Rah, I hope you enjoy your stay."

"We will," Arsen says with blunt confidence. He grips me around my middle, lingering on my hip and sending butterflies through my veins.

The floating slats rock under me, threatening to topple me into the water. Arsen holds me tight so there's no chance of that. I press my fingers lightly on his on my hip, driving his touch in harder. He shoots a look at me—hot and hungry.

Grinning slyly, I walk fast onto the proper, solid wood of the docks. All around us are long paths, their stilt legs jutting into the ocean under our feet. Further out are the dark gray shapes of thatched roof villas. The breeze is warm, it teases my hair, drying the nervous sweat from the flight on the back of my neck.

"This place is beautiful."

"Wait until you see our room."

"I can't wait," I say with glee. I shake out my long skirt that's sticking to my legs. "I need to change into something more comfortable."

"We'll show you to your room, Mr. and Mrs. Isakov," a man with wild, curly black hair and eyes as blue as the water says. He stands before us with my purple roller-bag by his feet. The other men with him are younger, possibly teenagers, their lanky bodies tan in the sun. The billowing white shirts they wear are open in front, their pants cut off at the calf.

I tense up suspiciously before recoiling backwards. "How did you know our names?"

The man blinks owlishly. "The captain told us. Plus, it's all over your luggage." He points at the tags.

Everyone is staring at me. *I shouldn't be so anxious. I have to get a grip.*

"Sorry, I'm just tired from the long flight."

"Understandable," he says, waving a hand to dismiss my apology. "I'm Luke, by the way. You'll be seeing a lot of me, I'll be your personal concierge during your stay. If there's anything you need, feel free to let me know." He starts off over the docks.

I begin to follow, but Arsen scoops up my wrist, slowing me down. "Are you alright?" he asks with a worried frown.

"Of course," I say firmly. I make sure my smile is big and bright. It has to be... I don't want to worry him on our honeymoon. "Let's hurry before they leave us behind."

Arsen nods in agreement, and the pair of us tagging behind the group. They handle our bags with ease, not even out of breath by the time we cross half the docks. On the other side, separated from the main resort, extending out onto the water like an island all its own, is a large bungalow. I spot a white square floating beside the entrance.

"Is that a hot tub?" I ask in wonder.

"Yes!" Luke laughs. "Your bungalow comes with a private hot tub boat!"

"We'll have to make use of that," I say under my breath.

Arsen glances down at me, and I shrug with a sheepish blush. He studies the hot tub with a half smirk, clearly imagining what we can do with it, too.

Using a small key, Luke unlocks the front door, allowing his companions to shuffle inside with our luggage. "If you need anything, just press the button beside the phone inside."

"Thank you," Arsen replies. He digs in the pockets of his light gray pants, handing over a thick stack of bills to Luke. "I'll try not to bother you too much."

"It's my pleasure to make sure you have a wonderful stay." Sticking the money in the front of his pants, he waves with both hands at us before walking down the path with the others following.

Ducking into the doorway, I survey the bungalow with rising elation. There are windows everywhere, and a set of French doors have been propped open to allow the ocean air to waft inside.

Turning in place, I exhale lightly. "I can't believe this place, Arsen."

"You mean you don't like it?" he asks, shutting the door. He scans the room with a mild frown. "I could always ask for a different room, if this one isn't good enough."

"Stop it," I giggle, tapping him on the arm. "It's perfect."

"No, this is." Scooping me up with his hands planted on my ass, he lifts me until our lips meet in a kiss. I wrap my legs around his body, eager to feel his hair in my fingers, his teeth under my tongue. He continues to kiss me while walking towards the French doors. The sun warms my neck and upper back, as well as my bare thighs.

He moves down the steps; they lead to a large slope of sand, the edge of it being lapped by the calm waves. "What are you doing?" I giggle around his lips.

He tugs at my bottom one with his teeth. "Enjoying my honeymoon, as promised."

"Out here?" I gasp, pulling away so I can scan side to side, checking for anyone around us.

"No one can see," he assures me. His hands squeeze my ass, massaging the soft plumpness. Fire radiates in my lower belly instantly. "And I've been waiting the entire plane ride."

I laugh. Below the nerves my arousal is budding. "What about the sand?"

He knots up his eyebrows, seeming to get my meaning. Looking around, he motions with his chin.

"Then we can get on those loungers."

They're meant for sunning, but they're more couch than anything else. The cushions are a pale white, a shade darker than the sand, with elegant aqua designs curling all over.

Carrying me like I'm weightless, he settles on one of the loungers. My knees spread on either side of his waist, thighs scissoring. I'm sitting right on top of his massive erection. Knowing how turned on he is from us just kissing has my heart thudding.

"You really can't wait, can you?" I ask.

"Not a second longer." His voice is thick with desire. Gently, but with the knowledge he'll get what he wants, that it's inevitable, he pulls me in for another kiss. I drag my nails over his shoulders with a groan; he takes advantage, plunging his tongue in deep enough to trace the ridges on the roof of my mouth. I'm dizzy from the rush of pleasure.

He slips the top button of my blouse open, then the second, moving down with efficient speed. The air feels amazing on my exposed skin. I help him glide the garment off, abandoning it on the sand. Underneath I'm in a basic lilac bra, the cups stained by sweat from the long hours of travel.

"I should change into something cleaner," I chuckle.

"After," he says, kissing the top of my breasts. "When we're done."

A single finger rolls down my spine; he unclips the bra, yanking it off my arms by the straps. I don't know where it ends up after that.

His hands palm over my naked breasts, covering them fully. He pushes inward, my soft skin pressing through the gaps of his fingers as my chest overflows from the pressure.

Gasping, I toss my head back, enduring the hard jolt of delicious pleasure. My nipples firm and dig into his palms; he loosens his hold, making light circles over my nipples, playing with me until I see stars.

"Oh!" I moan. "Yes."

I rub myself against his pelvis, ramping the speed, the force, until I expect smoke to start forming. The friction is perfect on my clit. If I keep at it, I'll come just from this. He hikes my skirt up, rolling my panties downward. I'm not satisfied by this; the texture of my skirt is too much for my sensitive skin. I rip it up, over my chest, until it comes over my head.

Arsen stops moving; he levels a look on me, taking in the view of my nudity. His cock flexes beneath me. "Take off your pants," I demand.

He pops the top button; I rise up on my knees so he can shimmy the clothing off entirely. I start to lower myself, but he catches my hips, shoving me down firmly on top of his shaft. It sandwiches between us, sizzling with heat, the girthy tip poking my navel.

Capturing my chin, he leads me to him until our mouths connect. The kiss is quick; he nips my tongue, my brain fizzling like it's full of pop rock candy. "On your knees," he whispers.

The lounger isn't big enough for me to do that without kneeling in the sand. I don't consider the consequences, I just hop off, my breasts resting on his thighs while I fist the base of his cock. I'll never be bored of the feel of him in my mouth. I lap at the wavy veins, then swirl around his cockhead. The flared base is pleasant on my tongue.

Coating him in saliva I work him down my throat. My gagging is audible, but his groans are louder. I've made him wet enough that I can pump my hand along his cock while suckling the head. Arsen rocks side to side, unable to hold still. This is one of the few times I have power over him, and it's insanely hot.

"Fuck," he breathes, grabbing at my shoulders. "Stop, I don't want to finish in your mouth."

Too bad.

Ignoring his plea, I fist him faster, my fingers squeezing. His cock throbs in my throat, promising me the sweet taste of his jizz. Reaching down I finger myself. I want to be the one in control, but I can't resist my own need to come.

"No," he snarls. "If we're doing this, we're doing it right."

He lunges forward, scooping me around my middle. In a powerful flex of his upper body, he lifts me from the sand. Falling backwards, he contorts us until I'm kneeling over his face, my mouth still over his cock. It's a proper sixty-nine and I am *here* for it.

Spreading my thighs, Arsen pets my pussy from behind. I see spots of color, nearly fainting sideways off the lounger. "Oh my god," I whine.

He taps my ass lightly. "Back to work." His tongue curls around my slit, the circles of it tightening as he draws near my clit. Taking his cue, I focus on his cock in front of me. I lather the tip, enjoying the bead of precum. It tastes like the ocean, which is fitting for where we are.

Faster and faster, I stroke him in my palm. I widen my jaw, slapping the tip of his dick on my tongue. I can't take him deep, not when he's eating me out. I need to *breathe* or I'll black out.

With perfect aim he flicks over my sensitive clit. Tremors have begun in my belly, my legs shaking, knees locking. His cock swells in my mouth. Our timing is lining up, both of us chasing orgasm while doing our best to please the other.

He groans behind me, the sound crunching like the

earth itself is splitting apart. He's lost in his passion, but still, he rubs my clit. The man is devoted to making me come... it's instinctual.

The first explosion of his seed on my tongue sends me over the cliff. Panting wildly, I shiver as I come. I'm sweltering, my body coiled and tight, my pussy a flurry of blissful quakes. As violent as my orgasm is I dutiful gulp down Arsen's cum, refusing to spill a single a drop on the parched sands.

Arsen spins me around, kissing me, letting me taste myself on his lips.

"That was amazing," I say dreamily. "But we should go inside before we get sunburned."

"I could just get some sunblock and rub it all over you," he suggests with a smirk.

My heart thrums at the idea. "We're here for a few days."

"Fine," he concedes reluctantly. "I could stand to rinse off in the shower, anyway. Let's freshen up."

He helps me off the lounger, and as I kiss him lightly on tip-toe, he gives me a wolfish grin. Before I can react, he smacks my ass, the sound cracking in the air. It's not a hard slap, just enough to make my skin tingle and my pussy throb.

"That ass is distracting. You're right, we should protect something this precious from the sun."

I giggle before sprinting towards the bungalow. He chases after me, catching up once I'm at the outdoor rain shower. We drench ourselves in the pleasant water, removing sweat and sand until I feel lighter.

"Look, they gave us robes!" I yank one of the white cotton robes off of a peg hanging near the outdoor shower. Sliding it on, I belt it into place. "Fancy."

"They go all out here," he agrees. Dressing himself in a

robe, he smooths his wet hair off his forehead. "Wait until you see dinner spread they do."

"Dinner?" I chew my knuckle lightly. "Is it really that good?"

"Three Michelin stars. Almost as good as Danil's cooking."

I roll my eyes with a groan, and Arsen pauses, watching me with the look of a man who wants round two.

"I don't want to miss that. Let me dry my hair, figure out what I'm wearing."

Inside the bungalow I find the bedroom. Someone has arranged rose petals in a heart on the blanket. In a damp silver bucket on a small table is a bottle of champagne. We were too busy fucking on the beach to notice what the resort has arranged for us. Laughing in chagrin, I sit on the mattress and flick at the petals. The next thing I know I'm stretching out on top of them with a yawn. *This bed is incredible! I'll have to figure out what brand the mattress and pillows are, then Arsen can buy us one for our home.*

Our home.

It's crazy to realize we've been living together for over nine months. I tried to convince Mom to move in with us, explaining the mansion had the space, but she stubbornly resisted. The one concession she made was to stay there and help with Steven while we went on our honeymoon.

Steven. I rub my belly. It's a hard habit to break. My baby is happy and healthy and real, but he isn't with me. I wish he was. *It's okay to have fun with your husband.* That, too, is real now. Arsen had gathered the documents, and we signed them with my mother as a witness the week after Steven was born. I didn't care about the papers, Arsen had felt like my husband for months, having it documented was incidental.

But having my *mother* there to be part of the event, small as it was, meant everything.

"Galina?"

I sit up; Arsen is standing in the doorway. He's replaced his robe with a loose button down the shade of palm-bark and long shorts that stop at his calves, showing off the thick muscles. He looks amazing in such a casual outfit with his hair still damp. "Sorry, I got distracted," I say.

"Can't blame you. Bed looks very comfortable." His eyebrows rise playfully. If I gave a hint of agreement, he'd jump on me right now. It's incredibly hard not to crook my finger at him and let him do it.

I nod at his outfit. "Let me get my clothes from the luggage. I can be ready to go out in ten."

"Take your time," he says.

"You don't mind?"

His smirk could saw a tree in half. "As long as I get to watch, you can take as long as you want."

Blushing, I allow him to help me pick what to wear. Arsen has me try on multiple outfits—I think mostly because he's enjoying seeing me take everything off each time—before settling on a flowing, thigh-high yellow strapless dress.

"You think this is the one?" I ask, turning side to side and playing with the pleats. Arsen rises off the bed, placing his hands on my hips. My blood becomes lava—I've been getting worked up putting on a show for him.

His eyes are half-hooded. "It'll be perfect for dancing in."

"Dancing?" I ask with a surprised laugh. "What kind of dancing?"

"My hands all over your body while you grind those beautiful hips of yours." He rocks mine for emphasis, and I exhale sharply. "Let's go before I decide to say fuck it all and throw you on this bed."

It's a challenge to leave the bungalow, but my growling stomach is dictating my needs.

Once we eat, I'll have plenty of energy to test that bed out with him.

Arsen wasn't kidding about the food.

Three massive buffets, all run by staff in chef coats who are either hand-cooking, carving, or serving dishes, stretch out on the beach. The sun has started setting, creating a hazy purple that morphs into the deep blue of the ocean. There are no waves, it looks like a pane of tempered glass.

On one side of the sand is a live band. They pound on their instruments, notes whistling in the evening air that's finally cooled down to a pleasant temperature. Other couples are eating, while some dance on the huge platform that's been set up to keep people from twisting their ankles in the sand.

"You made it!"

I turn, startled by the sight of our concierge Luke. He's wearing a casual, floral-patterned top with a deep V-neck and cargo shorts.

"Oh, hey," I say.

He looks at us, grinning. "When you didn't call me for anything after we left, I worried I'd upset you somehow."

"No, not at all!" I insist. "I swear I was just overtired before. I'm sorry, again, about how I acted."

His shrug is aloof. "I imagine you took a nap."

I hope he doesn't notice me blushing. "Yup." *Something like that.*

"Well, good!" He claps me on the shoulder the way a coach would do to a player at a sporting event. "Enjoy the rest of the evening. Don't miss the sunset, it's more stunning than any other in the world."

Once he's walked off into the crowd, I shake my head, turning in place. Arsen is behind me with a pair of purple-orange drinks. He's looking at where Luke went. "Everything okay?"

"Yes, he was just checking in." Taking one of the glasses, I sip from it to find an excuse not to keep explaining. "Wow, this is delicious! Hey, want to go check out the music?"

He keeps staring into the group of other people. "Yeah, okay."

Eager to escape the uneasy situation I power-walk to the stage. Half my drink is gone by the time I set my sandal-clad foot on top of the smooth wood. Arsen studies me with a frown that refuses to go away. "Try your drink," I suggest. Once he does, I take the glass, then set it and my own on the tray of a passing waiter. Arsen blinks warily, his confusion growing when I take his hands, pulling him deeper onto the stage. "You promised me we'd dance."

There—the frown morphs into a pleased smile. He grips my hands more firmly. "I did."

I let him take the lead, enjoying how he takes me to the center with confidence. I've seen how he carries himself in day-to-day life, his dexterity in the kitchen, his speed and strength when saving me from danger. I'm expecting great things from his dancing.

The band changes the tune they're playing. Two men blast on tubas, another on a sax. It sounds like the type of music Arsen put on when we were driving to the safehouse. His eyes flash, a vibrant energy coming over him. "Ready?"

"Sure," I half-laugh. "You don't need to look so intense."

He smirks ear to ear, one hand gliding down my arm, over my elbow, leaving pleasant ripples everywhere he touches. He ends by gripping my lower back, just above my ass. Suddenly it's harder to draw a full breath.

I was wrong. He's not great.

He's *incredible*.

Arsen spins me in a circle, and to my personal horror, I stumble. Catching myself, I narrow my eyes, my competitive nature roaring to life. I haven't made a mistake on a dance floor since I was a child. "You're alright," I tell him lightly.

His chuckle is razor sharp. "Just alright?"

"Were you trained?" I ask, my feet tapping around his, matching his pace. His palm smooths over my hip, grazing my thigh as he lifts my leg to hook onto his middle. It's not fair that he can throw me off balance with sexy moves like this. I try to maintain a cold expression, but it's impossible when he dips me low, his face inches from mine.

His teeth glint in the fairy lights strung above. "I taught myself."

"Bullshit," I scoff.

The smugness in his laugh creates hot swirls in my heart. "So you *are* impressed."

"Fine, maybe a little."

That time, his laugh is warmer—kinder. It coaxes a smile out of me. Hoisting me up to my feet, he holds me close, our bodies swaying in unison. "It should come as no shock that I think you're amazing, too. Your movements have the power of ballet, the grace, but can you do anything else?"

Taking it as a challenge I prop my hands on his shoulders. Rocking my hips, I grind myself against the front of his pants. His eyes widen—it's ambrosia to me. Spinning, I set my ass against him next, continuing to swivel. His hard-on is instant. "I might have some other moves," I say slyly.

He breathes across the back of my neck. "You tease." Sweeping my hair aside, he kisses behind my ear, rolling his body into mine. We dance slowly, ignoring the tempo of the high-energy brass band. We're in our own world. Everyone else has vanished.

The music dies out, people laughing and exiting the stage. Arsen cradles me tight, not letting me join them. He's not ready to be finished here. Alone in the middle of the stage, the sun setting on the horizon, we kiss until we can't any longer. Gasping for oxygen, we grin like teenagers who've escaped their parents. Our love is so over the top it feels like we're getting away with something criminal just by being together.

"Come on," he says, pointing at the ocean. "The stars are out."

My body is floating. I have to double check to make sure I'm touching the ground, scanning to confirm I'm leaving footprints in the sand.

The voices of the others on the resort fade away the further we go. Arsen keeps us out of the water, but a few times the tide tries to tag us, and we dodge away with laughter. Up above the purple sky has become an ink wash packed with glitter. The stars are numerous, I could never count them all, not even if we stayed here for a hundred years.

"Look!" I cry, crouching down to dig an orange shell from the sugary sand. "Isn't it pretty?"

Arsen takes the shell and holds it up. He levels it beside my face, his voice softer than velvet. "Next to you it's forgettable."

How can he still make me blush? I sit on the sand,

drawing my knees to my chest and hugging them. Arsen joins me, our arms grazing as we watch the ocean roll elegantly just a few feet away. "I could stay here forever," I sigh.

"Should we move here with Steven?" he chuckles.

"My mother would hate that. She can't be away from him for more than a few hours."

"I'm sure she'll manage."

I smile in agreement. "She's probably having a blast right now with him. That, or freaking out. She can panic about the oddest things." I chuckle, but Arsen doesn't join in.

He's gazing at the water with a faraway look in his eyes. The look doesn't change when he shifts enough to stare down at me. "What happened earlier?"

I go stiff as Rebar. "What do you mean?"

"The way you reacted when we first met Luke. He said our last names and it set you on edge."

"Oh, that?" I laugh too loudly. "I said I was tired."

"You looked scared, Galina."

Hesitating, I lower my eyes to avoid his. Kicking off my sandals, I drag my toes in the sand, creating swirling shapes without purpose.

Arsen slips his foot forward, caressing his ankle on mine until I stop making the shapes. "Talk to me."

"I don't want to make you worry."

"The last thing I want is for you to hide something because you think it's for my sake."

Lifting my shoulders up, I exhale until they slump lower than before. "I *was* scared earlier. He knew our names, and it freaked me out. What if he was here to hurt us? Yevgeniy is dead, but I've been struggling with these little bursts of anxiety for a while. I hoped they'd go away by now, but..." I shake my head to clear my thoughts. "I want to shrug off the terrible things we went through, but it turns out I'm not strong enough for that."

"You've got it all wrong." Arsen pulls me against him, stroking my hair as he speaks in a low baritone. "You don't have to be strong. What happened to us, we went through it together. Shouldn't we deal with the aftermath together as well?"

"Arsen..."

"Lean on me. Rely on me. Use me and allow me to support you through your fears, Galina."

"You mean that?" I hush.

He smiles indulgently, his thumb outlining my bottom lip. "What else could being in love possibly be about?"

I WAKE up to the sun in my eyes. Grimacing, I throw up my arm to shield myself. *What time is it?* I didn't bother to charge my phone. I've been trying to be 'present' on this trip, leaving my mother instructions to call the resort if something is wrong instead of me directly.

Sitting up on the bed I stretch until my joints crack in a satisfying way. Then I freeze, noticing Arsen isn't beside me.

"Arsen?" I call uncertainly. Sliding my legs over the edge of the bed I walk in my bra and underwear—I was too tired to change into anything else when we got back—and explore the bungalow. Finding no sign of my husband, I step out through the French doors to our private beach.

Arsen is standing ankle deep in the ocean. He's wearing his forest green swim trunks and nothing else. With him facing away, I'm able to see his glorious tattoos. It's my first time seeing them in the sunlight, they've always been something shared behind closed doors. The things struck me as a grim secret. But here, with the sunlight, they look like works of art hanging in a gallery.

They're beautiful. Just like him.

Blessed with an opportunity to simply *look* at him without him looking back, I take a moment to enjoy myself. His wide shoulders with their indents of chiseled muscle create a taper for his trim waist. He's a healthy olive tone, polished like a gem and sharp like one as well. It would be easy to worship this man.

He's not a saint... he's my soulmate. I'll never bow to him, but I'll always love him.

His head turns, his jugular flexing. He's spotted me. "You're awake."

"I didn't mean to sleep in," I say, stepping down on the warm sand to approach him.

Arsen waits for me where he is. The ocean laps at my toes, and it delights me how pleasant it feels. "You were tired. It's fine, we're here to enjoy ourselves, and that includes sleeping in."

"I guess I haven't done that much since Steven was born," I chuckle.

He loops his fingers in mine, pulling me deeper in the gentle waves. "Are you missing him?"

"Of course," I say quickly.

Arsen nods knowingly. "I am, too." Bending down he kisses me; not a brief kiss, but one with full lips and tension pacing in the shadows. He doesn't expand on his admission; he doesn't need to. He feels the way I do, and I appreciate knowing I'm not alone.

I crane my neck to kiss him back, before wincing as the sun peeks over his ear and blinds me. "It's bright already."

He frowns in thought. Suddenly he's smirking, pulling me towards the shore. "You reminded me of something I've been dying to do." He's taking me over to the lounge chairs. The sight of them sends my pulse rocketing upward, my body heating up like a fever is coming on. I can't think of anything other than what we did here yesterday.

"Lie down," he tells me. "I'll be right back."

Laughing a bit nervously, I stretch out on the lounge cushions on my back. I shoot multiple looks after him as he jogs inside our bungalow, trying to predict what he's up to—and also enjoying the view of him running. His muscles are particularly sexy when they're flexing.

I'm briefly alone. I don't take my eyes off the bungalow, but the position I'm in to see the French doors is twisting my neck. Giving up after a minute, I slump on the cushions with my head tilted back, eyes closed to protect me from the sun that's blazing above. *I wish I'd brought my sunglasses.*

Arsen clears his throat; his shadow falls over me, blocking the sun.

"Here." He offers me my pink rimmed sunglasses.

I take them with a surprised laugh.

"You can read my mind, it's confirmed." I set them on my face and adjust them. "There," I say, angling my chin to gaze up at him. "Now I can see you without going blind."

He makes a circular motion with his finger. "Roll over."

My brow scrunches, but then I spot the bottle of sunblock in his hand. The little flutters are back in my belly, stronger than ever. I flip onto my stomach on the lounge chair. I'm wearing nothing but my bra and panties, which isn't that different than a bikini, but it suddenly feels obscene.

I can't see Arsen, but he can see a *lot* of me.

"You're going to lotion me up?" I ask coyly. "Just that concerned about me getting burned?"

His chuckle is thick and gritty, it vibrates into my blood

until I'm shivering deliciously. "The only person who can make this ass red..." His hand lightly slaps my right cheek. "Is me."

I swallow with difficulty. Resting my cheek on my folded arms, I try to remain still as I listen to the sound of him squirting lotion into his hand. Everything is louder because I'm not looking. My heightened senses extend to my skin—his palm settles on my upper back and I jump. "Sorry," I whisper-laugh.

He glides his hands down my spine, making circular motions over my shoulder-blades. When he encounters my bra strap he undoes it wordlessly. Now he can smooth the lotion from the base of my neck to the curve of my hips without anything interrupting him.

The man is an expert with his hands, I think in a daze. He rubs in harder until I gasp, and when he massages down my hamstrings I whimper and groan. My toes curl as he works over my calf-muscles. He's not just putting sunblock on me, he's luxuriating in touching my body. I've never felt so lucky.

Or so turned on.

The buzzing in my core has been constant since I saw him standing in the ocean. With him running his hands all over my body, the buzzing has become an earthquake. This thirst is intense. My insides ache for him to do more than massage my legs and back.

"You're shifting around a lot," he whispers darkly in my ear. "Are you alright?"

"You know what you're doing to me," I counter. I try to sound annoyed—his fingers sweep low, rubbing into my ass, forcing me to groan. I arch into his touch, seeking more of it. I want to encourage him to use his damn hands on other parts of me.

He breathes out, sounding like he's straining. I turn to

try and see him, but the angle is wrong. All I spot is the sand and the ocean on either side of me. His shadow dances on the white grains. It moves as he does, warning me, only barely, before he rolls me onto my back. My breasts flash in the air. I move to cover them with my arm out of habit. He frowns, eyes narrowing, and I stop halfway.

That's right, we're alone here. No one can see us.

I hope they can't hear us either...

"You don't want to get a burn on this half of your body," he says hoarsely. He stands over me; I glimpse the large shape of his cock straining against his swim trunks. My clit throbs sympathetically. Arsen holds up the sunblock, shooting a fresh dose into his palms. I watch with my breath tangling in my lungs. He's fixated on my breasts. The anticipation of what he's about to do has me rocking on the lounge, unable to hold still as waves of arousal rise higher than the ones on the actual ocean surrounding us.

He lowers his hands to my chest, smoothing slippery lotion over my breasts. My eyes roll in my head and I bite down on impulse. The rush of pleasure is immense enough that I think I'm losing my eyesight, until I remember I'm wearing sunglasses. His fingertips, lubed by sunblock, toy with my nipples, sliding around them without any friction.

"Oh my god," I whimper, grinding my knees together. Reaching down, I brace my hand against his erection. It jumps in my hand; he pushes his hips forward, giving me better access. While Arsen spreads sunblock all over my upper chest, I massage his cock through his swim trunks.

His growl would frighten me if I didn't know him. "That feels incredible, Galina."

"That does, too," I moan, shoving my breasts into his hands by sitting up on the lounge chair. He tugs my nipples lightly, then lets go of one, slipping a hand down to the junction of my thighs. His hands, covered in sunblock, glide over the front of my underwear. The fabric is pushed inside of me; he pulls it upward against my clit, then side to side, releasing bursts of wicked pressure in my pussy.

Maneuvering my panties out of the way, he pets two slick fingers over my lower-lips. I squeal, panting eagerly while lifting my hips to encourage him. I don't stop palming his shaft through his trunks. We're masturbating together, the knowledge erotic enough to have me on the edge of orgasm. By the time Arsen wedges two fingers knuckle deep into my pussy I'm ready to explode.

Throwing my head back, I let out an obscene cry of pleasure. My sunglasses topple off my face and onto the sand, but my eyes have shut; I'm too lost in pleasure, accidentally sparing my eyes from the ball of white-hot sun.

The glow seeps through my eyelids. It's inside of me, it *is* me—my muscles tremble and my pussy thrums around Arsen's fingers as I come. I jerk on the lounger, squealing as my muscles go haywire. Every inch of my skin is slick from sweat or sunblock.

The tremors are fading along with the orgasm. I start to catch my breath and say something now that we're done. Arsen drives his fingers into me harder. *He's* not done.

He's only getting started.

48

ARSEN

I'VE BEEN LUCKY ENOUGH TO SEE MANY BEAUTIFUL THINGS IN my lifetime. Expert oil paintings, hand crafted statues, flowers that took years to cultivate into a special shade of maroon.

Galina outshines all of them.

I'm knuckle deep inside of her, my other hand cupping her left breast and teasing her hard nipple. She's mewling beneath me, the sound of it making me wild. My cock is hard enough that it hurts. A moment ago, she was jerking me off through my trunks, but she's too busy coming to do anything but quiver.

Turning her brain and body into mush is addicting. She's the strongest, most intelligent woman I've ever known, but in my touch she falls apart. The power of that... it thrills a dark part of my soul, a hungry, primal piece of me that wants to conquer.

Galina tries to look at me—her sunglasses are gone, and her face is scrunched up in the sunlight. I lift an arm over her head to create shade, lowering my face to hers in a passionate kiss. This works even better because she shuts her eyes instinctively.

We should get out of this sun. The sunblock was a ruse to drive her crazy by massaging her everywhere. It worked. But now I want to be away from the scorching heat, especially when there's a hotter fire growing inside both of us. We're bound to melt on the sand at this rate.

But not yet. One more before we move. I curl my fingers inside of her pussy; she gasps down my throat. Wiggling my fingers side to side independently, I use my thumb to pet her swollen clit. I've always been a perceptive man, but I'm on high alert with Galina. My goal is to know what she loves... what will make her heart thud, her thighs tremble. I've become a master at reading her body.

Her inner walls clench on my fingers. I count the twitches, waiting for the tell-tale sign that she's going to come again. *There!* She tightens up, her lips going slack, though I continue kissing her anyway. Galina is electric in my arms as her climax swings through her body. My cock swells, ready to burst as I'm taunted by how warm and tight she is around my fingers.

"Arsen," she moans my name.

Scooping her up, I carry her over the sand. She stirs, looking around as she clings to my shoulders, trying to make sense of why I'm moving. Taking us inside our bungalow, I don't slow down until I enter our bedroom. "We've had this amazing bed since yesterday, but we haven't taken advantage of it once."

Galina laughs, her skin bouncing against mine from the tempo. "How rude of us."

"Exactly," I chuckle. Setting her on the blankets that are askew from us sleeping in them—we haven't had a chance for the staff to show up and make the bed—I kiss her again.

My hands drop on either side of her head in the pillows, my weight settling on her until her breasts dig into my hard chest. I love the way that feels.

Lowering myself, my lips encircle one of her nipples. Galina sings her excitement, her fingers tangling in my hair to keep me where I am. I allow it—for a bit—but I have other goals. Inching further across her silken body, I kiss her navel, her pelvic bones, enjoying the hard parts of her as much as the soft ones.

The sweet scent of her pussy weakens me. I inhale deeply, pushing her thighs wider to give me access. She clamps her knees around my face, muscles trembling in anticipation. My thumbs spread her apart, then I dip my tongue inside of her, savoring her flavor.

"That's so good," she hisses, grinding herself against my face. I flatten my tongue, a string of saliva connecting from it to her clitoris as I rise up on my hands. She sees and flushes pink. The way she bites her lower lip makes my pulse quicken, rendering me unable to wait any longer.

"I need you," I say thickly. Kneeling on the bed I slip my swim trunks off my ankles. We're both naked, a fact so simple yet so arousing. The large window is wide open, the breeze coming off the water making the curtains stir. Everything smells like sea salt and cocoa butter.

"Should we use a condom?" she asks me, her eyes big as dinner plates.

"No." Aiming myself carefully, I push inside of her with as much patient control as I can manage. Tingles roll from my belly to my brain; I hiss through my teeth. "No, no condoms."

"But— ah!" She loses her voice when I fill her up. "But I could get pregnant again!"

"So?" It's a simple response that says a million things.

Her lips drop open, as red as the heat living in her cheeks. "You're sure?"

Does she really believe I wouldn't relish another child? If I had my way we'd have multiple children. A family is something to treasure. There's no world where I wouldn't be delighted at being told I'm a father over and over again.

"Yes. I want this, I want whatever happens from this."

There's something beyond pleasure in her dark pupils. Maybe bigger than *love,* though I don't have a word for it. She puts her hands around my hips, guiding me inside of her all the way, and when I pull my hips back for a second thrust, she grips on, leading the pace.

I'm panting in hot bursts of air. The lust has already surged to a peak, my shaft hard as rock as I slam into her on the bed. Galina wraps around me tighter than a ribbon. Every gyration of my body she meets with her own.

I heave forward, the bed shaking from the effort. Galina hugs around my cock, enveloping me like silk. Her pussy flutters each time I plunge inside. Every stroke takes me closer to the delirious release of orgasm, and god, I need it badly. I'm hot all over, as if my skin can't contain the energy inside. It has to go somewhere... it has to go into *her.*

She cries out on the cusp of every thrust. "Arsen! Oh my god, Arsen, yes! Don't slow down don't you dare slow down!"

Obediently I drill into her with new energy. I'm driven by the climax I'm chasing, but also by seeing her lose control. Her nails bite into the flesh around my upper back, straight into the ink of my tattoos.

"Fuck!" I breathe huskily. The pain is sharp, it wakes up more of my awareness; my very cells are on fire. If this is the last thing I experience, I could die contently.

It's as if a storm goes off inside of her. Little electric tingles, muscles flexing, pulsing. "I'm coming!" she screams at the top of her lungs. As secluded as we are, there's a chance the resort guests hear her.

Her orgasm is the lighting of my fuse. Bracing my jaw, my neck bunching, I lean into her on the bed. I hook her ankles around my elbows to spread her wider, getting a few inches more of the traction I need. Massive pressure builds in my chest, darting into my lower core. Droplets of my own sweat stain the bed sheets, making darker designs on the fabric.

Grunting until my throat feels raw, I start shaking. My cock expands, the tip hot and heavy, pleasure immense enough to leave me lightheaded. I come in spurts, filling Galina up with each final thrust of my hips.

Both of us shudder together, like we've shed some sort of burden and can finally relax. All my muscles loosen, but my skull is tight. That's what happens when you connect with someone with your whole being. No part of you, body or mind, is left untouched.

Galina hugs me close. Her fingers run over my back, grazing the tender spots her nails dug in. She doesn't know she did that. She's a total prisoner to her body when she's turned on, acting without thought as she pursues relief. I understand of course.

Revenge isn't lust, but it's controlled me in the past just the same.

"I love you," I tell her, kissing her forehead.

"I love you, too." Galina takes me by the jaw, moving me so our lips press snugly. It's wonderful to lie on our bed and enjoy each other's quiet presence.

Eventually Galina shifts, then sighs. "What a workout," she giggles.

Sitting up, I gather her in my arms. She doesn't have time to ask what I'm doing until I've carried her, naked as she was born, out back into the sunlight. She sees the hot tub as we approach it and smiles. "You don't mind a change of scenery?" I ask.

"No, not at all."

Together we sink up to our necks in the hot tub. The jets are on, the bubbles rolling against our bodies. My muscles appreciate the sensation—I let out a soft sigh. Galina reclines beside me, her eyes shut, enjoying the moment.

Her thick lashes tickle her cheeks. There's a mild smile playing over her red-tinged lips.

There have been many times where I wondered what Galina was thinking. She's capable of being mysterious, her wit allowing her to mislead me when she had no other options. I've cursed myself for my inability to read her mind when it really counted. But this time, I don't have any trouble.

She's happy.

She doesn't have to say it out loud for me to know.

49

GALINA

He leaps across the room, his reflection copying him in the floor to ceiling mirrors. One spin, a second and a third, before he bends forward, arms stretching long enough they give him the illusion of being taller than he is.

When he finishes his last pirouette, Ruslan faces me with his eyes ablaze. Some of his dark hair is stuck to his forehead.

I clap enthusiastically. "That was wonderful, Ruslan!"

His smile deepens his dimples. There's pride on his face, but his voice still has the fragility of an unsure child. "Thanks. But I keep messing up on the pivot."

"You'll get it, just keeping trying."

Cocking his head, he frowns to himself. Looking in the mirror he does a few quick half-bends, like he's testing my theory. "You're sure that's enough?"

Putting my hands on his shoulders from behind, I study our reflections. Ruslan has changed in a short amount of time. It began the night he was forced to witness his father's death. The kindness that was always in his heart has crawled fully into the light, allowing him to trust others, and to trust that he, himself, will never be like his father.

Under my hand I feel the rough patch of skin where his tattoo used to be. It's amazing that a single session was all it took to wipe the ink away.

He locks eyes on mine in the mirror, searching me, waiting for my answer. I smile easily. That's what's changed for me—smiling comes as often as blinking these days. "Yes, it's enough."

Leaving my star pupil to drill his movements, I walk to the front of the studio. The walls are plastered by photos of my family. It was tragic how many pictures were lost in the fire, but thanks to my husband, I was able to get copies of some, as well as brand new ones.

They look better out here, in the public eye, than hidden away in a tiny office.

Sitting behind the front desk I do a quick check of the schedule. My studio has had an endless list of students signing up. I never imagined having to limit class sizes before, but there's no choice. I don't even care that the reason has nothing to do with me or my teaching skills.

Once word spread that Astana Bukharova was running workshops, our phone didn't stop ringing. Sighing, I scribble down a few notes for myself on a chart. *Don't be miserable, you wanted success, and now you have it.* I'm grateful...

But I also miss the quiet beach in the Maldives.

I glance up, catching my mother just as she pushes the door open with my son in her arms. My heart bursts to its limit. *Who needs a private island when I've got him?* "Hi, Mom," I say, hurrying around to take Steven.

He's dressed in a breathable cotton onesie the color of a

tangerine. Cooing at me, he waves his fat little fists. Pressing my face into his hair I breathe in until I'm dizzy.

"I don't mind watching him, of course," Mom says, "but I hope you're not working too hard. You know I'd be happy to take more shifts."

"You already teach half the morning classes, Mom. It's really fine." I kiss each of Steven's cheeks. "Did you have fun with *babushka*?"

He tucks one of his hands into his mouth, gnawing it with a smile.

The door opens again. Arsen stands there, the warm air billowing into the studio. He's wearing a short-sleeve moss green shirt that hugs his biceps. His faded jeans cover the tops of his tan boots.

"Arsen," I say, smiling happily.

He lays a kiss on my cheek before taking Steven in a single huge arm. His son squeals in excitement. They share the same eyes, and I wonder when Steven grows up how much he'll look like his father. "Are you ready to go?" he asks me and my mother.

She nods her head towards the dance room. "Let me tell Ruslan it's time."

Arsen and I are alone with Steven. We come together naturally, hugging our son with our heads bent together. I crave moments like this, but today, I also need it.

I GENTLY AND carefully brush the dirt off the grave. When I'm done it's nearly polished. "Hey, Dad," I whisper, kneeling down. "Sorry about the mess. These summer rains are making everything muddy."

The grass has grown thick in the cemetery. Yellow

dandelions have cropped up around my father's grave in thick blankets that lure honeybees. A few buzzes near me in drifting motions, settling here or there but leaving me alone.

That's good. I need to be alone.

"Steven is growing up really fast, I can hardly believe it. One day he's crying in the hospital, the next he's starting to roll onto his back. He's going to be a spunky one, I think." I'm smiling, but tears well up in my eyes; I wipe them away. "I wish you could meet him. I wish... I wish you were here. I miss you more than you know."

I pick out Steven's laughter on the breeze. I'm far enough away that I can barely make out my mother across the cemetery. She's holding Steven high, turning him like he's flying. I let her visit Dad first, explaining I had things to say in private. She didn't argue.

Just to her right, I see Arsen looming over a grave, his head bent so low his whole face is shadowed. Beside him is someone else. Mila's black and blue moto jacket shimmers in the sun. She's cut her hair recently, the strands ruler-edged to line up with her jaw.

I can't read the name on the grave they're standing at. I know who it is, though.

Kostya's death has weighed heavily on them both. At his memorial, Arsen spoke proudly about his bravery and how honorable he was. It feels strange to recall I used to hate Kostya. He'd been cruel to me, but in the end, his loyalty never wavered.

He'd saved Arsen once and died trying a second time. No one will forget his sacrifice.

Mila glances up suddenly, sensing me staring. I stiffen because even at this distance her eyes are hawkish. She considers me for a long while with the wind ruffling her short hair. Finally, she turns, whispers something to Arsen, and walks off with her hands in her jacket pockets.

She's always acted aloof, but I know how big her heart is.

It's thanks to her that I got this back. Clutching something in my cardigan, I lightly trace each letter of my dad's name on the grave. I hesitate before repeating it with his surname. My heart thuds quicker, curling on itself as I fight a wave of sadness.

"Until next time." Placing the rose brooch on top of the grave, I lean forward, tapping my lips on the stone in a gentle kiss. "Bye, Dad."

"This is so good! Your chef is amazing!" Audrey gushes. She stuffs another forkful of salmon into her mouth; some of it drips onto her golden dress, and she winces, dabbing at it with a napkin. Josh hides an entertained smile behind his second glass of wine. He's drinking more than the rest of us, especially Audrey, who hasn't touched hers.

Giggling politely, I point my fork at Arsen. "He cooked this, actually."

Audrey freezes with her fork in her mouth. Wide-eyed, she swallows the food, washing it down with some ice water. "He *what?* Well, I was already happy for you, but this confirms you've got yourself a real catch."

"It is pretty tasty," Josh admits reluctantly.

"Don't be like that, you've polished off half your plate," Audrey chides him.

Josh pulls a face before putting his fork down. "Because I'm hungry."

Audrey rolls her eyes at me, and I can't stop myself from giggling. It's surreal that we're sitting here in the mansion. It wasn't long ago that I'd had to sneak Audrey into the cellar in a crate of fruit. "I'm glad we could all have dinner together," I say.

"Me too," she agrees, "I've been looking for an excuse to get everyone in the same room."

Arsen stiffens, casting me a curious look. I shrug to indicate I don't know what she's talking about. "What do you mean?" he asks warily.

Her grin is so big the corners of her eyes vanish in deep crinkles. Clearing her throat, she pushes her chair back, standing and tapping the edge of her glass with her knife dramatically.

"Josh and I have an announcement. We're having a baby!"

Gasping, I shove my chair away so I can rush around and hug her. "Audrey, oh my god, congratulations!" She laughs, tears squeezing down her cheeks as we jump up and down together. *My best friend is going to have a baby! Our kids can grow up together!*

Arsen peers at Josh over his hands with a kind smile. "You'll enjoy being a father."

At first he looks unsure how to react. I let go of Audrey, eyeing Josh nervously, unsure if he'll say something rude or snide or what. As nice as things have gotten, he has every right to hold a grudge against Arsen for what he was put through.

Taking a big breath, Josh inclines his head in a knowing way, like they're swapping stories. "Thanks, I hope so. No backing out of it now."

Audrey scoffs playfully while lightly tapping Josh on the arm. He pretends to flinch, but his half smile reveals how much he enjoys their game.

When we're all back in our sets, Arsen raises his glass.

Now I get why Audrey hadn't touched her wine. "Cheers to your new family," he says loudly.

"And cheers to no more late nights at Tsar's," Audrey says. She gives me a side-eye and smirks. "Though I can't pretend I won't miss it."

Everyone descends into chatter, conversations overlapping. I listen, but my mind is elsewhere. I'm traveling along that string of thought Audrey just handed me. *Tsar's* was another lifetime ago. The woman I was then doesn't exist anymore, not really. I'm still Galina Stepanovna, but I've grown enough to understand what that *means.*

I've witnessed death and trauma, passion and love.

I lost many things on my way here. But when I lift my head, gazing at Arsen, hearing my son cry upstairs in a nursery that was once locked away and covered in dust, I'm positive of one thing.

Life can't get any more perfect than this.

EPILOGUE

Galina
Three years later

I'M GOING TO BE LATE!

It's the one thing I was dead set on avoiding. I'd looked Arsen in the eye this morning, kissing him as I climbed into my car, and assured him I would definitely be on time for our date.

How arrogant of me.

It's not my fault, the Nutcracker performance is in just two weeks. It's our biggest show and it has to be perfect. It's baffling that in just a few years my studio has blown up to be recognized as the top ballet studio in the state. Maybe the entire coast, though I try not to let my ego get wind of that.

But none of that matters. Today is about celebrating my three-year anniversary with Arsen.

Which is why I should NOT be late. Ugh.

Driving through downtown, I take a familiar road that I'd be able to navigate in the dark. Street lamps being out because someone busted the glass with a rock for fun wouldn't be strange—in the past, that is.

Big globe lights propped on black poles dot the entire sidewalk, glowing like a row of tiny moons and lighting up the storefronts. Many of them are brand new. The lack of potholes *and* shady people huddled in alleys is what really shows off how far this city has come.

The Grachev Bratva has maintained a tight leash on the crime levels. Arsen kept his word to Josh, staying under the radar while his organization flourished. And, credit to Josh, he's stayed out of their way. How those two have gotten along without killing each other is a mystery. Perhaps fatherhood has tamed them both?

My car's headlights glint over the painted lines along the curb in front of *Tsar's Lounge*. I haven't been here since that fateful night years ago, when I was shoved into the backseat of a car by a man I used to hate.

I hope he hasn't been waiting long, I think, parking my car. I double-check my makeup in my center mirror. There'd been just enough time between leaving the ballet rehearsal to dodge into the studio's bathroom, throw on the slinky red dress I'd brought from home, then toss my hair up in a messy bun before patting on a quick bit of rouge lipstick and mascara.

I'm not *actually* worried about how I look. Arsen would tackle me if I was wearing a trash bag, but I want him to know I'm excited about tonight... that I'm trying to put in the effort. *Oh, don't forget that!* Ducking over to the passenger seat I grab the tiny silver package.

Locking my car, I shiver in the brisk night wind. The air has the stale taste of a snow storm on the cusp of arrival. I'd forgotten to pack a tasteful cardigan or bolero, so I accept my penance and cross the street in nothing but my heels and glittery dress. I glance around furtively, hoping nobody will catcall me... and I notice there's no one around.

It's not that late, there should be a ton of cars parked outside. I don't see any people loitering, either. Approaching the lounge gives me a funny sense of deja vu. Nudging the front door open, I wait for my eyes to adjust to the dim lighting. Once they do I confirm what I suspected. *Nobody is here?*

Frowning uneasily, I shut the door and walk further inside. There's a rhythmic beat piping through the speakers in the walls, purple lights shifting all over the room to create long shadows that change with every second. "Hello?" I call out.

Crossing my arms, I tap a finger on my bare elbow, scanning for evidence that Arsen is here because I'm *sure* he is. I can read him like a book.

My attention zips to the VIP section. Nodding to myself, I take long strides, my heels clicking on the hard floor as I go.

"Arsen?" I peel the beaded curtains aside to reveal the interior of the private room.

His back is to me; he turns, a bottle of champagne in one hand and a bouquet of roses in the other. They're white and a shade of red so deep they verge on black. Flowers from his own garden. The chocolate brown dress shirt strains to contain his broad chest, and when he approaches me with his angled smirk, I catch a whiff of sandalwood.

"I was beginning to think you'd bailed on me."

"Oh god, no!" I assure him. "I'm really sorry. Work got crazy. I should have called you so you'd know why I was late."

Arsen rakes his eyes over my body. I swear I can *feel*

them on the curves of my breasts and hips in my tight dress. "You're forgiven."

I tremble from how hot his desire gets me. I make sure he sees me checking him out as well. "Here," I say, passing him the silver package. "Happy anniversary."

He looks at the present with his brow scrunching. "When I planned this date, I imagined giving you your gift first." We trade items; me, the flowers, and him the present. He places the champagne on the knee-high table in the middle of the room.

"I hope you like it," I say with a tiny smile. The roses smell amazing, I inhale them a few times while watching him unwrap his gift. Arsen holds up the crystalline bottle shaped like a swan. "It's vodka," I explain. "I wanted to find a goose, but no one makes bottles like that I guess."

Laughing as understanding warms his eyes, he turns the bottle in his hands to study it. "Our trip to my cabin really left an impression on you. Your turn." Setting the vodka carefully on the table he plucks a green velvet box from his pocket.

I take it, opening it with reverence as my heart begins to thud. "Oh, Arsen," I whisper. The necklace inside the box is as gold as the sun. The chain links are delicate enough that I'm afraid they'll break when I lift it. In the center of the necklace is a pendant shaped like a bird's cage.

Turning it in the light makes the bird inside twinkle.

He's watching me intensely, an eagerness in his face that transfers to his hands; they flex at his sides. "What do you think?"

The necklace twirls as it dangles in my fingers. *Ptichka.* Once upon a time, I'd used his nickname for me against him. But I'm not longer trapped in a cage. Bars don't surround me to throttle my ability to fly, they're a barrier to protect me from enemies who wish me harm.

"I love it."

Approaching me, he motions for me to pass the necklace to him. I do, spinning to face away. Arsen sweeps his fingers lightly over the bare skin of my shoulders. I've thrown my hair up, there's nothing for him to brush away—he's just looking for an excuse to touch me. He places the necklace around my neck, his breath tickling on my skin as he clicks the latch.

"Three years."

"At this rate we'll hit ten before we realize," I laugh.

"I'm looking forward to celebrating our hundredth. I love you, my *ptichka.*"

My chest tightens from the swell of emotion. "I love you, too," I whisper, reaching to cup his jaw. His lips graze my ear. I moan on impulse, leaning my weight into his chest. Arsen slips his palms down my naked arms until he traces the insides of my wrists. His aim shifts, hands running up my stomach, over my ribs, through the valley of my breasts.

My hips grind backwards, finding his erection at full force. Heat attacks my pussy; I push my knees together, enjoying how squeezing my legs makes the pressure building in me feel even better. Sliding my hand between us I rub the front of his pants—he hisses through clenched teeth.

"Are we really alone in here?" I whisper.

"Very much so," he promises me.

"Good." Grinning, I back away, then push him as hard as I can. He topples to sit on the huge black sofa, staring at me in surprise. "I don't want anyone to hear us celebrating."

THE END

Want to read Galina and Arsen's searing hot celebration?

Scan the QR code

Printed in Great Britain
by Amazon